THE DEVIL GETS HIS DUE AND OTHER MYSTERY STORIES

To Cindy,
Happy Reading!
Elizabeth
Elwood.

Elizabeth Elwood

First Printing, 2017
Printed in North Charleston, South Carolina
ISBN: 0978272447
ISBN 9780978272449

Published by Elihu Entertainment
www.elihuentertainment.com
info@elihuentertainment.com

For Barbara Kay

TABLE OF CONTENTS

THE DEVIL GETS HIS DUE

I

It was past closing time, but the dimly lit window of the second-hand bookstore silhouetted a solitary hooded figure standing in front of the glass. The man studied the haphazard display of paperbacks inside the shop, then moved on, dissolving into the shadows and materializing again as he passed a gleaming row of bridal boutiques. When he reached the Palace Theatre, he paused, then turned, the eyes below the cowl scanning the street to see who might be watching. An occasional car drove by, heading for the main arterials that led west towards Vancouver or south to the Alex Fraser Bridge, but otherwise, Columbia Street was eerily silent. The street was deserted. No stragglers were out walking on this bitter January evening when the ice-cold air stung the skin and thrust like a dagger into the lungs. Hard piles of snow still lined the curb, frozen remnants of the white Christmas of 2010, its greeting-card beauty now reduced to grime-streaked mounds of ice. More snow was threatened, but not yet. Luckily the roads

1

were clear, for snow would have jeopardized his plan, but in two more days, it would no longer matter. The man glanced at his watch. It was half past six. This time tomorrow, there would be activity—stage manager, singers and crew would be hurrying up from the parking lot and bustling through the stage door—but tonight, the theatre was dark, the box office empty, the glass window sealed.

He swept his eyes along the ornate cornices of the theatre's façade. The stone walls were golden where the beam of the street lamp cast its light. The old building still looked exactly as he remembered it from his childhood. The three storeys that fronted onto Columbia Street were deceptive, for the theatre was built on the steep slopes of New Westminster so that the rear of the building was augmented by an additional thirty feet of storage and work space. He knew every inch of the Palace, from its wide, shallow stage, designed for vaudeville in the early part of the last century, to the labyrinthine corridors that surrounded the auditorium and led backstage. He had explored every level, from the horseshoe balcony and the upper offices to the basement scene shop that opened through a loading dock onto Front Street at the rear of the theatre.

Being here again brought memories of his mother, who had graced the stage in plays and pantomimes during the seventies—but this was not the time for sentimental reminiscences. He forced his mind from the past into the present. He had a part to play tomorrow night and his focus must not waver. The lights were not on under the canopy, so the poster for Bellemere Opera's production of *Faust* was barely visible in the dim light, but an errant splinter of light from the street lamp spilled below the canopy, angling down to illuminate the bottom of the poster and pinpointing the name that was burned into his brain: Grégoire Chalon as Mephistopheles.

The role was appropriate, he thought calmly. Tomorrow, the Devil would get his due.

⚔

Dr. Faustus finished his anguished outpouring on the loss of youth, and right on cue, the Devil materialized in a puff of smoke. Brilliant, thought Genevieve Marchbanks, watching from the sixth row of the auditorium. Thank heavens for a Mephistopheles with enough agility to haul himself through the trapdoor and strike a dramatic pose before the haze cleared. It was such a coup to get Grégoire Chalon. The hard-won sponsorship that had paid his fee would not normally have been sufficient to bring him to sing with a small company like Bellemere Opera and she knew she was lucky to have him there. He was doing the role partially as a favour for her, in return for her mentorship in the days before he had become an international star, but mainly in order to raise the profile of his stepdaughter, the young mezzo who was singing Siebel. Genevieve smiled to herself. There had been several fine mezzos audition for the role of Siebel, at least one of whom was a far stronger performer than Christa Van Luven, but choosing Christa had not been entirely a politic move designed to entice her stepfather into the production. The girl had a richly mature, well-trained voice and, in Genevieve's opinion, only needed some solid stage experience to round her out so that she was ready to embark on a professional career.

Genevieve watched closely as the first scene unfolded. Mephistopheles tempting, Faust gradually weakening. She was pleased to see that local tenor, Pablo Alonso was holding his own. It would do wonders for his career being able to add a performance with Chalon to his resume. Chalon's stepdaughter was not the only one benefiting from his appearance. All the singers would gain attention by appearing with a star of such magnitude. Philippa Beary would definitely profit from the experience, Genevieve thought shrewdly, for the young soprano was at a crossroads in her career. She had been performing a lot of musical comedy lately, but she was going to have to make a decision soon whether to go the easier route, or take the long, demanding road to an operatic career. Singing Marguerite was the kind of challenge that would help her make that choice.

Genevieve sighed. There were so many factors other than talent that decided who would successfully make the transition from small local companies to the professional opera circuit. No one could make it alone. A strong support network could make all the difference for an aspiring singer, and Philippa certainly had the backing of her relatives. Genevieve had noted several members of the Beary family in the auditorium before the lights went down. Councillor Bertram Beary and his wife, Edwina, were in the seats at the end of the sixth row. With them was Philippa's sister, Juliette, who, along with her husband and children, had come down from the Sunshine Coast to see the show. Philippa's oldest sister, Sylvia, was sitting two rows forward with her husband, Norton, although Genevieve knew that the Barnwells were also present to see their children who had been included as extras in the village scene. Next to them was Philippa's brother, Richard, who was a detective inspector with the RCMP. Every one of Philippa's relatives had arrived wearing a glow of proud expectation, and with justification, thought Genevieve as she turned back towards the stage.

The dark wall of the study, illuminated from behind the scrim, had disappeared to reveal Marguerite at her spinning wheel. Philippa looked radiant. Her red curls and fine features made her appear a Rossetti angel under the golden light. Without singing a note, she managed to emit an aura of alluring innocence. The inevitable outcome dictated by the libretto was utterly believable. Faust gave in and the pact with the devil was made.

In the pit, Amar Johal, fierily bouncing on his podium, urged the small orchestra into the crashing chords that climaxed the scene. With another flash and a cloud of smoke, the Devil disappeared the way he had come.

Faintly, under the noise of the orchestra, Genevieve thought she heard a short, high-pitched shriek as Mephistopheles descended into Hell. Not in the score, but it sounded eerily effective all the same.

Of course, what she did not realize was that Grégoire Chalon had just made his final exit.

When Mephistopheles did not appear for his next cue, the stage manager began to panic. Billy Curtis was the stagehand sent to find him. Billy checked the dressing rooms and the green room to no avail. Queries to the other singers made him realize that no one had seen the Devil since his exit through the trapdoor, and with a sinking feeling of apprehension, he hurried down the stairs that led to the scene-shop loft where Grégoire Chalon should have landed after his descent.

Billy opened the door and peered along the walkway, which, supported by a series of trusses, ran the entire width of the scene shop and provided a secure landing for actors coming down through the trapdoor. He could see the thick foam where Chalon should have landed and the ladder that the actors climbed to enter through the trapdoor, but there was no sign of the singer.

Billy was about to leave when it struck him that something was not quite right. The mattress was on the wrong side of the ladder. Swearing under his breath, Billy walked out to investigate. His eyes were on the mattress, and he wasn't watching his feet, so it was only at the last moment that he noticed the yawning gap before him. The swear words stopped abruptly. Stunned into silence, Billy clutched the edge of the truss and looked down into the scene shop.

Sprawled on the cement floor, thirty feet below, was the immobile form of Mephistopheles. Suppressing the wave of nausea that washed over him like a tidal wave, Billy turned and ran for the exit.

Philippa Beary was in the wings when an ashen-faced Billy raced in to tell the stage manager what had happened. Catching enough of his story to realize that a request for a doctor was only going to take care of one aspect of the terrible accident, she quietly informed the stage manager that he should also ask her brother to come backstage.

The stage manager's announcement produced no less than three members of the medical profession, and the SM quickly whisked them away and led them down to the scene shop. Philippa remained in the backstage corridor, waiting for her brother to appear. As she stood there, Christa van Luven emerged from the dressing room to find out why the orchestra had stopped playing. The young mezzo's shock at the news soon became a desperate determination to go to her stepfather's side, and Philippa was still trying to restrain her when Richard appeared in the wake of a white-faced Genevieve Marchbanks and a pale young woman who turned out to be Christa's older sister. At the sight of her sister, Christa broke down into sobs. Her sorrow was heart-wrenching. She personified the expression, *bathed in tears*, thought Philippa. Christa's sister attempted to comfort her, and was clearly trying to keep a grip on her own emotions, but the tension in her shoulders was palpable.

Quickly assessing the situation—Philippa had kept Billy waiting with her so that he could tell the detective what he had seen—Richard arranged for the young women to follow the ambulance to the hospital. Then he instructed Genevieve to keep all cast and crew backstage and have the house manager close the auditorium until he gave permission for anyone to leave. He made the necessary calls to the Integrated Homicide Investigation Team and the New Westminster City Police, after which he told Billy to lead him down to the loft. It could be worse, he told himself cynically, as he followed Billy off the stage. It could have been a Vancouver Opera production in the Queen Elizabeth Theatre, which seated twenty-seven hundred people. At least in The Palace, he only had two-hundred disgruntled patrons to interview.

Richard took note of the route as he walked behind Billy. It was only a short distance from the stage to a double set of stairs, one flight ascending and one descending. The upper flight, Billy informed him, led to the dressing rooms. Richard followed Billy down the other set of stairs and through the door that led to the loft. Then, telling Billy to remain by the door, Richard walked out between the trusses.

A wide gap yawned in the middle of the walkway. Through it, Richard could see a cluster of people surrounding the prone figure below. He called down to them. A grey-haired gentleman glanced up and shook his head. In the distance, Richard could hear the wail of an approaching ambulance.

He looked back at the walkway. It was easy to see what had been done to set the trap for the singer. A cordless drill lay by the edge of the gap and the section of plywood that should have covered the hole had been slid back. Several screws were scattered on top of the wood. Someone had pulled the mattress aside and systematically removed the flooring beneath the trapdoor. Instead of a short drop onto the mattress, Mephistopheles had plummeted forty feet to his death.

Billy came out onto the walkway and looked over Richard's shoulder.

"It was done after the opera started," he pointed out, unnecessarily since Richard had seen the Devil rise through the trapdoor with his own eyes. "The platform couldn't have even been partially disconnected because Roger always comes down and checks the mattress before the opening curtain."

"Roger?"

"The stage manager. Whoever did that had no more than ten minutes to pull the plywood up."

"It wouldn't take that long. Do you recognize that cordless drill?"

Billy nodded.

"Yes. It belongs to the theatre. See those letters on the side. They label all their tools. The drill will have been brought up from the scene shop."

A blast of cold air and a rattling sound made Richard look down. The doors were opening onto the street and an ambulance was waiting to come through. Knowing there was nothing he could do below, Richard turned back to Billy.

"How many ways are there to get into this loft?"

"Just the way we came through, or from the scene shop below." Billy pointed to a wooden ladder attached to the wall.

"So how do people get to the scene shop, other than descending that ladder or going through from Front Street? You must have a way to transport your sets up to the stage."

"There's a service elevator that goes from the shop to stage left, but it's kept locked. We're renting the theatre for the show. The resident techie helped us load in our sets and bring them up to the stage, but once we were in, he closed the elevator off. The exterior doors of the shop are locked too. There's a stairway that connects to the theatre, but it goes to the front of house. You'll see an alcove in the lobby with a door that says *Staff Only*. If you go through it, you'll find stairs up to the lighting booth and another flight down to the shop."

"Who was in the booth?"

"Janie Kim is our lighting technician. There's no way she went AWOL. Roger was talking with her on the headset the whole time. There are quite a few lighting cues during the first scene."

"What about the cast or crew? Did any of you have access to that set of stairs?"

"Not without being seen by a lot of people," said Billy. "There are only two doors that connect front of house with backstage. One's the exit door at the foot of the auditorium—"

"The one I went through to come backstage?"

"Yes. Then there's a door on the other side of the theatre that connects the stage-door foyer with the bar, but anyone going that route would be seen by the house manager. They'd have to cross the lobby and she's there throughout the performance."

"The whole time?"

"Yes, it's a liability issue. Someone has to be on duty in case of emergencies. No one in the show could have got to the scene shop via the door in the lobby."

Billy warmed up to his topic. Having recovered from the initial shock, he was beginning to enjoy being a key witness.

"Of course," he continued, "anyone could come the way we did and climb down the ladder to fetch the shop drill, but that would be pretty hard for a member of the cast, given the costumes they're wearing—and the crew's all accounted for, except our wardrobe mistress, but she's over seventy and is seriously overweight so there's no way you'd catch her clambering down that ladder."

Richard frowned.

"I can't rule the cast and crew out," he said. "Anyone involved in the production could have come in early enough to slip down to the scene shop before the opening curtain. When your stage manager went down to check that the mattress was in place, he wouldn't have searched the entire loft. There's nothing to say that the cordless drill wasn't hidden behind one of the trusses, all ready for use when the killer came through to the loft once Mephistopheles had made his entrance. I venture to say that none of you are off the hook yet."

Billy fell silent.

"Any other bright suggestions?" asked Richard.

"The Phantom of the Opera?"

"Serious suggestions." Richard was not amused.

"I was serious . . . well, sort of. I suppose I meant that this whole thing is about as far-fetched as the Phantom of the Opera. It doesn't make sense."

"What doesn't make sense?"

"Killing Mephistopheles," said Billy. "He may have been playing the Devil, but in real life, everybody loved him. He was one of the nicest guys ever to grace the opera stage. Nobody had any reason to harm him."

II

Given the high profile of the victim and the nature of the murder, Detective Constable Mike Burrows of the New Westminster City Police was happy to have a senior detective from IHIT on hand. To facilitate the process, and to prevent the bussing of so many people down to the police station, the house manager volunteered her office for police interviews. Richard and DC Burrows commandeered another uniformed officer to take notes and followed the house manager round to the lobby. Her office was on the right side of the foyer, immediately next to the door to the ladies' washroom. Directly opposite, on the other side of the lobby, Richard could see the men's washroom, and beside it, the alcove that contained the door to the stairway that Billy had described earlier. Having mentally noted the geography of the area, Richard followed the house manager into her office and seated himself on a chair in the corner. DC Burrows settled himself behind her desk, and after a brief collaboration with

Richard, decided to question the HM first, then have her send for the stage manager. After this, they would see each member of the crew and technical staff. Once these interviews were done, they would talk with the performers. Richard sighed. It was going to be a long night.

It was also to prove a baffling night. Three hours later, Richard had to conclude that Billy, the stagehand, had known what he was talking about when he said the murder did not make sense. Every person interviewed expressed the same horror at the singer's death. Grégoire Chalon seemed to be universally liked. No one could offer any suggestions as to why the popular baritone had been killed.

Billy had also been correct when he'd told Richard that most of the people in the production were accounted for. The chorus had been called on stage as soon as Mephistopheles made his entrance. With the exception of four people, everyone backstage was either waiting in the wings, where they would have had to pass by the stage manager in order to leave, or in the women's dressing rooms in full view of the makeup ladies and the wardrobe mistress. The four exceptions were the baritone singing Valentin, who was alone in his dressing room, one male chorister, who was in the washroom and responded to the chorus call several minutes later, the young man doing props who had slipped down to the green room for a cup of coffee, and Philippa Beary, who had come down from her dressing room prior to positioning herself behind the scrim for the vision scene.

None of the cast or crew had come through to the lobby via the connecting door in the stage-door foyer, for the bartender had remained at his post for fifteen minutes after the start of the opera and would have seen anyone who went by. This was confirmed by the house manager, who was overseeing the box-office count. The exterior box-office window was no longer used; instead, patrons entered the front doors and lined up to pick up their tickets at a window inside the building. Therefore, the house manager had a clear view of the theatre lobby, and she insisted that no one had come through once the opera had started. The house manager was also adamant that no one could have entered the theatre from outside. The only doors that were not locked were the front doors, which she could see, and the exterior kitchen door, which was in full view of the two ladies who were catering the reception. All other exit doors were set with crash bars that allowed patrons to get out but did not allow anyone to enter. To further demonstrate her efficiency, she explained that the ticket sales from the box office, combined with the opening-night comps, tallied with the stubs that the ushers had turned in, which meant that all the people who had purchased tickets had taken their seats. The police had to search for their suspects among those who were involved in the production—and once Philippa was discounted, DC Burrows was left with a principal baritone, a chorister and a stagehand.

It's almost too easy, thought Richard, looking at the list of three names. There has to be a connection between Chalon and one of these men. We just have to find what it is. He turned to Mike Burrows.

"Let's get my kid sister back in here," he said.

Philippa was torn. She was genuinely appalled by the tragic death of Grégoire Chalon, but another part of her was seething with frustration.

"My first opportunity to sing a major operatic role and I didn't even get to open my mouth. I suppose you're going to shut us down now that the theatre's a crime scene," she grumbled to her brother.

"That's not my decision," said Richard, nodding towards DC Burrows.

Burrows eyed Philippa warily. Red hair and a nose right out of joint. On top of that, she was the DI's sister. Tread carefully with this one, he thought.

"When was your next performance scheduled?" he asked.

"Saturday."

"Two days away. No, I'm sorry. We won't be finished by then. Are there any more shows after that?"

"Thursday and Saturday next week. Those were the last two."

"Those can go ahead, barring anything unexpected. I assume, since you asked about continuing the run, that you have an understudy on hand."

"No," said Philippa, "but I know someone who does the role and I think he's available."

"Well," said Burrows, not entirely impressed with the determined glint in Philippa's eye, "now that we've dealt with your problem, perhaps we could get onto the reason why we asked you to talk with us."

Philippa looked apologetic.

"I'm sorry," she said, genuinely abashed. "I must sound awful. Of course I want to help. Grégoire Chalon was a superb performer. His death is a dreadful loss to the world of opera. I can't imagine anyone wanting to harm him."

Richard interrupted.

"Leaving aside his professional life, what did you think of him personally? We've heard 'handsome' and 'charming' and 'diplomatic'. He's been described as a generous performer and a real trouper. If everyone is to be believed, the man was a paragon. You concur with these descriptions?"

"Yes, I would say so. He was a good family man too, judging by the way his stepdaughter talked. She's the mezzo singing Siebel. She's only nineteen and studying in the UBC opera workshop. It sounds as if he's been wonderfully supportive of her ambitions."

"Never mind what other people have said. Did you like him?"

Philippa paused and thought for a moment.

"Yes, I did—and not just because he was handsome and charming. Actually, he was a bit too handsome and charming for me. I like men with a bit more grit," she added, thinking of the sparks that flew between herself and Vancouver detective Bob Miller. "But Grégoire Chalon was so easy to work with and he managed to keep the most volatile performers in a good frame of mind. He encouraged other singers, passed on tricks of technique, that sort of thing, and he was great with young people—Sylvia's three absolutely adored him. You'd have thought Santa Claus was in the production, the way they carried on."

"That's my oldest sister's children," Richard explained to Burrows. "They're in the opera as extras."

Philippa continued as if her brother hadn't spoken.

"Grégoire was disciplined, but never autocratic," she explained. "If other singers were not pulling their weight or were at odds with each other, he had a knack for bringing them into line without upsetting or offending them. He was very persuasive in a genial way." A shadow crossed Philippa's face. "I suppose you've been in touch with his fiancée?" she said. "He was going to be married next month."

"That's news to us," said Burrows. "Do you have any idea who he's marrying? She's obviously not here, so we'll have to contact her."

"He's marrying a long-time friend from Ontario. The only reason I know is because Christa mentioned that she'd be going back to Toronto for the wedding. She said it was to be a fairly quiet affair since it was a second marriage for both."

"That's good enough," said Burrows. "The stepdaughters will be able to give us an address." He stood up and went to the door. After speaking briefly with the constable outside, he returned to his seat at the house-manager's desk.

"A second marriage, eh?" he said thoughtfully. "So what happened to Chalon's first wife? Is she still around?"

"She died years ago. Cancer, I think."

"What else do you know about Chalon's personal life?"

"Only what I've read in his profile. He started out as a teacher, but quit to follow his singing career. He studied with Julia Berti in Toronto, and that's when things started to come together for him. Everything took off when he won the regional Metropolitan Opera auditions, and after that he was offered a contract with COC and he's been on a roll ever since."

"Canadian Opera Company," interjected Richard, seeing Burrow's quizzical expression.

"If you want to know more about Chalon's background, the person to ask is Genevieve Marchbanks," said Philippa. "She knows him from way back. She's the one who set him up with Berti in the first place. She could tell you a lot more than I can."

"All right, we'll do that. Let's move on. The motive may be a mystery, but we can deal with opportunity. Can you give us some idea of the time you left your dressing room?"

Philippa nodded.

"I can do better than that. I can tell you exactly when. We started right on time, so when I came down, it would have been fourteen minutes past eight."

"Did you go directly to the wings?"

"Yes."

"No detours?"

"No."

"How long do you figure it took you to get to the stage?"

"Less than a minute. It's not far."

"Did you see anyone on the stairs or in the corridor?"

"No. Not a soul." Philippa frowned. "I did hear something though. It was a muted sort of bang. It could have been a door closing . . . or something being dropped."

"Where did it come from?"

"It happened just as I came out of the dressing room, so it was definitely below me, not behind."

"From the steps to the basement?"

"Possibly. I couldn't tell the direction. I wondered if someone had left the audience through the door at the front of the auditorium and gone out the emergency exit onto the street. I checked the doors as I went by, just to make sure they were properly shut—and they were. But someone could have gone through."

Richard shook his head.

"No. No one left the auditorium that way. I was sitting near the front. I would have noticed."

Burrows glanced at the list on the table. Catching Richard's eye, he thrust the list into Philippa's hand.

"What can you tell us about these three individuals? Does any one of them have any special connection to Chalon?"

Philippa stared at the names, puzzled.

"None of them do," she said firmly. "George Mackinnon is a singer with the UBC opera ensemble. He did the role of Valentin in the opera workshop, which is why Genevieve chose him for the part. He's only nineteen, the same age as Christa. His father is dean of the music school and as far as I know, he's never met Chalon in his life. Curtis Yee is a chorus singer I met during HMS *Pinafore* last year and he's another young, enthusiastic performer who's never been anywhere outside Vancouver."

"What about this stagehand? Carl Jorgensen? The one who does props?"

"Another local. Genevieve roped him in. He's married to the lady who directs for Burnside Musical Theatre. His wife is a good friend of Genevieve's and they're always helping each other out. I have no idea if he's ever met Grégoire Chalon before, but somehow, I doubt it. I've chatted with him several times and never had a hint of a connection. But there again, Genevieve is the person to ask. Bellemere Opera is her baby, so she can tell you a great deal more than I can."

"All right," said Burrows. "You can leave. We know where to find you if we need you. Could you ask Genevieve Marchbanks to come up before you go home?"

Philippa nodded. With a smile to her brother, she left the room.

"Interesting young woman," commented Burrows to Richard.

"That she is. Smart too," said Richard.

"Sounds like she's determined the show can go ahead. How come she can produce a Devil out of her hat like that?"

Richard grinned, sensing the detective's distrust and amused at his clumsy attempt to be tactful.

"She didn't have a keen understudy waiting in the background for Chalon to drop dead, if that's what's worrying you. These opera singers learn roles that suit their voices and they make the rounds performing them with various companies. There will be a whole raft of baritones who sing Mephistopheles and can come in and adapt to the production at the drop of a hat—and I bet I know who this particular one will be."

"Oh? Who?"

"Probably Adam Craig. Philippa's ex-boyfriend."

"Looking for an excuse to get back together, is she?"

"No, not at all. This will be strictly professional. Philippa is much more interested in a young VPD detective that she met, believe it or not, when he arrested her a couple of years back—and don't even ask. It's too long a story. Needless to say, it proved an embarrassing mistake for VPD."

"Hm." Burrows grunted and rapped his fingers on the desk. "I wonder if this Marchbanks woman is already burrowing around for a replacement."

"We'll see," said Richard. "Genevieve Marchbanks is an interesting woman too," he told Burrows. "She started the Bellemere Opera ten years ago. It's a small company, but it gives local up-and-coming singers the opportunity to try their hand at major roles. Vancouver Opera only gives them chorus or minor parts, so Bellemere provides an important stepping-stone in their careers. Marchbanks is the driving force that keeps it going. She works tirelessly applying for grants and sponsorships to fund the productions."

"So why was she bringing in this big star if she wanted to showcase local talent?" asked Burrows.

"Money, according to Philippa. His name resulted in a sponsorship that was large enough to fund the entire production."

The door flew open and Burrows looked up to see a gauntly elegant woman in black framed in the doorway. Her hair was short, with silvery spikes, and her dark eyes burned into Burrow's own.

"It's about time," she said curtly. "This is my company and I need to know what's going on."

The power of her gaze drew Burrows to his feet and he gestured politely to a chair on the other side of the desk.

"Come in, Ms. Marchbanks. I'm sorry it's taken so long to get to you, but we needed to talk with the people who were backstage. Please sit down."

Genevieve sat and folded her hands in her lap.

"It's Mrs. Marchbanks," she said shortly.

Ignoring the hostile tone, Burrows sat back down. Keeping his voice level, he said, "Mrs. Marchbanks, we need to know more about Grégoire Chalon. I gather, of all the people in the company, you knew him best."

"Yes, Grégoire and I go back twenty years or so. I met him in 1989. I was directing an operetta for a community group in Scarborough, Ontario and Grégoire auditioned for one of the roles. Right away, I recognized his potential and arranged an audition for him to sing for Julia Berti. She agreed to take him on as a student, and because I had such faith in his ability, I paid for his initial lessons. Don't look at me like that, young man," Genevieve snapped, seeing the quizzical expression on Burrow's face. "It was strictly a business relationship. Grégoire was to pay me back once he was established—and he did, too."

"How old was Chalon when he first auditioned for you?"

"He was twenty-one. Fabulous voice. Just an incredible natural instrument—"

"Let's leave aside his talent for a moment," Richard interjected. "Where had he come from? I'm assuming he was French Canadian."

"Yes. He'd recently moved from Montreal."

"What was he doing for a living? Was he already earning money from singing, or did he have some other job? Was his family supporting him?"

"Grégoire's parents were dead and he didn't have any siblings. He had been teaching music to support himself, but he'd decided to take the plunge and try making his living as a singer, so he'd quit his job the previous year. That's why I took him in hand and said I'd pay for him to study with Julia Berti. I didn't want to see him ruin that voice by taking any and every job he could get. I knew he had a future in opera, and I was proved right."

"Did you have to wait long for him to pay you back?"

"No. I didn't have to help him out for long either. He married Mary van Luven in 1992, and she ended up supporting him until he got on his feet. She had as much faith in him as I did. She did well out of it, too, because it wasn't long before he was raking in very big fees. They were very comfortably off."

"Mary van Luven? Is that the lady who died?"

"Yes, she developed cancer. She battled it successfully for several years, but she died in 2006."

"Was she a singer too?"

"Mary sang chorus and small parts with amateur groups. That's how Gregoire met her, but she didn't have any ambition to do more, even though she had a lovely contralto voice—which her youngest daughter has inherited. Unlike her mother, Christa is ambitious, so I think she'll go far."

"I gather Christa van Luven is Chalon's stepdaughter."

"Yes."

"So Mary van Luven was married before?"

"That's right. She was a widow with three children. Her first husband had left her very well off, which was why she was able to support Grégoire while he studied and got himself established."

"Was it a happy marriage?"

"As far as I know. I moved away from the Toronto area soon afterwards, but whenever I ran into Grégoire, he always spoke of Mary with great affection. They did have some serious problems with two of the children from Mary's first marriage—but Greg and Mary always pulled together and coped with whatever life threw their way. They were married for fourteen years, after all, so the girls became like Grégoire's own daughters."

"They still keep their father's name though," observed Richard. "The young mezzo who was crying her heart out is listed in the program as Christa van Luven, not Christa Chalon."

"Grégoire never actually adopted them. It was something to do with a clause in Mary's first husband's will. It didn't make any difference though. He took full responsibility for the girls and helped Mary cope when the older two became so hard to handle."

"What sort of problems did they have?"

"The oldest girl went haywire as a teenager. Boys, drugs, the works. Totally promiscuous and self-destructive. She committed suicide around the time Mary became ill. Then Susanna—that's the middle girl—"

"Christa's older sister? The one who was here tonight?"

"Yes. After her sister's death, Susanna became rebellious and difficult. According to Grégoire, she was so angry that her sister had died and her mother was ill that, instead of being supportive of her mother, she became hostile and hard to handle. Mary couldn't manage, given her failing health and all the treatments she had to go through, and ultimately, she decided to send the two girls to stay with her sister who lived at the army base in Trenton. Her mother lived there too, so the girls had their aunt and their grandmother to care for them. After Mary died, the girls stayed there and were raised by the sister and her husband because Grégoire was travelling constantly with his work—but he used to visit them and he contributed financially to their upbringing and paid for their education. He had a strong sense of responsibility—he was a devout Catholic, you know—and he was fond of the girls. He was very pleased that Christa wanted to follow in his footsteps and have an operatic career."

"So Christa van Luven was the good daughter? No problems there?"

"No, Christa was fine. . . lovely girl, lovely voice, lovely nature too. I certainly never heard of her causing her parents any worry the way her sisters did."

"How well do you know Chalon's stepdaughters?"

"I don't know Susanna at all. Until the night of the opera, I hadn't seen her since she was small, and I only met Christa when she auditioned for *Faust*. But of course, I'd heard all about them from Grégoire. He updated me on family news whenever we met through our professional engagements."

"Did he talk about the children a lot?"

"Just the usual proud-parent stuff: graduations, degrees, jobs, that sort of thing. Obviously, he was very pleased about Christa's scholarship to UBC."

"What about the older sister? Did he give you the impression that she'd sorted herself out?"

"Susanna? Yes, she's turned out all right. She completed her education degree and is now teaching high school. She lives in BC because she married a local boy—which is one of the reasons Christa applied for opera school at UBC."

"So the sisters live together?"

"No. Christa is in residence on campus. Susanna and her husband live on the North Shore. She's actually married to Larry Hayes' cousin."

"Larry Hayes?" Burrows looked confused.

"Tricia Hayes' ex-husband." Genevieve stopped abruptly. "Oh, sorry. You wouldn't know. Grégoire was engaged to be married. His fiancée's name is Tricia Hayes. She lives in Toronto. She'll have to be contacted. She's going to be devastated. You'd better get onto her before this hits the news."

"That's in hand," said Burrows. "I just didn't have her name. What did you say it was?"

"Tricia Hayes."

"And you say she's a divorcée?"

"Yes."

"And what's this connection between her ex-husband and Susanna van Luven?"

"Susanna married Geoff Caruthers, who happens to be Larry Hayes' cousin."

"Good heavens!" Richard interjected. "How did that come about?"

"Larry Hayes was in the armed forces. He and Tricia lived next door to the aunt in Trenton who raised the girls after their mother died. That's how Grégoire met Tricia—through his visits to the girls—and Susanna met Geoff Caruthers the same way."

"When he came to visit his cousin at the army base?"

"Yes, but why this interest in the girls? You surely don't think either of them had anything to do with Grégoire's death? You must have seen how upset they were. Besides, Christa was backstage and Susanna was in the audience, sitting two rows in front of me. She was there with a girlfriend. They were in the same row as you, actually—in fact, now I think of it, they were right next to you. So neither Christa nor Susanna could have sabotaged the trapdoor landing, unless you've figured out some brilliant way they could dismantle screws and wooden planks by remote control. I can't see how all this family background is relevant," Genevieve said tartly. "It's more than likely that Grégoire's death was an accident."

"Mrs. Marchbanks, it wasn't an accident. Someone deliberately set a lethal trap, and you have to help us find out who it was. It must have been a person involved in the show—someone who knew about the use of the trapdoor in the opening scene."

"Anyone who watches the national news would have known. CBC did a feature on the production. We were going against tradition having Mephistopheles drop through the trapdoor at the end of the first scene. Normally, he exits with Faust, but we were going for a little extra drama." Genevieve bit her lip as she noticed the irony in her words. "Anyway, CBC filmed the trapdoor sequence at a rehearsal last week. Oh, my goodness!" Her face paled. "Perhaps the publicity is what did it. There are a lot of insane people out there. Maybe some religious fanatic decided to set the trap, simply because Grégoire was playing the Devil."

"That's a bit far-fetched," grunted Burrows.

"No, it isn't," said Genevieve. "It's far more likely than saying anyone in the production was responsible. Believe me, no one in the cast or crew had any reason to harbour a grudge against Grégoire. None of them had ever met him before."

"Are you sure of that?" Burrows glanced down at his notes. "What about George Mackinnon, Carl Jorgensen or Curtis Yee?"

Genevieve stared at him as if he were mad.

"Those three? They have no connection with Grégoire. Why single them out?"

Burrows sighed and explained how the other cast, crew and audience members had been eliminated. Genevieve's tone became even more scornful.

"We had a big crowd tonight," she said. "There were only a handful of empty seats so the front-of-house staff would have been run off their feet. They may be efficient, but they're not infallible."

"Every ticket sold was turned in to an usher and no one left the auditorium once the opera started."

Genevieve snorted.

"What was to stop someone from slipping out before it started? People take their seats and then go out to the washroom or the concession stand. The usher wouldn't think anything of it if the person didn't come back because there are two entrance doors to the auditorium. The person could have just as easily gone back through the other door."

"But the house manager was in the lobby. She'd have seen anyone who remained there after the show began."

"Not if they hid in the washroom," Genevieve pointed out.

Richard slapped his hand to the side of his head.

"And the men's washroom is right by the alcove with the stairway that goes to the scene shop! He could have been down the stairs and into the shop before the overture had finished. He'd be lurking there waiting to go into action the minute Mephistopheles had gone up through the trapdoor. Don't forget the sound Philippa heard. She said it could have been the emergency door closing. Our character could have left that way and be long gone before Chalon made his fatal final exit."

"Great," grunted Burrows. "That means none of the names we're taking of audience members will be any use at all."

"Not necessarily," said Richard. "We may not know the motive, and maybe Mrs. Marchbanks is right and we're dealing with a nutter, but if the killer was in the audience before the show, someone may have noticed him leaving. Also, the box-office staff may remember a solitary male buying a ticket. We'll get him yet."

III

By Monday of the following week, Richard felt less optimistic. The autopsy results had come in and confirmed the obvious. Chalon had died from the injuries sustained in the fall. His legs were broken, there was massive trauma to his internal organs, and the back of his head was smashed from the impact as he fell back against the concrete floor. One touch of irony had been revealed in the report. Under his devil's costume, Chalon wore a gold chain with a cross. Perhaps, thought Richard, the man's faith had conversely worked for him when he played Mephistopheles. The man had probably believed that the devil really existed.

The investigation had been handed over to IHIT and the team had focussed on any ticket holder who had the opportunity to commit the crime, but none of the interviews with audience or front-of-house staff had produced results. The only solitary ticket purchasers had been female and no one in the audience recalled any patron who left his seat prior to curtain time and didn't return. The audience appeared to be a remarkably continent group who had no need of last-minute trips to the washroom, for the ushers insisted that only four people, all women, had come back out to the lobby, and all four had returned to their seats prior to the start of the opera. One of these had been Susanna Caruthers.

Richard and DC Burrows were both present for the interviews with Grégoire Chalon's stepdaughters. It did not take the detectives long to ascertain that neither one could have been responsible for the trap. Christa had arrived at the theatre at six-thirty and had gone straight to her dressing room, where she had remained until Philippa saw her emerge after the crisis erupted backstage. Her presence there was confirmed by the wardrobe mistress and two makeup ladies, both of whom assured the police that Christa had not left the room at any time.

Susanna's alibi was equally solid. Geoff Caruthers did not share his wife's interest in opera, so he had opted to watch the hockey game with his cousin that night. Susanna had given his comp to a friend, but she had driven him to his parents' home in South Burnaby before picking up her friend in Metrotown. It was only another ten minutes to New Westminster, and by the time the two women had parked, walked to the theatre and taken their seats, it was quarter to eight. Susanna had made a quick trip out to the washroom just prior to curtain time, but was back in her seat before the lights went down.

Both Chalon's stepdaughters had seemed deeply saddened by his death. They insisted that he had been a wonderful stepfather, and even after their mother's death, he had generously provided for their upbringing. Richard's hope that he could garner more information from the aunt and uncle who had raised the girls was dashed when they informed him that the couple had died in a car crash shortly after Susanna was married. By that time, Christa was in residence at UBC. Their grandmother, who was now eighty-nine and afflicted with dementia, was left without a home, so Grégoire had brought her to BC and was paying for her care in High Hill House, one of the most expensive senior homes in the province. Neither sister could provide any motive for Chalon's death. Each one parroted the mantra that Richard was increasingly frustrated at hearing: Everyone loved Grégoire Chalon.

As Richard was reviewing his case notes, Detective Sergeant Bill Martin came in and deposited a coffee on his desk.

"You look like you could use this," he said.

"Yes, I could. Thank you." Richard picked up the mug gratefully. "How was your holiday?" he added. Martin had just returned from his annual trip to England to visit his elderly mother.

"All right, I guess. Confirmed my feeling that I was right to emigrate when I did."

"Mum OK?"

"She's fine. She likes living with my sister's family. Speaking of sisters, I see yours has landed herself in the midst of another mystery. Is she helping you solve it or is she just teed off at having her show cancelled?"

"Actually, we're letting them back in today. Genevieve Marchbanks has managed to extend the theatre rental, so the run will go ahead with the original number of performances. They're just starting late. They open on Saturday."

"So Philippa will be able to sing and sleuth to her heart's content. That'll make her happy."

Richard rolled his eyes. "I'm not sure what's going to make Philippa happy at the moment," he said. "I've never seen her so lacking in focus."

"Surely she isn't losing interest in her career?"

"No, but she's ambivalent," said Richard. "Her agent has been trying to line her up for some parts on the national scene, so her career could be taking a quantum leap any time now."

"Well, that's fantastic. Why should that make her ambivalent?"

"Well, for one thing, she's reaching a point where she has to choose between opera and musical comedy, and naturally, her agent and her singing teacher have totally opposing opinions."

"What's the other thing?" asked Martin.

Richard grinned.

"If she opts for the musical-comedy route, she could be away for months at a time, especially if she nails a role in any of the big festivals back East, so I think she's worried that her friend in VPD isn't going to miss her as much as she'll miss him. She's scared he won't be around when she gets back."

"He will if he has any sense. Your sister's a gem."

"I know," said Richard.

"Has she come up with anything useful for you on this trap-door murder?" asked Martin.

"Not a great deal, but I'm sure she's keeping her ears open. It's a tough one, though. The victim doesn't seem to have made any enemies. Everybody appeared to love him."

"What about financial motive? Chalon must have been worth a few bob. Who inherits?"

"That's a dead end. He created generous trust funds for his first wife's daughters—she was a widow with children when they married, and he wanted to make sure the girls didn't lose out as a result of his upcoming marriage—so they're well taken care of. His fiancée would have inherited a bundle if they had already been married, but as it is, she gets nothing. Under his existing will, the only beneficiaries are various opera companies and scholarship funds."

"My, that must have upset the wife-to-be. Have you met with her?"

"No. She's back East. According to the Toronto DC who interviewed her, she's devastated by Chalon's death."

Martin peered over Richard's shoulder and eyed the picture in the file.

"Tricia Hayes?"

"Yes, that's her. Very attractive divorcée in her early thirties."

"She was married before?"

"Yes. It would have been a second marriage for both of them."

"Why did her first marriage break up?"

"She was married to a soldier. That's how she met Chalon. She and her husband lived next door to the McKenzies at the army base in Trenton. That's the couple that raised Chalon's stepdaughters after his wife died. Miriam McKenzie is Chalon's first-wife's sister. Chalon visited them often, so he got to know Tricia Hayes quite well."

"Was he the reason she divorced her husband?"

"No, it doesn't sound that way at all. Jack Hayes was seriously wounded in Afghanistan in 2006. He returned and recovered physically, but emotionally, he was a wreck. He was discharged from the army on medical grounds, and he became very hard to live with. According to what his ex-wife told the Toronto police, Hayes always had a tendency to be controlling and assertive, but after his return from Afghanistan, he became angry and possessive to the point where she felt she was being suffocated. She divorced him in 2008. It wasn't until the following year that she became reacquainted with Chalon. She attended a COC production of *Trovatore* and went backstage to congratulate him after the performance. By then, of course, his wife had died, and when he realized she was divorced, they started dating. They became engaged in 2010."

Sergeant Martin frowned.

"I'm surprised you say that Chalon had no enemies. The soldier ex-husband wouldn't be joining his fan club."

"No, obviously not. I did have Hayes tabbed as a possible suspect, especially as it turns out that he's originally from Vancouver and is back on the West Coast now—he lives in a basement suite in his uncle's home on the south slope of Burnaby—but he proved another dead end. We ran a check on him, and it sounds as if he's pulled his life together. He took counselling—I have a report from a psychologist vouching for his stability—and he now works as a security guard for the Royal Bank. I sent Constable Jean Howe round to the house too. Hayes was at work, but she talked with his aunt and uncle. They told her that Hayes is now engaged to a lovely woman and very happy. It seems the divorce galvanized him into sorting himself out. On top of all that, he has an alibi, so he's out of the picture."

"What sort of alibi?"

"Home watching the hockey game with his cousin, who'd come over to visit while his wife went to the opera with a friend."

Richard explained the complicated network of relationships that had resulted in Chalon's stepdaughter marrying the cousin of his fiancée's ex-husband.

"It wasn't just the aunt, uncle and cousin vouching for him," Richard continued. "The next-door neighbours verified that he was there. They were over for a bridge night. Geoff Caruthers and Larry Hayes were watching the game in the basement suite, but they were back and forth a couple of times to raid the Nanaimo bars the aunt had baked for her guests. They both came up again at quarter to nine when Susanna phoned to let her husband know what had happened. Hayes promptly offered to drive Caruthers out to join the women at the hospital—which he did. His intention was to later drive Christa back to UBC and let Susanna and her husband go straight back to the North Shore, but as it turned out, Christa was so upset that she decided to spend the night with her sister and Hayes came home alone."

Martin frowned.

"Are the neighbours certain that both Hayes and Caruthers came upstairs during the hockey game? Bridge players become pretty focussed on their game. They wouldn't see what was going on in the kitchen."

Martin had a suspicious mind, and a highly devious one. Richard suspected it was a result of being raised by a mother who had read everything written by Agatha Christie. Oblivious to his superior officer's train of thought, Martin continued, "What if Hayes and Caruthers were in it together?"

"A conspiracy theory? That's a bit far-fetched."

"Not necessarily."

"Not really practical, either. How could they pull it off?"

"Caruthers could have pretended to be calling to Hayes—giving the illusion that they were both raiding the fridge. If that were the case, there would be about an eighty-minute gap … just enough of a window of opportunity for Hayes to drive to the theatre, fix the trap, and return in time to show his face when the phone call came to say there'd been an accident."

"Hayes' van was in the driveway all evening," said Richard. "It was in clear view of the bridge players because their table was in front of a picture window that overlooked the front lawn. The sheers were drawn but the curtains were open, and the streetlamp lit up the whole drive."

"What about transit? The Skytrain line runs through South Burnaby. Is the house anywhere near a station?"

"Not by road—at least a half-hour walk—but it's beside a forested ravine with a trail that cuts through to the Edmonds Station. It's equivalent to one block via the short cut. But that doesn't wash either. There was a bomb threat at six o'clock that night. The line was shut down for the next two hours. And no, there weren't any cabs called to make trips along that route and Hayes doesn't own a bike—not that even a champion marathoner could make that trip there and back in the time frame unless he was on a motorcycle. No, every way you look at it, it would be a pretty far stretch to put the ex-husband in the frame."

"So you're well and truly stuck?" said Martin. "Not a lead anywhere?"

"That's about the size of it. I'm almost ready to fall back on Genevieve Marchbanks' theory. Maybe the killer is a nutcase who got the idea when he saw the CBC feature on the opera production."

"Well," said Martin gravely, "the first rule if there are no definite suspects is to concentrate on the victim. You should go back further, to his childhood if necessary. Somewhere in Chalon's life will be the reason for his death."

"That's in hand," said Richard. "Jean Howe is working on it. Trouble is, there's very little to go on. Chalon doesn't seem to have talked about his early life at all. It's as if his life only began with his singing career."

"He was an opera star," said Martin philosophically. "What do you expect? He probably did figure life began with his singing career."

"Well," said Richard grimly, "it certainly ended with his singing career and he's left us one hell of a puzzle. Who orchestrated the fall of Mephistopheles?"

Philippa was always happy to perform at the Palace Theatre since it was only a ten-minute walk along the Quay from her condo. Therefore, after Adam Craig arrived in town to assume the role of Mephistopheles, it was easy for her to fit in extra rehearsals while he familiarized himself with the production. By the end of the run-through on Tuesday, it was obvious that Adam was going to step in with ease and confidence. The following day, Genevieve scheduled some time to polish the staging of the principals' scenes, and after an exhilarating afternoon reviewing the final trio, Adam suggested that the group go for an early dinner at the Boathouse. Since Genevieve had a prior engagement, and both tenor and rehearsal pianist declined, Philippa found herself walking to the restaurant with her ex-boyfriend.

Although it was only twenty past four, the light was fading as they cut down Antique Alley and strolled past the odd assortment of second-hand shops that lined the lower road. They crossed the railroad tracks and headed for the Quay where the ornamental lampposts were already lit and casting golden pools of light on the walkway. The day had been clear, but cold, and the temperature seemed to drop another few degrees as they reached the boardwalk, for the icy chill from the river permeated the already crisp air. The path was treacherous, encrusted with ice where the snow had melted and frozen. With visions of broken ankles and sinusitis dancing in her head, Philippa slowed her pace and pulled her muffler up around her nose.

Adam solicitously took her arm. He seemed as cheerily impervious to the cold as the giant tin soldier who towered over the entrance to the market.

"Like old times," he said. "Remember how we used to walk along Spanish Banks after our opera-workshop sessions? We've come a long way since then."

"You've gone further than I have," said Philippa. "Your two years in Dresden have established you on the international scene. That's going to guarantee you roles with North American companies."

"Hopefully," said Adam. "It's been a great learning experience, even though I've only had small roles. I've worked with some major stars."

As they reached the Inn at the Quay and cut around to the front of the building where the Boathouse entrance was located, Philippa asked, "Did you ever perform with Grégoire Chalon?"

"Yes. Once. That was *Faust* too. He flew in to take over four performances when our Mephistopheles was ill. I was singing Valentin."

"Did you enjoy working with him?"

"He was fine. Very courteous, always the perfect gentleman. Only time he displayed any emotion was through his singing."

"That's not unusual."

"No. I know." Adam aggravatingly changed the subject. "So how are your parents?" he asked. "I always got a kick out of them. Are they still busy with local politics?"

Philippa sighed. It had always been impossible to keep Adam going in whatever direction she wanted him to take. Dutifully, she responded, "Yes, but they're a bit preoccupied with other things right now. Dad had a rather amazing windfall recently, but it's a bit of a mixed blessing."

"Oh? What's going on?"

"One of his elderly fishing buddies died and left Dad his house . . . well, not really a house. It's a tiny little cottage on Lac La Hache, but, of course, Mum's shopping for things to furnish it because she says Guthrie—that's the old guy who died—had ghastly taste so she wants to start from scratch."

"That's going to prove an expensive inheritance."

"That's what Dad says." Philippa paused at the top of the steps and let Adam go ahead. "By the time they've finished fixing it up, they'll probably have to sell it to break even," she said.

Adam held the door for Philippa and then followed her into the restaurant. They were greeted by a welcome blast of warm air and a smiling hostess who gushed rather too obsequiously as she led them to their table. Once she had taken their drinks order—wine for Adam, mineral water for Philippa—she left them with their menus. Adam devoted his attention to the list of entrées. Philippa prompted him back to the subject on her mind.

"What else can you tell me about Grégoire Chalon?" she asked. "I'm still trying to come to terms with why he was killed. It's so hard to make sense of it all."

"He was generous with advice to young singers," said Adam, his eyes still scanning the menu. "He gave me some great tips on how to do my role."

"Did you talk to him about anything else?"

"Not really." Adam grinned. "The one I chatted with was his fiancée. She was a bit of all right. I got along with her really well."

Philippa rolled her eyes.

"I bet you did," she muttered, remembering exactly why her ex was her ex. "So, what was she like, other than being good-looking?"

"Very proper, unfortunately," Adam admitted ruefully. "Most of our intimate conversations were her telling me how wonderful Grégoire was and how much she adored him. All so sweet and sugary it was nauseating."

"That seems to be the story from everyone who ever met him."

"Still," added Adam, "reading between the lines and interpreting the glint in the lovely Tricia's eye, I suspect she thought he was much too magnanimous with the stepchildren from marriage-number-one. She figured they were old enough to look after themselves. She never came right out and admitted it, but I think she resented the fact that he still felt responsible for them, not to mention the dotty old grandmother."

"Dotty?"

"She has dementia. Grégoire was paying for her to live in High Hill House."

"Ooh. Expensive. I bet she could tell a few tales if you caught her on a good day. Richard should check her out. Granny ought not be discounted."

"If Tricia had her way, I suspect she would have been, right alongside the stepdaughters. Shouldn't you stop grilling me about Chalon and read your menu? I'm hungry and our waitress will be here any minute."

"I know what I'm having. I always order stuffed prawns at the Boathouse. Go on, tell me why Tricia Hayes doesn't like Grégoire's stepdaughters? Are they being difficult with her?"

"I don't think she has anything to do with them, but she figures they put Grégoire through hell. Evidently there was an older girl who went haywire as a teenager . . . slept around with anyone and everyone, then got into drugs and finally committed suicide. Then the second girl became difficult, right around the time his poor wife was diagnosed with cancer. I don't think daughter-number-three caused any trouble, but Tricia obviously thinks that all the trials and tribulations with the first two made Grégoire's life miserable and she thinks he should stop worrying about them and move on."

"If she was trying to cut Grégoire off from his former family, then the stepdaughters must have felt threatened by his upcoming marriage," said Philippa.

"I doubt it," said Adam. "It sounds like they had a lot of money from their mother. Grégoire's first wife was rich. She's the one who put him on his feet."

Their waitress appeared and took their dinner order. Once she had left, Philippa returned to the subject at hand.

"Is Chalon's wife-to-be wealthy like his first wife?" she asked curiously.

"Don't think so. I got the impression that she was very much looking forward to the upgrade in lifestyle that came with being attached to a rich, successful singer. She must be really ticked to have missed her opportunity. Poor old Grégoire. What a way to go. Almost Miltonian, isn't it? The fall of Satan, except Chalon didn't fall from grace, he just fell. It was a hell of a final exit."

"It was the fall of Mephistopheles," corrected Philippa. "He's not actually Satan, is he? He's a demonic tempter and a seeker of souls. I read somewhere that his name is Hebrew for destroyer and liar, but he has that same air of urbane sophistication that's associated with Lucifer."

"I was told his name was Greek for Lord of the Darkness, so whichever way you look at it, he's a devil, if not The Devil. Honestly, Philippa, you should sing more and read less. You might make a bit more headway. And you'd better concentrate on staying in shape to sing Marguerite and not get sidetracked wondering who set that trap for Chalon. This is a demanding role, so you can't split your energies by sleuthing between scenes. Leave that to your brother and your VPD pal—if, of course, he's still around." Adam left the statement hovering in the air, too obvious a question to ignore.

"He's away right now," said Philippa, "but he'll be back in town next month."

Adam's eyes lit up.

"Oh, well, if you're at a loose end, we'll have to make the most of my time here."

"We certainly will," said Philippa. "We have to make *Faust* a topnotch production, and as you said yourself, the roles are too demanding to allow ourselves to be sidetracked."

"That's true," said Adam smoothly, "but there's nothing wrong with combining early nights with congenial companionship. Are you quite sure you wouldn't like to join me in a bottle of wine?"

"Absolutely," said Philippa.

"Absolutely no wine, or absolutely, we can combine companionship with an early night?"

"Both," said Philippa sweetly. "I fully intend to benefit from your congenial companionship over dinner, after which I shall head back to my condo to have an early night . . . on my own. Now, here comes our dinner, so stop pouting and enjoy your meal."

IV

Richard stared at Constable Jean Howe in disbelief. He was astounded at what he was hearing.

"What do you mean, Grégoire Chalon doesn't exist?" he demanded.

Jean Howe shrugged apologetically.

"Just that. There's no record of Grégoire Chalon between the date on his birth certificate and 1987 when he turned nineteen and applied for a SIN. The birth certificate was obviously forged, because the hospital has no record of the birth, nor any records pertaining to the names of the parents. The SIN was for a job he was taking as a waiter at a restaurant in Montreal, one that has long since been out of business, so there's no joy to be had there. It wasn't long after that that he met up with Genevieve Marchbanks, so she's still your best source of information."

"She said Chalon had been teaching music. That was the job he gave up."

"If he was, he must have been coaching students privately and pocketing the money. There's no record of him in the public-school system, nor in any private school in Quebec."

"Marchbanks specifically said, 'He gave up his job.' That doesn't imply a private studio. It suggests that he was at a school. Besides, given his age, he couldn't have afforded a studio and he wouldn't have qualified for the public system, so a private school is the best option."

"I'll check the other provinces, but given the fact that the name is false, it's going to be tough to trace. Plus, it's possible he made the whole thing up."

Richard frowned thoughtfully.

"He obviously had a reason for adopting a new identity, but people usually cling to some things that are factual. The music teaching has a ring of truth. The other significant thing Marchbanks told me was that he had been orphaned young. She also said he was a devout Catholic, and that's substantiated by the cross he wore. Put all those items together and we have a definite lead."

Jean nodded.

"A Catholic orphanage and private school . . . one where he could have been taken in as a child and later acted as an assistant teacher in return for his keep."

"Precisely. No need for an SIN until he broke away from the school. Now we have to find out why he left and was determined to create a whole new life. If we ascertain that, we may discover why he died. I wonder if Mary van Luven knew about his past life. It was only two years later that he married her. He might have confided in her."

Jean sighed. "It's too bad the sister who raised the stepdaughters is dead," she said. "If Mary had known about her husband's past, she might have confided in her sister, but the children would have been much too young to know anything."

Richard tapped his fingers thoughtfully on the edge of his desk. "The grandmother is still alive," he said. "She's eighty-nine. I have the details here," he added, nodding towards a printout on top of a pile of papers. "She's in a care home on the North Shore."

Jean raised her eyebrows. "Doesn't Chalon's mother-in-law have Alzheimer's?"

"No. Vascular dementia," said Richard. "The result of mini-strokes. Loss of short-term memory. Basically, she's senile, but she could still have the odd good moment."

"But could we rely on anything she said?"

"Probably not, but you never know."

"It would be tricky," said Jean. "Somehow, I can't see the care-givers giving a policeman carte blanche to grill one of their residents. You'd have some bossy nurse standing alongside running interference the entire time. I suppose I could go in undercover, but there would be a lot of negative repercussions if it came out."

"Yes, you're right," said Richard. "Not a good idea, and probably a waste of time. Still, I think I'll drive over to the North Shore and have a talk with the older girl. There's always a chance that she might recollect snatches of conversation between her mother and her grandmother. She could know something that she doesn't realize is significant. It would be worth picking her brains to see what she can dredge up from her childhood memories."

Richard phoned to ascertain that Susanna Caruthers would be home that evening and arranged to drop by at seven o'clock. By the time he left his office, it was well past six, so he stopped en route at McDonald's to pick up a hamburger, and then slid into the tail end of the rush-hour traffic to the North Shore. He took the Lynn Valley exit and headed up the hill, observing how, in the higher elevations, the gardens were still blanketed with snow. More flurries were predicted in the next few days so the area could become a white-out. He was glad he was getting the interview in today.

When he reached the Caruthers' home, the first thing he noticed was the propensity of sports equipment stacked at the side of the carport beside the two-door Chevy Cavalier. Hockey sticks, a kayak, cross-country skis, toboggans and two eighteen-speed racing bikes filled the space between car and wall. The equipment was top-of-the-line. There was money in this family far beyond Susanna's salary as a teacher. Richard was not surprised to see a Dodge Ram pickup truck with a canopy parked on the road in front of the house. Something large would be needed to transport the outdoor-recreation gear.

Susanna and her husband were both home. They had finished dinner and were drinking coffee. Susanna politely invited Richard to join them at the dining table and offered him a cup. Richard accepted and sat down. Susanna poured him a coffee, passed it to him, then sat back and waited for him to speak. Her husband watched, equally quietly, from the far end of the table.

There was a coolly courteous impassiveness about Susanna Caruthers, thought Richard. He did not know quite what to make of her. He could not tell whether her lack of visible emotion was her natural manner, or whether it was the result of tension due to the police presence. However, when he explained the reason for his visit—that he wanted to know more about her stepfather's early life—the mask slipped momentarily. She was taken aback. Richard also detected a note of relief, though it vanished almost as quickly as it had appeared. But in spite of her apparent readiness to answer his questions, after half an hour, Richard had learned no more about Grégoire Chalon than he had known to start with.

Susanna confirmed that Chalon had been present a lot during the early years of his marriage to her mother. The couple had lived in Toronto while he was studying with Julia Berti and during the years he was under contract with the Canadian Opera Company. It was only later that Chalon had spread his wings onto the international scene. Susanna understood that her stepfather had taught music before he met her mother. She had never met any members of his family, and she had been told that his parents had died when he was young. No, she didn't recall hearing her mother and grandmother ever discussing her stepfather. As far as she was concerned, he had always been good to her mother and had taken great care of the family. How had she felt about his marriage to Tricia Hayes? Anxious, Susanna admitted frankly, in case money that should have been hers and Christa's ended up going to his new wife, but once it was clear that their mother's money was to be settled on her and her sister, she had stopped being against the match and wished him well. Geoff Caruthers listened throughout the interview, watching his wife solicitously, and occasionally cutting in with a comment that reiterated whatever Susanna had said. A guardian parrot, thought Richard, thoroughly irritated, wishing the man would leave, although it was abundantly obvious that Geoff Caruthers had no intention of doing so. Frustrated, Richard drained his coffee, thanked Susanna and stood up. As he headed for the door, he had a sudden thought.

Turning back, he asked, "What about your grandmother? I know she's had a series of strokes, but it's possible she and your mother would have talked privately about matters they didn't want you girls to hear. Does she have lucid moments? Perhaps a word with her would be helpful."

At last, Susanna's reserve dissolved.

"No," she said shrilly. "Don't even consider that. Granny has dementia. She becomes terribly confused if you try to make her remember things, and then she gets distressed. I wouldn't dream of putting her through a police interview, and the nursing staff would back me to the hilt on that. If she became agitated, you could bring on another stroke."

Richard raised his hands to stop the outpouring.

"That's all right," he said. "I get your point. It was just a thought, but we'll respect your concerns."

Richard allowed himself to be shown out, but as he walked down the driveway, he glanced back at the couple standing in the doorway. Geoff Caruthers had his arm around his wife's waist and her head was tilted towards his shoulder. In the light from the porch, he could have sworn he could see the glint of tears on Susanna's cheek.

The following morning, he arrived at his office early. The printout on the nursing home was still at the top of the pile on his desk. He eyed it thoughtfully. Martha Gage, mother of Mary and Miriam, grandmother of Christa and Susanna. Susanna Caruthers was probably right that the staff wouldn't like their charge being subjected to a police interview, and he was sure that Susanna would have called the care home to demand that her grandmother be protected from any form of official questioning. However, there was no reason why a young woman who was a friend of the family couldn't pay the old lady a visit.

Richard smiled to himself. Philippa was always eager to help with his cases. Here was the ideal opportunity for her to do something useful without endangering herself or interfering in police business. A visit to a care home was a no-risk activity and he had no qualms about sending her there. He was very curious to know whether Susanna's reaction had been the result of concern for her grandmother's wellbeing or anxiety for what her grandmother might divulge. Impatiently, he glanced at his watch. He couldn't call Philippa yet—her dress rehearsal with Adam had probably gone late last night. He would give her the morning to rest, but come noon he would phone and tell her his plan.

V

Philippa was delighted to get Richard's call. It was two days since her dinner with Adam and she was anxious for opening night to arrive. A full-dress rehearsal had been mounted for Adam's benefit the previous evening and the opera had proceeded with metronomic precision, but it was clear that the singers needed an audience. They were past the point where a rehearsal could be exciting. With a full day off before the opening, the afternoon had yawned ahead interminably. The mystery novel she was reading hadn't held her attention, for her mind kept wandering back to the death of Grégoire Chalon. Richard's request offered release from hours of restlessness and boredom.

Cheerfully, Philippa tossed her book aside. Then, assuming that the elderly Mrs. Gage would be from the pre-jeans generation, she changed into a skirt and sweater. As an afterthought, she put on the gold chain with the tiny cross that her parents had given her on her twenty-first birthday. It was dainty, crusted with small diamonds, and the most tasteful piece of jewellery she possessed. Then she threw on her coat and headed out the door. The threatened snow had not yet arrived and the day was bright. She stopped at Starbucks to pick up a coffee for the road; then she headed for the freeway.

Twenty minutes later, she was on the Second Narrows Bridge, racing towards the breathtaking panorama of snow-packed mountains that swept across the North Shore. Humming to herself, Philippa slid into the passing lane and whipped by a Winnebago that threatened to spoil the spectacular view. Too quickly, she was across the bridge and heading up the cut that bisected Lynn Valley.

The day darkened as she drove up the hill. Philippa assumed that the steep rocks had cut off the sunlight, but when she emerged at the top, she saw that the sky had clouded over. She hoped the threatened snow was not going to appear before she made the return trip.

As she pulled into the parking lot of High Hill House, a cyclist cut across her path. Philippa glanced round as the rider accelerated onto the access road. The blonde ponytail flowing below the helmet looked familiar. She had only met Grégoire Chalon's stepdaughters the night of his demise, yet she was ready to swear that the cyclist was the older sister, Susanna.

At the front desk in the lobby, the receptionist confirmed Philippa's suspicions. Susanna Caruthers had been visiting her grandmother, but had just left. Philippa ruthlessly suppressed twinges of conscience and managed to imply that she was an old family friend. She expressed her disappointment at missing Susanna and compounded her deceit by adding that she ought to say hello to Mrs. Gage while she was there. Unsuspecting, the receptionist directed Philippa to the wing where the dementia patients were located. Philippa repeated her fabrication when she reached the nursing station. She was promptly welcomed and led to a room at the end of the hall.

"Mrs. Gage is having a good day," the nurse informed her. "She'll be delighted to have another visitor. Of course, she won't know who you are. She doesn't even recognize her granddaughters most of the time, but she still enjoys their company."

The nurse threw open the door and ushered Philippa through.

"You have another visitor, dear," she announced. "One of Susanna's friends. Isn't that nice?" Without another word, she went back out and disappeared down the hall.

Philippa stepped into the room. It was clean and tidy, but the beige and brown décor gave off little light. The colour scheme seemed gloomy, although the furnishings appeared new and modern—with one exception. A well-worn burgundy-striped wing chair with Queen Anne legs was placed by the window. A tiny woman sat in the chair, her wizened face palely illuminated by a thin shaft of light that filtered between the curtains. Her eyes were on a flickering television screen in the far corner—Philippa recognized a Nigella Lawson re-run—but the sound had been turned off. Nigella was pounding her chicken in silence. On a table beside the wing chair stood a half-drunk cup of tea and a vase that held a fresh bunch of pink carnations.

A low armchair was placed opposite the wing chair, so Philippa seated herself there and introduced herself as a friend of Susanna's. As an afterthought, and happy to be saying something truthful, she added that she was a singer who had worked with Susanna's sister and stepfather. Mrs. Gage looked at her blankly. Her eyes were glassy, and seemed to be focussed on something past Philippa's shoulder. Philippa wondered if she had undergone cataract surgery. Plastic lens implants might create that strangely reflective effect, she thought, but when Mrs. Gage spoke, it was apparent that the glazed expression was from bewilderment.

"I don't know a Susanna," she said anxiously.

"Your granddaughter," Philippa prompted. "She was just here to see you."

The blank look disappeared. Mrs. Gage smiled sweetly, and her eyes landed on Philippa with an alertness that was sudden and disconcerting.

"Oh, no, dear. I don't think so. You're my first visitor today."

Philippa's spirits sank. This was going to prove useless. Having never talked with anyone who suffered from dementia, she felt at a loss. Her sister, Juliette, should be here, she thought. She'd know what to say. Juliette had spent years as a volunteer at a senior centre. Philippa tried to remember what Juliette had told her about her experiences. *Talk about anything. It doesn't matter what you say. Accept their reality and don't worry if the words don't make sense.*

Philippa took a deep breath and tried again.

"Those are lovely flowers."

"Aren't they pretty? Did you bring them, dear?"

"No, I think that must have been Susanna."

"That's right. She's such a nice nurse. She looks after me very well." Mrs. Gage turned towards the window. "Is it cold out today?" she asked. She took one of the curtains in her claw-like hand and pulled it back a couple of inches.

As Philippa followed her glance, she noticed a spattering of faint stains on the drapes. Following them down to the floor, she saw that the carpet had been marked in places too. Someone had diligently cleaned up the spills, but the telltale marks remained. Philippa eyed the half empty teacup. There was probably a very good reason for the brown and beige décor, she decided.

"Yes," she replied, suddenly aware that she hadn't answered the question. "It is cold today. They say it might snow."

"I don't like snow."

"No. It's pretty, but it makes driving difficult."

"Do you drive, dear?"

"Yes. I came in my car."

"Susanna always comes on her bike," said Mrs. Gage. "She likes to keep fit."

Philippa blinked. She felt a surge of excitement.

"Susanna? Your granddaughter?"

But the moment of lucidity had gone.

"Could you get me a cup of tea, dear?" said Mrs. Gage. "And open the curtains so I can see out."

Disappointed, Philippa nodded and rose to her feet. She opened the curtains. Then, taking the teacup, she left the room. No one was manning the nursing station, so she found her way back to the front desk. The receptionist directed her to a small lounge, which was well stocked with drinks and snacks for the residents. She filled a fresh cup from the tea-urn and returned to Mrs. Gage's room. As she entered, she noticed a set of framed photographs on a stand by the door. One was a group picture, and as she peered at it closely, she recognized a younger Grégoire Chalon. He was posing with an attractive fair-haired woman and two young girls. Philippa took the tea to Mrs. Gage. Then she returned to fetch the photograph.

Mrs. Gage sipped her tea.

"Lovely," she said. "Nice and hot." Her eyes strayed to the television set. "I can't hear it," she said. "What's wrong with it?"

Philippa picked up the remote and turned up the sound. Nigella was extolling the virtues of turmeric.

"I like her," announced Mrs. Gage. "She's nice. Susanna always puts her on for me."

Philippa smiled. The food network was the perfect station for someone in Mrs. Gage's condition—a one-on-one visit with the person on the screen talking directly to her audience. Susanna knew how to cater to her grandmother's needs.

"Susanna is a good girl, isn't she?" said Philippa.

Mrs. Gage gave a throaty laugh.

"She is now," she said.

"Is this Susanna?" Philippa thrust the photograph forward. Mrs. Gage's eyes slid from the television screen and scrutinized the picture.

"When she was good, she was very, very good, but when she was bad, she was horrid," she crooned. "It was Mary's fault. Mary never listened. She never paid attention."

"Susanna was bad? What did she do?"

Suddenly Mrs. Gage let out a cackle of laughter and her eyes grew wild. "Mary used to say, 'She was full of Old Nick.' Silly fool. She was right, and she didn't know it."

The glassy eyes became expressionless again. Mrs. Gage turned her blank gaze on Philippa's neck.

"That's pretty," she said, eyeing the diamond-studded cross. "I like that."

"My parents gave it to me," said Philippa.

"You're a good girl," said Mrs. Gage. "You can wear a cross. He didn't have the right to, though. That's why Susanna wouldn't go back. Everyone thought she was just difficult, but she was right not to go. Mary was a fool."

Philippa leaned forward eagerly.

"Right not to go where? What did Susanna refuse to do?"

Mrs. Gage's mind had wandered onto another track.

"I like your hair, dear," she said. "It's pretty. I had a friend with red, curly hair when I was young. She was a nurse in the war. Are you a nurse?"

"No," said Philippa. "I'm a singer. I was singing in the opera with Grégoire Chalon."

"Who?"

"Susanna's stepfather . . . the opera singer. We were in *Faust* together. I was Marguerite. He was Mephistopheles . . . the Devil."

Mrs. Gage sighed.

"Old Nick. His head used to turn when I called him that, but then he'd get so mad. Mary got cross too. She was a fool. She never listened to me." Her eyes slid sideways and lit on the vase of flowers at her side. "Those are pretty," she said, smiling happily. "That was nice of you to bring me flowers, dear."

"Those weren't from me." Philippa leaned forward and patted the frail hand. "Susanna brought those for you."

Mrs. Gage's eyes glided back to Philippa, but they were smooth impenetrable mirrors again.

"Who is Susanna?" she said. "I don't think I know her." The eyes returned to the television screen. Nigella was making dessert. "I like her," said Mrs. Gage.

Philippa remained for another half hour, but the only remarks forthcoming were about the flowers, the television—Mrs. Gage liked Emeril as well as Nigella—and Philippa's cross and her red hair. It was like being on a miniature railway with a single loop. One kept going past the same checkpoints, over and over and over. When the first sporadic snowflakes began to drift past the window, Philippa knew it was time to leave. She fetched Mrs. Gage one more cup of tea, gave her a hug, and bid her goodbye. As she opened the door, she turned to look back. Mrs. Gage's eyes were fixed on the television screen, but she seemed to sense that Philippa was still there. Without looking up, she said, "It's all right, dear. It's quite safe for you to sing with him."

Philippa froze in the doorway.

"Why?" she asked quietly.

Mrs. Gage's eyes were fixed on the flickering screen.

"You're too old," she said.

The snow started to fall in earnest as Philippa drove down the cut. Traffic had slowed and was threatening to grind to a halt. Philippa put the heater on high, but no matter how much hot air blasted into the vehicle, she could not get warm. The memory of Mrs. Gage's final words had chilled her to the core. She had admired Chalon for his artistry and his generosity to his fellow performers, and she felt sickened to think of the dark side that might have lurked below the charming persona. She shivered, suddenly remembering how the children in the chorus had flocked around him, including her own sister's children. What had she said to Richard? They acted as if Santa Claus was in the production. Good old St. Nick—but how ironic. According to Mrs. Gage, there was nothing goodly or saintly about Chalon. He was simply Old Nick, the Devil incarnate.

Cursing the snow and the traffic, which was now crawling towards the Second Narrows Bridge, Philippa wished she had had the foresight to pick up another coffee for the return trip. She was anxious to report back to Richard, but couldn't risk phoning from the car, no matter how slowly she was proceeding. Frustrated, she pulled a disc from the glove compartment and inserted it into the CD player. The glorious tones of Montserrat Caballe singing "O, Mio Babbino Caro" floated from the dashboard, but the aria brought no comfort to Philippa. If she had correctly interpreted what she had heard at Hillside House, Mary van Luven's daughters had lost their own beloved father and had him replaced by a charming predator.

By the time Philippa was home, she had listened to four of the CDs from the six-disc set. Wearily, she took off her coat, put the kettle on and picked up the phone. Predictably, she only reached Richard's voicemail, so she left a message for him to call her. Then, hoping to receive an answer to a question that had been nagging at her all the way home, she phoned Adam. He sounded mildly puzzled at the reason for her call, but he told her what she wanted to know.

"Yes," he said, "Tricia Hayes does have children. Three girls. She has sole custody because of the state her husband was in when he came out of the army. . .. How old? I don't know, all under ten, judging by the picture she showed me. They look like three little blonde angels. Why do you want to know?"

"Just curious," lied Philippa.

"They'll be sad about Grégoire too," said Adam. "According to Tricia, they absolutely adored him."

⇒┼⇐

Richard called half an hour later. He was astounded when Philippa told him what she had learned on her visit to the nursing home.

"Are you absolutely sure you understood correctly?"

"I'm telling you exactly what she said. The poor old soul is right out of it, so I could be way off base, but I don't think so. Every so often, she'd zoom in on an idea and seem perfectly lucid. When she did, I had the distinct impression that she thought her son-in-law had been preying on the children, and that her daughter had been either too blind or too intimidated to do anything about it. She said Susanna had refused to go back . . . which has to refer to the fact that the children remained in Trenton with their aunt and grandmother."

"What you've found out could certainly explain his change of identity," said Richard. "If there was an incident in his past, something perhaps not proved but causing mistrust, it would mark him for life."

"Or impede his opportunities to repeat the behaviour," said Philippa sourly. "Did you know that Chalon was about to marry another woman with young children? Tricia Hayes has three small daughters. She has sole custody too."

"Does she, indeed?" said Richard. "That wasn't mentioned in the report from the Ontario police. Given that the fiancée was in Toronto and had nothing to gain and everything to lose from Chalon's death, we paid very little attention to her. But she'll have to be interviewed again. We need to find out if anyone had tipped her off. Obviously, I have to interview the stepdaughters again, too. It would help a lot, though, if we could find more information about Chalon's early years. If child abuse is his dirty secret from the past, there may be someone else he's harmed that we know nothing about."

"What are you doing to trace him?"

"His photo has gone out all across the country. For now, we're checking Catholic schools and orphanages in Quebec, New Brunswick and Manitoba, but we'll do the whole country if necessary. Hopefully, someone will recognize him. The beard is a bit of an obstacle, because he'll have grown that to go with the name change, but there are other identifying factors. We're pretty sure he was teaching music, and he left the school around the time he was nineteen."

"You know," said Philippa slowly, "Mrs. Gage told me something else that might be significant. She said that when she called Chalon Old Nick, he'd turn to answer, but then he'd become angry. That could mean he responded to the name, and then was mad because he'd been caught out."

"It could indeed," said Richard. "Clever kid, you are. What's the French for Nicholas?"

"Nicolas, I think," said Philippa. "Sounds the same, just doesn't have the *h*."

"Right, well off you go. I hope you didn't get chilled being out in the snow. Don't want to ruin your opening night tomorrow. You'd better have a hot drink and turn in early."

"I'm already in my PJs," said Philippa, "and I'm drinking mint tea with honey. I'm going to have a light supper and watch TV. Then I'll say a prayer that the snow won't ruin our audiences tomorrow, after which I'm heading for bed."

"Not to worry." Richard glanced out the window of his office. "It's already turning to rain."

"That's in Vancouver." Philippa glowered at the thick flakes gliding past her window. "It's still dumping on New Westminster."

"You'll survive. After all the publicity you've had, a bit of snow won't keep your audiences away. Have a good show, and don't be offended if I can't make it this time."

"Do try. All the original seats are reserved as they were for the first opening night, so Mum and Dad and the rest of the gang will be there."

"I'll see," said Richard. "And whether I'm there or not, for heaven's sake, don't drop any more baritones into the scene shop."

"I wouldn't dream of it," said Philippa pertly, "even if Adam is my ex."

She rang off with a sigh. Flippancy helped, but it didn't cover her sadness at the thought of the frail old lady in the nursing home whose fragmented brain was tormented with snatches of dark secrets from the past. Nor did it cover her own sorrow at her disillusionment with a performer she had greatly admired. Yet the more she reflected on the behaviour of Chalon's stepdaughters—the oldest girl's suicide and the rebellion of the second daughter—the more she believed that her conclusions were correct. Had Chalon intended to go through the whole family? Was the oldest girl's promiscuity and subsequent suicide the product of his abandonment of her in favour of her younger sister, and was Susanna's rebellion the result of her discovering first hand what had been going on? Her determination that she and her sister remain with their aunt could have been a ploy to prevent her younger sister from ever going through the same trauma. It could also explain Christa van Luven's untroubled personality and genuine grief at her stepfather's death. She was the one who had been shielded from his dark side. Uneasily, Philippa recalled the lithe figure she had seen cycling away from the nursing home. If Susanna Caruthers had been fiercely determined to protect her sister, she would not have turned a blind eye to the future fate of Tricia Hayes' children. But what had she done to set the fatal chain of events into motion?

VI

"We've got him, sir." Jean Howe waved a computer printout at Richard as he walked into the incident room. "His name's Nicolas de Mornay, and he was raised in a private Catholic orphanage school in New Brunswick— St. Dominique's. He stayed on as a music teacher after he graduated, but was forced to resign due to the suspicion that he had a sexual relationship with an eleven-year-old female student. I talked with the detective who sent us the report," she added, "and he said that 'suspicion' was a euphemism. The school authorities had known that the abuse had taken place and were just trying to shuffle it under the carpet. One of the nuns took DC Baird aside after he left the administrative offices and told him flat out that de Mornay was caught in the act, so there's no doubt about it. Basically, de Mornay seduced the child. He was seventeen when he started teaching her. He had gradually established a close friendship with her over a period of eighteen months, taking her on outings and giving her treats. He was nineteen when he was hauled in to account for his behaviour."

Richard took the report silently and began to read. Jean continued talking.

"There's more from the Ontario branch too," she said, "and everything they found confirms the fact that the man was a pedophile. The team that went through his Toronto apartment uncovered a mass of computer files and links to kiddy-porn. They also discovered that ever since his stepchildren went to live with their aunt, he has taken an annual holiday in Thailand, possibly to satisfy the urges that he could no longer take out on the van Luven girls. Sergeant Martin has sent a photograph to the Thai police, so if Chalon did travel there to visit underworld brothels that cater to pedophiles, somebody should be able to come up with a witness."

"If Chalon had a history of child abuse, there could be a lot of people out there who would have liked to see him dead," said Richard. "I wonder where the girl from St. Dominique's is now. She'd be about the same age as Susanna Caruthers, wouldn't she?"

"That's a dead end, sir," said Jean. "The girl died in a car accident two years ago."

"What about her family?"

"No family. She was one of the residents at the orphanage. But, of course, there will have been others along the way."

"Yes, but let's concentrate on the people already in the frame. Get back to Ontario and ask them to go back to Tricia Hayes and present her with what we've discovered. Her reaction should tell us a lot. At this end, we'll bring her ex-husband in to see if he had any idea of Chalon's propensities. God, can you imagine how he must have felt if he'd been told that his ex-wife was about to marry a pedophile? That's a hell of a motive for murder."

"I thought Larry Hayes had an alibi, sir."

"Yes," grunted Richard. "He does. But his alibi happens to be Susanna's husband—and if Susanna had been abused by her stepfather, Caruthers would have a motive too. Something here stinks to high heaven."

"So are we bringing in the stepdaughters too?"

"No, not yet. For one thing, I don't think Christa van Luven can tell us anything. I saw her after the accident. She was devastated, and I'm ready to swear her grief was genuine. I suspect that she has no idea that Chalon is anything other than the indulgent father figure that she adored. But Susanna is another story. I think she may have been behind everything that happened. Susanna is the key to the whole mystery. But how in heaven's name are we going to break through that stony wall of silence?"

⋙⋘

Richard was at his desk by eight-thirty on Saturday morning. The moment he sat down, his phone rang. It was his Toronto counterpart, DI Toby Welsh, reporting on the results of an interview with Tricia Hayes.

"You caught her early," said Richard. "I'm only on my first coffee of the day."

"It's eleven-thirty here," said Welsh. "Mrs. Hayes was heading up to Kingston this afternoon so she came in to see us before nine o'clock."

"What was her reaction when you told her what we'd discovered about Chalon's history? Anything interesting?"

"Very interesting," said Welsh. "Total denial."

"What!"

"She said she'd heard it all before and that the accusations were complete fabrications."

"You're kidding. She knew about his past?"

"Evidently. Shortly after she and Chalon became engaged, she received an anonymous letter accusing him of molesting his stepdaughters. She says she showed the letter to Chalon, and he told her everything—well, his version of everything. The man was an even more cunning villain than we imagined," grunted Welsh. "He told her that he had been falsely accused of molesting a pupil when he was teaching music at the orphanage, and, as a result of the incident, he had changed his name. He said his wife had known all about it, and had never doubted for a moment that he was innocent. He also told her about all the trouble he and his first wife had had with her children—well, the first two—I gather the youngest girl had never been a problem. He said that the oldest girl had gone haywire…that she had run with a bad crowd and was sexually promiscuous and experimenting with drugs by the age of fifteen. When his wife became ill, he had to take more control of the children, and after the oldest girl's suicide, he saw Susanna heading in the same direction so he cracked down on the rules to make sure she didn't follow in her sister's footsteps. What he didn't realize was that Susanna had overheard him and her mother once discussing the case at St. Dominique's, and when he tried to rein her in and control her behaviour, she countered by accusing him of molesting her and her older sister. She also tried to blame the sister's suicide on him. The situation became impossible, and that was why the girls were sent to live with the aunt in Trenton."

"All pretty plausible," said Richard, "if we didn't know better. Well, Philippa said he was a remarkably persuasive man. How did he explain the anonymous letter?"

"He told his fiancée that Susanna was angry because he was taking on a new family and had sent the letter in an attempt to break up the engagement. He said she was greedy for more money, even though he'd given both girls extremely generous settlements in addition to all he'd spent on their education and upkeep over the years."

"Poor Susanna," said Richard. "She was simply trying to protect Hayes' children, just as she'd protected her younger sister all those years before."

"But Hayes didn't believe her. She chose to believe Chalon."

"What sort of woman is this Tricia Hayes? I find it hard to believe she didn't feel some twinges of anxiety, given that she's the mother of three young girls. Let's face it, Chalon fits a well-known pattern, twice marrying, or trying to marry, women with young children. Didn't she feel the need to follow through and at least check up on the facts?"

"She definitely didn't strike me as the brightest bulb on the chandelier," said Welsh, "but she did follow through in one way. She says that she contacted the younger sister and told her about the anonymous letter. She says she asked Christa flat out if the accusation was true. Predictably, the girl was horrified and denied it absolutely."

"Predictably, because Chalon never did molest Christa. Susanna made sure of that by insisting that they remain in Trenton. Susanna protected her sister in other ways too," mused Richard, "because she kept her in ignorance and allowed her to retain her idolized image of her stepfather, the singer in whose footsteps she intended to follow. But by doing that, Susanna undermined her ability to make Tricia Hayes believe her when she tried to warn her against the marriage."

"You think this Caruthers girl took matters into her own hands?"

"I don't know," said Richard. "She certainly wasn't the person who set the trap, because she was sitting right next to me in the lower orchestra at the theatre. But I'm quite sure she'd confided in her husband about her past. Geoff Caruthers treats her as if she's a Dresden doll, which is ludicrous when you consider that she's an athletic young woman who goes in triathlons for weekend entertainment, so his concern must be over her mental and emotional state. He hovers over her as if she might break at any second. I can't believe that she wouldn't have discussed the danger to the Hayes children with him. And when the anonymous letter didn't work, I think they turned to the only other person who would be motivated to protect the children. The father. Tricia Hayes' ex-husband."

"You think the three of them somehow planned it together?"

"I'm sure of it. I just don't know how they did it."

"So where do you go from here?"

Richard smiled.

"Well," he said, "tonight, I think I'll go to the opera."

⚒

The snow was falling heavily in New Westminster but the roads had been ploughed and the steady flow of traffic was keeping the streets passable. Still, Richard was glad to have four-wheel drive for there was no telling what the conditions would be like after the opera. At least the weekend traffic was relatively light. People were staying home if they didn't have to go out. He hoped his sister's audiences were venturesome types. She would be bitterly disappointed if her big opening was ruined by a white-out.

When he pulled into the covered parkade, he saw that the first level was almost full. That augured well for the opera. As he drove along the row of cars, he passed by two women getting out of a white Chevrolet Tracker. He recognized Susanna Caruthers right away. Her companion looked familiar too. It was the same woman who had been sitting with her on the first abortive night of the opera. Good, thought Richard. He had calculated that Susanna would be there again, though he'd wondered if she'd be backstage providing moral support for Christa. With any luck, she would be sitting next to him as she was before.

By the time Richard found a parking space, Susanna and her friend had disappeared. He walked out of the parkade and navigated the half-block to the theatre, keeping to the narrow, snow-free section of the sidewalk that was protected by the store canopies. He held the glass entrance door open for two damp-looking women who had been shaking out their umbrellas under the marquee; then he followed them inside. There was already a crowd milling about the lobby and he spotted his mother standing near the coffee bar with Sylvia and Norton. Richard waved to them, and then joined the line at the box office. Once he received his ticket, he worked his way over to join them.

"Where's Dad?" he asked.

"Parking," said Edwina. "Keep an eye out for him. I have his ticket."

"Do you want coffee?" asked Norton. He was standing by the counter. "I'm getting your mother one."

Richard shook his head. He turned to watch the patrons streaming through the front door. The line at the box office was twice as long as it had been when he arrived. A lot of people were standing to one side, ridding themselves of umbrellas and dusting snow off their coats as they waited for friends or partners who were picking up tickets. Within the lobby, two bulging circles had formed in the vicinity of the auditorium doors. Some patrons were filtering off to the upper level, but the main floor was becoming uncomfortably crowded. Finally, the ushers opened the auditorium doors. As the ticket-holders started to flow through, the crowd in the foyer diminished.

Sylvia and Norton left to go to their seats, but Edwina was still drinking her coffee, so Richard stayed to keep her company.

"Where's Juliette?" he asked, suddenly realizing he had not seen any members of his other sister's family.

"They couldn't come down this weekend. It's too bad, but since they're not here, you can sit with us. I'll tell Sylvia and Norton to move back to our row too."

Richard cursed inwardly. The possibility of a switch in seats had not occurred to him.

"They may have resold those seats," he countered. "We'd better stick to what we've got."

"Nonsense. Even if the seats are taken, we can ask people to shift so we can all sit together."

Richard sighed. One could never get around his mother through guile. She had been a formidable high-school teacher and an even more formidable administrator. Experience had taught her every diversionary tactic in the book, and retirement had numbed none of her instincts. He decided he'd better level with her.

"Look, Mum, I have to sit in my own seat. Sorry. I don't want this to be public, but I need to talk with the people who will be sitting next to me."

Edwina gave him the gimlet eye.

"You're working? You're not just here to see Philippa?"

"Well, what do you think? The case is still open and the opening-night crowd have been given their original seats. That's as good as a re-enactment from my point of view. Just don't make a fuss about it, OK? And if Sylvia suggests moving, find a way to put her off."

Edwina sighed.

"Very well. I suppose what you're doing is important. I just hope there aren't any more calamities tonight. Mind you," she added sharply, "if Adam went through the trapdoor and landed on his head, it would serve him right." Adam's defection when he had abandoned Philippa for a mezzo in Germany still rankled with Edwina. "And if your father doesn't hurry up and arrive, I'll be wishing him a similar fate," she said testily.

Five minutes later, Beary had still not shown up. Edwina's tone was becoming increasingly acerbic. She drained her coffee and deposited the paper cup in the garbage bin.

"What on earth is your father doing?" she snapped. "He could have walked the length of the parkade three times over by now."

"It was crowded up there. He may be having trouble finding a parking spot."

Edwina sniffed.

"More likely, he walked through the Army and Navy and stopped to check out the fishing equipment."

Richard thought she was probably right, but refrained from agreeing. Fortunately, at that moment, his father's head bobbed into view at the rear of the box-office line. Edwina waved imperiously and pushed forward, cutting across the line of people entering the auditorium. Beary saw her coming and stepped aside to join her. Edwina handed him his ticket, steered him into the line by the left-orchestra door and beckoned to Richard to join them. Richard worked his way across and slid into line beside his parents. He followed them through the doors, handing his ticket to the usher as he went by. As he took the stub that she returned to him, he saw his sister coming up the aisle. Sylvia waved her stub at the usher, mouthed the word *washroom* to her mother and wriggled through the tide of bodies pouring into to the auditorium.

Richard walked down the aisle behind his parents. He helped his mother off with her coat and saw her settled in her seat beside his father. Then he clambered past Norton, who was sitting on the aisle two rows down, and slipped into the seat next to the young woman who was with Susanna Caruthers. As he leaned forward to greet Susanna, he noticed that there were two empty seats on her other side. Susanna did not look pleased to see Richard.

"Oh, of course," she said coolly. "I'd forgotten the reason you were originally here. You're Philippa Beary's brother, aren't you?"

"Yes. Like you, I'm very proud of my sister. This production is a great opportunity for both of them. How is your sister holding up? I guess tonight is going to be hard for her emotionally."

"She'll get through." Susanna opened her program and began reading it with an air of deliberation. Her friend smiled apologetically at Richard.

"It was very sad for both of them," she murmured. "Neither of them has got over it, but the show must go on, mustn't it? Christa's stepfather would have wanted her to sing tonight."

"I'm sure he would," agreed Richard. He glanced up, seeing a familiar figure hurrying along in front of the orchestra pit. It was Sylvia returning to her seat. She turned up the aisle and waited while Norton got to his feet to let her by. Then she slipped into the seat beside Richard.

"You came back the long way," said Richard.

"I thought I wasn't going to make it. They're taking forever to bring a wheelchair through. I gave up and came back through the doors on the other side." Sylvia swivelled her head to include Norton in the conversation, but Richard did not hear what she said, for he suddenly perceived how simple it had been for an extra person to get inside the theatre without the house manager noticing any discrepancies in the ticket count. He turned back to Susanna Caruthers' friend.

"We haven't officially met," he said. "I'm Richard Beary. My sister, Philippa, is singing Marguerite."

"Lovely to meet you," the woman responded. "I'm Joan Greenwood. Susanna and I work together."

"You're a teacher? What's your subject?"

"Music. That's why I was thrilled when Sue offered me her husband's comp. I'm really looking forward to this production."

"This whole row must be comps," said Richard. "Friends and family out in full force."

"Such a luxury. We didn't even have to stand in line," said Joan. "Susanna had the tickets ahead of time."

I bet she did, thought Richard. And I bet she had the extra comps that cover the seats beside her. She would have used two when she and Joan entered the auditorium through the left-orchestra door, but she would have had an extra ticket tucked in her purse. Her last-minute visit to the washroom was merely a ruse to come out to the lobby.

Richard visualized the scene: Susanna standing near the theatre entrance, holding the extra ticket, appearing to be another wife whose husband had dropped her off and gone to park. When her accomplice arrived, she would have waved the ticket and whisked him into the theatre lobby, bypassing the box office line. Once safely inside the crowded foyer, the accomplice could slip through the connecting door that led to the scene shop and Susanna could return to the auditorium through the right-orchestra door, giving the usher the third ticket instead of using her own stub to get back in. A balanced ticket count for the box office, and an intruder with deadly intent moving unnoticed within the building.

As if in keeping with the darkness of Richard's thoughts, the theatre lights began to dim. *Faust* was about to begin.

In spite of the palpable tension in the audience, *Faust* proceeded without any unexpected incidents. When the curtain fell, most of the patrons cleared the auditorium quickly, keen to get home before the weather deteriorated further; however, friends and family of the singers stayed to mingle, well aware that a reception was to follow and that food and wine would be appearing shortly.

Richard saw a group of people surrounding Genevieve Marchbanks. He was about to join them, but Genevieve noticed him approaching and came to meet him. Richard wasn't surprised that she didn't want to introduce him to her friends. People rarely wanted to advertise the presence of the police.

"Congratulations," he said as she drew him aside. "Well done!"

Genevieve raised her eyebrows wryly.

"For the show itself, or for getting through without killing any more singers?"

"I meant the show," said Richard. "Excellent production. But, yes, I'm glad there were no more casualties. Everyone must have been pretty edgy, especially Adam Craig, given that he was the one who had to drop through the trapdoor."

"Don't worry. I had a stagehand on duty for the entire evening. He remained on the platform from the opening curtain right through to the end."

"Sensible."

Genevieve sighed.

"So are you any further discovering who set that awful trap? Everyone keeps asking me and I have no idea what to say."

Richard shook his head.

"It's complicated," he said. "Nothing has been resolved yet. But I'm not here to investigate," he lied. "I came to see Philippa do her stuff."

"Of course you did. Lovely girl, lovely performance. I expect you're very proud of her. You're staying for the reception? It probably won't last long, given the weather, but I hope you'll join us. It'll be starting soon. We're just waiting for the lobby to clear and the singers to come out."

Genevieve drifted away. Richard looked around for the other members of his family. The only one he could see was his father. Beary was in an alcove at the far end of the lobby. He was studying a display of photographs of past shows and performers and keeping a surreptitious eye on a door in the corner. Richard wandered over to join him.

"What's so interesting over here?" he asked.

Beary nodded towards the door.

"The kitchen is in there. That's where the wine and canapés will make their entrance."

"Good plan. I'll join you. Where are the others?"

"Your mother's in the washroom, and Sylvia and Norton have gone backstage to gather their children and congratulate Philippa. They're not staying for the reception. Sylvia has an early meeting with a corporate client and Norton has to be in court first thing. Look at those old photos," Beary added fondly, changing the subject. "Some of them date back to the pre-World War I era. The Palace is a grand old building, even if it does need a bit of shoring up now and then."

Richard was barely listening, for a studio photograph of a glamorous blonde in evening dress had caught his attention.

"She's a looker, isn't she?" said Beary, following his son's glance. "You saw her on stage once," he added. "She was the principal boy in your very first pantomime, not that you'd remember. You were only four at the time. But your mother and I saw her in a couple of plays as well. Tamara Hayes was quite the star here all through the seventies."

Richard seemed mesmerized by the photograph. Beary glanced away, and then nudged his son.

"Never mind ogling sex goddesses from the seventies," said Beary. "There's a very attractive miss giving you the eye from the other side of the lobby."

Richard turned to see Joan Greenwood looking his way. When he met her glance, she smiled.

"There's an invitation you can't ignore," said Beary, "and you don't need your old father tagging along. Go to it. I'll stay here and watch for the wine."

Richard was glad to follow his father's suggestion, although not for the reason that Beary had implied, however attractive Susanna's friend might be. He joined Joan Greenwood and said, "I've been looking over the photographs on the end wall. There's one of Tamara Hayes. Wasn't she related to your friend in some way?"

Joan smiled.

"She was the sister of Sue's father-in-law."

"Geoff Caruthers' aunt? That must have been nice for him. Did he get to hang out at the theatre and go to all her shows for free?"

Joan shook her head.

"No, she died in 1979, four years before Geoff was born. His cousin Larry was a theatre kid, though. Tamara divorced her husband when Larry was two so she raised him on her own. He was carted around everywhere with her. He knew this theatre like the back of his hand—which was useful for this production. He helped load the sets in at the start of tech week."

Richard's eyes narrowed.

"He did?"

"Yes. Geoff has a pickup truck, so the two of them helped transport scenery from the rehearsal hall. That's why I was surprised that they weren't interested in coming to see the opera. Still, it's not everyone's taste, and since the Saturday-night competition was hockey…" Joan shrugged and let her expression say it all.

Richard studied her keenly.

"You know Larry Hayes well?"

"I've met him a few times. Nice fellow. He had a hard time in Afghanistan but he's come through it all. He's in great physical shape too. He borrowed Geoff's bike last month for a competition up at Whistler and placed in the top three."

"Was that the Wilier I saw in their carport? It was a beauty. The Ferrari of bicycles!"

"Yes. Larry's the only other person Geoff will trust with it."

"He must be reliable."

"Very. He's engaged to a lovely girl now, and we're all hoping he'll regain partial custody of his children again, now that he's back on his feet. Quite honestly—" Joan leaned in and lowered her voice— "from what I've heard, his first wife was pretty self-centered and unfeeling. If she'd been a more caring person, he'd have recovered a lot sooner."

"You obviously like him?"

"Yes, he's very kind under that gruff surface. He came out like a rocket last week after he'd heard what happened. He brought Geoff to the hospital to meet up with Susanna and Christa, and he drove me home." Joan's eyes widened and she unashamedly batted her eyelashes at Richard. "He's like you," she said. "Austere on the outside, but he makes you feel that he could always take care of you in a crisis."

Richard had no time to decide how to respond, because Joan's expression abruptly changed from flirtatiousness to dismay. He swivelled round to see Susanna Caruthers. She had come up behind him. Her eyes were blazing as she took her friend's arm.

"I don't think we can stay after all," she said. "Christa is upset. It's been a hard night for her, and I have a migraine coming on." Susanna looked Richard straight in the eye as if anticipating the fact that he was about to offer Joan a ride home. "I'm going to get you to drive," she added to Joan. "You're good at handling the car in the snow. You don't mind, do you?"

Joan clearly did mind, but knew it would look unkind to refuse. She nodded and turned back to Richard.

"Well, it's been lovely talking to you. I hope we'll meet again."

"I hope so too. Drive safely."

Joan laughed. "No problem. Susanna's car handles well in the snow. But it's a good job this weather didn't hit last week. The Tracker was in for servicing so we were in Geoff's pickup truck."

With a furious glare at Richard, Susanna tightened her grip on her friend's arm and steered her towards the exit doors. Richard watched as the two women left the theatre. Then he retreated to a quiet corner in the auditorium, pulled out his cellphone and punched in Sergeant Martin's number.

"You were right from the very beginning," he said. "All three of them were in it together."

The snow continued to fall throughout the night, and by morning, the south slope of Burnaby resembled the smooth white ski slopes of Whistler. The ploughs had been out, but the roads were still only navigable by those with snow tires or four-wheel drive. Even Richard's SUV was mildly fishtailing as he negotiated his way down the winding road where the senior Caruthers' home was located. When he reached the bottom of the hill, he continued past the house and slid the car into the deep snow that blanketed the wide gravel strip beside the wall of snow-laden evergreens.

He turned off the car engine and sat for a moment, reflecting on the clever scheme that Susanna had concocted with her husband and his cousin. He was certain he was right about the trio's complicity. It was the only scenario that made any sense.

Geoff Caruthers must have had his racing bike in the back of the Dodge Ram pickup when he and Susanna drove to his parents' house. Before Susanna continued on to the opera, he and Hayes went downstairs to watch the game, but Hayes slipped out the basement door and climb into the back of the truck. The canopy windows had tinted glass, which would have partially screened him, but he probably lay down alongside the bike and covered himself with a blanket to make sure he wasn't spotted when Susanna picked up her friend. At the other end, he would have remained hidden while the girls parked and walked to the theatre. Once they left, he'd have made his own way there. Susanna got him into the theatre with her extra ticket, and once in the scene shop, he hid there until Chalon went up through the trap door. After removing the plywood, he left through the emergency exit. That was the bang that Philippa heard as she was heading for the stage.

It would have taken him less than five minutes to retrieve the bike from the truck and get to the path below the Skytrain. From there, he could have been back in twenty minutes. Maybe a couple more minutes to bounce down the trail by the ravine. He'd have left the bike in the bushes, and he and Caruthers could have picked it up when they drove to the hospital in Hayes' van. It would have been easy for them to transfer it back into the pickup truck before joining Susanna and Christa.

Richard sighed. It was a great theory, but as Sergeant Martin had pointed out, it was pure speculation. There was no proof. Even if DNA evidence could be found to link Larry Hayes to the scene shop, the truck or the racing bike, there were legitimate reasons to explain his presence in every case. And Susanna Caruthers wasn't going to break. She was the coolest young woman Richard had ever come across. Now that the snow had come again, the investigation seemed irrevocably stalled, the trail as cold as the icy wind-chill that cut the frigid winter air. Yet perversely, Richard was determined to find some small sign to vindicate his conclusions, even if it were not enough to prove the case. He hoped he would find it here in the shelter of the forest.

He put on the wellington boots that he kept in the back of the SUV. Then he got out of the car and plodded round to the entrance of the trail. He paused at the stanchion at the opening of the path. A smooth white expanse stretched between the rows of trees, its pale surface only broken by the foot- and paw-prints of early dog walkers. However, on the far side of a snow-crusted log that sat like a marzipan-coated Christmas cake at the edge of the trail, there was a startling patch of green where the sun had penetrated a small clearing sheltered by a dense stand of hemlocks. Hoping to find more bare patches further along the trail, Richard set off, carefully treading in the furrows created by the previous walkers. The air was colder in the wood, for the trail was lined with tall cedars, their branches so heavily weighted that the trees were shaped like arrowheads. Sun filtered through the occasional gap and cast streaks of gold against the dark trunks.

Around the corner, the cedars retreated into the forest and frosted branches of alders and vine maples bowed over the trail, forming a fairy-like barrier of intricate white whorls that resembled a series of elaborate wrought-iron gates. Richard ducked his way through the maze of branches. On the other side, the trail dipped suddenly between a grove of fir trees. In their shade, the morning darkened and the chill air became even more penetrating. Then, on a patch of brown across the path, he found what he had been seeking. A long strip of earth, protected by the trees, was bisected by a hollow where the post-Christmas rain had accumulated and turned the ground to mud. It had frozen over when the January temperatures plummeted, but the ice had cracked and the clear imprint of a tire track traversed the soft ground below.

Richard whipped out his phone and snapped a photograph. Then, with a small smile of triumph, he texted the picture to Sergeant Martin. Almost immediately, his phone rang.

Sergeant Martin remained skeptical.

"Is that really enough?" he asked.

"If the tracks match Caruthers' bike, possibly."

"But do you have enough evidence to convince a prosecutor to move on it? What have you really got? A lot of theory and one paltry mark where the snowfall was intercepted by the trees. Your case is as thin as the ice over that pothole. Even if the Crown did decide to proceed, it's a hard one to prove, and no jury is going to convict on anything as circumstantial as that."

"I know, but I still have to report my findings."

"Yes, I know you do, but if Chalon had lived, can you imagine what the future of the Hayes children would have been? Susanna wasn't so much an avenging angel as a protective one, determined that no other child should suffer as she did. Think how the jurors will react when they hear the story of Chalon's life. All the evidence will be overshadowed by the one thought that will be shared by every person in the courtroom."

Richard had a sudden vision of his young nieces and nephews as they had appeared in the children's chorus. What had Philippa said? They had acted as if Santa Claus was in the production. He let his eyes range over the winter wonderland that had obliterated all but one small trace of the journey that had led to the murder. He wondered what he would have done in Larry Hayes' shoes.

"Yes," he said. "They'll be thinking, the Devil got his due."

THE HOUSE OF ONCE BEFORE

1964

It was the house that enthralled Anne. She had expected a tower-ing Mont Royal mansion, evoking Victorian splendour to match the grandeur of the literary aristocrats who owned the dwelling. Instead, the home was a charming Lower Westmount townhouse, an airy confection of open areas with vaulted ceilings and tall windows that revealed a restful panoply of towering elms on the street and a small walled garden at the rear, a courtyard-like sanctuary that seemed to offer a refuge from the hubbub of the world. Anne felt as if she was stepping into an enchanted sphere where the serenity of the environment muted the shrill chatter and the vibrant clothing of the artists and writers mingling within the room.

A nudge from her date brought Anne out of her reverie and she allowed Teddy to propel her forward. His uncle was moving into the crowd. If she wanted the coveted introductions that she had come here to achieve, she would have to stay close to Dr. Kent. Teddy's uncle was a professor at McGill and a respected historian.

Though frequently included on guest lists, he was a reluctant visitor, as skilled in inventing tactful excuses for his absence as in writing the books that had made him famous. However, he had a fondness for his nephew, and had agreed to attend the Paradis-Donaldson party when Teddy explained what it would mean to Anne if she could come along as a guest. The pretty brunette was also at McGill, in her case, a student working on her master's degree in English literature, and the chance to meet the owners of the townhouse was irresistible.

As Anne followed Dr. Kent into the throng, she found herself in a sea of familiar strangers, faces she knew from book covers and magazine articles, but faces that only returned her stare of recognition with polite smiles. Somehow, the people seemed smaller, less grand, than the images she had seen staring from the glossy pages. Her eyes swept the crowd, looking for the literary legends who were hosting the affair. After a moment, her glance landed on a tall, grey-haired man who stood by a round table laden with appetizers. With a start, she realized he was Hugh Donaldson, the host she had been searching for. She regarded him analytically. He was every bit as handsome as the covers of his novels suggested; yet the dynamic quality of the photographs was not present in the living being. He seemed more stolid than magnetic, a diligent scribe rather than a dashing adventurer. He also looked tired. He was talking with a cluster of admirers, but his manner seemed stilted, and periodically, his eyes would slide towards the fireplace on the far side of the room.

Anne followed his glance. Three people had gathered by the fireplace, and immediately Anne understood why he looked there. At the centre of the trio was Michelle Paradis. Anne was startled to see how tiny the poet was. Yet in spite of her diminutive figure, Paradis burned with all the dynamic energy that her husband lacked. Her copper hair, with its sea-urchin spikes, and her glittering turquoise tunic, slashed with vivid stripes of pink and orange, would have dashed a lesser individual into oblivion. Paradis's beauty was incandescent—one writer had coined the phrase, *mouth of an angel*, to describe her smile—but her dark eyes smoldered with a feverishness that made Anne afraid for her. The poet's fragile health had been well documented. Many articles had mentioned her heart condition and described the early bouts with tuberculosis that had ravaged her system, yet the blazing intensity of her personality belied the stories.

The young man standing beside Paradis seemed unable to take his eyes off her. Anne, too, found it hard to draw her eyes from the poet. But after a moment, she became conscious of the younger woman who formed the third member of the group. The woman's face was unfamiliar, so if she was a fellow writer, she was not in the illustrious league of her hosts. She was not pretty or striking in any way, but her clear-eyed countenance was calmly pleasing. She, too, watched Michelle Paradis, but her expression showed concern rather than fascination, and occasionally her glance flew upward to meet that of Hugh Donaldson on the far side of the room. A strange dynamic, thought Anne: the solemn middle-aged man and the quietly attractive woman, with their linked glances encircling the exotic poetess. A bird of paradise nesting incongruously in a shaded garden of elms and oaks.

There was something quietly arresting about the second woman, Anne thought pensively. Her glance was drawn to the windows at the front of the house as a ripple of breeze set the branches of the elm trees dancing outside the tall glass panes. As she watched the fluttering leaves, framed in the graceful lines of the tall windows, the beauty of the architecture enfolded her and the hum of the crowd in the room diminished to a gentle murmur. What I would give to live and write in a place like this, she thought. It was then that she realized what had struck her about the woman who stood with Paradis. It was her aura. She was as serene as the house itself.

2011

Edwina's face darkened as she read the editorial page of the *National Post*.

"Your favourite columnist isn't going to be flavour-of-the-month back home," she grumbled. "She's coming out in support of the British Columbian merchants who use uni-lingual Chinese signs. She might keep her opinions to issues on her own side of the country. *Merci*," she added to the waiter who had come to refill her coffee cup.

Bertram Beary looked up from the financial pages. "She *is* writing for a national newspaper," he said. "*Un plus café au lait, s'il vous plait, garçon*," he added ponderously, seeing the waiter waving the coffee pot in his direction. The waiter smirked, poured the coffee and said in perfect English, "You are most welcome."

Edwina rolled her eyes.

"What's wrong with my French?" Beary demanded. "At least I'm trying. When in Quebec, do as the Québécois do, and all that— and on the subject of our stay in Montreal," he added warily, "I'm going to be visiting Anne Kent while we're here."

Edwina slapped down her section of the newspaper and adopted her frostiest stare.

"You're not!" she snapped.

Beary, deliberately ignoring his wife's glacial tone, shrugged.

"We arranged it by email," he said. "Can't back out now. She invited me for coffee tomorrow afternoon."

Edwina's chilly gaze slipped a few more degrees.

"I'm not included?"

"I told her you were going shopping. I'll meet you back here afterwards—" Beary pointed to the bright marquee of the bistro on the far side of the square— "and take you out to dinner."

Edwina's glare made it clear that the dinner offer failed to mollify her.

Beary shrugged apologetically. "Well, I didn't think you'd want to come, given the fact that you hardly ever read her columns."

"I do read them. I just don't slaver over them with the ridiculous adulation she seems to inspire in you . . . and I don't agree with all her ultra-conservative views."

"You agree with some of them," Beary pointed out contrarily. "You just have your nose out of joint because she stands up for the male of the species in today's feminist world. Anyway, her opinions aren't the point. I don't always agree with her either, but I like the way she speaks her mind."

Edwina sniffed.

"Yes, well, you don't need someone to encourage you to do that. One of these days you'll speak your mind once too often and that'll be the end of your seat on Council."

"Nonsense, people like the way I speak out. I refuse to cower before political correctness, and so does Anne Kent. That's why I look forward to meeting her. Besides, she's working on a very interesting project."

"Oh. And what would that be?"

"A biography of Michelle Paradis."

"The poet? Wasn't that done back in the seventies?"

"The authorized bio was, but according to Anne, it was a highly sanitized version written by one of her acolytes. This one sounds like it could dispel a few of the myths."

"Really? That is interesting." Edwina thawed a little. "How did she light upon the project?"

"That's a story in itself," said Beary. "It goes back to 1964. When Anne was a student, she was invited to a party hosted by Michelle Paradis and Hugh Donaldson."

Edwina nodded approval.

"I like Hugh Donaldson's books a lot more than I like his wife's poems," she said. "At least there's some solid Canadian history in his novels. Her poetry, from what I saw of it, was all gloom and angst. So hypocritical when you consider that she had pots of money and a marriage that was the stuff of legends—both of which allowed her to stay home and write instead of having to go out and get a job like the rest of us ordinary mortals."

Beary waited until Edwina wound down. Then he continued: "She was a troubled soul with genuine health problems. She was manic-depressive—what they call bi-polar today—and she had a heart condition that ultimately killed her. That alone would have caused her to dwell on her mortality."

"She must have been very hard to live with."

"Probably, but Donaldson was devoted to her, witness his suicide after her death."

Edwina frowned. "What a waste. He was by far the greater talent. He must have published the best part of thirty novels over his lifetime. All Paradis did was win a few prestigious awards and put out two small volumes of poetry. I'm surprised that Anne Kent was dazzled enough to want to write her biography."

"Actually," said Beary, "what dazzled Anne Kent was not so much Paradis, but the townhouse where she lived. She found it quite magical."

"So?"

"So a couple of years back, the Kents decided to downsize. They started house hunting, and lo and behold, they discovered that the Paradis-Donaldson home was on the market."

"It must have changed hands a few times since the literary giants owned it," said Edwina. "They died back in the seventies, and as I recall, they didn't have children."

"Actually, Donaldson had a son from his first marriage, but he was killed in a motorcycle accident, so the house was left to their secretary for her lifetime, and then kept in the family via nephews and cousins. It was only when the latest great-niece decided to unload it that it became available."

"Interesting. So Anne Kent is living in the house she fell in love with in the sixties."

"She is." Beary beamed with delight. "Imagine writing a biography while living in your subject's home."

Beary had been an English teacher prior to retirement and a second career as a city councillor. His enthusiasm had turned him quite pink. Edwina was unimpressed.

"There's hardly likely to be any memorabilia after all this time," she said. "The family probably gave all the papers and artifacts to the university, and those will have been raked over by every serious Can-lit student of the past forty years."

"That's true, but there's a current resurgence of interest in both writers. There's even a thematic tour on their work at the history museum right now. We'll have to pop in and see it while we're here. It's a fashionable topic."

"It might be fashionable, but it's all been said before. What is Anne Kent going to add to the Paradis-Donaldson myth?"

"Well, for one thing, she thinks their famed marriage might not have been such a great love story after all."

"I've never considered it a great love story," Edwina said dismissingly. "It was an obsessive relationship, but I doubt if it was a happy one. Between Paradis's mental troubles and her eye for attractive young men, she probably led Donaldson quite a dance. The secretary who inherited the house provoked a bit of talk, too, didn't she? Seems to me, the only thing that keeps the 'grand passion' myth alive is the fact that Donaldson killed himself after his wife's death." Edwina frowned. "Didn't he do it on their wedding anniversary?" she added.

"He did. Downed an entire bottle of wine loaded with his wife's leftover heart meds. What a way to ruin a good cabernet." Beary tutted disapprovingly.

"Foolish, but definitely a statement that he couldn't live without her—so how can Anne Kent come up with a new interpretation of the events?"

"With ease," Beary said smugly. "She's come across a cryptic reference to Donaldson's epitaph, which happens to be a quote from one of his books. The quote also has a connection to Paradis's last poem. Anne thinks there's a message for posterity within the words."

"I remember Paradis's last poem," said Edwina. "'Into the Night'—we had to study it in school."

"Yes. It was published after her death. Well, actually, not until after they both died. It was still on the Grade 10 curriculum when I was teaching."

"So what's the cryptic message within the text?"

Beary shook his head.

"I don't know, but I'm looking forward to finding out. That's why Anne Kent wants to meet me. She knows I'm good at puzzles. She's very fired up about the project, and—" Beary brushed his hand lightly against his chest and attempted to look modest— "she's asked me to look over what she's concluded to date."

Edwina looked sceptical.

"What can you contribute that any other ex-English teacher couldn't throw into the equation?"

"Ah, but you see, it isn't just a literary mystery," said Beary. "The Kents have made a few renovations to the house, and, in the course of tearing out the wooden stairway, they discovered a small hidden compartment under what must have been a loose tread. The tread had been hammered down again, but not before someone had concealed a couple of very interesting items, wrapped in a section of newspaper that was dated October 12, 1970."

"The year Paradis died."

"Not just the year, the actual date of her death."

"Good heavens!" What was wrapped in the newspaper?"

"A syringe and an empty vial of digitalis," said Beary. "Anne Kent suspects that Michelle Paradis's death was not the heart attack it was presumed to be. She thinks Hugh Donaldson murdered his wife."

> *When winter claims the heart, it forms*
> *layers of ice around the core,*
> *Freezes the soul, numbs care, and makes one dare*
> *To walk into the night, needing what's most precious at the end,*
> *For comfort in the shadow of the grave.*

Anne Kent stared at the words on the last page of the book. "Into the Night"—Michelle Paradis's final poem. It was a disturbing contradiction: the stoicism of the first two and a half lines, and then the softness, the neediness of the last phrases. None of Paradis's other work demonstrated such inconsistency, but then, who was to say that consistency of emotion would be the norm when one was facing death. Anne had read enough treatises about Paradis to know that other writers had struggled with the same paradox that had struck her when she read the poem. But now, with the discovery of the vial in the secret compartment, it was hard to know what to think. If only the secretary had written a memoir, or left letters or a diary, but dutifully discreet to the end, she had stayed on in the house and catalogued the papers. She had lived quietly, giving no interviews, and had died equally quietly in 1979, when cancer had claimed her at the relatively young age of fifty-three.

Anne closed the poetry book and pushed it aside. She leaned back and looked with pleasure around the cheerful room that she had claimed for her office. The long, extended surfaces and bright light made for a delightful workspace, aesthetically pleasing and functionally practical. A whiffle from the corner indicated that Harley, the black Lab, was chasing rabbits in his sleep. Anne smiled, then stretched and turned back to the pile of notes spread out along her desk. What did she really know about Paradis and Donaldson? Very little, she thought wearily, and all second-hand.

It was infuriating how few people were still alive who had known the couple well. Teddy's uncle, the historian, had been a great provider of literary gossip over the years, but in hindsight,

Anne realized that he had merely served to confirm what was general public knowledge. Mentally, Anne reviewed what she knew about the couple.

The Paradis-Donaldson love affair had been a volatile and passionate relationship right from the start. Donaldson had been a married man with a two-year-old son when they first met. It was 1933 and he was riding the fame of his first novel, which had been published the previous year. Michelle Paradis, at twenty-two, was already a controversial public figure, loved by some, despised by others. She had won a national poetry contest at the age of thirteen with a sonnet that the judges considered a miracle of literary brilliance from one so young, and critics dismissed as a mere echo of everything said by the famous war poets. However, the combination of her lyric use of words and her magical smile as she accepted her award had earned her the phrase that was echoed time and time again throughout her life—*the mouth of an angel.*

By the time Paradis met Donaldson, she had won several prizes and had published a string of pacifist poems in prestigious magazines, but she was known as much for her beauty and her extravagant lifestyle as for her writing. She was from a wealthy family that had withstood the economic downturn of the thirties—her grandfather had substantial gold holdings and owned a vineyard in France—and while the rest of the world struggled through the Depression, she travelled, absorbing art and culture, and acquiring a cosmopolitan sheen that, combined with her stunning appearance and clever mind, presented a package that few men could resist. The studious, handsome Donaldson was no exception. Their affair began within a month of their meeting. Six months later, he abandoned his family and moved to Montreal to live with Paradis. They were married as soon as his divorce was finalized.

Within two years, they were the toast of the literary world. He wrote another successful novel; she published her first book of poems. Their love for each other was the stuff of fairy tales. Even when the first signs of mental instability began to manifest in his wife, Donaldson continued to be devoted to her. His world revolved around his marriage and his craft, but Paradis did not share her husband's compulsion to write. Her passion was for life. Poetry was an extension of her feelings, not an art to be cultivated for its own sake. She craved excitement and constant adulation, so when Donaldson was secluded in his study, working on his latest novel, she would surround herself with other men who could provide her with the attention she needed.

Anne thought back to her first meeting with the couple. She found it easy to recall how they had looked that day, although it was less easy to visualize Faith Gibbon, the secretary who had been hired by Donaldson in 1945 after he returned from serving in the armed forces. The few nondescript photographs of Gibbon in the Paradis-Donaldson biographies did not evoke the sense of calm serenity that Anne remembered. She tried to visualize the man who had been the third member of the trio that Donaldson had watched so carefully. Thoughtfully, she pulled a book from the pile on her desk and flipped it open to the photographs at the centre. Donaldson's son from his first marriage stared back at her, a shadowy version of his handsome father. Hamish MacLeod had died tragically only a few months before his famous father. A motorcycle accident had taken his life. Was it her imagination that placed him in the room with Gibbon and Paradis all those years ago? Had he been the young man who could not take his eyes from Paradis. Anne sighed. She simply wasn't sure. It was just as likely that, having seen his photograph, she had superimposed his image on her memory of the scene.

So many questions, Anne thought wearily. Had son, like father, fallen for Paradis? Had Donaldson overlooked his wife's frailties, or had he been worn down by her erratic behaviour. Had he continued to adore her, or had time and acrimony doused the flame? Every source she had read indicated that his love for his wife had never wavered, but so much of that was founded on the fact of his suicide so soon after her death. But had his motive been guilt, rather than grief? The Paradis-Donaldson myth would have been vastly different if someone had found what was hidden in the staircase at the time of the poet's death.

Sighing, Anne pushed the book aside. Tomorrow, she would run her findings by the friendly councillor from Vancouver who seemed so interested in her project. Today, she had work to do. Time to check her messages and then get on with her next column. Quickly, she brought up her emails. Typical. One solitary thank-you from a reader who considered her the voice of common sense, countered by two hostile missives from pit-bull owners, a minatory one-liner demanding that she stop criticizing treatment of women in other cultures, an offensive letter objecting to her defence of a Montreal restaurateur who dared to use the word, *pasta*, on his menu, and a vituperative barrage from a radical feminist who objected to a recent column that displayed an unbiased view towards both sexes. Anne's eyes glinted. She had lots more to say on the same subjects. Just let them wait.

Beary was looking forward to his meeting with Anne Kent. Edwina, rather huffily, had abandoned him at the Atwater Station and set off to explore the downtown area on her own. Beary had checked his map, and then found his way to the address that Anne Kent had provided. He found himself on a pleasant tree-lined street, standing before a picturesque red brick townhouse, which was set back from the road to accommodate a small front garden. The gabled roof and tall windows gave the house a charming, old-world air. Beary liked what he saw. He walked down the path, mounted the steps and rang the doorbell. As he admired the vivid colours in the fanlight window over the entrance, the front door opened. A smiling Anne Kent greeted him.

Beary's first thought was that the columnist's newspaper photograph did not do her justice. She was a very attractive woman, and although he knew she must be in her sixties, she could easily have passed for a decade younger. Her short dark hair was neatly styled and highlighted with silver streaks, and her eyes sparkled with intelligence and humour. Although casually dressed, her dark tailored slacks and red wool sweater were smart and stylish. She stepped back and welcomed Beary into her home.

As soon as he stepped inside, Beary saw why Anne Kent had been so enchanted by the interior of the townhouse. The rooms were independent, yet there was an airy openness that breathed comfort and tranquility. The mix of contemporary—the metal staircase and Japanese gas fireplace—with traditional—a vibrant Persian rug, and the grand piano in front of the vaulted windows—managed to be dramatic, yet soothing. He followed Anne into the kitchen, which was a pleasing modern room with its own traditional touch in the form of a tall, blue armoire that served as a pantry. The coffee was ready. Anne poured two mugs; then she led Beary through to the study. He observed the array of books and notes spread along the work surfaces and nodded approvingly.

"You've been doing your homework," he said.

"You've no idea," said Anne. "I've read every single version of their life stories."

"How many are there? I've only read the one from the seventies written by Terence Troy."

"That's the authorized version that came out in 1974. Troy was an interesting character. Fellow poet, close friend of Paradis. You know, back in the forties there was speculation that he was her lover, but that disappeared in the sixties once he came out of the closet. Too bad he isn't still alive. He was probably the closest person to the couple after Faith Gibbon."

"He died of AIDS, didn't he?"

"Yes. In 1979."

"Did he ever write anything else about them?"

"Only a couple of articles debunking the other bio that came out in the seventies. He took exception to the way it compared Donaldson's domestic situation to Noel Coward's *Design for Living*. Troy went to his grave insisting that Donaldson's love for Paradis never wavered and that Faith Gibbon was never anything more than a valued research assistant and editor."

"But being a loyal friend of Michelle Paradis, he would want to preserve her image at all costs."

"Yes. He would have been appalled at the bios that were published during the next two decades, especially the one that came out in the nineties. It was a radical feminist version that vilified Donaldson as the cruel, cold husband and postulated that the real love affair was between Paradis and Gibbon."

"*Faith and Michelle?* Yes, I remember the furor over that one. They turned it into a TV movie. You figure there's no substance to it?"

"Definitely not. No one I've been in contact with has even hinted at bi-sexuality, though the *Design for Living* version did raise the issue and leave it open to interpretation." Anne pulled a book from the pile on the desk and slid it across to Beary. "This biography from the eighties could have some validity, though."

Beary glanced at the title: *All Passion Spent.*

"That's Milton," he said. "*Samson Agonistes.* Can't see Donaldson and Paradis as Samson and Delilah," he added gruffly.

"Neither could the author," said Anne, "but she did compare them to Vivien Leigh and Laurence Olivier. She also suggested that Faith Gibbon was the Joan Plowright in Donaldson's life."

"Yes, well that's more appropriate," acknowledged Beary. "Did no one ever think to tackle a biography of Gibbon?" he added thoughtfully. "What was behind her unassuming exterior? There must have been some emotion simmering under all that quietly self-contained devotion."

"An Ontario writer attempted the project after the scandalous nineties bio came out, but she gave up after a few months of research. There just isn't enough to develop into a book. Gibbon was a BC girl, by the way. She grew up in Powell River, the only child of doting parents."

"Really? So what took her to Montreal?"

"She won a scholarship to McGill. Her parents died in a car accident during her third year and, by then, she was working for Donaldson. She never returned to the West Coast. Everyone I've talked with believes that Faith Gibbon was in love with her employer, even though she never admitted it. She showed her love in her actions. She ensured that his surroundings were serene and she strived for harmony in the home, knowing that Donaldson needed peace in order to work. She never failed in her care for Paradis, either, because she knew that would help him too."

"Happy wife, happy life?"

"I suppose so. She sounds almost too good to be true, doesn't she? But then, her preferred area of literature was the Victorian novel, and her favourite book was *Jane Eyre*. She probably felt she was living the role."

"With the madwoman out of the attic and very much in evidence in the living room?"

"Exactly." Anne rapped her fingers on the cover of the biography. "I've been trying to get hold of a man called Gerald Marsh who was listed in the author's acknowledgements. He was at McGill with Faith Gibbon."

"He must be a bit long in the tooth by now."

"He's eighty-three, but supposed to be sharp as a whip. If he ever gets back to me, I'll set up a meeting. He's the one who related how Paradis became hysterical when she read about Olivier's marriage to Joan Plowright. Evidently, she threatened to kill herself if Donaldson ever left her."

"Strong stuff. Do you think it's accurate?"

"Yes, I think it could be. Paradis's health problems were similar to Vivien Leigh's and it's obvious from her poetry that she identified with talented, fragile women—especially ones who felt diminished by their husbands' success. She wrote a poem on that theme in 1949 after the death of Zelda Fitzgerald."

"I know that one. It starts with a stinging quote from Ring Lardner: 'Mr. Fitzgerald is a novelist and Mrs. Fitzgerald is a novelty.' You're right. The poem does reveal a lot of sympathy for Zelda."

"Yes, but it isn't just the poetry that makes me feel the biography is accurate. One of Donaldson's novels has a plotline that you could swear was based on the Leigh-Olivier marriage: a famous actor, a mentally unstable actress, a passionate love affair that disintegrates until, at last, he leaves her to find peace with a gentle, loving woman half his age."

Beary shook his head. "Even if Donaldson did reach the breaking point, that doesn't mean he murdered his wife. He had no qualms walking out on his first wife. He could have decided that he was ready for mate-number-three."

"Paradis was Catholic. Divorce wouldn't have been an option."

"That's true, but co-habitation wasn't that big a deal by the nineteen-seventies. He could have set up house with Gibbon elsewhere. And if he did intend to leave, it's quite conceivable that Paradis would have followed through on her threat. Even if she did die from an overdose of digitalis, it might have been self-administered."

Anne pushed back her chair, disturbing Harley, who clambered to his feet and came over to his mistress. She fondled the Lab's ears. Then she said, "I could believe in the suicide theory if it weren't for the vial and the syringe. Paradis couldn't have injected herself with an overdose of digitalis, and then pulled up the stair tread, hid the evidence and reattached the tread. Besides, she took her medication in oral liquid form, so why would she use a syringe?"

Beary continued to play devil's advocate. "To ensure it stayed in her system and did the job properly. It would have been easier to administer an overdose that way. Donaldson could have hidden the vial and syringe, not because he was guilty of murder, but to conceal the fact that his wife killed herself. As you pointed out, she was Catholic. Suicide would have been a mortal sin. She couldn't have been buried in consecrated ground."

"That," Anne pointed out, "was why the doctor issued the death certificate without ordering an autopsy. Well, not entirely why," she added, seeing Beary's questioning stare. "Paradis's heart attack was not unexpected. She'd been a cocaine user in her youth. She suffered from congestive heart disease and she'd become increasingly frail in the two years prior to her death. The doctor could still have asked for a post mortem, but he made the decision not to, and I quote his widow: 'Out of consideration for the living and pity for the dead.'"

"Did that quote come from one of the books?"

"No. I traced the doctor's widow and talked with her a couple of months back. She was the nurse at her husband's clinic, by the way, so she knew Donaldson and Paradis well. She says her husband knew that suicide was a possibility because Faith Gibbon had told him how concerned she was about Paradis's mental state. The doctor's widow also admitted that a vial of digitalis had been missing even though Paradis's prescription had only just been renewed."

"How come all this hasn't come to light before?"

"Because, even though lots of writers approached the doctor over the years, he would never tell them anything and his wife felt bound by his silence. I was luckier than my predecessors. Now that her husband's dead, the widow is more forthcoming. She made it quite clear that her husband acted the way he did out of kindness. She'd have been horrified if she realized that I believe he was inadvertently covering up a murder."

"But if Donaldson killed his wife because he wanted to marry Faith Gibbon, why did he kill himself? That hardly makes sense."

Anne nodded. "I know, but if I've interpreted events correctly, Donaldson didn't kill his wife so he could marry Faith Gibbon. It was something quite different that triggered the crisis."

Edwina was still feeling miffed. She had not bothered to correct Beary's assumption that she would spend the day exploring the Montreal shops, but browsing along the storefronts was only part of her plan for the afternoon. She intended to chart a course that would end up at the museum where the Donaldson-Paradis memorabilia was on display.

The day was bright, but very cold, and she was glad of the hat and scarf that augmented her winter coat. She noticed that a good number of the shop windows featured furs. Now that she was experiencing Montreal weather in March, she understood why. She was glad to go inside Westmount Square to warm up, buy a latte and study her city guide. Having finished her coffee and decided on her route, she strolled around the mall, admiring the distinctive fashions in the dress-shop windows. She ventured into one particularly inviting boutique, but balked when she saw a sweater priced at five hundred and seventy dollars. Hastily exiting the store, she did up her coat and braved the cold again. She would settle for window-shopping and a visit to the museum.

She was looking forward to viewing the Paradis-Donaldson exhibit. It would be highly gratifying, she thought smugly, to surprise Bertram with tidbits of knowledge that he had failed to acquire. She easily found her way to the museum, which turned out to be a low structure with grounds at the rear that resembled a miniature estate garden. Once inside the building, she strolled through the displays on Montreal's history before making her way to the Paradis-Donaldson exhibit on the lower floor. When she arrived downstairs, there was only one other person in the room, a studious-looking young woman who was taking notes on her iPhone. She was already more than halfway around the displays, so Edwina enjoyed a leisurely sense of isolation as she viewed the memorabilia.

The early photographs of the couple were enlargements of pictures Edwina remembered from the biographies, but it was a long time since she had read the books and she studied the pictures curiously, searching for clues in the expressions and body language that might reveal more about the relationships between the people caught by the camera. She stared at a photograph of Donaldson with his first wife, a sweet-faced woman who stood shyly beside him, holding a laughing toddler in her arms. These were the two people that the novelist had abandoned for Paradis: Jean McLeod, who had reverted to her maiden name after the divorce, and her son, Hamish, who had used his mother's name. There was no sign of wealth or ostentation in the family portrait, but the contrast to the next display was striking, for it featured Donaldson's 1934 wedding to Paradis.

No indication of the Depression here, Edwina decided. Michelle Paradis, exquisite in French lace, clung to Donaldson's arm with an air that suggested triumph rather than affection. Donaldson wore a vaguely bewildered look, as if he'd just come out from his study and found a party in progress. Another photograph showed the couple on their European honeymoon. Edwina gazed admiringly at the embroidered kid gloves and the crystal glasses in the display case below the picture. Beside the stemware stood a bottle of Château Lafite Rothschild Cabernet Sauvignon

and propped against it was an ornately engraved card which carried the words, *Never forget!* She raised her eyebrows as she read
the written words below the inscription. Michelle Paradis's grandfather had laid down fifty bottles of the wine for the couple to
celebrate their wedding anniversaries. Not champagne, the card
explained, for Paradis had abhorred sparkling wines. For her, only
the rich, dark reds. Edwina blanched as she read the dollar value
attached to the vintage wines. Definitely not a family affected by
the Dirty Thirties, she thought wryly. Spread around the display
were arrangements of cards. Some were small florists' tags signed
by Donaldson, and some, elaborate anniversary cards signed by
Paradis, but every one of them carried the words, *Never forget*, amid
the other flowery phrases. Edwina sighed. If Beary were to have an
anniversary slogan, it would more likely be *Ever forget.*

Edwina moved on. The next display was filled with writing
paraphernalia from the forties. Over it was suspended a pair of
timelines, one for each writer. Reading the placards, Edwina saw
that Donaldson had begun work on his second novel shortly after
returning from his honeymoon. Edwina remembered the book:
Denial, a moving story of two Parisian women, both musicians, one
a Jewess and one a Catholic. Obviously, Donaldson's time in France
had made him apprehensive about the future of Europe and the
prospect of war. After his third novel was published in 1939, he had
enlisted and fought overseas with the Canadian Armed Forces.

The second timeline showed what Paradis had been doing
while her husband was in the army. Edwina's eyebrows arched disapprovingly. Paradis's most significant act of 1941 was to befriend
Terence Troy, the gay poet who became her confidante and ultimately wrote her biography. There was no mention of any contri-
bution to the war effort, although the entry for 1945 indicated that
Paradis's health had declined during the war years. Edwina's eyes
glided upwards to the earlier entries. Paradis's first book of poetry
had been published in 1937, the same year as Donaldson's second

novel. The first signs of the poet's manic-depressive behaviour appeared the following year.

Letting her eyes skim back and forth, Edwina scanned the rest of the timeline. Donaldson came home after the war and resumed teaching at McGill. In November of 1945, he hired the nineteen-year-old grad student, Faith Gibbon, as his secretary, although in time, she was to become far more, serving as an invaluable research assistant and editor for both him and his wife. Three years later, Donaldson gave up teaching to concentrate on writing.

The next ten years were significant—a stream of novels from Donaldson, a trickle of poetry from Paradis. There were very few pictures of Donaldson other than his back-cover portraits, but many photographs of his wife with assorted members of the literati and the artistic world. In 1957, Jean McLeod died. A year later, Donaldson and Paradis moved to their townhouse in Montreal. Intrigued, Edwina noted that it was not until 1963 that Hamish McLeod was reconciled with his father, and it had come about due to the young man's collapse and hospitalization after a complete downward spiral due to alcoholism. After that, he recuperated, joined AA, and, judging by the series of photographs from that era, became a regular visitor to his father's home—until, in 1970, drinking once more, he had exploded with rage, stormed out of the house, and was killed in a motorcycle accident.

Edwina stared at the photograph of the thirty-year old Hamish. He was a handsome man, just like Donaldson, but unlike his father at the same age, his eyes were unhappy. He bore the tormented look that Edwina had seen on the faces of students who could not accept what life had thrown their way. The inability to cope, she thought, was in the genes. Some students came from disastrous backgrounds and still managed to forge ahead and succeed. Others with every advantage let discontent weigh them down like the Mariner's albatross and allowed their resentment to define their future. Surprising that the docile Jean McLeod and the studious

Donaldson had produced such a child, but who knew what lay in each parent's family background. Hamish might have coped if his environment had presented no challenges or disadvantages, but he couldn't deal with the rejection of a father who had abandoned him or a mother who had died relatively young.

A newspaper clipping contained a photograph taken at Hamish's funeral. Faith Gibbon stood beside a stony-faced Donaldson. Paradis was conspicuous by her absence. She was not in the picture and her name did not appear in the guest book. Edwina scanned the article. A line at the end indicated that the poet had been too ill to attend. Too ill, thought Edwina, or not welcome. Another photograph showed the couple at the last awards ceremony they had ever attended. The date was two months after the death of Hamish McLeod. Donaldson wore the same granite-hard glare. He stared at the camera, but the rigidity of his pose suggested he was not trying to accommodate the photographer, but staring straight ahead so that he did not have to look at his wife. Paradis, thought Edwina, simply looked demented.

Edwina came to the end of the display. In a bed of white satin that resembled nothing so much as the inside of a coffin lay the last bottle of cabernet sauvignon that Donaldson had ever drunk. Beside it was another florist's card inscribed *Never Forget* and signed by Donaldson. She felt a chill down her spine as she read the placard beside the display. The card was from the flowers that Donaldson had given Paradis on their thirty-fifth anniversary and had been clutched in her hand when her body was found. Twenty days later, it had been found on the table beside Donaldson's cold body.

The last exhibit was a photograph of the graves where the two writers were buried. Indignantly, Edwina read the placard that told how Faith Gibbon's ashes had been scattered between the graves of Donaldson and Paradis. It was as if their valued assistant had no identity of her own. Bristling, Edwina moved away and left by the door that went out to the gardens at the rear of the building.

As she strolled between the hedged boxes of plants, she saw that there were three sections: a vegetable garden, a flower garden and an orchard garden. Whimsically, she equated each garden with the characters she had been contemplating: Gibbon, Paradis and Donaldson: sustenance, flamboyance and the fruit of creativity. But where did Hamish McLeod fit in? What had induced him to start drinking again? Which of the three had driven him back to his self-destructive behaviour? And was his death the trigger for the other two that followed so closely? Had the combined loss of wife and son driven Donaldson to suicide? Had he stoically decided that his life no longer had any meaning, and that he would send Paradis before him into the night that she wrote about so touchingly in her final verse? All three gone within four months of each other; how could there not be a connection?

She was beginning to understand why Anne Kent had become so fascinated by the fate of the poet. There were far too many questions and no answers at all.

Beary was surprised by Anne's declaration.

"If Donaldson didn't want his freedom so he could marry Faith Gibbon, why would he have hastened his wife's death?"

Anne scratched Harley's ears and looked thoughtful. Her answer, when it came, was indirect.

"I think the key lies in his final novel," she said. "It's on the Phaedra theme—the trio being the husband, the wife and the son from a first marriage."

Beary raised his eyebrows incredulously.

"Are you implying that Michelle Paradis was having an affair with Donaldson's son?"

"Not necessarily an affair, but there's no question that Donaldson's son was in love with his stepmother. Paradis left a trail of discarded suitors and damaged relationships throughout her life. Hamish was just one on a long list, but in his case, the infatuation proved fatal. You should see the police report on his motorcycle accident. There's a statement from Donaldson's cleaning lady. Here, I'll show you."

Anne flipped through the papers on the desk, extracted a document and slid it across to Beary. Fascinated, Beary read the witness statement. According to the cleaner, Hamish had been an unstable young hothead. Beary smiled, visualizing the down-to-earth charlady who had no patience with anything that smacked of artifice. Her indignation leapt off the page:

Mrs. Donaldson turned the boy's head with a lot of talk about love poems and other literary claptrap. It's no wonder he misinterpreted her attention. When he shot out the door and pushed by me, I could tell he was all churned up. I could smell the alcohol on his breath. He should never have been driving, not in that state.

"She was no fan of Paradis's writing," Beary said wryly.

"No fan, period. She thought Paradis phony and insincere."

"She could have been wrong. Maybe Paradis did fall for her stepson."

"I don't think so. You only have to read her poems to see that. There are a lot of love sonnets, but always about her husband. Nothing in the poems suggests that she was in love with anyone else, let alone Hamish McLeod. Her flings and flirtations were for excitement, and maybe a dash of ego-stroking, but that's all."

"They could have been attempts to get her husband's attention," Beary said charitably.

"Well, perhaps, but either way, they didn't touch her heart."

"So you think she led Hamish on, then slapped him down, and he turned back to the booze?"

"Something like that."

"And you believe Donaldson blamed his wife for his son's death?"

"Yes. That could be his motive for murder. It also provides a credible reason for the despair that drove him to suicide." Anne pulled a book from the shelf and opened it to a photograph of a grave. "Donaldson's headstone contains a quote from his last novel. It says, 'All accounts told, all accounts paid, I go willingly into the night.'"

"'Into the Night'—interesting. That's the title of his wife's last poem."

"Yes," said Anne. "I suspect Paradis deliberately used the phrase from the novel when she wrote the poem. It has a nice ring to it. But don't you see how the inscription ties in with Donaldson's suicide? The 'accounts told' are his stories. The 'accounts paid' would be avenging his son's death."

Anne removed Harley's head from her lap and stood up.

"Come and look at this," she said.

Beary got up and followed Anne into the kitchen. Harley padded after them. They went out the back door onto a deck that overlooked the walled garden. A flight of steps descended to a patio bordered with wooden tubs, which, Anne informed Beary, were filled with geraniums during the spring. At the far end of the garden, an L-shaped rockery had been fashioned from granite, perennial shrubs and variegated ivy.

Anne led Beary down the steps and across the lawn. When they reached the rockery, she said, "Donaldson had this put in a few months before he died. It was heavily overgrown when we moved in so it was quite a marathon cutting the ground cover back. Take a look at the stone at the far end."

Beary bent down and peered at the slab. Under the fronds, he could see scratches on the stone.

"Lift up the ivy," said Anne. "Read the inscription."

Beary raised the trailing branch and stared at the words carved in the rock.

At my grave, the truth lies.

"So that's why you believe the inscription on Donaldson's headstone contains a message," he said, nodding thoughtfully. "But it could still refer to a double suicide. Why are you so positive that you're dealing with murder?"

Anne looked back towards the house. In the fading light, the red brick walls had taken on a lavender hue, and the golden light from the study window cast a spectral glow on the shadowy elm at the side of the garden. Overhead, mottled patches of lilac and purple streaked the sky. Anne shivered.

"I have a recurring dream," she said. "It's only happened since we moved into the house, but it haunts me all the time. I dream that I wake in the night and hear a woman's voice. It's very faint. She's whispering. I can't make out the words, so I get up and go out to the landing. I can see a shadowy figure coming up the stairs. Her face is concealed by the darkness, but as she moves towards me, a sliver of moonlight from the landing window lands on the spiked red swirls of her hair. Then I know it's Michelle Paradis. She seems to know I'm there and she calls out to me."

"What does she say to you?"

"Murder! It was murder."

⇒╬⇐

Beary had arranged to meet Edwina for an early dinner at five o'clock. As he exited the subway station, his cellphone rang. It was

Anne Kent. Her voice had returned to her usual crisp, sensible tone. The disturbing account of her dream might never have taken place.

"Guess who called me ten minutes after you left?" she carolled. Without waiting for a response, she went on. "Gerald Marsh! How would you like to meet him?"

Beary blinked.

"Gerald who?"

"The man who knew Faith Gibbon at McGill."

"Right," said Beary. "Excellent. What did he have to say?"

Anne's voice gurgled with amusement.

"He said he enjoyed my columns and would like to meet me, so I invited him to come and hear the speech I'm giving at the university on Friday. It's at four o'clock. There's a reception to follow and I thought we could chat there. Why don't you come, and bring your wife?"

"What's the speech on?" asked Beary.

"The rights of fathers in family disputes."

"Ah, yes. You'll be going into the bias of family courts towards mothers?"

"Absolutely. It's time someone stood up for the men."

Beary smirked inwardly, visualizing Edwina, torn between inner fury and the social requirement of courtesy as an invited guest.

"Excellent. We'll be there," he said. "Edwina will be most impressed. She's very hot on fair play. She was interested in your column on bi-lingual signage too. She's always nagging me about not offending ethnic groups in the electorate. I look forward to introducing her to you."

"Wonderful," said Anne. "There will be drinks and finger-food galore at the reception so you won't need dinner, but Teddy says why don't you come back here for coffee and dessert afterwards? Then we can talk over what we've learned. Did you tell your wife about the research I'm doing?"

"Yes. She's interested in that too," Beary acknowledged, this time truthfully. "She'll jump at the chance to talk to this Marsh fellow. Did he admit to being the source for the suicide threat mentioned in *All Passion Spent*?"

"Yes, he did, but he said he'd only been repeating what he'd been told by Faith Gibbon. We didn't talk for long. We'll be able to grill him at the reception."

Anne gave Beary the event details and ended the call. Beary slipped his phone back into his pocket and set off down the street. Not being as proficient with street maps as his wife, he took a circuitous route from the subway to the restaurant. With the help of a charming lady, distinctively Gallic in beret, scarf and modish cape, he found his way to the row of restaurants and gift shops that he remembered from the previous day. As he walked the last few blocks in the fast-vanishing light, he noticed that the streets looked prettier in the dark. The buildings glittered with light and the cheery restaurateurs stood promoting their menus outside the cafés. Ahead, he could hear music. A few more steps and he reached the square. It was a lively scene. A young man, rosy cheeked and warmly wrapped in a wool coat, gaily striped scarf and bright red toque, was singing while his girlfriend encouraged members of the crowd to dance. Edwina was nowhere in sight. Looking at his watch, Beary saw that he was fifteen minutes late. His efficient wife would already be waiting inside the restaurant.

Sure enough, he found Edwina seated at a table by the window. She was savouring a mug of dark ale as she watched the antics in the square. A second mug of ale was set on the other side of the table. Beary's eyes lit up.

"Who would think we're in Montreal?" he said. "Good choice."

"I knew you'd like this place," said Edwina. "I've ordered sausages and chips for dinner. It doesn't hurt to indulge once in a while, though you'll have to go for an extra-long walk tomorrow to work it off."

Beary sighed happily. On the scale of dietary watchdogs, Edwina tended to be a pit bull.

"How was your day?" he asked affably. "Did you find anything nice in the shops?"

"Lots," said Edwina, "but I didn't buy anything. The clothes here are tremendously stylish, but they have designer-label prices. My sense of thrift got the better of me."

"That's never stopped you before." Beary thought back to a particularly pricey trip to New York when Edwina had doubled the cost of their holiday in a single day of shopping.

"No," said Edwina regretfully, "but I was pulling in a big salary last time we went travelling. Now we're both retired, and with the way our benefits are being cut, I thought I ought to be more careful."

"You might want to buy yourself one little item to take back," Beary said congenially, lulled into a generous frame of mind by the ale and the prospect of a sausage dinner. For all Edwina's annoying ways, he was quite proud of her appearance. Unlike himself, Edwina kept in shape and was always smartly turned out. Besides which, the occasional shopping excursion was usually guaranteed to assure a few days of reduced nagging.

"That would be nice." Edwina looked wistful. "The fashions here are elegant, and there are lovely pieces for women my age. If we were doing anything other than sightseeing, I might consider it. Still, I hardly need to be dressed up for tramping through museums."

"Actually," said Beary, "you will have an opportunity to dress up. Anne Kent is giving a lecture at the university Friday afternoon, and there's a reception to follow. We've been invited."

Edwina's eyebrows arched.

"Really? Both of us?"

Beary ignored his wife's acerbic tone.

"Yes. Her husband will be there too and he's invited us to come back to their house for dessert afterwards."

"Is he as outspoken as his wife?" asked Edwina.

"No idea, but I'm sure we'll like him. He sounds a real charmer, and talented too. I gather he's a great skier and tennis player, and he's the one who plays the grand piano in their front room."

"So what's the speech about?" asked Edwina, still mildly suspicious.

"Um, not sure," Beary lied, "but I'm sure you'll enjoy it. Besides, someone will be there who knew Donaldson's secretary well. We'll be able to talk to him at the reception."

"Now that does sound interesting." Edwina's tone altered immediately. "Faith Gibbon is practically the invisible woman," she said tartly. "Not even a proper gravesite; just melted into the grass between her employers' plots. I've never heard anything like it. I'd love to hear what this man has to say."

"Right. That's settled."

Beary blinked, suddenly registering what his wife had said.

"How do you know that Faith Gibbon didn't have a gravesite?"

Edwina told him. Beary chuckled. He should have known that his wife would refuse to be relegated to the sidelines.

"And I think I will pop back to the shops tomorrow," Edwina added, smiling complacently. "I can't go to a reception at McGill wearing jeans and a sweater."

The waiter appeared and set two appetizing plates of sausages in front of them. Conversation ceased as they tucked into their meals. While they ate, they watched the street entertainers and listened to the songs, melodies they recognized, even though they could not understand the French lyrics. Montrealers were hardy folk, Beary decided, watching the number of cheerful individuals joining in the fun.

Once dinner was over, Beary and Edwina enjoyed a leisurely café au lait while Beary described his visit with Anne Kent. Edwina listened intently.

"It's bizarre, isn't it?" she said, when Beary had finished. "Three people living together for all those years, and no one can say for sure how they felt about each other. I can't help but think they'd have continued rolling along as they were if Donaldson's son hadn't entered the picture."

Beary nodded.

"That's what Anne thinks. She believes his relationship with his stepmother caused Hamish's lapse back to alcoholism—which, in turn, led to his death—"

"—and Donaldson's decision to murder his wife."

"Precisely. Anne may well be right. Her theory ties in with the inscription in the rockery."

"It does, doesn't it, but how can she hope to prove it?" Edwina furrowed her brow. "And how does that poor secretary fit into the picture? There are still far too many variables to be certain of anything."

"That's why it's such a beguiling puzzle," said Beary. "A mystery to relish. A regular four-pipe problem."

"Well, at least a four-latte problem," chipped in Edwina.

"Good idea," said Beary, and waved the waiter over to order two more of the same.

Anne Kent's speech had been well attended and the reception was packed. The columnist had spoken well and looked particularly elegant in a soft grey suit that Edwina guessed had come from one of the Westmount stores she had admired and bypassed, due to the prices of the designer-label ensembles. Since Anne was surrounded by admirers who were rhapsodizing over her speech, Beary and Edwina found a corner where they could wedge themselves safely and sip their drinks without fear of circulating bodies sending their wine glasses flying. Beary had to strain to hear the snatches of conversation.

"How are you enjoying Montreal?"

The speaker was a suave elderly gentleman who appeared to have taken a shine to Edwina. Grudgingly, Beary admitted that his wife was looking her best in the chic olive-green dress that she had purchased that morning. Edwina had also visited Anne Kent's hairdresser, who had styled her short blonde hair into a bob with a distinctively soignée French touch. Beary had glumly looked at the charge receipts and regretted his impulse of the previous day. Expensive sausage dinner, he thought gloomily.

Oblivious to Beary's mood, Edwina continued to lap up her companion's Gallic charm.

"Very much," she cooed. "Of course, my high-school French is terrible, but everyone has been so kind. The minute they hear me struggling, they switch to English."

"That usually is the best way to get French-Canadians to speak English," Anne Kent said breezily, slipping in to join the group. "They can't stand hearing their mother-tongue being butchered."

"I wonder if that would work with Mandarin," Edwina said, pointedly delivering the aside to her husband. Eyes glinting, she turned to the white-jacketed waiter who was hovering nearby and helped herself to a prosciutto-wrapped spear of asparagus.

Beary pretended he didn't notice the puzzled look Anne threw his way. Assuming a benignly innocent expression, he reached for a canapé and changed the subject.

"Didn't you say there was someone here who knew Faith Gibbon at university?" he asked.

"Yes, Gerald Marsh. That's why I was coming to fetch you. He's over there by the buffet talking with Teddy. Come on, I'll introduce you."

Edwina tore herself away from her admirer and followed the others across the room. There was only one person by the buffet who was old enough to have known Faith Gibbon, and he was talking animatedly with Teddy Kent. Gerald Marsh was a tall, distinguished-looking man, with an abundance of grey hair and an amiable countenance. He smiled when Anne greeted him, and made a jocular remark about her latest column. Teddy chuckled and winked at Beary and Edwina. The three of them stood back and waited patiently while Anne and Marsh exchanged a good-natured round of repartee. Then Anne turned to introduce the Bearys.

Gerald Marsh greeted them congenially.

"So Anne has you hooked on her project, has she?" he said. "The Paradis-Donaldson enigma: Happy couple or romantic triangle? No one has ever been able to decide for sure."

"What do you think?" asked Beary.

"A bit of both," said Marsh. "Grand passion with his wife; platonic romance with his secretary, which may or may not have progressed to more towards the end. Hugh was a good-looking fellow, but pretty staid, so he wouldn't have embarked on an affair unless his marriage had started to break down."

"His wife must have been uneasy having Faith Gibbon living with them?" Beary persisted. "Wasn't she jealous of her?"

"Not in the early days. Faith was a useful slave who typed and edited the manuscripts, and ran the household to boot. Faith was also a very private person. She loved the work, but shunned the limelight, so she was no threat to Michelle in that regard. Later on, I think some resentment crept in. Hugh and Faith shared such a passion for his work, and though they didn't intend to make Michelle feel excluded, I suspect she did."

"Did you know Faith Gibbon well?" asked Edwina. "Anne said you met her at university."

"Faith and I moved in the same circles for a good many years, even after university," said Marsh. "I worked for the publishing house that handled Hugh's novels, and Michelle's poetry too.

Faith may have been hired initially as a secretary, but in time, she became Hugh's research assistant—and she was an excellent editor too. Faith loved working on his novels. They became her life work as well, so she and I communicated regularly. We got along famously."

"You were her friend?"

"Friend, but not confidante. Faith was the most self-contained person I've ever met."

"She never talked about her feelings?"

"Faith? Not a chance. She was the original stoic. You never really knew what she was feeling. The only time I ever saw her break down was when she received the news that her parents had been killed."

"Really?"

Marsh nodded.

"Really. She cried her heart out, poor girl. She was riddled with guilt as well as grief, because when she won the scholarship to McGill, she'd promised her parents that she'd return to the West after she graduated, but then she accepted the job working for Hugh and she put off going back to visit them. And then, of course, it was too late."

"Didn't she cry after Donaldson's suicide?" asked Edwina. "That must have hit her hard."

"Oh, it did. We all assumed that Hugh was going to marry Faith after Michelle died, and I'm sure Faith believed that too. There's no doubt in my mind that she was in love with him. Of course, she probably shed some tears in private. I didn't see her until a couple of weeks after Hugh's death, so by then, she'd had time to pull herself together. She came in to bring us Michelle's final poem."

Anne looked surprised. "Hadn't you already received it?"

"No. Michelle knew she was likely to die many years before her husband, and she didn't want to be a mere historical footnote when his time came, so she'd placed a copy of the poem in a letter and left it with her lawyer. He was instructed to deliver it to Faith after Hugh was dead. If Hugh hadn't committed suicide, the world wouldn't have seen that poem for years."

"Good heavens!" said Edwina. "How very calculated. It sounds as if she was absolutely determined to have the last word."

Marsh laughed.

"Yes, you're probably right," he said.

"You said 'a copy' of the poem," broke in Beary. "What happened to the original?"

"No one ever knew. Faith looked through all the papers at the house. She never found it." Marsh laughed at Beary's sceptical expression. "Don't look so suspicious. Even with the Photostat, we could see it was Paradis's writing, and the letter was a handwritten original."

"What did it say?" Anne asked.

Gerald Marsh deftly exchanged his empty wine glass for a full one from a passing waiter's tray. "Schmaltzy stuff," he said. "All about Donaldson and Paradis being together in death as they were in life. The letter charged Faith with the duty of ensuring the publication of the poem and co-operating with Terence Troy in the collating of all the papers to assist him with the official biography. It closed with the typical Paradis touch. 'With my final poem, you know the truth. Now tell it to the world.'"

Beary and Anne exchanged puzzled glances, but before they could comment, Marsh continued. "Personally," he said, "I think Paradis had a highly glorified sense of her own importance. She was given to self-dramatization. That was the basic difference between her and Faith. Faith said once that the reality of everyday life was what counted, not public image. She knew what was important. Michelle, sadly, was all about image and public perception. It wasn't enough to have a love affair; the whole world had to acknowledge it as a great love affair. So ultimately, it wasn't about love, it was about ego."

"Hugh Donaldson's love for her must have been real," said Beary, setting his glass down and helping himself to a smoked-salmon canapé. "Otherwise, he wouldn't have left his first wife for her."

"Oh, yes," said Marsh. "Hugh was besotted with Michelle. Who wouldn't have been? She was gorgeous and clever and loaded with sex appeal, but eventually, her neurotic behaviour wore him down. Faith was the one who made his life bearable. He was a fool to kill himself when he could have enjoyed a serene old age with her. He'd have probably churned out a few more good novels too. Sad state of affairs, the whole thing."

"More than sad," said Edwina sharply. "I'd call it cruel. What a slap in the face for the secretary who'd served him loyally all those years."

"Faith was left well provided for," said Marsh, "but I know what you mean. Along with the house and the money, she was stuck with the job of perpetuating The Myth, which must have been horrendously trying since Hugh had made it plain that he didn't want his wife's dark side blazoned to the world. I told Faith to throw caution to the winds and write a rip-roaring, tell-all bestseller, but she declined in her quiet way and insisted that she would follow Hugh's wishes. I have to say, though, that I sensed a degree of anger under her impassive exterior. For the first time, I was aware that she actively disliked Michelle and felt constrained by Hugh's attitude."

"Why was Donaldson so anxious to whitewash his wife's character? He'd bared his soul in his novels, so wasn't it a bit hypocritical to insist that the non-fiction version kept the ugly stuff under wraps?"

"Hugh felt guilty after Michelle died. He became maudlin. Said Michelle's problems had been his fault—that he'd been too preoccupied with his work and that he hadn't loved her enough."

"Do you think that was true?" asked Teddy.

"Not really. No one could have loved Michelle enough. It was an impossible task. She drained people dry and spat out the dregs. Still, I think Hugh's feelings of guilt were genuine. I suspect he'd finally reached the point where he was ready to leave her, but then she died and he blamed himself. Faith tried to make him see that it wasn't his fault, but obviously without success. It still amazes me that she wasn't able to pull him out of his depression."

"Poor girl," said Edwina. "She seems to have got a raw deal at every turn."

"Yes," agreed Marsh. "It was strange, though," he added. "When I commiserated with her over her personal loss, she made an odd reply. She said she had been devastated at first, but now she had come to terms with it, because she knew she had never really lost him."

"What on earth did she mean by that?" asked Beary.

Gerald Marsh smiled wryly.

"I can't say for sure, but I suspect she had already been diagnosed with the cancer that ultimately killed her. Perhaps she knew she wouldn't be long joining him."

"She lived on for a full nine years after his death," Edwina pointed out. "She didn't join him that quickly."

"No, that's true. Well, who knows what she meant? Faith was a great one for playing with words. I can still see her sitting in the cafeteria at McGill whipping through the cryptic crossword. She was a very intelligent girl, and in spite of her reserved manner, I believe she enjoyed her life far more than most people think. She wouldn't have remained like a third arm in that household for all those years unless she'd been happy there. She wouldn't have stayed on afterwards either. Even if she couldn't sell the house, she could have rented it out for a pretty sum and lived it up elsewhere. But she carried on, working on the papers in the winter, nurturing the garden in the spring and summer."

Teddy caught Anne's eye.

"She must have seen the inscription in the rockery," he said. "She would have known what it meant."

"What inscription?" asked Gerald Marsh.

"It's a reference to Donaldson's grave," said Anne. She frowned. "At least, I've assumed it is, but after hearing about the letter left for Faith Gibbon, I can't help wondering if I've interpreted it correctly. Paradis must have been around when the rockery was built. Perhaps she was the one who arranged the inscription." Anne turned to Beary. "Could 'the truth' lie at *her* grave? What do you think?"

"What's written on her gravestone?" asked Beary.

"Her last poem," interjected Edwina. "'Into the Night'. I saw a photograph in the museum."

Gerald Marsh looked bewildered. "You've all lost me," he said. "Where is this inscription you keep talking about?"

"On a stone in the rockery at the end of our garden," Teddy explained.

"Which part of the rockery?" asked Marsh.

"What difference does that make?" said Anne.

A waiter glided by with a tray of hot canapés. Gerald Marsh swivelled round to capture a scallop wrapped in bacon. Then he turned back to Anne.

"Quite a lot," he said. "You see, Donaldson started the work in the garden, but Faith was the one who completed it. She put in all those little pathways, and the herb garden at the side of the house, too—but she wanted a more natural area for bluebells and primroses and the like, so she added another section to the rockery. Faith loved wildflowers," he reminisced. "Her favourites were blue cornflowers. Every spring, she would have some in a vase on her desk—" Marsh paused, realizing that his monologue on Faith's floral arrangements was not what his listeners wanted to hear.

"Which part of the rockery did she build?" demanded Anne.

"The piece along the side wall," said Marsh, gesturing with his tooth-picked scallop before popping it into his mouth.

"Good heavens!" said Beary. "That changes things."

"Doesn't it?" Anne looked utterly bewildered. "That means the inscription on the stone was Faith Gibbon's doing. But how can that be? How can the truth lie at Faith Gibbon's grave when she doesn't have one?"

Gerald Marsh swallowed his scallop and re-entered the conversation.

"Faith has a grave," he said.

Anne stared at him. She made no attempt to hide her amazement.

"What do you mean?" she exclaimed. "Faith's ashes were spread on Donaldson's grave."

"Only some of them," Marsh said blandly. "Her ashes were divided."

He looked gratified at the gasps from his audience.

Teddy was in the process of extracting two mini-quiches from a passing tray, but he was listening to the exchange. He thanked the waiter, handed one of the appetizers to Anne and said: "You know, we shouldn't be surprised. It makes perfect sense. Faith kept her promise to her parents."

Gerald Marsh nodded.

"Of course she did. She went home, but nobody thought it worth commenting on. There was a lot of hoopla about the ashes that were spread on Donaldson's grave because that was a sentimental gesture that the media could capitalize on, but no one gave a damn about the other half. Faith just wasn't that important."

"So where are the rest of her ashes?" Beary asked.

"In a cremation plot in Powell River. They're interred in the cemetery where her parents are buried."

"Well, I'm damned," said Beary. "The so-called 'truth' has been waiting in BC all the time."

Teddy finished his quiche and slipped an arm around his wife's shoulder.

"It's poetic justice," he said. "I rather think the unobtrusive secretary will have the last word after all."

The rest of the evening was pleasantly relaxing. After the reception, Teddy reiterated his invitation for the Bearys to come back for dessert, and they accepted with genuine pleasure. Edwina was looking forward to seeing the townhouse that had inspired Anne's book. Beary, imbued with a sense of well-being brought on by gourmet appetizers and full-bodied burgundy, was also reluctant for the day to end. Anne, as guest of honour, made a final circuit of the room to thank the organizers, then joined Teddy in the lobby, where he was waiting with her coat. Edwina rounded up her husband, and they all made their way out to the parking lot where the freezing air transformed their breath into coiling wraiths that drifted upwards and vanished into the darkening sky.

Beary had taken full advantage of the wine at the reception, so Edwina was glad that their hosts were driving them. The journey was mercifully short, but a surreptitious nudge was still required to halt the occasional snore that erupted in the back seat of Teddy's Jeep Grand Cherokee. Once at the townhouse, Beary folded himself into a comfortable armchair, but Edwina, captivated by the elegant architectural lines and the airy sense of spaciousness, took in every detail from the modernistic steel staircase to the tall, graceful windows that overlooked the street.

After the bustle of the reception, the peaceful ambience of the townhouse was soothing to their over-active minds. The afternoon had produced a startling revelation that boded well for Anne's book, but the conversation was no longer focussed on the enigmatic trio who had lived in the house so many years before.

A sense of accomplishment, combined with the knowledge that nothing further could be done that evening, infused the room's inhabitants with a leisurely feeling of good will. Harley's amiable presence prompted an exchange of pet stories. Beary and Edwina were missing their husky, MacPuff, and their feisty cat, Minx the Manx, both of whom were being pet-sat by Juliette at her home in Pender Harbour. Before long, Beary and Teddy were engaged in an animated discussion on outdoor recreation, while Edwina found herself congenially comparing notes on children and grandchildren with her hostess. Anne had been a talented performer in her youth, but born in an era when girls were advised that the stage was a diversion, not a profession; therefore, she was interested to hear Edwina talk about the trials and tribulations of Philippa's career. Edwina, in turn, was completely engrossed as Anne recounted her son's adventures in the newspaper world. By the time they had both admitted to a shared teenage enthusiasm for the columns of Ann Landers, the evening was an assured convivial success.

Knowing that they had to start their return journey in the morning, Edwina and Beary called for a cab at eight o'clock. With promises to Anne and Teddy to contact them the moment they reached the grave in Powell River, they set off. Normally, they were sorry when a trip was drawing to a close, but this time, they couldn't wait to get back to British Columbia. Not that they intended to stay home for long. A short overnight stop to check on the house, then it would be time for the journey to the Sunshine Coast. First, Powell River, and the solution to a mystery; then a return trip via Pender Harbour to pick up their beloved pets.

The air in Powell River did not carry the biting chill of the Montreal winter, but Beary and Edwina were glad they had bundled up in heavy winter coats. They had returned from the bright, cold days of the East Coast to West Coast wind and rain, and the damp seemed to gnaw right into their bones.

They found the cemetery at the end of a winding road that branched off the highway and meandered down towards the water. When they arrived, Edwina's first thought was relief that she had worn long boots. The graveyard was an unruly grassy expanse, overgrown in patches, and bordered on three sides by forest, with a low picket fence running along the side adjacent to the road. The wind had died down, but the day was dull, and the tops of the surrounding evergreens were swathed in low-lying cloud, which shifted and parted to render fleeting glimpses of grey mountains far in the distance. In the misting rain, the landscape appeared monochromatic, a pale scene viewed through a soft-focus lens.

Beary followed Edwina through the wooden stile at the cemetery entrance.

"Not overly populated," he commented, looking at the sparse spattering of headstones.

"Not well-tended either." Edwina noted the overgrown shrubs and the long clumps of grass projecting haphazardly between the graves.

"It's nice," said Beary. "Restful and natural. The deer can amble in to have a chew at the bushes. The neighbourhood dogs probably prowl through as well. Much better than the manicured plots in town. This is my kind of graveyard."

"Yes, it would be," said his wife tartly. She stepped carefully around a sunken patch of dirt and set off to explore the headstones.

Beary took a deep breath and let his eyes sweep the area. The graveyard was no bigger than a neighbourhood park so he felt no urgency to hurry. The task would not be daunting. Edwina was already stalking methodically through the sites, but Beary bent to reorganize a sad arrangement of silk carnations, blown over by yesterday's windstorm and plastered by rain against the concrete slab of a cremation plot. He propped up the flowers as best he could and moved on. Edwina had already reached the far side of the graveyard.

"Spotted them yet?" called Beary.

"No." Edwina craned her neck and scrutinized the boundary. "There are some slabs up by the trees," she said. She stepped between the headstones and made her way to the wide stand of hemlocks that marked the upper border. A moment later, she cried out jubilantly and beckoned to Beary.

"Here! I've found them!"

Beary hurried to join his wife. Edwina was staring at three slabs, inlaid side-by-side in the grass. The outer stones were weatherbeaten and black with lichen, but the names of Alec and Marjorie Gibbon were still faintly legible. The centre stone was Faith Gibbon's. The slab was formed from a highly polished granite that had more successfully resisted the weathering of the elements and the verse etched onto the surface was easily decipherable.

Silently, Beary read the inscription.

Needing becomes taking as woman drains the lifeblood of her mate,
Shadow becomes darkness, when love resembles hate,
Mingled forever, myth has governed fate.

Yet those whose souls were kind and brave
Need no myths. The love they gave
Still lives on beyond the grave.

"Good heavens!" exclaimed Edwina. "Was she trying to be a poet too? That verse can't be another of Michelle Paradis's efforts."

"No. It has to be Faith's," said Beary.

Edwina did not try to hide her disappointment.

"It's no more than an outcry from a frustrated mistress who despised her lover's wife."

Beary stared at the rhyme on the stone, willing the words to tell him something more than their surface meaning.

"Not necessarily," he said. "It's more riddle than poem. You heard what Gerald Marsh said about Faith. She loved codes and cryptic crosswords."

"It may be a riddle," said Edwina, "but her meaning is crystal clear. Paradis was as loving as a black-widow spider and the so-called myth of the Paradis-Donaldson love match is just that—myth, rather than reality. According to this, the real love was between Faith and Donaldson. That hardly tells us anything that we hadn't already figured out. I suppose it's confirmation of a sort, but that's all."

"No, there must be more to it than that. Anne may be able to enlighten us. She's spent far more time than us studying the books and poems." Beary glanced at his watch. "What time is it in Montreal? Noon, right?"

"Three hours ahead. Yes, I think so."

"I'm going to call her."

Beary whipped out his cellphone and punched in Anne Kent's number. To his disappointment, he only reached her voicemail.

"There's no point in telling her the verse over the phone," said Edwina impatiently. "She'll need time to read it over. Save the call for when we've all had time to think. Send her a photograph."

Beary took a picture with his iPhone, but the inscription was only barely legible. Edwina frowned and shook her head.

"Here, give me her number," she said. "I'll text it to her."

"The whole thing!" Beary protested. "We'll be here all day."

"Nonsense. It might take you all day, but it'll only take me a couple of minutes."

Pulling out her own phone, Edwina efficiently tapped in the text of the poem and sent it to Anne. Then she put her phone away and turned towards the gate.

"Come along," she said firmly. "Mission accomplished. We can struggle with the interpretation over a cup of coffee. I'm frozen."

Without glancing back, Edwina set off for the exit, but Beary paused, feeling the need to linger a moment longer. The mist had thickened and was closing in, swirling around the ornamental crosses and obliterating the road so that the cemetery took on a dreamlike air. The mountains had completely disappeared from sight, and even Edwina had vanished from his view. If there were such a thing as spirits, thought Beary, Paradis would materialize in the haze and repeat her whispered accusation. Uneasily, he realized that he was afraid of what this might be, for he had started to feel an affinity for Faith Gibbon. As he watched the curling patch of fog that hovered over the grave, his thoughts were as black as the lichen crawling across the stones. Had Faith hated Paradis so much that she had given her the fatal dose of digitalis? Had Donaldson killed himself when he understood what she had done? Beary stared at the tendrils of mist, willing them to morph into a ghostly manifestation, but as he watched, they dissolved and faded into the surrounding haze. The air was still, the silence, absolute.

Alone at the gravesite, Beary contemplated Faith Gibbon's words. As he read the verse again, he found himself recalling Paradis's poem, and at last, the meaning of the inscription fell into place. He felt a flash of sorrow as the full significance struck him, and he felt a surge of admiration for Faith Gibbon. He would have liked her a great deal, he decided. He wondered if Anne Kent would make the connection between the poems too. He believed she would.

Beary was about to leave when, from the corner of his eye, he noticed a splash of colour. An urn with silk wildflowers was nestled against a stone memorial that overlooked several well-tended graves. The arrangement had withstood the windstorm for it had been protected by the tombstone, but a few of the flowers had blown free. Amid a tangle of yellow primroses scattered on the grass was a single blue cornflower. It was fate, Beary decided. With only a minor twinge of conscience, he extracted the flower and walked back to Faith Gibbon's grave. He placed the cornflower at the centre of the stone. Then, filled with a curiously gratifying sense of peace, he set off to join his wife.

The Kents had just settled down to lunch in their favourite Montreal bistro when Edwina's text came through. Anne heard the signal, but waited until they had finished their meal before she checked the message. Her eyes widened as she read the words; then, silently, she passed the phone across to Teddy. Abstractedly, she sipped her coffee while her husband read the message. Frowning with concentration, she said: "There's something vaguely familiar about it. I'm not sure if it's the rhythm or the word patterns. What is she trying to tell us?"

"Whatever it is, it's still only Faith Gibbon having the last word," Teddy cautioned her. "And a very roundabout last word too. It's really too bad she didn't write the tell-all biography that Gerald Marsh proposed."

"Yes, well, we know why she didn't. Donaldson was adamant that he wanted his wife's dignity preserved, no matter what she'd done. Faith wouldn't go against his wishes."

"Then why contradict them in such a devious way? She's still blaring 'He loved me' to the world, even if the message is only received by the handful of people who amble through that obscure country graveyard."

"She's telling us more than that," said Anne. "What is it about that verse that seems reminiscent of Paradis's poetry?"

"I know," Teddy said suddenly. "It's the words, *needing* and *shadow*, in the first verse. They occur in the final couplet of Paradis's last poem."

"Oh, my goodness!" Anne's eyes lit up with excitement. "I think I see what she's done. 'Needing becomes taking' and 'shadow becomes darkness'!"

Anne brought up the notepad on her phone and typed in the final couplet of 'Into the Night'.

"Now," she said, "see what happens when I change those two words."

Teddy stared at the verse and shook his head in amazement.

When winter claims the heart, it forms
layers of ice around the core,
Freezes the soul, numbs care, and makes one dare
To walk into the night, taking what's most precious at the end
For comfort in the darkness of the grave.

"I knew there was a murder," Anne said triumphantly. "I just had it backwards."

Teddy was still absorbing the changed text.

"Come again?" he said.

"Donaldson didn't kill his wife," said Anne. "She murdered him."

Six months later, Beary received an email from Anne Kent. Attached to the message were several photographs and a word file with a segment from the biography which was nearing completion. It was the chapter that dealt with the deaths of the famous literary couple. Anne wanted Beary's feedback before she went to publication. As Beary opened the attachment, Edwina came into the study. When she saw what was on the screen, she hovered behind her husband's chair and read over his shoulder.

The doctor who issued the death certificate for Michelle Paradis covered up the evidence of an overdose because he believed she had committed suicide. He was right. Michelle Paradis did take her own life. Her reason? Her husband had finally made the decision to leave her for Faith Gibbon. The death of his son had hardened his resolve, and he blamed his wife for Hamish's death.

Paradis realized that, this time, threats and pleas were not going to change his mind. Her health was failing. She was unbalanced and depressed, and she decided to end it all. However, she had no intention of leaving Donaldson and Gibbon to enjoy life after her death, so she resolved to take her husband with her. Flamboyantly creative to the end, she wrote a poem obliquely expressing her intentions, fully aware that Faith Gibbon would interpret the verse correctly and know what she had done. Vindictively, she arranged for the poem to be published through Faith, knowing that the secretary's commitment to literature would ensure that her instructions were carried out. To make certain that foreknowledge did not interfere with her plan, Paradis specified that her lawyer retain the poem and letter of instruction until after Donaldson was deceased.

Paradis, by now, was frail and debilitated, weakened further by the shock to her system over Hamish's death and destabilized by her husband's anger and rejection. The radiant smile that had inspired columnists to rave about the 'mouth of an angel' was no longer there. Illness had ravaged her system and removed any vestiges of conscience. She waited until a day when she was alone in the house. Using a syringe, she doctored the bottle of wine that had been designated for the thirty-sixth anniversary of her marriage to Donaldson. She knew her husband well enough to realize that, even though he had no intention of celebrating with her in life, guilt would propel him to acknowledge the occasion after her death. She wrapped the empty vial and syringe in a piece of newspaper and hid the parcel under a loose tread in the stairway. Then, getting out the card that had come with her husband's flowers on their last anniversary, she took an overdose of digitalis. She died holding the card inscribed Never forget.

Edwina straightened up and sighed.

"What a wicked creature," she said. "Why on earth did Donaldson have to drink that wine? Foolish sentimentality, and it killed him."

"Realistically, he'd have drunk the wine at some point," said Beary, "even if he hadn't acknowledged the anniversary."

"Not necessarily," said Edwina waspishly. "We know *you* wouldn't have wasted the wine, but Donaldson might have had a conscience about drinking it and simply given the rest of the bottles away."

"On the other hand," said Beary smoothly, "he might have been so glad to get rid of his wife that he celebrated by sharing it with Faith Gibbon, and then they'd both have died."

Edwina's eyes narrowed suspiciously, but Beary's face remained impassive. "Of course," he continued, "Paradis wouldn't have cared about that. Still, you can see why Faith Gibbon said that she'd never really lost Donaldson. Once she received the poem, she knew Donaldson hadn't killed himself. She must have changed the two words, made a Photostat, destroyed the original, and then released the poem in its altered form. That's why scholars have found it so contradictory all these years."

Edwina sniffed disapprovingly. "Ridiculous subterfuge. She should have let the world know what had happened and told everyone what a poisonous creature Paradis was. I mean, really! Hugh Donaldson wouldn't have been so keen to maintain his wife's reputation if he'd known she'd poisoned his wine."

"Perhaps not, but Faith obviously felt she could not go against the promise she'd made. But you know," Beary mused, "there's another angle to this. She might have felt she was thwarting Paradis."

Edwina's expression brightened.

"That's a good point. Paradis didn't just want Faith to know what she'd done; she wanted the world to know."

"Highly vindictive, when you think how it would have panned out in the press. Paradis would be the dramatic avenging angel. Donaldson would appear as—what? —the unfaithful husband who got his just desserts for driving his wife to suicide? The sap who was suckered all his life by a brilliant woman who could always make him dance to her tune? Donaldson's death would have been diminished and every headline would have been about his wife."

"Still," said Edwina, "I'm glad Faith decided to leave some evidence of the truth. Even if no one ever discovered it, she left a record of her story."

Beary chuckled.

"You heard what Gerald Marsh said about her. She loved codes and cryptic puzzles. I bet she felt a great deal of satisfaction leaving a trail for posterity. I shall make a point of taking cornflowers to her grave every spring."

Beary exited the word file and brought up one of the photographs. It was a portrait of Paradis taken in 1932 at the height of her beauty. He stared at the picture and wondered why it had taken them all so long to see into the poet's soul. With the knowledge of hindsight, he could recognize the vacuum in the eyes where empathy should have been.

"My goodness," said Edwina. "Look at her. The mouth of an angel, the eyes of a cobra. Anne should title her book, *Ice at the Core.* Is that the photograph that's going on the book cover?"

"No, actually," said Beary. "Anne's bio has taken a slightly different turn."

"Oh," said Edwina. "In what way?"

"In quite a dramatic way. She's pretty much started over and rewritten the whole thing. I know you're going to like it, though. And you'll definitely be pleased with the new title."

"Really," said Edwina. "What is the book called?"

Beary clicked the mouse and brought another photograph onto the computer screen. He gazed at it for a moment. Then he leaned back and smiled.

"Faith," he said.

A TALE OF VICE AND VILLAINY

R ichard Beary hated state dinners. The pomp and pageantry
that delighted the select individuals on the invitation list
merely signified a huge headache for the Force. All police departments in the Lower Mainland had been called in to take part, but
the main burden fell on the RCMP. Every known troublemaker
and terrorist organization had been watched and monitored for
months, and the combined United States and Canadian plainclothes and uniformed officers were ready to take their places,
along with the guest of honour's personal security team—but
now, with the American vice-president's visit only one day off,
E-Division had just been notified that a text message had arrived
on the Vancouver police chief's cellphone.

*What would make the vice-president's visit really special? How
about an assassination?*

Most likely a crank, thought Richard, irritation causing his
breakfast to form what felt like a boulder in his stomach. But he

couldn't be sure. No one could be sure. The only thing certain was that he would be very glad when tomorrow evening was over.

⟞⊹⟝

Edwina radiated disapproval as she surveyed the crowds lining the long, narrow concourse outside the Hyatt Regency ballroom.

"The invitation distinctly specified black tie," she sniffed, smoothing the folds of her emerald brocade gown and glowering at the short woollen frock that was parading by on the Rubenesque figure of a prominent cabinet minister's wife. "*She*, of all people, should know better."

Beary tugged the jacket of his tux over his ample middle and enviously eyed the business suits sported by a number of his colleagues. "*I* should have known better," he said. "Only half the men here are wearing penguin suits."

"That's not the point," said Edwina. "The vice-president will be wearing a tux and his wife will be in a long gown. All these day dresses are an insult to the guests-of-honour." Edwina scowled at the display of business suits and day dresses milling about the room. "The most annoying thing," she said crossly, "is that people like that make those of us who observed the dress code appear to be overdone. Our American visitors will think the West Coast Canadians are a bunch of ignorant hicks."

"Well," said Beary, "when you consider that the people who are invited to these events are drawn from a 'safe' list of local politicians and the various members of the boards of their riding associations, that's probably a very good description of the crowd that's here. You can tell it's a municipal-election year," he added. "There must be a dozen mayors working the room. Look at Mrs. Thatcher, the sequel, and Pinko Rogers countering each other's efforts." He nodded to the far end of the concourse where an opulently gowned woman was carving a smooth and stately procession through the crowd, while an amiably ineffectual-looking man in an ill-fitting tuxedo followed in her wake.

Edwina's lips tightened.

"For heaven's sake, call people by their proper names," she muttered. "One of these days, Gwendolyn Pye is going to hear you spout your Mrs. Thatcher joke, and that'll be the end of your nomination for a place on her council slate."

"Gwendolyn has been trying to get me off the slate for years," said Beary, who prided himself on his independent outlook. He enjoyed picking his issues and attacking the proposals he deemed unfit, regardless of which party had put them forward. "And Pinko doesn't care if I slap a left-wing label on him, because he knows I give him credit for not being afraid to say what he thinks. Unlike certain others," he added, seeing Merve Billings approach. Merve also sat on the Burnside Council and was a notorious fence-sitter. "Look at him. He's twisting himself into a pretzel trying so hard not to say anything that could be construed to offend."

"Hello, Beary," said Merve. "Big night, this. Hope we don't have any burglaries in Burnside. I've never seen so many police in one spot." He peered anxiously around the room. "I suppose all these coppers vote, don't they? Should one say hello, just in case they live in our riding, or would that just annoy them because they're on duty? One doesn't want to offend by ignoring them. Rather tricky, isn't it?"

Beary pointed towards Gwendolyn Pye, who was proceeding to her targets with the smoothness and precision of a heat-seeking missile.

"Why don't you jump into the wake of Our Lady Mayor?" he suggested. "Chat to the people that she thinks worth talking to."

Merve beamed.

"What a good idea. Thank you, Beary. If you see Marge, just tell her I'll meet her at our table." He slipped away through the crowd.

Edwina's frown deepened.

"Why are you tipping off your competitors with good advice that you should be following yourself?"

"Don't be silly," said Beary. "Gwendolyn hates anyone tagging along on her coattails. She'll consider him as irritating as a gnat, and after five minutes, she'll probably swat him too. Figuratively speaking, of course—and speaking of people who are sufficiently irritating to deserve swatting, here comes George Lacey."

Edwina looked round to see an angular man in a navy suit coming towards her husband.

"Hello, Beary," said the newcomer. "Here for the free dinner? I believe we're at the same table." The tall man proffered his hand. He had a gauntly aristocratic face framed in leonine salt-and-pepper hair, and a fluid expression that constantly shifted between arrogance and charm, depending on whether his glance was focussed upon men or women. His companion, who followed a few paces behind, was gowned classically and elegantly in full-length claret-coloured velvet that emphasized her tall, slender figure and gave her creamy skin and dark brown hair a radiantly warm glow.

"Hello, George," said Beary. He turned to Edwina who was hovering at his elbow. "Edwina, I don't believe you've met George Lacey. He's the new riding association president for the Coquitlam Progressive Conservatives. And this," he added, waving his glass of Scotch in the direction of Lacey's companion, "must be your lovely wife. We haven't met," he said, turning to the woman in the velvet gown, "but Edwina reads your books all the time. Edwina, this is Alexandra Lacey. She and George moved here last year from Toronto."

Edwina's face lit up.

"You're the mystery writer! I love your books. How very nice to meet you."

"You're probably going to see a lot more of us," Lacey announced peremptorily. "We're negotiating to buy a cottage on the Sunshine Coast. It's a skip and a hop from your daughter's house."

Alexandra smiled. "The little blue one," she said. "Right by the path to the pub. It'll be the perfect place for me to get away and write."

Her husband's eyes swept along the row of double doors that ran the length of the concourse. The guests were starting to funnel through into the ballroom. "Quite the crowd here tonight," he said. "If anyone wanted to wipe out the federal, provincial and municipal politicos of British Columbia, this would be the place to do it. They must make up fifty percent of the assembly, and the other fifty percent seems to be the Force."

"All the deaf men are security," noted Beary, eyeing the ubiquitous gentlemen in suits who had wires attached to their ears. "The entire massed forces of the Lower Mainland must be here. What a bonanza for criminals around the rest of the city."

"Is your son here tonight?" asked Lacey. "He's RCMP, isn't he?"

"Yes, Richard will be on duty somewhere."

Edwina pointed over Beary's shoulder and waved.

"Speaking of police," she said, "there's Philippa's nice young friend. Doesn't he look dashing?" she added, noting the tux with approval.

Beary looked round to see DC Bob Miller approaching. He smiled and greeted Edwina courteously, then shook Beary's hand.

"Busy night for you boys," said Beary. "Is there a big contingent from VPD?"

Miller nodded. Beary noticed that the young detective's eyes continued to sweep the crowd, even though he appeared willing to stand and chat.

"Such a shame Philippa couldn't be here tonight," Edwina cooed. "But she's performing this evening. It's an opera night."

"Just as well," said Beary gruffly. "This lad doesn't need any distractions."

Lacey took his wife's arm and moved her towards the stream of people pouring into the banquet hall.

"We'd better get to our table," he said. "It's about that time."

"You go ahead," Beary said to Edwina. "I have to take a quick bathroom break."

Edwina looked annoyed.

"That's because you've already downed three drinks. You'd better hurry up."

She left Beary and fell into line behind the Laceys.

"Mrs. Beary's right," Miller told Beary. "You'll probably have to go by security again when you come out. Better make it quick."

Beary hustled off in the direction of the foyer where the washrooms were located. Miller remained where he was and continued to watch the people trailing past. The assassination threat had put every member of the Force on edge, and he wondered if the danger was real, or if the note was merely the product of a disturbed mind—a sociopath who enjoyed creating tension but had no intention of acting. He wondered, too, what success the RCMP was having in tracing the writer. Yet surely an assassin who was intent on a successful mission would not be foolish enough to forewarn the police. Who could tell? A terrorist might keep an operation covert, but a madman might revel in taunting his adversaries, and he would be no less dangerous.

Miller glanced back towards the concourse entrance. His new partner was positioned by the first set of doors. A frown crossed Miller's face. He had been glad that Phil Ho had won a well-deserved promotion to detective sergeant; however, Miller regretted the loss of his former partner. Phil had been far easier to work with than Darlene Brady, the constable who had replaced him. Brady had the kind of movie-star good looks that were unusual in her chosen profession—she could have passed for a young Elizabeth Taylor—but there was no warmth or softness in the violet eyes. Still, there was no doubt that she was a capable officer. She had come through training highly commended, with top scores for marksmanship and physical training, and she was serious and ambitious. Yet Miller found her abrasive, humourless and hard to read.

As Miller watched, Darlene Brady turned in his direction, but her eyes looked beyond him to the end of the concourse. In spite of her voluminous evening jacket that was far better suited to concealing the prerequisite shoulder holster than the males' suits and tuxedos, Brady looked exactly like what she was—a plainclothes policewoman on security detail. She also looked extremely tense. Miller wondered if his own visage revealed the same degree of anxiety.

The concourse was emptying fast. Miller glanced at his watch. The vice-president was due to arrive in ten minutes. Looking up again, Miller noticed Beary coming through the doors at the end. The wily councillor was sporting an ear-to-ear grin. He lumbered back to Miller, eyes gleaming wickedly.

"You were right," he said. "When I came out of the loo, the copper outside said he had to search me, so I pointed at the winsome corporal outside the ladies' toilet and said, 'If I have to be frisked, I want *her* to do it.'"

Miller grinned.

"And did she oblige?"

"Cheerfully," said Beary. "She thought it was funny. Not like that humourless lass on duty at the end there," he added, tilting his head in the direction of Darlene Brady. "I cracked my all-the-deaf-men-are-security joke to her and got a look that could freeze a nuclear reactor."

"That's my new partner," Miller informed him.

"Oh," said Beary. "My sympathies."

Miller grinned.

"Accepted," he acknowledged. "Darlene's all business and so efficient you wonder which drawer she has you filed away in. She's very sharp though. We just finished dealing with what appeared to be a routine domestic murder and thanks to Darlene picking up a coded file in the victim's computer, we found he was linked to Hezbollah. We were able to send a massive list of contacts off to CSIS."

"Impressive."

"You're telling me. She's smart, but you'd get more camaraderie from a boiled egg. Not that I'll have to put up with her for long. There's a good chance I'm going to get an overseas posting for a few months, in which case someone else can deal with Darlene."

"Overseas? Where?"

"Afghanistan."

Beary nodded sagely.

"Ah, I read about that. Several VPD officers have served there in recent years, haven't they? What's your mission? Military intelligence?"

"Nothing that exciting. I'll be helping with community building and reconstruction. I'll be back by the fall. Hopefully, by then, Darlene will have been promoted and I'll have someone a bit more compatible to work with."

"Well, even if you are stuck with her, you won't have to worry about my daughter being jealous. Your new partner may be a looker, but she has all the sex appeal of a hydra. Speaking of fearsome creatures, I'd better get in there before the veep arrives. Edwina's tongue will be clicking like a beetle with delirium tremens. I'll never hear the end of it if I'm late."

Miller walked with Beary to the doorway and pointed to a table on the aisle. Beary made his way across the room and seated himself between his wife and Alexandra Lacey. Ignoring Edwina's frosty expression, he introduced himself to the other members of the table. The couple immediately opposite were members of the same riding association as George Lacey. Their names were Reginald and Flora Burton. Not scintillating company, Beary decided. The husband was a formidable-looking individual with a military bearing and a steely, fanatic glint in his pale blue eyes. His cowed wife looked like a permed rabbit, with tight grey curls and a beleaguered air, which was accentuated rather than diminished by her red sequined evening sweater. Clearly Reginald was not prepared to fork out for a new gown for his wife in honour of the vice-president's visit, thought Beary. The sweater and long black skirt had probably been trotted out for every Christmas dinner for the past two decades. The fourth couple at the table turned out to be a city manager from Mission and his wife. Trish and Vince Harper seemed a pleasant pair, with no strong political views and no axes to grind. Beary decided they would be well suited to deal with the Burtons so he focussed his attention on his attractive neighbour. He reached for the bottle of white wine at the centre of the table, filled his own glass and poured Alexandra Lacey a refill. She smiled and thanked him graciously.

"So," said Beary, "are you sitting here thinking up a mystery set at a state dinner?"

"Yes, actually," admitted Alexandra. "New settings always give me ideas for plots."

Beary emptied his wine glass and helped himself to a refill.

"Who are we going to bump off tonight?" he asked. "Not the VP, I hope."

"Definitely not." Alexandra shook her head. "I write cozy mysteries, not suspense thrillers. I would probably poison off one of the guests and there would have to be a personal motive."

"How about dispatching an over-indulgent city councillor?" Edwina's tone was icy.

Before Beary could comment, he felt a hand on his shoulder and he looked up to see his son.

"You must have overheard us," Beary chuckled. "This lady is planning a murder," he added, gesturing towards Alexandra. "Hope you're not going to arrest her."

Richard raised his eyebrows but did not look amused.

"Only in print," said Alexandra. "I'm a writer. But I always enjoy meeting policemen. They're so helpful, filling me in on protocol or telling me if my plots are viable."

Richard gave a thin smile of acknowledgement but his attention was obviously elsewhere. He turned to greet his mother, and then prepared to move on, but Trish Harper spoke up and detained him.

"Inspector Beary, you must know my brother. He's your equivalent rank with the Vancouver City Police. DI Barry Mackinnon? He's here this evening."

"Yes, of course. We've collaborated on a number of cases."

Richard nodded politely and excused himself.

"Oh dear," said Alexandra. "I shouldn't have babbled on like that."

"Nonsense." Beary topped up his glass again and gave Alexandra a reassuring smile. "He's preoccupied. Normally, he'd have been dazzled by your charm and stayed to chat for as long as you wished."

Edwina sniffed. Her son's single status, given that he was one year shy of his fortieth birthday, was a very sore point with her.

"Richard overworks constantly and has very little social life," she complained, "but he usually manages a normal degree of courtesy. His obsession with work is becoming rather an irritant. He's going to have to change his attitude if he's ever going to settle down."

"Policemen have a hard time balancing work and family." Trish Harper spoke mildly. "My brother is hardly ever home so my sister-in-law pretty well has to raise the children single-handed. Khari's an angel," she laughed. "Barry's a very macho male, and we always tease him that he married an Iranian woman because no western female would put up with his archaic attitudes. You should hear him. Pink jobs and blue jobs. The guys go out and do the fun stuff while the women stay home to cook and clean."

"Sounds reasonable," said Reginald Burton, earning himself a glower from Edwina, which he ignored, "but what the hell is a policeman doing being married to an Iranian? Doesn't that hold him back in his job? These days, anyone from that part of the world is suspect."

"Khari has no love for Iran," said Trish. "She's a Baha'i. Her mother was a brilliant woman—a concert pianist—and her father was a history professor. They were both hanged two years after the Islamic Revolution. Khari's grandparents managed to get her and her brother out of the country. Then they were raised by an aunt in Lebanon. The brother is still there, so Khari goes back to visit now and then, but Canada is her home."

"How did your brother meet her?" asked Alexandra.

"They met in France when they were both on holiday. It was a whirlwind courtship. Barry went back to Lebanon three months later, married her and brought her back."

"A fellow who knows what he wants," said George Lacey.

Trish laughed.

"A fellow who usually gets what he wants," she said. "He's quite the ladies' man. I suspect Khari was the one who said it was marriage or nothing. Still, it's worked out well. They've been married twelve years now and have two sons. Khari adores Barry and he's devoted to her."

"No more the ladies' man?" Lacey raised a sardonic eyebrow. "I suppose it comes to us all in time."

"Yes, well, it's about time it came to Richard," sniffed Edwina. "Especially when bachelorhood is turning him into such a curmudgeon that he's rude at a social event."

Trish reached over and patted Edwina's hand.

"I doubt if Barry will even acknowledge my presence tonight, so you certainly don't have to apologize for your son. At least he came over to say hello."

George Lacey poured Edwina a second glass of wine and soothed her ruffled feathers.

"We're not offended," he assured her. "Big responsibility to-night, looking after the vice-president. I wouldn't want his job. Still, hopefully the only killing will be in the form of a new plot for Alex."

"Doesn't it worry you," interjected Vince Harper, steering the topic of conversation into safer waters, "having a wife who spends her time thinking up ways to murder people?"

"Not at all," said Lacey. "Alex is so gentle she has trouble bring-ing herself to swat a mosquito. The only things on the planet that she endangers are houseplants. In that regard, she's a serial killer."

Alexandra nodded ruefully.

"That's true. I'm good about the garden, but indoors I get busy writing and I never remember to care for anything in a pot. I'm quite hopeless."

"You can do other things, dear lady," barked Reginald Burton. "Flora spends a ridiculous amount of time nurturing her spider plants, but in nigh-on fifty years of marriage she's rarely managed to write a coherent sentence, let alone a book."

"Really?" Edwina was nettled. She threw Burton a withering glance. "You handle all the family correspondence, do you? The Christmas cards? Personal letters?"

Burton flushed.

"I was speaking figuratively, of course."

"Oh, I see." Edwina patted Flora Burton's hand. "Husbands do tend to overuse hyperbole, don't they? It's a way of compensating for their limited language skills."

Beary smirked. He always appreciated Edwina's sharp tongue when it was directed at someone else.

A stir suddenly rippled through the room, and the conversa-tions faded to silence as an imposing gentleman took his place on the podium. The newcomer stood erect and announced with a broad smile: "Ladies and gentlemen, will you please rise for the vice-president of the United States."

As one, the invited guests rose to their feet. Everyone's eyes swerved to the entrance at the far-left aisle as the vice-president and his entourage walked in. To Edwina's delight, the party swept right past where she stood, so she had a close view as the VIPs passed by. She noted with satisfaction that she had been quite correct regarding the dress code, for the vice-president wore a tuxedo and his wife was elegantly attired in a long, sequined gown of a gloriously vibrant crimson. Then, in a blink, the couple had passed and were proceeding towards the podium.

But before they reached their destination, there was a cry from the far side of the room.

"Gun!"

Edwina hardly knew what happened next, for her husband pulled her down below the table. She heard a shot ring out—and then chaos seemed to ensue. A series of shrieks and screams followed. When she stood up again, the vice-president, his wife and his security men had disappeared, but the focus of the crowd appeared to be at the other end of the room. Before anyone at the table could move to see what had happened, members of the police force positioned themselves about the room and instructed the guests to remain where they were.

"Well," said Beary, as he sat back down and peered gloomily at the empty wine bottles on the table, "if there was going to be an attempt on the veep's life, I wish the assassin had waited until we'd eaten. This could be a long, dismal evening."

"Your priorities are appalling, Bertram," Edwina snapped. "For all we know, someone may have been hurt."

"Not the vice-president," said Beary. "His secret service men closed ranks and hoofed him and his lady out of the room at the speed of light. If anyone was hurt, it'll be one of the poor buggers who tried to protect him."

"Well, we'll hear soon enough. Even if no one tells us anything tonight, it'll be on the news by the time we get home."

Reginald Burton's eyes glinted.

"Can't you find out from your son? He'll know what's going on."

"We aren't likely to see Richard again this evening," said Beary.

"As a matter of fact, you're wrong," drawled Lacey. He pointed over Beary's shoulder. "Your son is approaching right now."

Beary swung round to see Richard coming through the doors from the concourse, but instead of speaking to his parents, he stopped beside the Harpers and quietly asked them to come out to the lobby.

Trish Harper's face paled and she looked as if she might faint. Her husband took her arm and helped her to her feet. Edwina watched as the couple followed Richard from the ballroom. Then she looked back at her table companions. Their countenances revealed that they had been gripped by the same feeling of icy dread that she was feeling now.

Finally, it was Alexandra who spoke the words that everyone was thinking.

"Oh, Lord," she said. "It must be Barry Mackinnon."

Barry Mackinnon was pronounced dead on arrival at the hospital. Darlene Brady, who had fired the deadly shot after seeing Mackinnon pull his gun and aim towards the vice-president, was put on suspension, and the hornet's nest that was uncovered by the incident had become a nightmare for the Vancouver Police. It also became a nightmare for Richard Beary, for the RCMP Integrated Homicide Investigation Team was given the responsibility of heading up the investigation.

By the end of the week, the IHIT investigators had reviewed all the surveillance tapes and conducted interviews with every member of the detective branch of VPD, but Richard chose to bring back DC Bob Miller and interview him himself. Mackinnon had been Miller's superior officer and Brady was his partner, and Richard knew enough about the young detective to trust in his reliability and integrity.

"I just don't believe it," said Bob Miller. "There's no way Mackinnon attempted to shoot the vice-president."

"Two of my investigators have watched the surveillance videos. They say it's very clear from the security cameras. Mackinnon was the first person to draw his gun. The camera on the side wall caught his actions quite distinctly and there are times on the tapes. Brady drew immediately afterwards and fired—there was a camera directly behind her on the wall of the concourse, beamed right onto the doorway, so there are two clear views of the whole thing taken from different angles—but there's no doubt that Mackinnon drew first."

"Did anyone else see him?"

"No. All eyes were on the vice-president. Mackinnon was stationed just inside the doorway. The only reason Brady saw him was because she was positioned behind him on the other side of the double doors. She hollered, 'Gun!' when she saw Mackinnon draw—several people heard her call out, including several secret service men who had their own guns out instantly. Then everyone in the blessed room must have been hollering the word *gun* and screaming and ducking. Mackinnon raised his gun and pointed it in the direction the VP was moving. Brady had no time to analyze or process the situation. So she fired."

"But Mackinnon could have been zeroing in on a target that he considered to be a danger. That's what you need to figure out. What caused him to pull his gun? Maybe he recognized someone in the crowd near the vice-president and realized that the assassination threat was real and about to happen."

"And when Brady misinterpreted his action and fired her shot, the real assassin was foiled because the VP was rushed out of the room by his security guard."

"Yes. That has to be the solution."

"It was a pretty bold step for Brady to take. She's very shaken up by the whole experience. She said it was the hardest judgement call she's ever had to make. It's actually amazing that she was able to act so decisively," Richard added, "and that brings me to another matter. You're her partner. Perhaps you can answer this. What is she like with other ethnic groups? She admitted to me that the thing that made her take action, given that she was facing a dreadful dilemma with only a split second to make a decision, was the fact that she knew Mackinnon was married to an Iranian."

Miller looked uncomfortable.

"Darlene is pretty hot on terrorism, but I don't think she harbours any particular prejudices. I do recall her saying something about meeting Mackinnon's wife at a barbeque. Something Khari had said jarred with her. I remember her asking me about the background on the marriage. She seemed reassured by what I told her, but maybe she wasn't."

"Mackinnon's wife is hardly likely to be a terrorist," said Richard. "The Mullahs executed her parents."

"I know. That's what I told Darlene. No, I'm quite sure she was acting with good intent. I don't particularly like her, but she's an excellent police officer. I've never come across anyone as meticulous. Unfortunately, I think she's so paranoid about the terrorist threat that she made a grave error, and as a result, your real would-be-assassin got off scot-free."

"Well, CSIS is going back over every single person who was in that room, including you and me," said Richard. "If you're right, they're bound to come up with something." He stood up to signify that the interview was over. Miller started towards the door, but before he reached it, it flew open and PC Jean Howe came hurrying into the room.

"Sir!" she cried to Richard. "We've just received word from CSIS. They've been running checks on Mackinnon, his family and his friends. Nothing showed up until someone ran his Lebanese brother-in-law through the database. Amin Al Aboud was on a list of people with connections to Hezbollah. What's even more significant, Khari Al Aboud was on the list too under her maiden name. Mackinnon was married to a terrorist!"

Miller phoned Richard the following day.

"What's happening?" he asked bluntly.

"CSIS are heavily involved now. Both Mackinnon's wife and brother-in-law have been brought in for questioning."

"Interrogation, more like. I still can't credit this. I've met Khari Mackinnon. She hates fanatics and she's one of the most thoroughly westernized women I've ever met. It's inconceivable that she'd be involved with Hezbollah. And I've known Barry Mackinnon for years. He mentored me right from when I joined VPD. I don't believe he was a rogue cop."

"I'm having a hard time believing it too," agreed Richard, "but we haven't come up with any other possible alternative for his actions. I'm about to view those surveillance tapes myself. Why don't you come over and join me? Maybe we'll see something that was missed before."

A half an hour later, Miller entered the room where Richard was preparing to watch the videos. Staff Sergeant Bill Martin was putting in a tape, and he waved Miller over to a chair.

As Miller sat down, Jean Howe bobbed her head around the door.

"Your father is on the phone, sir," she said. "Can you take it now?"

"Tell him I'll call him back," said Richard.

PC Howe nodded and left the room and Bill Martin started the video. As the tape began to play, Miller asked a question.

"Why hadn't CSIS already identified Khari as a terrorist? Isn't this one hell of an oversight, considering we were coming up for a state visit?"

"I asked that," said Richard. "They only just acquired a list with her and her brother's names. It was on that computer that you found during your murder investigation."

"The list that Darlene turned up?"

"I believe so."

Miller looked thoughtful.

"Could we find out when Khari's name was added to that list? Surely the computer geeks will be able to pull that information off the laptop."

"I've already asked, actually," said Richard. "I wondered that too."

The screen flickered and Barry Mackinnon appeared, standing by the doors of the ballroom. His eyes were directed to the far corner of the room, where, although not in view on the screen, the vice-president was walking towards the podium.

"Handsome sod was Barry," said Martin. "Had a hell of a way with women. I could see him turning some female's head and making her act against her own instincts, but there's no way he'd let a woman influence him to turn traitor. I'd vouch for his integrity on the job, no matter who he was married to. Look," he added sharply. "Here it comes."

Suddenly the figure on the screen leapt into action. The gun was out in a flash. Mackinnon's arms were extended as he swung his body round. He paused, the gun pointed towards the podium. Then abruptly his body hurtled forward and crashed to the ground.

"He was definitely pointing where the veep was walking," said Martin.

"But that could have been because the threat to the vice-president was nearby," Miller insisted. "Can we see the video of Darlene Brady?" he asked.

"Coming up," said Martin. He ejected the tape and inserted a second video into the slot. The three detectives watched silently as the picture flashed onto the screen. The camera had been on the back wall of the concourse, so it was a few feet above the policewoman's head and probably about thirty feet behind her. Like Mackinnon, Brady's stance made her appear vigilant and alert. She stood directly facing the double doors, her body still, almost soldierly. Then she seemed to stiffen, and she stepped forward. Her body turned slightly, and although there was no sound on the surveillance tapes, the viewers could see her mouth open as she cried out. Then she drew her own weapon and fired.

"Just the way she described it," said Richard. "She definitely went rigid, which would be when she saw Mackinnon draw."

"Can we zoom in on these tapes?" said Miller suddenly. "Look, you don't know Mackinnon like I do. There has to be an explanation for what he did. I know you can't see his eyes because of the angle, but a close-up might tell us more."

Martin switched the tapes again and brought the video into close-up. Mackinnon's head and shoulders filled the screen. Then, suddenly, the head jerked, momentarily looked down, and then levelled again for what seemed only a couple of seconds before it disappeared from the screen.

"Bloody hell," said Sergeant Martin. "Something startled him. He didn't just casually pull his gun."

"No," said Richard. "And his head swivelled before it steadied. We may not have been able to see his eyes, but I'm willing to bet he was scanning the room to locate the threat. Let's do the same with the tape of Brady."

Martin amiably switched the tapes a second time, and soon the trio was staring at a close-up of the back of Darlene Brady's head. Martin pressed play.

"Go back," demanded Richard. "Put it in slow motion."

The tape ran through a second time.

"Jesus, did you see that?" said Martin.

"Yes," said Richard grimly. "Here, try an experiment," he added. "Turn your back on me and yell, 'Gun!'"

Martin obliged. Richard and Miller watched the stiffening of Sergeant Martin's shoulders and the momentary visibility of his jaw. Then they looked at each other and nodded.

"She didn't stiffen because she was startled," said Miller. "That's when she yelled, 'Gun.' I think she hollered *before* Mackinnon drew, and then yelled out a second time, by which time everyone was hollering and screaming. Check the time against the other tape. If that's the case, it was her cry that startled him. What the hell did she think she was doing?"

"I don't know," Richard said grimly, "but we need to find out why DC Brady wanted to kill her boss."

Once the RCMP shifted the focus of their investigation, the answers came quickly. Darlene Brady had been remarkably discreet in her personal life. However, the nurse who lived in the apartment opposite was able to identify a photo of Barry Mackinnon as the gentleman who had visited her neighbour occasionally during the first four months of the year, and then had vanished from the scene as abruptly as he had appeared. She also said that Brady had been extremely cheerful during this period and had once even forgot herself sufficiently as to drop hints about marriage and promotion. But the sunny mood had evaporated by the middle of May.

CSIS confirmed that the addition of the Al Abouds to the Hezbollah contact list was dated the same day that the computer had been confiscated as evidence by Darlene Brady. Equally damning was the fact that the stolen cellphone from which the assassination threat had been sent turned out to belong to a petty criminal who had been charged by Brady for breaking and entering.

To Richard's astonishment, when confronted with the evidence against her, Brady did not attempt to deny her crime. If anything, she seemed happy to gloat about what she had done.

"He said he was going to leave his wife," she said, "and he promised me a promotion. He was just using me, and he got exactly what he deserved. That Iranian bitch will get what she deserves too. I'm never going to admit to adding those names to the Hezbollah list, so even if her name is cleared, the mud is always going to stick to her and her rotten offspring."

"Not if I have my way," Richard told his father, when a week later, he got around to returning Beary's phone call. "Mackinnon may have been a philandering fool, but the least I can do is make sure that his wife and children don't suffer any more than they already have. Anyway, enough of my news," he said. "What was it you called me about?"

"It's no longer relevant," Beary said cheerfully. "Believe it or not, I got a tip from Merve Billings of all people, and I thought I should pass it along. But you've already wrapped up the case so it doesn't matter any more."

Richard was intrigued.

"Billings? Isn't that the one you call The Ubiquitous Vacillator? The way you talk about him, I wouldn't have thought he had enough brains to pick up clues, let alone provide you with any insights."

"Not in the usual way, but Merve fancies himself as a bit of a ladies' man in an ineffectual sort of way. He'd never actually dare to be unfaithful to Marge, but he loves to chat up anything female under the age of thirty. He deludes himself that he's charming them, whereas in actual fact, they all think he's a bore, but he's harmless, so no one is mean enough to disillusion him."

"So what was Billings' brilliant deduction?"

"Well, since it's an election year, Merve wanted to do a bit of campaigning, so I suggested he follow Gwendolyn Pye around . . . naughty of me, of course, because I knew Dame Pye would be irritated as hell by him dogging her footsteps. Anyway, Our Lady Mayor stopped to speak to Barry Mackinnon because it happens that he lives in her neighbourhood. Merve, being a couple of steps behind and seeing the luscious Miss Brady, stopped to try his charm on her. Naturally, it didn't work and he was given the deep freeze, but Gwendolyn saw him and slapped him down with a pointed comment about getting back to his wife."

"And?"

"Evidently Mackinnon broke into a huge grin and muttered, 'Good advice, man,' to Merve as he went by. Merve was embarrassed— of course, being Merve, that's not an unusual state for him—but he wasn't so flustered that he failed to notice the venomous look Darlene Brady gave Mackinnon. Afterwards, when he heard who the victim was, Merve phoned me to say there was a possibility that the shooting had a personal motive. Hell hath no fury like a woman scorned, and all that. It's going to make Merve's day when he finds out that he actually managed to get something right."

Beary rang off and Richard turned back to his report. He knew many excellent officers on the Vancouver City Police Force, but the scandal that was about to erupt would sadly touch them all. The police had been focussed on security for the vice-president, but the vice they should have been worried about was within their own organization. Richard sighed. Lust and revenge were the oldest troublemakers in the world. He was very glad that this particular tale of vice and villainy was over and done with.

SOCIAL WORK

Sylvia Barnwell's thoughts were as black as the raven that glowered down at her from the Robert Bateman wildlife painting on the wall of the lounge. Staying at a lodge, she decided, was like being on a cruise. One could get trapped by excruciating bores who dominated the dinner-table conversation and hunted you down in whatever corner you were hiding in the hope of having your nightcap in peace. Corin and Janina Heath were the worst kind of offenders, both sanctimonious and pedantic, and Sylvia and her husband, Norton, had been dodging them all through the May long weekend. Smugglers' Point held an abundance of lounges and fireside nooks, but Corin and Janina inevitably found the one that Sylvia and Norton inhabited.

Corin was a lanky, earnest man of early middle age, who was not only preoccupied with his own health, but also felt the need to lecture others on the importance of proper nutrition. In spite of his vapid appearance, he held down a senior bureaucratic position in the Ministry of Social Services. His wife shared his underfed-Greyhound appearance, although the thinness of her frame was disguised by the long, flowing blouses she adopted that made her look like an aging flower child. She also shared Corin's professional interests, for Janina Heath was a social worker. She and Corin had never produced any offspring, yet both were confident that they knew everything about raising children, particularly in regard to the things other people did wrong.

Sylvia and Norton were well-heeled and slenderly proportioned, in Sylvia's case through exercise and careful diet, and in Norton's case, through his nervous metabolism, so Corin and Janina had gravitated towards them, judging them to be more suitable holiday companions than the sturdily athletic hikers or florid-faced, elderly couples who inhabited the other tables. Norton's receding hairline and wire-rimmed glasses gave him a vaguely intellectual look and Sylvia's blonde elegance and expensive casual clothes reeked of success and affluence. Once Norton let slip the fact that he and Sylvia were lawyers in a prestigious downtown firm, their fate was decided. Fellow degree-holders and professionals must stick together. From then on, the couple had proceeded to ruin Sylvia's hopes of a peaceful retreat with her husband, and by Monday evening, she was spitting nails.

Anxious to appease his feisty wife in case she tossed good manners to the wind and said exactly what she thought of the unwelcome intrusions, Norton came up with a solution. It was a clear evening, if cool. They would sneak down to the lower terrace and light a fire in the outdoor barbecue pit, having pre-arranged with the bartender to bring them two of the particularly delicious rum- and kahlua-laced coffees that were a specialty of the house. Thus, when dinner was over, they pleaded fatigue, went up to their rooms, donned warm coats and toques, grabbed blankets for cushions, and crept down the outside stairway. A few minutes later, they were tucked snugly on the bench, warming their feet by the flickering fire and looking out over the Pacific Ocean, which gleamed golden in the slowly setting sun.

Sylvia leaned her head on her husband's shoulder. This was bliss. The children were safe and happy, enjoying a weekend with her parents. They would be indulged by her father—Beary was a soft touch with his grandchildren—and kept in line by her mother. Edwina, even when she relaxed her discipline was never much more pliable than granite. Sylvia had inherited her work ethic from her mother, and she was proud of the fact that her colleagues considered her both Supermom and Superlawyer, but it was heavenly to leave it all behind for a few days.

Suddenly, a loud voice interrupted Sylvia's tranquil mood. She sat up straight and looked around. Norton's expression warned her of what was to come. The Heath's were coming down the steps, each one of them carrying two Smuggler's coffees.

Janina's high-pitched monotone penetrated the air like the whine of a dentist's drill.

"The bartender was going to bring these down to you, and we thought, what a wonderful idea, so we ordered two more and came to join you." She scrutinized the bulkily folded blankets. "You know, if you spread that blanket along the whole bench, we can all fit."

Sylvia obstinately hunched down more firmly on her pile of wool. She had no intention of budging. Avoiding his wife's glance, which could have speared a bull elephant at twenty paces, Norton politely stood, stretched out his blanket to accommodate the others, and resettled himself as close to Sylvia as he dared. Janina offered him the drink in her right hand, then squeezed in beside him, leaving a couple of inches to spare at the end of the bench.

Corin handed Sylvia her coffee.

"Sunsets are gorgeous on the west coast of Vancouver Island," he informed her unnecessarily. "Just after the sun goes below the horizon, there is a green glow," he added with the air of a Knowledge Network commentator. "It's just a spot, but you must watch for it or you'll miss it."

"We'll try not to be distracted," said Sylvia tartly. Oblivious to her tone, Corin wedged himself into the gap beside his wife. As he sampled his Smuggler's coffee, there was a moment of blissful silence, but Sylvia knew it wouldn't last. Corin was one of nature's pontificators. He had a lecture for every occasion. Sure enough, after a couple of sips, the monologue began.

"British Columbia is a spectacularly beautiful province. We're very lucky to live where we do."

Corin always began by stating the obvious. Sylvia regarded this as a ploy to ensure no one would interrupt or disagree. A few more mind-numbing phrases usually followed, after which the listener tuned out and allowed the stream of verbiage to flow on, for fear that debate would protract the encounter.

"However, with that good fortune, goes the responsibility to step forward and be willing to interfere when we see others less fortunate who need assistance. Hence, our choice of profession. We assess problems, and reposition people to alleviate their stress and enable them to cope. That's why it's called social work." Corin delivered the last sentence in a tone that would have been appropriate in a kindergarten class.

Sylvia wondered if sarcasm would stem the flow.

"And isn't it nice," she said acerbically, "that in our professions, stepping in to help others adds to our own good fortune?"

Janina looked shocked.

"Oh, Sylvia. You don't mean that."

"Yes, I do," said Sylvia bluntly, rather enjoying the offended look on Corin's face, which was clearly illuminated by the flickering firelight. She hoped he was sufficiently dumbfounded that the flow would stop permanently. However, to her disappointment, Corin's face relaxed into a smile and he said, "Ah, Sylvia, that wit of yours must serve you well in court. Lawyers must have their little joke, mustn't they? Janina and I can appreciate that. We have a sense of humour."

Sylvia realized it was hopeless. They had hides like elephants. Her irreverence was forgiven. With barely a pause to take breath, Corin continued his lecture. The sun went down over the Pacific, the horizon glowed a magical, momentary green, the stars came out and the night grew chill—and Corin droned on and on and on.

≈≈≈

"Well, they are social workers," said Norton philosophically, as he and Sylvia came down for breakfast the next morning. "They probably consider it their duty to be social."

Sylvia was not amused.

"They're booked in for the entire week," she snapped. "I'll go mad. We're going to have to move on somewhere else."

"There isn't anywhere else at this late date." Norton looked glum. "Besides, I prepaid for the week. We can't get a refund. We'll just have to find some other couple to befriend."

"What good would that do? It won't stop the other two from buzzing around like hyperactive gnats."

"Well, it would be a bit of a buffer—dilute them a bit."

"Don't be ridiculous. Anyway, we didn't come here to socialize with anyone. We do enough of that with our jobs. We came for quality time together—as in me-and-you quality time. Not converse-with-the-whole-bloody-world quality time."

"I agree, but in the interest of the lesser of two evils—" Norton paused in the doorway and looked around the dining area. His eyes came to rest on a young couple seated at a table for four in the far corner. The other two seats at the table were vacant. "Over there," he said, firmly steering Sylvia across the room. "They're a nice congenial pair. I chatted with them on Friday when they were signing in. They're on a belated honeymoon. The husband's recently back from serving in Afghanistan. They were married eighteen months ago, before he went overseas."

Sylvia eyed the pair curiously. The man certainly looked like a soldier. He was burly, with short-cropped hair and a darkly tanned face, but his expression was amiable, and the way he was looking at his young wife made it clear that he adored her. The woman was a petite, pretty brunette with large brown eyes, a sweet smile and a radiant rosy glow that exuded blissful happiness. The plates in front of them were empty, but they were lingering over coffee, and they looked up with friendly smiles as Sylvia and Norton asked if they could join them.

Norton was right about the couple, Sylvia thought, after chatting with them while waiting for breakfast to arrive. Jane and Brock Reed were charming and polite. Jane was a dress designer with a home-based business that must be doing fairly well since Sylvia recognized the label as one she had seen in a North Shore boutique. However, at present, all the profits were going into the business. The couple cheerfully admitted that they could never have afforded a week at the lodge on what they earned. Their holiday was a gift from Jane's aunt.

After ten minutes of courteous exchanges, Jane looked up and said, "Oh, here comes your breakfast. We should go and let you eat in peace."

Sylvia looked round eagerly. For once, she had decided to indulge in the house breakfast-special and she was looking forward to breaking her usual strict diet. Sure enough, Horton, the portly lodge chef, was approaching bearing two plates loaded with bacon, eggs, sausages and hash browns. Behind him was a less welcome sight. The dining room door was opening and Janina and Corin Heath were coming through, followed by a middle-aged couple that Sylvia had not seen before. She turned back rapidly and laid a hand on Jane Reed's arm.

"Of course you don't have to go. Have some more coffee and keep us company."

Horton laid the plates on the table and wished them *bon appetit*. Seeing a nearby diner waving to get his attention, he sidled away to the adjacent table. Sylvia kept her head down and started on her sausages, but the gap left by the chef created a clear view across the room. Janina's piping voice penetrated the hum of chatter in the room.

"There they are, in the corner!"

Sylvia groaned and looked up. The Heaths were striding across the room. The middle-aged couple had also moved into the room, but they stood still, their eyes sweeping the room as they looked for an empty table.

Jane Reed had looked round when she heard Janina's voice. When she saw the newcomers, her face revealed a flicker of alarm. She tapped her husband on the shoulder, inclined her head towards the centre of the room, and to Sylvia's disappointment, the couple pushed back their chairs and stood up.

"No, really. We must go," said Jane. In a flash, the Reeds disappeared through the door that led out to the terrace.

"Perfect timing!" trilled Janina, sliding into Jane's empty chair and waving her husband towards the other vacant spot.

Corin slid into the other chair and peered at Norton and Sylvia's plates.

"All that cholesterol," he said, clucking his tongue. "Clogged arteries at fifty," he cautioned.

Sylvia's mouthful of sausage went down like a lump of lead.

After breakfast, Sylvia and Norton evaded the Heaths, packed a picnic lunch and went for a lengthy hike along the wilderness trail.

By the time they started back, they felt regenerated. Several hours without the Heaths had been most restorative. It wasn't that they disliked social workers, Norton mused. They knew several that were smart, capable and compassionate. But the Heaths epitomized the caricature of the self-important, interfering type for whom power took precedence over principle every time. The list of interventions Corin had crowed about the previous evening had been daunting. Norton couldn't blame Sylvia for not wanting to spend the rest of their holiday cornered by the aggravating pair.

It was four o'clock by the time they returned to the lodge. As they approached the steps, they paused to chat with an elderly woman who was walking her equally geriatric Scottie. The woman introduced herself as Agatha Bly. She was a friend of Marjorie Painter, the owner of the lodge.

"I always come for the May long weekend," said Mrs. Bly. "It's so relaxing. Marjorie has such a sensible attitude, only allowing families with children during the Christmas and summer holidays. The rest of the year, she advertises the lodge as a retreat and it's strictly adults only."

"It is unusual to find a place that bars children but allows pets," said Sylvia, giving the Scottie a pat behind his ears.

"Jock behaves himself and does what he's told," the woman said briskly. "Unlike most children these days. There's nothing worse than trying to eat a meal while you listen to parents trying to discipline their misbehaved offspring at the next table. Not that I don't love my grandchildren, but after all, a retreat should be a retreat."

"She's a fiery old bird," said Norton after Mrs. Bly had moved on. "Mind you, she's right about the no-children rule. It does make the lodge a very restful place to stay."

"It would be more peaceful if they barred some of the guests," grunted Sylvia. "Specifically, know-it-alls with verbal diarrhea."

"Don't look now," said Norton. "Here comes one of them."

Sylvia looked up to see Janina Heath coming down the stairs. Her usual complacent smirk had been replaced by a look of perplexity. She made a beeline for Sylvia and Norton. Without any preamble, she said, "There's something very odd about that young couple you were sitting with at breakfast."

Sylvia and Norton blinked, surprised. Norton was the first to speak.

"They seemed perfectly normal to me. Very pleasant, actually."

Janina pursed her lips.

"That may be, but they're up to something."

Norton was tempted to retort that he hoped they were, given that they were on their honeymoon, but knowing his wife's opinion of suggestive double entendres, he thought better of it.

"They're in the same wing as we are," Janina continued. "When I was walking down the corridor just now, Jane Reed was coming out of her room. She turned as if she was calling across the room to someone—in fact, I could swear I heard her using a rather silly, high-pitched voice, but then she must have heard me approach, and when she saw me, she shut the door in a hurry and looked quite guilty."

Norton decided that a comment about the purpose of the couple's holiday was relevant after all.

"She was probably embarrassed to be overheard saying a mushy farewell to her husband. They are honeymooners, after all. Practically newlyweds, when you consider that Brock has been in Afghanistan for most of their marriage."

Janina's eyes gleamed triumphantly.

"But that's just it!" she exclaimed. "When I reached the stairs, I saw Brock standing in the lower hall. So if there was someone else in the room, it wasn't her husband."

Janina seemed gratified by Sylvia and Norton's stunned silence. With an announcement that she was going to fetch Corin so they could discuss the mystery over a pre-dinner drink in the lounge, she turned and hurried back up the steps.

"That is a bit odd," Sylvia said to Norton, once they were alone. "I wouldn't admit it to Janina, but she does have a point."

"Jane Reed could have been talking to the maid."

"No, she couldn't. The maid makes up the rooms in the morning."

"Maybe they have a dog."

"You'd have seen it when they checked in. Or even if you didn't, they'd have had it out for a walk. Dogs are allowed at the lodge. Every time you turn around, there's somebody's mutt sniffing at your heels. So why should Jane look guilty?"

"Why don't you go and ask her?" suggested Norton. "Put yourself out of your misery."

"I can't just barge in and ask her if they've snuck an extra person into their room. She'd be terribly offended."

"Then stop fussing and get a move on. I had the impression that Janina expects us to join them. Let's go hide in our room before Corin appears for that pre-dinner drink."

"We shouldn't have to hide in our room," Sylvia muttered indignantly.

"No, but there are advantages." Norton grinned cheerfully. "After all, we may not be newlyweds like the Reeds, but there's no reason why this holiday can't count as a second honeymoon. I'll send down for room service."

Sylvia raised an elegant eyebrow and gave a little smile.

"If you want to have your wicked way with me, you'll have to wine me and dine me first. Do you think the lodge stocks champagne?"

"Probably," said Norton, "but if they don't, I'm sure a couple of Smuggler's coffees will do the trick."

Janina accosted Sylvia and Norton in the hall the moment they came down the next morning.

"Whatever happened to you two last night?" she demanded.

Something very pleasant that was none of your business, thought Sylvia. However, she said, "We were tired after that long hike so we just had a bite to eat in our room."

"Oh, well never mind. Come and join us in the breakfast room. Do I have news for you!"

Feeling curious, for once Sylvia and Norton followed willingly. Corin was already at the corner table, steadily wading through his fruit and granola. He looked gravely preoccupied, and did not even manage a reproachful glance when Norton and Sylvia ordered Smugglers' Bennies with extra sides of bacon.

Janina leaned in and spoke in a stage whisper.

"You know the Bartons. They're the couple that arrived yesterday."

"No," said Sylvia.

"Those ones." Janina nodded her head towards the other corner where a middle-aged couple sat eating their breakfast.

Sylvia recognized them. They were the people who had followed the Heaths into the dining room the previous morning.

"I had a long chat with them last evening. She's a pre-natal instructor." Janina's voice dripped innuendo.

"A worthy profession," said Norton. "Why is that significant?"

"Because," said Janina, "Jane Reed was in her class a year ago."

"That's hardly earth-shattering news," said Sylvia. "The Reeds were married eighteen months ago."

"You don't understand," Corin added, spearing a piece of cantaloupe and waving it in the air for emphasis. "Jane Reed came into the lobby as we were talking with Mary Barton, and she was clearly upset at meeting her. There was a very cursory exchange, and Jane escaped as soon as she could. However, not before Mary Barton had asked after her little one and Jane had muttered something about her mother looking after her so they could have this holiday."

"What's wrong with that?" said Sylvia. "My mother is looking after our brood. Sitters are expensive. Probably right out of reach for a couple like the Reeds. They told me that their stay here is being paid for by an aunt—though I'm surprised that Jane didn't say that they had a baby," Sylvia admitted. "Most people are only too eager to bring up their camera rolls and go on interminably about their offspring."

Corin sucked in his cheeks and raised his eyebrows knowingly. Sylvia thought he looked like a desiccated owl.

"The first time I met Brock Reed," said Corin, "he told me that Jane was raised by her aunt because her parents had been killed in an accident when she was a toddler. Jane doesn't have a mother to baby-sit their infant."

"Oh, well, she was probably referring to Brock's mother," said Norton.

Corin looked smug.

"No. Brock's parents live in Edmonton."

"What on earth are you insinuating?" said Sylvia.

"We're quite sure," hissed Janina, "that the Reeds have their baby in their room. They'll have smuggled her in to avoid paying for a sitter."

"I find that hard to believe," said Sylvia. "How would they keep something like that secret from the room-service staff?"

"They aren't using the house staff," said Janina. "I checked with the maid. She's been told not to do their room. They're taking care of everything themselves."

"Including garbage." Corin nodded tellingly. "Twice now, I've seen Brock sneaking down to put bags in the dumpster out by the sheds."

"So what are you going to do?" asked Norton. "Report them and get them kicked out?"

"If I discover that we're right," said Janina, "I won't be reporting them to the front desk. I'll be reporting them to the Ministry.

They've been out of that room for hours at a time. It's a classic case of child neglect. Utterly appalling."

Sylvia furrowed her brow.

"Oh, for heaven's sake, there must be some other explanation," she said.

"Why are you telling us all this?" Norton asked practically. "How do we come into it?"

"Well, you're lawyers. We wanted to find out the legal implications. It's not as if this is an official case for us. Do we know enough to report them, or do we need to have proof?"

"I think you'd better ask them outright, rather than make assumptions," Norton advised. "If you're wrong, it would be a pretty serious accusation to fling about."

Sylvia's brow cleared and she interjected firmly.

"No, why don't you let me talk to them?" she said. "They were very friendly with us. Jane is far more likely to open up to me than to someone like yourself who is obviously suspicious. I'll go up and have a word with her after breakfast. Then I'll report back to you."

Janina smiled beatifically.

"Oh, Sylvia, how very kind of you. Thank you. Yes, that would be much better. We're really very grateful."

Corin beamed approval too. He even restrained himself from comment when the hollandaise-slathered eggs arrived. Gratitude indeed.

As it happened, Sylvia found an opportunity to speak to Jane Reed the moment she left the dining room. She saw the young woman purchasing postcards at the front desk, so she invited her to join her for a cup of coffee in the adjacent lounge. Jane looked surprised, but pleased, and once she'd finished her purchases, she joined Sylvia in the next room. Sylvia had already poured the coffees and was seated in a cozy nook at the end of the lounge. It was a private space, just large enough to fit two well-stuffed armchairs and a small coffee table with legs fabricated from the branches of an arbutus tree.

Sylvia had already decided there was no point in beating around the bush. She came straight to the point and said, "I have to warn you that there could be some trouble brewing for you and your husband. Corin and Janina Heath are convinced that you and Brock are not the only ones in your room. They are all set to lay a complaint, but I put them off and said I would talk to you and try to straighten things out."

Jane paled.

"Oh, no! I knew someone would find out. Now there will be such a fuss. If only Judy hadn't been called out of town!"

"Judy?"

"My sister. She was going to look after Baby, but she had to back out—and as sitters are so expensive, we eventually decided we'd just bring her along and keep her in our room so no one would know."

Sylvia was aghast.

"You just left her up there, even when you were out hiking all day."

"Well, yes. She was fine. Auntie knew she was there. I told her how Judy had backed out on me, so she said we could bring Baby along as long as no one else knew about it. That's why she told the maids not to bother with our room." Jane noticed Sylvia's blank expression and elaborated. "Aunt Marjorie. She owns the lodge. That's how we got the free holiday."

"Oh, I see." Sylvia felt a wave of relief. "So your aunt was able to look after your baby when you and Brock wanted to go out."

Jane looked puzzled.

"Why would she need to do that?"

"Well, you can't leave a baby—"

Sylvia paused. Jane had dissolved into laughter.

"Oh, my goodness," she said. "You thought we had a baby up there?"

Sylvia nodded. "Yes. Of course I did. Why else the secrecy? Your aunt would be very embarrassed given the no-child policy if guests knew she'd allowed you to bring an infant along."

"Auntie doesn't just have a no-child policy," said Jane. "There are pet restrictions too. Dogs are allowed, but cats are prohibited because a lot of people have allergies and Auntie doesn't want the rooms smelling of kitty litter. That's why we had to be so secretive. Baby is my cat. Auntie made an exception as I was stuck but she doesn't want the other guests to know."

Sylvia felt a huge wave of relief. She broke into a big smile.

"Well, that's sorted," she said. "Don't worry. I won't say a word to anyone else, and I'll put the Heaths straight for you. But there is one thing that puzzles me," she added. "According to Janina Heath, there was an interchange between you and one of the other guests—a Mrs. Barton. She's a pre-natal coach?"

Jane's face grew serious.

"Yes," she said. "I was in her class last year, but two weeks after the course ended, I was in an accident and I had a miscarriage. I was dreadfully depressed at the time, especially with Brock overseas. That's how Baby came into our household. Judy bought her for me because she felt that it would force me to get back on my feet if I had a kitten to look after. It worked too. Caring for that helpless little bundle gave me a reason to get up in the morning. She's the sweetest little thing, and very gentle, which is just as well because—" Jane paused and flushed. "Well, there's going to be a real baby in a few months to keep her company," she said.

Sylvia beamed.

"Oh, how lovely! Congratulations."

"We're very happy about it. And I know everything will be fine this time."

"So why did you not tell Mrs. Barton? Why the story about your mother babysitting for you?"

Jane sighed. "Seeing Mrs. Barton brought it all back . . . the accident, and the depression that followed. I just didn't want to go there again. Mrs. Barton is a dear, but she never stops talking, and she has to know every single detail about every aspect of your life. I'd have been there for the next hour, suffering through a well-meaning inquisition and listening to her gush sympathy and dispense advice. I couldn't bear going over it all again. I know people say that you should talk about traumatic events, but that's not necessarily so. Sometimes talking about things just takes you right back to the stress you felt before. It was easier to lie and move on," Jane said simply.

Sylvia drained her coffee cup and stood up.

"I understand completely," she said. "I'll sort everything out for you."

"Perfect. Thank you." Jane stood up and gave Sylvia a hug. "Now, I must be off. Brock and I are going on a two-day hike along the Western Wilderness Trail. He's getting our camping gear organized as I speak. We're off within the hour. And don't worry about Baby," she added with a smile. "Auntie is going to keep her dishes topped up and her litter box clean."

Sylvia's eyes were sparkling as she rejoined Norton in their own room. He took one look at her face and said, "Well, obviously, that went well. Janina got it wrong, did she?"

"Did she ever." Sylvia recounted her conversation with Jane. Norton's grin soon matched her own.

"I bet you can't wait to set the Heaths straight," he said. "That'll teach them to jump to conclusions."

"Yes," said Sylvia. "Mind you, they'll still be smug and unbearable, because they were right that there was something going on. They'll probably complain about the cat too. They're such a self-righteous pair. We'll have to listen to them crowing for the rest of the week."

"True, but the alternative is worse, so you'd better go and have a word with them now."

Sylvia nodded and left the room. However, she looked thoughtful, and when she reached the wing where the Heaths were quartered, she paused. Jane and Brock Reed would be leaving soon and would not be back until late the next day, so any repercussions would not affect them as long as they occurred after they had left and before they returned. She looked at her watch. Then, resolutely, she turned back and made her way down to the lobby. She would have another cup of coffee and check her messages on her iPhone. That should kill just enough time to let the Reeds get clear of the lodge. Then she would go to see the Heaths.

Late that afternoon, three people arrived at Smugglers' Point. Two were from Social Services and one was a police officer with a search warrant. Janina and Corin Heath were in the lobby to greet them, and after some acrimonious discussion with Marjorie Painter, the newcomers were shown upstairs to the Reeds' room. What ensued was even more acrimonious, although now, the people on the receiving end appeared to be Corin and Janina Heath. Within the hour, the three newcomers had left, and when Norton and Sylvia came across to the lounge for their postprandial drinks, they were treated to the spectacle of the Heaths, chastened and glowering, surrounded by their suitcases at the front desk. They were paying their bill and checking out.

"I thought you were going to put them straight," said Norton, once he and Sylvia were settled in the cozy end nook with two extra-large Smugglers' coffees.

"I did," said Sylvia. "I told them what was going on."

"They called in Social Services over a cat?"

"It seems so." Sylvia looked smug.

"You're not Baby," said Norton, "so stop looking like the cat who swallowed the cream. What precisely did you say?"

"I repeated word for word what Jane had told me."

"And what was that?"

"That Jane's sister was going to look after Baby, but she'd had to back out. And since sitters are so expensive, they decided they'd just bring her along and keep her in their room so no one would know. Oh, and I pointed out that they figured Baby would be fine being left in their room for two days while they were hiking the Western Wilderness Trail as they'd arranged for Marjorie Painter to go up and feed her periodically." Sylvia peered across the top of her Smugglers' coffee mug and batted her eyelashes at her husband. "How was I to know they'd completely misinterpret everything?" she said sweetly.

Norton rolled his eyes.

"Clever Dick," he said. "You really are utterly unscrupulous."

"I think I handled everything rather well. The Heaths are gone, the Reeds are off on their hike, Baby is being spoiled rotten by Aunt Marjorie and you and I can enjoy the rest of our holiday in peace."

"Talk about manipulating everybody as if we're pieces on a chessboard," said Norton.

"No," said Sylvia firmly. "I merely carried out an intervention. I assessed the problem and repositioned the people, thus alleviating everyone's stress and enabling us all to cope."

She smiled.

"It's called social work," she said.

THE DEADLY SCORE

"I t's a deadly score, in more ways than one," moaned Philippa. "If I'd known what the composer had in mind, I'd never have agreed to take the job."

"At least you're enjoying a paid trip to the Coast," said Detective Constable Bob Miller. "You can stay with your sister, have a nice visit, and pocket your out-of-town allowance."

Philippa raised her eyebrows at her cellphone as if Miller could see her expression.

"Did I hear that right? Coming from a cop, yet!"

Miller ignored the reprimand.

"So what's so awful about this opera, other than the fact that it's modern and non-tonal?" he said.

"Atonal," Philippa corrected. "The intervals are horrendous, the tessitura is in the stratosphere and there's no melody to cling to anywhere. I'm going to sound like a steam kettle crossed with a grandfather clock. Are you laughing?" she added suspiciously.

"Not at all," lied Miller. "I wish I could be there to see the production."

"You could," Philippa said sourly, "if you were doing regular police work instead of constantly going off on special assignments. Why on earth did you volunteer for duty in Afghanistan?"

"Social conscience."

"A craving for adventure, more likely."

"That too. It's quite a challenge."

"Dangerous too. Are those sirens I can hear in the background? If the line goes dead, am I to assume you've been blown up?"

"Possibly. Still, you don't seem too worried, so stop grumbling. Tell me about this opera. It sounds like a once-in-a-lifetime experience."

"I sincerely hope it is," said Philippa. "The wretched composer has written the thing as a one-acter, so I have to struggle through his vocal acrobatics for a solid eighty minutes without a break. It isn't just the music that's getting me down, though," she said soberly. "It's the subject matter. I didn't understand why I was receiving strange looks and comments from the locals, but it turns out that the composer has based this piece on a local misery-guts who has alienated every person on the peninsula. Sort of a Peter Grimes à la Pender Harbour."

"In that case, you'll probably have sold out houses for the entire run."

"Perhaps, but it's a very uncomfortable feeling to be acting out the community feuds. I have this horrible feeling that the opera is going to escalate the situation. Who knows what might happen?"

"So who is this Peter Pender character, and what has he done to put everyone's backs up?"

Philippa looked up as her sister came into the living room with a tray of coffee. Juliette set a mug beside Philippa, settled herself in an armchair and discreetly picked up a book to read. Philippa smiled at Juliette, fortified herself with a swig of coffee, and then answered Miller's question.

"The man's name is Victor Ferguson. He owns a dilapidated waterfront home in Pool Bay. He's rumoured to be very wealthy, though you wouldn't know it from the condition of his house. But then, he's also supposed to be extremely miserly, so I guess that explains the lack of home maintenance. He doesn't have to work for a living, and his only activities seem to be fishing, feuding with his neighbours and launching lawsuits. He has an ongoing property dispute with the people on either side of him—one of whom is the president of the music society that's staging the opera—he's driving his nephew into the ground by challenging his sister's will, he's suing the owners of the pub, claiming he got food poisoning from their tartar sauce, and he's accused Juliet's next-door-neighbour of child abuse."

"That last one is pretty serious," said Miller. "Any foundation?"

"No. It's a personal vendetta. Since Ferguson's wife died, he's been on the lookout for a replacement, and when a pretty widow with a five-year-old son moved into the bay, he made a play for her. She wasn't interested, but she did end up remarrying—"

"—let me guess . . . she married the neighbour he accused of child abuse."

"Exactly. Of course, it was proved to be nonsense—Tim and Jenny Burns are the nicest couple you could hope to meet—but it had to be investigated. You can imagine the pressure it put on them and their relationship, and all because of pure malice. Ferguson is so enraged over Jenny's rejection that he does everything he can to make their lives miserable. They love the harbour, but they're putting their place up for sale and moving away because they can't stand it any more. Such a shame."

"He sounds like a real piece of work," said Miller. "You'd better steer clear of him. Does he know about the opera?"

"That's what worries me. He's such a loner that the harbour grapevine doesn't reach him at the speed it goes to everyone else, but he's bound to find out at some point, and then all hell will break loose."

"So who are you playing in this real-life soap opera?"

"The woman who rejected him."

"Jeez, you'd better stay out of his way."

"I'm laying low and staying out of everyone's way," said Philippa. "The whole harbour is in an uproar. The arty types at the music society think it's great and justify the enterprise on the grounds that it's 'significant', and their president is egging them on because he's mad about the boundary dispute, but the reality is, there's a degree of spite about the whole thing. The composer has a personal grudge against Ferguson over some past slight or other, and I think he's deliberately set out to stir things up."

"Sounds like he's succeeded."

Philippa and Juliette looked round as they heard the front door open. A moment later, Juliette's husband strode into the room. His eyes were bulging with excitement and his body language screamed a newsworthy announcement. Telling Miller to hold on for a moment, Philippa turned to hear what Steven had to say. When she returned to the phone, her voice was approaching the steam-kettle register she had complained about earlier.

"You won't believe this!" she trilled.

"Try me," said Miller.

"Victor Ferguson was found dead this morning. The local police are all over the property. The word is that he's been murdered."

"Good grief," said Miller. "Your composer really did stir things up. That's a new one. Murder by music—the deadly score."

"You don't know the half of it," said Philippa. "What killed him was a batch of frozen clams contaminated with red tide. The package had been planted amid the stock in his own freezer. A package of twenty," she added significantly. "As I told you earlier—in more ways than one, a deadly score."

⇥⊢ ⊣⇤

Detective Sergeant Alex Klein was not short of suspects. Victor Ferguson had more enemies than Pac Man. Every lead the detective followed, another foe would pop out from the sidelines and zoom into view. Ferguson, it appeared, craved power, and he had sufficient private income to be able to use his money to beat into submission anyone who annoyed him. Lawyers must have loved the man, Klein thought sourly. Ferguson single-handedly could have kept an entire firm of solicitors in business, judging by the number of actions he had initiated. Both of his next-door neighbours had been forced into expensive battles over boundary disputes that they could ill-afford; Ferguson's nephew, Jack Grogan, was in despair at seeing his inheritance being eaten away due to a spurious but costly challenge to his mother's will; Ian Brodie, the jolly Pool Bay innkeeper, could be facing bankruptcy through the lawsuit against the pub; and Jenny and Tim Burns had put their beloved home on the market rather than continue dealing with the persecution they had received at Ferguson's hands. It appeared to Klein that the entire harbour was going to benefit from Ferguson's removal. It seemed a shame to have to round up the murderer of such a scummy individual, but the law was the law, and he was its representative, so he dutifully knuckled down to tackle the case.

Ferguson's favourite activity, when not initiating lawsuits or tormenting his neighbours, appeared to be fishing. He had a particular love of shellfish, and spent many hours harvesting prawns, oysters and clams, which he would keep stocked in his freezer to ensure an ongoing supply throughout the year. Ferguson's death had been caused by eating a bowl of steamed clams, made from shellfish contaminated with red tide. The clams had been in his freezer, but the toxin was still lethal. DS Klein was familiar with the dangers of red tide, for he, too, liked to fish in his spare time, and he also harvested clams and oysters from the local beaches. He was well aware that the paralytic poison could not be boiled out, and could last up to two years in a freezer. However, a red-tide warning had come at the beginning of May, so, although the clams that had killed Ferguson could have come from a previous year, the likelihood was that they had only been harvested within the past three weeks.

Like many of the locals who fished for their own food, Ferguson kept a large chest freezer outside his house. Although these outdoor freezers could be locked, no one seemed to bother, any more than they locked their front doors during the daytime. Ferguson's freezer was in his carport, and well stocked with salmon, cod, oysters, clams and prawns. There was also a supply of frozen vegetables, both the commercial and homegrown variety. The smaller fridge freezer in his house was also full, but contained no seafood, only steaks, pork roasts and sausages. The dour woman who did Ferguson's bi-weekly housekeeping informed Klein that the outdoor freezer had been virtually empty when she defrosted it last June, and that any shellfish stocked inside had been put there since the fall. There were five bags of cooked clams frozen in their nectar. These were neatly piled in the lower part of the freezer. They were taken for testing, but proved harmless. However, there was no question that the fatal clams had come from the outdoor freezer, for the housekeeper insisted that she had seen one package in the upper basket the day before Ferguson died. She had noticed it particularly as the felt-pen numbers marking the date looked slightly different from Ferguson's writing.

When asked what she'd been doing in the freezer, she informed Klein that she routinely shopped for Ferguson and put away his supplies. She also explained that Ferguson had the habit of organizing his carport freezer so that the items that ought to be used first were kept in the basket of the freezer, and once those were used, he would restock the basket from the items below that had been frozen the longest. The basket had been piled full, as it contained not only two salmon and a trout, but also two tubs of frozen prawns and some packages of cod. The clams had been lying right on top. Ferguson did his own cooking, and would often make a package of clams his main meal, simply heating the contents of the bag in a pot and adding white wine and seasoning. However, in hindsight, she realized that someone else must have slipped this package on top of the other fish. She was adamant Ferguson would never have harvested the poisoned clams himself. He might have been an unpleasant man, but he was no fool, and he knew all about the dangers of paralytic shellfish poisoning.

The housekeeper's view was borne out with startling honesty by everyone Klein interviewed. All Ferguson's foes cheerfully acknowledged that the deadly batch must have been planted by someone else. Everyone appeared to think that the police should be awarding the perpetrator a medal, rather than rounding him up to face charges. DS Klein began to formulate *Orient Express* theories. Could the entire harbour have collaborated to remove Ferguson? Was there a conspiracy motivated by loathing for the victim, or was there another more commonplace reason for the man's death—such as money? Ferguson had been a very rich man.

Ferguson's wealth came from three sources. He had enjoyed a lucrative career in engineering, where his miserly instincts and profit-share contract had saved him and his corporate employer a great deal of money. The money he earned was augmented through a large inheritance from his parents and judicious investment of all his assets. Ferguson did not have a will, so with his death, his nephew, Jack Grogan had made the leap from prospective penury to undreamed of wealth. In Klein's eyes, this would make Grogan his prime suspect, but the nephew was an engineer like his uncle, and he had been working in Africa for the past six months, which put him out of the running as a harvester of toxic clams. Klein sighed. Who had hated Ferguson enough to be driven to murder? Far too many people for comfort.

A tap on the door of his office made Klein look up. Constable Adrian Wright stuck her head around the door.

"Sir, a word about this Ferguson killing."

Klein nodded and Adrian came into the room.

"Go on," he said.

"Did you know that the music society is producing an opera by a local composer that is based on Victor Ferguson's feuds with the people in the harbour?"

"Good God," said Klein. "You're not serious."

"I am. Actually, my cousin is starring in it. Would you like me to wander into a rehearsal and have a chat with her? You never know what these arty types might come up with. Their creative effort might contain a few grains of truth."

Klein gave a wolf-like grin. This was the best news he'd had all day.

"Go for it," he said.

The following day, Philippa did not have to be at the music centre until eleven-thirty, so she joined her sister for her morning dog walk. Philippa took Purdy's leash, for the good-natured Lab was easier to manage than Quasar, the huge German shepherd that was twice the size of the other dog. As they strolled beside the lagoon, Juliette took a deep breath and sighed contentedly.

"I love the harbour in May," she said. "The wild roses are glorious."

Philippa had to agree. The road was lined with a mass of pink blossoms, and the fragrant scent of the delicate petals permeated the air. The lagoon, sparkling in the sunlight, reflected three crisp, white storybook clouds that floated against a cerulean sky. A solitary loon splashed down onto the water, scattering the clouds and piercing the stillness of the morning with its flute-like tremolo. It was hard to believe there had ever been a serpent in this Garden of Eden, let alone one who had been done to death by another inhabitant of the earthly paradise.

"Had you and Steven ever had problems with Victor Ferguson?" Philippa asked her sister.

Juliette furrowed her pretty brow.

"Not serious ones," she said. "Fortunately, our property doesn't abut his, but if he'd proved his claim against our neighbours, we could have had a problem."

"How so? There are two houses between you and him."

"It's not that simple," said Juliette. "Our property is part of a big chunk of land that is enclosed between the waterfront and the three surrounding roads."

Philippa nodded. "The main road, the lagoon road, and the pub road, yes that's obvious enough. But there are six houses on it. There must have been a survey at some point."

"Yes, but there were never any fences, just a few steel surveyor's pins, which Ferguson claims have been moved. The trouble is, it was all handled very casually in the early years. The entire property was bought initially by two friends in the middle of the last century. The original lots shared access roads and the boundaries were pretty hazy. Then, in the eighties, the heirs decided to subdivide. They retained the largest piece of land, which stretches from the main road to the waterfront. It's wedge-shaped, so they divided it into two trapezoidal lots, one wide and one deep, both with access from the pub road. Then they created four smaller lots in the section that fronts onto the lagoon road. All the lots have been bought and sold several times since then. The two large lots are now owned by Ferguson on the waterfront side and the music-society president on the piece abutting the main road."

"And the four small ones are Colonel Codfish's fish-and-chip shop, your house, Tim and Jenny Burns, and—" Philippa paused. "Who owns that little cottage that overlooks the pub path?"

"That belongs to a local fisherman, but he had a stroke recently and his daughter had to move him into a retirement home—which is pretty expensive, so naturally she's anxious to sell. She has a buyer lined up, but Ferguson's boundary dispute has been making it impossible for the deal to go through."

They had reached the other side of the lagoon, and Philippa gazed across the water at the contentious stretch of land.

"Oh, I see," she said. "If Ferguson had proved his claim that the boundary between the large lots was further over, your property would have backed onto his as well."

"Yes. We could have been involved in litigation too. What a nightmare. I feel very guilty admitting it, but I'm so relieved that it'll never happen. I always had the feeling Ferguson was just waiting to add us to his hit-list."

"You mean he gave off nasty vibes, even though he couldn't touch you?"

"Oh, yes. And it was more than just vibes. He tried to harass us. He complained that the dogs were into his garbage, which is nonsense, because I never let them out unattended . . . and he tried to accuse the girls of stealing plums from his tree."

"Equally ridiculous," said Philippa. Her nieces were high-spirited, but had been raised to be respectful of other people's property. Besides which, they detested plums. "So what happened?" she added.

"Nothing," said Juliette. "You know what Steven's like. Not intimidated by anyone. He laid into Ferguson and told him where to get off. I was worried that he would escalate the situation, but actually it seemed to work. The man backed right off. Mind you," she added, "I did hear that he tried to have Steven's band barred from performing at the pub."

"I thought Ferguson was suing the pub. Hard to have influence when you've landed the owner with a lawsuit."

"That was before the lawsuit."

"Are there any grounds for his accusation that the pub food made him ill?"

"No, not at all. That was pure malice. The pub was sold last year and the new owners are doing a wonderful job. Jake and Myrna Larsen . . . they're the sweetest couple. The meals were pretty iffy before they came along. The locals used to say the chef's specialty was salmonella sauce. Steven and I stopped going there because the standard of hygiene was so awful. But the first thing the Larsens did was replace the chef with their nephew who trained at BCIT. The place is kept spotlessly clean now and the meals are excellent. However, the chef who was fired happens to be one of Ferguson's cronies—believe it or not, he actually had one or two people that tolerated him—so when the Larsens fired his drinking buddy and refused to take his side against Steven, he launched the lawsuit to get even with them."

"He really does sound horrid," said Philippa. "I thought the opera had to be an exaggeration, but I'm beginning to realize that it's spot on. Thank goodness he's gone. I guess your lovely neighbours will take their house off the market and stay on now," she added. "Ferguson can't hurt them any more."

Juliette nodded.

"Yes. Tim and Jenny are staying. She phoned me last night to let me know. Chloe Dobson will be relieved too."

"Who?"

"The fisherman's daughter. She's been staying at the cottage for the past two weeks."

"Oh, is that the little lady that looks like a cottage loaf topped with a Tilley hat?"

"Yes, that's the one. She'll be able to sell now and meet the payments for her father's care home. How's your time?" Juliette added, as they completed their circuit of the lagoon. "I always take the dogs down to the rocks so they can swim before we go back."

Philippa glanced at her watch. Lots of time. She followed Juliette onto the wide rock that projected into the lagoon. It was a familiar spot, for her nieces often used it for launching their dinghy or fishing for tiddlers, and on numerous occasions, Philippa had been sent down there to dispose of prawn tails and fish carcasses.

While Juliette threw sticks and the dogs swam, Philippa ambled around the rock, staring into the water and watching a school of shiners darting amid the waving fronds of sea grass. The floor of the lagoon was an intriguing landscape of sand and rock, a world in itself, but as she glanced toward the shore, she noticed a gleaming pile of pebbles at the water's edge. Peering more closely, she perceived that she had been mistaken. The shining objects were not small rocks. She was looking at a pile of empty clamshells.

If her estimate was correct, she thought, mentally totting up the number in the pile, she had found the deadly score.

Klein stared at the forensic report and shuddered. Ferguson had not stood a chance. Not only had he been a victim of paralytic shellfish poisoning; there was evidence of salmonella in his system. This was borne out from the examination of the bag that had contained the toxic clams as it, too, contained traces of salmonella. Ferguson had also drunk a daunting amount of alcohol. He had spent the afternoon at the pub at Rumrunners' Point, which was the venue he frequented since being barred from Pool Bay. He had drunk steadily all afternoon and not left to go home until five o'clock. Upon leaving, the innkeeper gleefully reported, Ferguson had proclaimed to all and sundry that he had no intention of paying through the nose for the overpriced crap on the pub menu, but was going home to throw some clams in the pot and enjoy a home-cooked meal while sitting on his balcony overlooking the bay.

Klein glowered at the thought of Ferguson's condition on his drive home. However, this answered one of the questions that had been bothering the detective. Ferguson had been too drunk to notice the slight variation in the labelling of the bag. The lab report had confirmed that the bag was the same brand that Ferguson used, but that the printed letters and numbers were different from those on the remaining bags in the freezer—which meant, Klein thought happily, that he only had to check the freezers of the local fishermen and locate a matching bag with the same writing. And at that point, he would have his killer.

Klein put the report away and stood up. As he came out of his office, he saw Adrian Wright hurrying towards him.

"Sir," she said. "Remember the cousin I told you about? The one that's starring in the opera?"

"Yes. Did you uncover anything exciting at her rehearsal?"

"No. I haven't been yet. I'm going on Monday. But when I called her to arrange it, she told me something rather interesting. She saw a pile of empty clamshells in the lagoon when she was out walking this morning."

"Could have been there for months," grunted Klein.

"No. I don't think so. Philippa wouldn't know the difference, but Juliette—that's her sister, my other cousin—is a local and she had a look too. Evidently the shells look pretty fresh. Juliette figures they must have been dumped there recently. She counted them too. There were exactly twenty."

Klein grinned his wolfish grin.

"Were there indeed? A deadly score, eh? That narrows it down. Our perp has to be somewhere within walking distance of the lagoon. This is going to wrap up in no time."

Adrian raised her eyebrows.

"Do you still want me to check out the rehearsal?" she asked.

"I'm hoping I'll nail the culprit before tomorrow night," said Klein, "but go anyway. Even if I've made an arrest, you could hear things that might help prosecute the case. Who knows? The composer may even have to rewrite the end of his opera."

⤝┼┼⤞

On Monday morning, Philippa and Juliette saw Steven and the girls off to school. Then they drove up to the Skookumchuck Narrows Provincial Park and took the dogs for a hike. They ate a picnic lunch while watching the whirlpools forming in the churning rapids, and then trekked back to the park entrance. On the way home, they stopped at the farm to buy vegetables, so it was well past one o'clock by the time they got back to the bay. To their surprise, as they were taking their bags out of the car, they saw the stout figure of Chloe Dobson hurrying along the lagoon road and waving to get their attention.

Juliette sighed.

"Something's up," she said. "Look at the bouncing brim on her Tilley hat."

Chloe puffed her way up the driveway. She seemed highly agitated.

"I saw you drive back," she said to Juliette, "so I hurried over. The most terrible thing has happened. The police were all over the bay this morning. They were searching people's freezers, and they've arrested Tim Burns."

"What! You can't be serious."

"I am. The bag that contained the poisoned clams had writing on it that matches the writing on Tim and Jenny's bags. What's more, Tim is the only person, other than Victor Ferguson, who harvests clams and lives right by the lagoon—and there was a witness who came around the pub path on Wednesday night, and he says he saw a man dump something into the lagoon and then go back up Tim and Jenny's driveway. It looks really bad for him. Jenny is absolutely devastated."

"Who's the witness?"

"Mick Seeger."

"That old drunk," said Juliette uncharitably. "After an evening at the pub, he wouldn't be able to see straight enough to recognize his own mother, let alone know what day it was."

"Well, to be fair," said Chloe, "he said he couldn't make out who it was because it was just a silhouette in the light from the street lamp by the inn. But he was sure it was a man, and he insists the figure went up Tim's driveway."

"What does Tim have to say about it?"

"According to Jenny, he's completely bewildered. Jenny says they were away on the weekend Ferguson died. They went downtown to take young Johnny to see his grandmother and didn't come back until Monday morning, which was when they heard the news. I suppose that could leave it open to interpretation that Ferguson went over and helped himself to some of their clams, but Jenny insists that the number of bags in their freezer tallies precisely with what they had before. They used a bag last Thursday, and she counted to see what they had left when she took it from the freezer. She also insists that there was nothing wrong with their clams, though, of course, the cops have confiscated their supply for testing. It's all quite shocking, but Tim a killer? I don't believe it for a minute."

"Me neither," said Juliette. Her pretty brow furrowed and she bit her lip anxiously. She had always been fond of Tim Burns and had been overjoyed when he'd found happiness with Jenny and her young son. The future had looked so bright for their little family until Ferguson had cast his menacing shadow over them.

"We have to do something," said Chloe stoutly. "I'm going to the pub. That's the best place to hear the gossip. Juliette, why don't you come with me? I know you can't, Philippa, because you have to rehearse tonight, but you can still keep your ears open."

Philippa blinked. The harbour grapevine continually amazed her. She might only just be finding out who Chloe was, but obviously, Chloe knew all about her. She smiled at the apple-cheeked woman and nodded.

"I can do more than that," she said. "Our cousin, Adrian, is a—"

"—policewoman." Chloe nodded sagely. Was there anything the woman didn't know? Unaware of Philippa's bemusement,

Chloe continued, "Excellent plan. You can track your cousin down and impress upon her that the police have got it wrong."

"I don't have to track her down," said Philippa, finally managing to come out with something that hadn't reached the grapevine. "She's coming to the rehearsal tonight. I'll have a heart-to-heart with her during the break."

"Do," said Chloe firmly. "No matter what Detective Klein thinks, there has to be another solution."

As it happened, Adrian arrived twenty minutes early at the community hall, so Philippa was able to pull her aside before the rehearsal started.

"It doesn't look good, Philippa," Adrian said soberly. "There are three sets of fingerprints on the bag that held the toxic clams. One set belongs to Ferguson, one, we're not sure of, but the other set is definitely Tim Burn's. Also, according to Tim Burn's fishing buddy, there were twelve packages of clams in the Burns' outdoor freezer two weeks ago, but when we looked, there were only eleven. Jenny Burns insists that she and Tim ate a package of clams the night before they went downtown, but we couldn't find an empty bag in their garbage. The little boy couldn't corroborate what his mother said, either, because he was at a sleepover at a friend's house. Jenny says that they came back from their trip to town to discover that a bear had raided their bins over the weekend. All their garbage was strewn around the yard, so she claims the bag could have blown away or been taken by an animal, but that's pretty thin."

"No, it could be true," said Philippa. "There was a bear around. It was Thursday around dinnertime. The darn thing ransacked Juliette's garbage bin too. Honestly, Adrian, you must have doubts yourself. You've known Tim Burns for long enough to know he's a decent sort."

Adrian frowned.

"I do know he's a decent sort," she said, "but he's been pressed very hard. Even decent people can do crazy things when they're pushed beyond a certain point. Tim had good cause to hate Ferguson. He probably didn't intend him to die, just have a rotten dose of illness, which the mean bugger probably deserved, given the misery he's inflicted on so many people. But the fact remains, planting those toxic clams was a criminal act."

"I know, but I still don't believe Tim Burns did it. He may have hated Ferguson, but he hasn't a criminal bone in his body. The psychology is wrong. To poison someone with toxic clams takes evil intent. The victim would die in agony. It's a terribly cruel way to kill, and Tim is one of the kindest people I know. There has to be someone else who fits the mould."

A call from the music director forced Philippa to end the conversation and take her position for the start of the run-through. She gave Adrian a draft of the program notes and slipped away. Adrian, thoughtfully, settled herself in a chair at the side of the hall and prepared to watch. In spite of what she had told Philippa, she was not completely satisfied, and she was curious to see what the local artistic community had made of the unpopular victim in the case. The composer had certainly stuck himself out on a limb, thought Adrian, as she glanced over the program notes. Even the names were close to the originals. Ferguson had become Fingerson; Jenny and Tim Burns were Jane and Tom Binns; Chloe, the fisherman's daughter, had become Clare, the fisherman's wife. If they hadn't already made an arrest, the composer could have been in line as a suspect. He would have had a major libel suit on his hands if Ferguson had lived.

Adrian was hoping to gain insight from the opera, but she did not have any expectation of being moved by the piece. However, as the rehearsal proceeded, she was surprised to find herself spellbound. At first, the atonal score jarred and disturbed her, but after a while, she stopped being aware of the music and became absorbed in the drama. From her knowledge of life in the harbour and her interaction with local residents, she had to admit that the composer had cleverly aced the various characters. There was satire and mischievousness in the piece, but there was genuine human emotion too. Philippa was heart-wrenching as the sweet widow who started as an object of the protagonist's desire and became a target for his malice. She had conquered the bizarre intervals that had been so difficult to learn, and the staccato lines were actually remarkably effective. The tenor playing her husband was suitably heroic in his attempts to shield her from the cruelty of Fingerson, and equally tragic as he descended into the mire brought on by the accusations that he was abusing his stepson. The neighbours with the boundary disputes and the jolly pub owner formed a cleverly crafted trio that bobbed in and out like a Greek chorus, furthering the action and providing comic relief amid the heavily dramatic sections where the hero and heroine struggled to restore their lives or when the bass portraying Fingerson growled his revengeful monologues.

As the opera drew to a close, only three characters remained on stage: Fingerson, and the couple he had driven away from the harbour. As Philippa and the tenor sang their sorrowful farewell to the home they had loved so much, Fingerson ground out a menacing counterpoint, gloating, remorseless, and vowing to turn his attention to those who remained within his grasp. The final sombre chords thundered through the hall, and the silence that followed seemed to ring in Adrian's ears. A thought was trying to formulate itself in her head but it wouldn't take shape. Then, suddenly, she realized that she could still hear ringing. It was her cellphone. The idea slipped away, wraith-like, into the ether. When she answered the call, she heard Klein's gruff voice.

"There are complications," he said. "The reason Mick Seeger was adamant that he saw the man on Tim Burns' drive on Wednesday night is because Wednesday is the day that his son comes by and brings him a cheque—which, of course, he immediately cashes and goes to spend at the pub. But when we talked with his son, it turned out that he came by a day late that particular week. It was Thursday that Seeger saw the man dumping stuff in the lagoon."

"And by Thursday night, Tim Burns and his family were in downtown Vancouver," said Adrian. "Then someone else was on their driveway. After all, a third person did handle the bag of toxic clams. There was that extra set of fingerprints."

"No, that doesn't help," growled Klein. "It turns out that the housekeeper knocked the bag down into the lower part of the freezer when she was stocking the things she'd bought for Ferguson. However, she retrieved the bag and put it back, and she insists it was the right one, because she recognized the slightly larger printing. We're back to square one. Did you go to that rehearsal?"

"Yes. I'm here now. It just ended."

"Any joy?"

"I'm not sure. Let me call you back."

Klein grunted a terse goodbye and rung off.

Adrian continued to sit on the sidelines, oblivious to the bustle of performers and crew who were dealing with notes and reorganizing the hall. Gradually, the idea that had been formulating in her mind began to filter back. It was to do with the words her cousin had spoken before the rehearsal had begun. *Full of hate and evil intent.* There was only one character in the entire piece that fitted that description.

Adrian looked up, suddenly conscious of eyes upon her. Philippa was standing in front of her. Their eyes met, and with an instantaneous flash of telepathy, they both blurted out the same name.

"Ferguson!"

"The only one who fits the mould," said Philippa.

By the following weekend, the harbour grapevine was abuzz. Everyone had known that Ferguson had been thriving on his vendetta against Jenny and Tim Burns. Victimizing them had been fuel to his fire, balm to his ego. What no one had comprehended was how enraged he had been that they were about to escape him by moving away from the harbour. Determined that they would not get away, he had formulated a plan. First, he gathered twenty clams from the cove that had precipitated the initial red-tide warning. He knew the Burns would be downtown for three days, and as the corner of his property touched the corner of their backyard and the adjacent lot was screened by blackberry bushes, he was able to stroll back and forth unobserved. Therefore, once the Burns had left for town, he went across and took a package of clams from their freezer. Probably, his intention had been to substitute the toxic clams for the good ones, but then he had seen the pile of garbage left by the marauding bear and had conceived an even more deadly plan. The empty bag was undamaged, but guaranteed to carry the beginnings of the salmonella bacteria. By freezing the toxic clams in the used bag, the results would be even more deadly. However, he still had to take the full bag, since the Burns might know how many bags had been in their freezer.

Ferguson went back to his own house. He placed the bag of good clams at the bottom of his freezer; then he cooked the toxic clams, and filled the discarded bag with the meat and a portion of the juice. He placed this bag in the basket of his freezer so it could solidify overnight. He wanted to be sure the bag looked just like the others before he put it in the Burns' freezer, and there was no rush since they were not returning for another two days. He would have time to prepare the good clams for his dinner the next evening, and while they were cooking, slip over to plant the deadly score and discard the empty bag. However, he needed to dispose of the shells right away, and he cut through the Burns' yard to get to the lagoon, knowing that Tim always tossed his shells there.

Then he went back the same way and turned in for the night, secure that his plan would proceed smoothly.

He spent the following afternoon at the pub, and he did not realize that his housekeeper had dislodged the package in the basket as she loaded shopping into the freezer. She had returned what she thought was the same package to the freezer basket. The printing on the bag was the same; however, there were two identical bags, and when she reached in to retrieve the bag she had knocked down, she picked up the wrong one.

Or the right one, as the jubilant residents of the bay decided. Nobody deserved more to be hoist by his own petard that Victor Ferguson. Never had the locals been happier with the results of a cause célèbre. Tim and Jenny were staying in their home, the lawsuits were dissolved, and Ferguson's nephew, who was a much nicer individual than his uncle, was fixing up the wreck of a house with a view to using it as a summer cottage. Drinks at the pub were on the house and everyone in the harbour was rejoicing.

"It's great that it turned out the way it did," said Philippa, when she called Bob Miller to tell him about the case, "but you wouldn't believe what a pain it is for me. All the locals keep saying it's justice on a grand scale, and I'm ready to scream if I hear that phrase again. It may be a grand scale, but I'm the one who has to sing it. The composer has written a whole new ending and I have to soar up a two-octave chromatic scale and end on a high F! I mean to goodness… it's…it's…"

Philippa paused, her frustration eloquent in her silence. Miller finished the sentence for her.

"You said it right from the start," he laughed. "It's a deadly score."

THE FACE OF MURDER

Edwina Beary sat in the shade of the tall conifers and scrutinized the picnickers and hikers who had assembled to watch the running of the tidal waters at the Skookumchuck Narrows. She had seen the whirlpools and rapids many times before, so she was more interested in the onlookers than in the swirling current below.

"More coffee, Mum?" Juliette held up the thermos that had been balanced between them on the bench.

"Please." Edwina held out her cup.

Juliette poured the coffee and replaced the lid on the thermos. Then she gazed upwards as the shrill shriek of an eagle penetrated the roar of the racing water and the hum of tourists' voices. "Look at that magnificent wing-span," she said, picking up her binoculars so she could follow the stately white-headed bird's progress as it glided across the cloudless blue sky.

Edwina's eyes were still scouring the rocky promontory. A steady stream of walkers continued to emerge from the hiking trail. She clucked her tongue disapprovingly as two earphone-clad hikers ambled by, faces and fingers glued to their iPhones. Then her expression brightened as she spied a couple at the edge of the woods.

"Oh, look!" she said, tapping her daughter on the shoulder. "I do believe that's the Laceys."

Juliette brought her eyes back to earth. They landed on a youthful woman, bespectacled and drably clothed in a shapeless tank top and baggy shorts that were the same faded blue as her shirt. Unkempt, mouse-coloured curls sprung out from under a Canucks cap that was perched inelegantly low over her forehead. Beside her walked a blonde, bearded giant whose Nordic appearance seemed at odds with his black T-shirt and grimy denim cutoffs. He was holding onto a large yellow dog.

Juliette was surprised. The couple did not seem likely acquaintances for her mother.

"The ones with the golden retriever?" she asked.

Edwina made a distasteful moue. "Not them. The pair to their right. The man in the Tilley hat with the brunette in navy and white. George Lacey is president of the Conservative association in our local riding. I don't particularly like the man, but his wife is charming. She's Alexandra Lacey, the mystery writer."

Juliette's face lit up.

"Oh, I love her books! Do introduce me."

"Of course I will. You ought to meet them. They've just bought the cottage by the pub path so you'll be neighbours during the summer months."

Juliette's smile broadened.

"So that's who bought it. Fabulous! It's been sitting empty since June and we've all been wondering who the new owners were. Chloe was very hush-hush about it."

"That's because Alexandra wants to use the cottage as a writing retreat. A nice anonymous escape from her busy life in town."

Juliette trained her binoculars on the newcomers. "Alexandra Lacey has an interesting face," she observed. "Intelligent, but kind. Is she as nice as she looks?"

Edwina nodded.

"She's a gem. Devoted wife, good mother, and successful with her work. I do wish Richard could find himself someone like that instead of the flighty bimbos he always seems to have in tow. You should see his latest. An overblown platinum-streaked creature called Giuditta, and if I hear her shriek 'Ricky cara' one more time, I shall scream."

"Richard used to fall for serious types," said Juliette soberly. "I think he rather went off clever brunettes after Janet Green. He doesn't trust them."

"Speaking of Richard, where has he disappeared to? Your father too?"

"They walked the dogs down to the lower point. There's a bunch of Australian daredevils riding the rapids there. They'll be watching the action."

"That could take forever," sniffed Edwina. "Maybe I should call and tell them to hurry up."

"No, you don't have to. They're coming." Juliette had turned her binoculars towards the southern slope. Her brother and father were making their way along the rocks, accompanied by MacPuff, Quasar and Purdy, all safely leashed so that they could not break free and fall into the churning water. As they drew near, Edwina set her coffee mug down and stood up. "Watch that the dogs don't tip my mug over," she said. "I'm going to pop over to see the Laceys. Bertram should come too."

She walked across the rocks, waving vigorously to her husband and beckoning him to follow her. Seeing his wife hailing him, Beary handed MacPuff's leash to Richard and hurried off in her wake. He caught up with her as she reached the Laceys, and as

Juliette watched, he began an animated conversation with George Lacey while Edwina chatted with his wife. By the time Richard had settled the three dogs, Edwina was returning with Alexandra in tow. She introduced her to Juliette, then gestured to Richard, who was hanging back and keeping the dogs in line.

"Richard you've met," said Edwina. "At the state dinner—though he was rather preoccupied at the time," she added, a note of disapproval creeping into her voice. "A policeman's lot tends to be a rather antisocial one," she added sourly.

"I expect a detective inspector's lot is a particularly onerous one," Alexandra countered graciously.

Richard redeemed himself. He flashed a charming smile.

"You're the mystery writer," he said. "Of course I remember you. How is your latest book coming along?"

"Very well, thank you."

"Well don't forget I'm here if you need any background material. I'll be more than happy to answer your questions."

Alexandra beamed.

"That's so kind. I might take you up on that offer some time."

"Excuse me!" A penetrating, high-pitched voice interrupted the conversation.

Edwina looked round, startled. The frizzy-haired woman in the faded shorts had come up behind her. She was holding out a camera. At close range, the woman appeared even more unappealing. Edwina was always impeccably groomed and she inwardly recoiled as she noted food stains on the woman's shapeless garments.

"Would one of you mind taking a photograph of me and my husband?" the woman asked. "It's our anniversary today."

"Richard, you take it," said Edwina, who hated handling other people's cameras. "Juliette can hold the dogs. Then we really should pack our gear and prepare to head back," she added sharply.

The pale-haired woman appeared impervious to Edwina's antipathy. Alexandra, however, picked up the vibes.

"I'll tell Bertram you're ready to go," she said. She gave Edwina a hug and slipped away.

Richard handed the leashes to Juliette and took the camera. The woman beckoned to her husband, who was standing a little way off with their own dog, and he moved towards them. Seeing the golden retriever approaching, Juliette judiciously relocated the Beary pack a few steps further away. The newcomer looked friendly, but MacPuff and Quasar both tended to be unpredictable, and the last thing she needed was a group of struggling animals and tangled leashes, especially with the turbulent water only a few yards away.

Richard expected the couple to pose on the rocks with the sweeping panorama of water and mountains in the background, but to his surprise, the woman asked Edwina if they could sit on the bench for the photograph. Edwina raised her eyebrows, then, with a visibly aggrieved air, moved her thermos and bag. Cheerfully oblivious to her irritation, the pair settled on the bench.

"This is where we met," the woman explained. "My sister and I were having a picnic right on this very bench, when Brett came out of the trail with Frisk. He started talking with us, and . . . well, two years later, here we are again. We live in Vancouver now, but Regina, still lives on the Coast, so we're visiting for the summer. Frisk loves it here. All the country smells. It's so much more exciting than town."

Her husband remained silent. He was having trouble controlling the dog, for it had caught sight of the trio of canines with Juliette and clearly wanted to play. He finally forced the retriever to sit, wedging him between his knees and firmly holding the dog's head so that it faced the camera, and he managed to look up to smile as Richard took the shot.

"Thank you so much," the woman gushed. "I'm Gudrun Ewell, by the way, and my husband's name is Brett. This picture means such a lot to us."

Brett grinned and nodded.

"It means a lot to *her*. It'll be in the computer and posted on Facebook the minute we get home. I'll be making the coffee while she yaks on-line with her friends and posts notes on their fairy-garden walls."

Gudrun laughed, although the sound held little warmth.

"He's always teasing me about my Facebook friends," she said, "but it's a great way to stay in touch with people. I've made new contacts all over the world on the different game sites."

Brett rolled his eyes. "Yeah, right. Admit it. You're addicted. Come on, girl. Time to hike back."

The couple moved away, dragging a reluctant Frisk who was still eager to see the other dogs. They disappeared into the trees, and Edwina plopped the knapsack back onto the bench and began to pack the picnic crockery.

"Fairy gardens indeed," she scoffed. "What's wrong with inviting a friend in for a cup of tea. All this on-line virtual living is becoming quite insane. Where did privacy go? I detest this modern world where everybody's business is everybody's business and people can't even come out to enjoy nature without being attached to their electronic devices. I can't say I cared for that young woman either. For all her voluble chatter, she had hard eyes. No wonder she communicates through a computer. She was as artificial as one of those annoying paperclip icons that bob up and interrupt when you're trying to write a letter."

"Everyone communicates through computers these days," Juliette pointed out. Her face had gone rather pink. "I have a Facebook site," she admitted. "I use it to promote the puppet company. I have a fairy garden too," she added, gently rather than defiantly, since Juliette was the peacemaker in the Beary family. "It's called Purdy's Paradise."

Richard chortled.

"You named your garden after your dog?"

"Yes. Why not?" Juliette said indignantly.

Still looking somewhat flushed, she gathered Purdy, MacPuff and Quasar around her and headed off across the rocks.

Edwina stared after her amazed.

"Well!" she exclaimed. "Dogs and fairies. Really!"

Richard laughed.

"And just think," he said, "we always thought Juliette was the sensible one."

"I heard that," Juliette called over her shoulder as she marched away. Then, surrounded by her adoring wall of dogs, she disappeared into the trail.

Bea Talbot was watering her dahlias when her neighbours' car pulled into the driveway opposite her own. She waved as the couple got out of the vehicle.

"Hello Gudrun. Hi Brett. How was the Skookumchuck?" She knew all about the trip as they had chattered to her about their plans a few days ago.

Gudrun waved and began to unload the knapsacks from the trunk. Brett called back across the road.

"Lovely, thank you. We had a wonderful hike. Frisk adored it."

"Come on over and have a cup of tea."

"We'd better take a raincheck," said Brett. "Gudrun can't wait to fire up her laptop and post her pictures. She's running an ongoing travelogue for all her Facebook friends."

He grinned apologetically and followed his wife inside the house. Bea shook her head in bewilderment and went back to her flowerbeds.

Ten minutes later, Brett was staring at the image on the computer screen. It was a good shot of him and Gudrun, both smiling happily, with Frisk wedged firmly between his knees.

"It's perfect, isn't it?" he said. "Has Marta seen it yet?"

"Yes. She was already on Facebook when I logged on so we've been chatting online. She's been drooling over the surfer pix. Right now, she's gone back to watering a bunch of fairy gardens, but she said she'd be back in a sec."

"Type in 'hello' from me," said Brett.

"All right."

Brett watched the words come up on the screen and waited for the reply to appear. After a moment, he raised his eyebrows.

"So what do you think?"

"She didn't sign off, but there's no response."

"Are you quite sure?"

"Yes. She doesn't seem to be there. But I'll hold on for a bit, just to be sure."

"Okay. I'll go make the coffee."

He walked away towards the kitchen. But five minutes later, when he returned with the drinks, there was still no reply from the other end.

Sergeant Hawkins of the Calgary RCMP glared at the constable who had delivered the dispatcher's report.

"Is this your idea of a joke?" he demanded.

The constable grinned.

"No," he said. "That's exactly what it says. A fairy from Tasmania phoned in to report another fairy missing. She said the missing fairy, whose name, by the way, is Bluebell, hasn't watered her garden in days, yet she didn't indicate that she was going away and, even more significant, or so I gather, she didn't freeze her garden. Her fairy friend is keeping the garden going, but she's worried that there's no response from Bluebell. The Tasmanian fairy doesn't have an address for Bluebell, but she knows she lives here and she wants us to investigate."

"Since the Tasmanian fairy is managing to water a bunch of plants in Calgary, I take it we're discussing a virtual garden," the sergeant said dryly.

The constable nodded.

"Yes, sir. It's a Facebook game."

The Sergeant groaned. "Heaven preserve us. What does this Tasmanian fairy expect us to do? Wave a bloody wand."

"So do we do anything about it?"

"Not until she uses her magic powers to come up with a name and address," growled Hawkins. "Go and get on with something useful."

The sergeant went back to his desk, and by the end of the day, he had forgotten about the report from overseas. However, when he came in the following morning, the dispatcher herself greeted him with the news that five more fairies had called to express concern about their missing friend. It appeared that Bluebell's disappearance had generated waves of apprehension in South Africa, the United Kingdom and three different American states.

While Hawkins mused on the fact that Bluebell seemed to have a lot of international friends who cared about her welfare, but no one in her own backyard, virtual or otherwise, who gave a damn, another call came in.

"This alert is different, sir. We have a name—Marta Greeley. She's a local travel writer. Her cousin is on the line now. Name of Gudrun Ewell."

Hawkins picked up the phone and took the call. The woman on the other end had a high-pitched, rather irritating voice, but she sounded genuinely upset.

"I haven't heard from her since the weekend," she said. "I've called several times but there's no reply. I've left messages, but she doesn't call back."

"Have you gone around to her home?" asked Hawkins.

"No, you don't understand. I'm in British Columbia, but we keep in touch regularly. Not so much phone calls, but we chat on-line all the time. It's totally unlike her to disappear like this."

"Have you tried contacting her neighbours, or the people where she works?"

"She works at home. She's a travel writer, and when she's busy with a project, people might not see her for days at a time. The house is pretty isolated because it's on a ten-acre property—but she always answers her phone calls and emails, and she never fails to check in on Facebook. I was talking with her online last week-end. I'd just posted a photo—it was my wedding anniversary and it was a picture of me with my husband and our dog. I'd put up some more photos too, and she said she'd look at them as soon as she finished watering her fairy garden—and then I waited, but she didn't come back. It's been five days now, and there hasn't been a word from her. Something must have happened. She's never away from her computer that long."

Sergeant Hawkins cut in with a question.

"Does this cousin of yours have an online name that she uses in these fairy gardens?" he asked.

He knew the answer to his question before he received the reply.

"Yes," said the woman. "Her name is Bluebell."

As it turned out, Gudrun's assessment of her cousin's habits was accurate, for Marta Greeley was not away from her computer. The constable who was sent to check on her received no response when he knocked at the front door, but upon going around the back of the house, he found signs of a forced entry. When he entered the home, he saw why Marta Greeley had not come to the door. She was slumped in the swivel chair at her desk, her lifeless eyes incapable of seeing the ironically apt screensaver message, *Peace at Last*, which ran horizontally and repetitively across the monitor.

A flick of the mouse produced the image of a couple seated on a bench, with a wall of evergreen trees behind them and a golden retriever tucked between the man's knees. A cluster of open reference books lay spread around the floor by the computer desk, and a handbag, its contents strewn all over the carpet, had been dumped by the chesterfield, though Greeley's wallet was conspicuously absent from the pile. The only additional item to mar the otherwise immaculate carpet was an eight-pound exercise weight with a rusty-looking stain at one end.

The major crime section, along with the forensic unit, was duly called in, and by the end of the week, the detectives handling the case could have used some magic from the conscientious fairies who had alerted the police in the first place.

DI Tidewell assembled his team in the incident room on the following Monday and waited to hear what progress they had made.

"She was hit over the back of the head with a metal exercise weight," Detective Sergeant Blake informed him. Blake was a phlegmatic older man who refused to be hurried or pressured into action unless he was certain he had the right result. He spoke slowly and clearly, ignoring the impatient look on his superior's dark countenance.

"We've established the probable time of death," Blake continued. "We believe she was killed on the afternoon of July third. She went out in the morning to visit her mother who is in hospital in the final stages of cancer. Greely arrived at the hospital around ten, but she was only there for an hour. She told one of the nurses that she was heading home to work on an article for a trade journal—and she must have gone straight back because the nearest neighbour, who lives on the forested piece of acreage adjacent to Greeley's home, passed her car on the road as she was leaving to go shopping."

"Was Greeley alone in the car?"

"Evidently."

"What's to say she didn't continue past her property and pick up someone before she went home?"

"Her driveway is the last one on a dead-end road. There's nothing but woods and a wide ravine next to her home."

"This was the last time she was seen?"

"Yes, but she was online leaving messages for several friends during the course of the morning."

"The fairies at the bottom of the garden," sniggered DC Johns, who fancied himself as the station comedian. He grinned at the burly uniformed constable in the corner of the room who had been assigned the job of tracking the Internet contacts. "Fill us in, Fairy Morton."

Sergeant Blake quelled DC Johns with a glare and nodded to the other constable.

"Go ahead, Morton."

"It's a Facebook game, sir," explained Constable Morton genially. "These fairy friends are all over the globe, and they leave messages on each other's garden walls. They were very informative," he continued. "Every one of them insists that no one but Greeley could have left the messages they received, since the comments referred to things that other people couldn't possibly know. Greeley was also online with her cousin from British Columbia, and it's pretty likely that she was killed very soon after she stopped responding to messages, which would be around two o'clock that afternoon."

"That tallies with the autopsy findings," DS Blake added for the inspector's benefit.

DI Tidewell furrowed his wide brow and glowered at the assembled detectives.

"What else do we have?"

"There's been no activity on any of Greeley's credit cards," piped up DC Johns. "There's no indication that the cards have been copied, or that the numbers have been used overseas. There's no way this was a robbery. Someone just set it up to look like one. The broken window on the back door could have been done after the murder. It's more than likely Greeley knew the killer and let him in. Or her," he added. "The murder weapon belonged to Greeley herself. It came from a rack of weights by the chesterfield."

"That hardly suggests premeditation," pointed out Tidewell dourly. "If someone has murder in mind, they usually come prepared with a weapon."

"Not if it was someone who was familiar with the house and knew the exercise weights were there," rebutted DC Johns.

"They *were* at the back of the room, sir," DS Blake pointed out, supporting his junior officer. "The killer would have had to walk past Greeley to get to them. She must have seen whoever it was, and there was no sign of a struggle. It's more than likely she knew the killer."

"Fine." Tidewell harrumphed, sending his jowly visage into the series of wobbles that his staff recognized as the precursor to a battery of questions. "But who wanted the woman dead?" he demanded. "What is the motive? Did she have a boyfriend? An ex? What do we know about her love life?"

"She was engaged," chimed in Constable Morton, "and about to be married—this weekend, actually."

"Strange timing," barked the detective inspector. "With her mother dying of cancer!"

"That was the reason for the rush," said Morton. "She wanted her mother to know that the marriage had taken place. She intended to have a quiet civil ceremony. I got that tidbit from the Tasmanian Fairy, who, incidentally was the first person to notice that Marta had disappeared from view."

"Never mind these fairies," growled Tidewell. "What do we know about the fiancé?"

DS Blake took over again.

"We know he's out of the frame as a suspect. He was in Russia touring with the Welsh Choir and there are more than a hundred witnesses to prove it."

"Why the hell didn't *he* call in to express concern about the girl? Everyone else seems to have. Wasn't he worried when he couldn't get hold of her?"

"He left three messages on the answering machine. He said for her not to worry about calling back as he was out of cell range and he'd call again when he had access to a phone. His last message included a comment about the fact that she wasn't home and wasn't answering her cell, so he hoped that didn't mean her mother was worse, but he told her to take care, and that he'd be back at the end of the week and would come right over. When he heard about her death, he was pretty devastated. I'd say his grief is genuine."

"What about assets? Did Greeley own the house she lived in? Must be a valuable piece of property if it's on a ten-acre estate. Who's her next of kin? Any chance it was this fiancé?"

DC Peake put up her hand and ventured the information. She was a polite, conscientious young woman, whose deferential manner belied a bulldog tenacity for getting to the truth. "The house belongs to Greeley's mother, who's also her next of kin," she said. "Greeley moved in there last year when her mother was diagnosed with cancer. Because Greeley worked so much at home, it was easy for her to help with the nursing. But two weeks ago, the mother was moved into palliative care at St. Regis and she's virtually comatose now. The staff says she won't last more than another week or two."

"Would Greeley have inherited the property if she had lived?"

"Yes, and quite a lot more," said the detective constable. "She was an only child, and her mother had well over a million dollars in investments and personal accounts."

DI Tidewell's jowls quivered. He reminded DC Peake of a Saint Bernard watching a slab of beef being broken into his dinner bowl.

"So someone is going to benefit considerably from the fact that Greeley pre-deceased her mother, and it obviously isn't her fiancé?"

"Yes, sir," said DC Peake.

"Now we're getting somewhere. Who does stand to inherit?"

"Her cousins in British Columbia. Their mother was Greeley's aunt—her mother's sister—but she died in a car crash some years back, so the nieces are next in line. However—" DC Peake peered apologetically over her gold-rimmed spectacles.

Tidewell waited expectantly.

"Well?" he demanded.

"Neither one of them could have done it," the young woman finished. "They were both on the Sunshine Coast. One of them lives there, and the other was visiting her from Vancouver. The resident sister is Regina Jinkerson, and she was at work on the day Greeley was killed. The other sister is Gudrun Ewell, and she and her husband, Brett, were at a provincial park at the north end of the peninsula. A picture of the two of them there was on Greeley's computer screen. Gudrun Ewell had just posted it and was chatting with her cousin online."

"The photograph could have been taken any time," pointed out Tidewell. "And anyone could have posted it."

"No, sir. We traced the man who took the photograph that day—and he's an incorruptible witness. He's an RCMP DI from Vancouver," she added ruefully. "He confirmed that he took the picture on the morning of July third."

"Is he sure the people he photographed were the Ewells? These days, with Photoshop, people can play all kinds of tricks."

"Inspector Beary interviewed them himself, just to be sure," said Peake, "and he took Ewell's camera and computer for analysis. The camera had already been formatted—but the picture on her Facebook page had been put into her computer with all the others she took that day, two of which actually have Inspector Beary in the background. They're all in the same file, numbered sequentially, so the photo had to have come from her camera. And it hasn't been doctored. The Ewells appear to have indestructible alibis, and Regina Jinkerson does too."

Tidewell bristled.

"Do they indeed? Well, I think you should get busy destructing them. I don't believe in perfect alibis." His eyes swept the room as he issued the detectives a challenge.

"Find the flaw," he ordered them, "because there has to be one."

DC Peake was not the sort of police officer who acted on hunches and then worked to make the evidence fit her theories, but she could understand why the inspector was suspicious of Regina Jinkerson and the Ewells. No one else had a motive to kill Marta, and the cousins had a great deal to gain. Their parents had never earned much money, so there had been nothing left but a pile of debts after the elder Jinkersons died in the car crash. Gudrun had taken enough business courses to qualify for a secretarial job, and her husband ran a used-car lot in Surrey, but they were hardly affluent. Regina had barely made it through high school, so she supported herself by working as a waitress at the pub, and augmenting her income through her artistic talents, which appeared to be acting and sketching portraits of tourists during the summer season.

The BC force meticulously checked the cousins' movements over the three-day period surrounding Marta Greeley's death, and the report that came back to the Calgary team was comprehensive. DC Peake's antennae began to quiver when she saw that Regina Jinkerson had left the Sunshine Coast on June second, the day before the murder, but as she read on, she saw that the woman's alibi was still intact. Regina had left the Coast to go to Vancouver, where she had an appointment to show her watercolours to an art dealer in Yaletown. After the interview, she spent the afternoon shopping in town, but she was back home by evening. The gallery owner, the store merchants and her neighbours in Madeira Park all confirmed this.

Gudrun and Brett had also travelled down the Coast that day, but had not left the peninsula. They had driven down to Gibsons, strolled through the gift shops, eaten takeout fish and chips for dinner, then driven back to Pender Harbour in the late afternoon.

The next day, June third, which was the day of the murder, Regina had gone out for her usual morning jog, after which she had returned home to work in her studio on a portrait commissioned by a tourist. This was the day that Gudrun and Brett had hiked across the Skookumchuck Provincial Park and met DI Richard Beary at the viewpoint overlooking the rapids. They had returned to the house around one in the afternoon, whereupon Gudrun had entered her photos into a Facebook album and gone online with her cousin in Calgary. Regina had emerged from her studio and been at her usual pub shift by four o'clock that afternoon. She remained there until ten o'clock, after which she was given a ride home with a neighbour who had been patronizing the bar that evening.

DC Peake continued reading. The notes on the next day did not disclose anything helpful either. Although Regina Jinkerson had worked late into the evening, she had been out for her morning jog on July fourth, and several neighbours had seen her and spoken to her. After she returned to the house, Gudrun and Brett had proposed that the three of them drive down to Gibsons for brunch, which they did. The restaurateur in Gibsons confirmed their presence in his dining room. Then, on the way back up the coast, they had taken Frisk for a walk in the Smuggler's Cove Provincial Park. Several witnesses had been found who had met the trio with the friendly dog while hiking the trail.

But like her commanding officer, DC Peake was still dissatisfied. She stared at the computer screen and studied Marta Greeley's final online chat:

Gudrun: Just posted pix of our hike at the Skookumchuck. Have a look.
Marta: I'm looking. Fabulous album. Can't believe those surfers. They must have nerves of steel.
Gudrun: I have some of them on video. Don't exit. I'm going to post that next.
Marta: Go ahead. I'll check it out in a minute. Right now I have to go water my garden. Have a wilting Bonsai.
Gudrun: It's that hot in Calgary?
Marta: Har har. See ya in a mo.

But she never came back, thought DC Peake, because at that moment, the killer must have arrived at the house. However, if it had been a stranger breaking in, Marta would have stood up—would have tried to escape or defend herself. And if a visitor had arrived and she had let the person in, why would she have gone back to the computer? It didn't make sense. Unless, she thought suddenly, it was a fellow computer enthusiast.

DC Peake noticed the fairy-garden icon at the left of the Facebook page. Feeling an urge to see what happened if she tossed Marta's final conversation out into Fairyland, she quickly typed out the lines, then opened the fairy site and pasted the insert onto Bluebell's garden wall. Then she returned to the main page and opened another of Marta Greeley's photo albums. It contained several photographs of her cousins. The two sisters were strikingly dissimilar, thought DC Peake. Whereas Gudrun Ewell had frizzy, beige-coloured hair, Regina's was short, spiky and white blonde. Gudrun's outfits were shapeless—casual wear in drab shades, looking for all the world as if they had come from the discount table in

Value Village—whereas Regina's clothes were tight-fitting ensembles in vibrant colours. One photograph, taken on what looked like an ocean promenade, cruelly emphasized the contrast between them, for Gudrun faded into insignificance beside her sister, who sported a fuchsia pink tank top, heart-shaped sunglasses in the same shade, and shorts so short that the full length of her slender, shapely legs was revealed. She appeared to be taller than her sister, but on closer inspection, DC Peake saw that the pink canvas sandals with crisscross ties were platforms with three-inch wedge heels. So, thought the constable, the girls were probably close in height. She studied another photo, which was one of a set from a wedding album. The photographer had caught the sisters in a candid shot, probably as they listened to the speeches, for they were both seated at a table and staring at someone beyond the camera. Gudrun's hair had been swept back for the occasion, and now a family resemblance was visible in the shape of the face and the colour of the eyes, which were a pale, icy blue. DC Peake felt a chill as she looked at the pair. The eyes were cold, she thought. That was the most startling similarity between them. One woman was flamboyant and dramatic, and one was self-effacing and understated, but they both looked capable of murder. As she stared into the empty, light-coloured eyes, a sudden thought struck her, and she picked up her phone. She needed to a make a call to Vancouver.

When DC Peake eventually got through to Richard Beary, she told him what was on her mind.

"During the period from the morning of July second, when Regina Jinkerson drove to Vancouver, until 11:00 am on July fourth, when she, her sister and brother-in-law were having brunch at the Sea Chest in Gibsons, neither sister was seen together."

"What are you suggesting?" asked Richard.

"The drive from Vancouver to Calgary is only fourteen hours. Regina Jinkerson was last seen in Vancouver when she picked up her watch on July the second at two o'clock in the afternoon. That's twenty-four hours before Marta Greeley was killed. Then there's another twenty-one-hour gap from two o'clock on July third until the two sisters were seen in Gibsons on July fourth. Lots of time for someone to drive to Calgary and back, and still have a few hours sleep in a rest-stop each way."

"You're thinking that one sister could have impersonated the other during that period?"

"Yes. The differences between them are superficial, related to dress and hair colour. Their actual height and body shape is close enough that with the proper clothes, make up, and a wig, one could be made up to look like the other. I don't think Gudrun Ewell could possibly have passed for Regina during her shift at the pub, but she might have got away with impersonating her downtown, because the art gallery owner and store clerks had never met her. They testified that they had seen Regina, but what had they really seen? A white-blonde woman with Regina's credit cards, who wore flamboyant clothes and heart-shaped sunglasses." DC Peake's voice rose in pitch as she explained her theory. "Suppose it was Gudrun who went downtown on the Wednesday. She could have left Regina's car at the ferry terminal, walked onto the ferry, and taken the bus to Vancouver, which is what her sister always did when *she* went into town. She had Regina's art portfolio, and she would have used her sister's charge card for the shopping. With dark glasses and a blonde wig tucked under a huge sunhat, she had a perfect disguise. Afterwards, she could have changed into jeans and put on a different hat for the drive to Calgary."

"In what vehicle?" Richard interjected. "You said she parked her car at Langdale."

"Brett Ewell works at a used-car lot in Surrey. He could have left a car for her. She could have taken the Skytrain to Surrey and picked it up. In the meantime, Regina would have gone for her usual run that morning. Then she could have put on a frizzy wig and her sister's clothes and gone with Brett to Gibsons where they were seen having coffee and ambling through the gift shops. Brett could have driven his own car back, and Regina could have discarded her disguise, picked up her car from the ferry terminal and driven it back up the coast in time to go to work in the pub for her evening shift. The next day, once again she'd have gone for her morning run. Then she could have donned the disguise and gone with Brett to walk the Skookumchuck, where they met you and had the photograph taken. After they returned to the house, Regina could have posted the pictures on Gudrun's Facebook site and talked with her cousin online. Later, she'd have discarded the disguise again to go to work at the pub."

"And while Regina covered for her sister, you figure Gudrun drove through the night, stopping to sleep a few hours beside the road, and arrived in Calgary in time to reach her cousin's home by early afternoon."

"Yes. Can't you just see it? Marta Greeley would have been amazed to see her, but all Gudrun had to do was say it was a surprise, and that Brett and Regina were online waiting for her reaction. What would Greeley logically do?"

"Laugh, and go back to the computer to send them a message from the two of them."

"Exactly. I couldn't figure out why she was sitting at the computer, but that would make perfect sense. She would have been looking at the screen—"

"—and would never have noticed her cousin picking up the weight and coming up behind her."

"Right. Once Marta was dead, Gudrun could have dumped the purse, stolen the wallet and smashed the back window to make it appear that the killer was a burglar who had broken into the house. Then she just had to leave and drive back. She could have abandoned the car in Surrey—the park and ride would be the perfect spot for pickup and disposal, because it's right by the Skytrain—then she'd have taken transit back to Horseshoe Bay and caught the first ferry to Langdale. Regina would have gone for her morning jog before driving down to Gibsons with Brett, and they could have met Gudrun at the restaurant where they were all seen having brunch together. After that, it was a breeze. They went back up the coast together, stopping en route for the hike at Smuggler's Cove."

"It's an ingenious theory," Richard acknowledged.

"It's doable!" insisted Peake. "It would work. But of course it comes down to one crucial factor—"

"And that is?"

"Can you swear that you saw Gudrun Ewell at the Skookumchuck Narrows, or can you only be sure that you saw a woman with mousy hair, drab clothes and a high-pitched voice? Are you positive the woman you interviewed after the murder is the same one you photographed at the provincial park?"

Richard paused and thought carefully before he replied.

"You're not going to like this answer," he said finally. "I didn't notice much about the Ewells at the time, because I didn't interact with them. When you're looking through a camera lens, you're concentrating on getting the image in the frame, not observing the people themselves. However, I had the picture on hand when Regina and Gudrun were brought into the station, and I'm ready to swear, having stared long and hard at both of them, that it is Gudrun in the photograph. It's a minor point, but she has a frozen little finger on her left hand. The joint is immobile and slightly swollen. I didn't notice it at the time, but it's easy to see in the picture. Regina, on the other hand, has immaculate hands."

DC Peake felt deflated.

"Are you sure?"

Richard could hear the disappointment in her voice.

"Sorry," he said, "but you can't get around it. It's not a detail large enough for them to have incorporated into a disguise, but it's significant enough to convince me that the shot I took was definitely of Gudrun Ewell."

Richard could tell that DC Peake was frustrated by his response, but he was certain that the photograph was genuine. However, he had to admit that the scenario DC Peake had presented was plausible, and the more he thought about it, the more he wondered if he had missed something. After mulling the situation over at length, he suddenly thought of Alexandra Lacey. A mystery writer could well be observant. He looked up her website and found her contact information. He punched in her phone number, hoping he would get through to the writer and not an agent or secretary, and after two rings, he heard Alexandra's mellow voice. She seemed delighted to be asked for her opinion on something other than a fictitious mystery. She listened carefully as Richard explained the details of the case. Then, after a pause, she spoke thoughtfully.

"There was one thing that struck me as peculiar," she said. "It was the fact that they posed for the shot with their backs to the forest. The photograph would have been much more effective taken with the sea and mountains behind them. Why did they choose to sit on the bench?"

"I thought that odd too," Richard admitted, "but they explained that they had met at that particular spot. It made sense, from a sentimental, if not aesthetic point of view."

"Did anyone check that they really did meet there, or that it actually *was* their anniversary?"

"Interesting point," said Richard. "I should have thought of that. You have a suspicious mind," he added.

"I have to. I'm a mystery writer."

"So what is the mystery writer implying?"

"That there might have been a previous photo, taken a few days earlier. It would be a lot easier to duplicate the scene if they were sitting on the bench with the dog between the man's knees. The evergreens don't change, whereas water and clouds can be variable, plus there could be other people caught in the shot if the rocks were in the background."

"You're right, of course, but we examined Gudrun Ewell's computer, and all the photos from the Skookumchuck were in the same file and numbered in sequence."

"But she could have trashed your photo, and the earlier picture would have been entered as the first one of the set. Could you see anything different about the image in her computer? Did anything strike you as not quite the way you recollect from when you took the shot?"

"No. That's the frustrating thing. It looks perfectly OK to me, but then, I was concentrating on the camera, not on them. There is one difference between the sisters that I noticed later on. Regina has perfect hands, but Gudrun has one swollen joint on her right hand. It's slight, but it was pronounced enough to be visible in the picture. Do you recall noticing her hands that day?"

"Honestly, no," said Alexandra. "I didn't pay much attention. As soon as they appeared, I went to tell your father that your mother wanted to start back, so I only saw them very briefly. But why don't you email me the photograph? I'll have a look to see if there's anything I can pick up that you might have missed."

"Good idea," said Richard.

He emailed the photograph as soon as he was off the phone. As an afterthought, he also included a photograph of the two sisters side by side. Alexandra's reply came quickly, but she was not able to help. Nothing struck her as extraordinary about the picture, though she did indicate her belief that the sisters could successfully impersonate each other if they traded clothing and had the proper wigs. In spite of the different hair colouring and style of dress, their features were similar and their eyes looked identical.

Richard frowned. The phone rang again. It was DC Peake.

"We've had a break-through," she told him. "A witness has come forward to say he saw a strange vehicle—a dark blue van—parked on his street around two o'clock on the afternoon of July third. This is the street on the other side of the woods that abut the Greeley property. There's a trail through the trees, so it would be easy for someone to cut through without being seen. The witness couldn't provide a licence number or the make of the van, other than saying it looked old and was rather battered, but what he did notice was that it had a BC plate. And," she went on triumphantly, "I called Surrey and they sent a squad car out to check Brett Ewell's used-car lot. There was a battered blue van there. It's been taken for analysis. We can check for DNA links to Gudrun Ewell, and if it was parked near Marta Greeley's property, there will be traces that will show up. It must have been Regina Jinkerson in that picture. There's no other way they could have managed it."

"No," said Richard. "It was Gudrun in the picture, but there is a way they could have worked it." Richard told her of his conversation with Alexandra Lacey. "If Regina had taken the photo of Gudrun and Brett at an earlier time, that would explain why the Facebook image is authentic. It just isn't the picture I took on July third."

"Damn," said Peake. "Why on earth didn't we think of that?"

"It takes the twisted thought processes of a writer of fiction," chuckled Richard.

"It's too bad there isn't some little detail that could be used to prove her idea," said Peake. "Still, we'll work with what we have."

She thanked Richard for his help and rang off.

Ten minutes later, the phone rang again. This time it was Juliette.

"Remember how you told me about the group of fairies who had put the police onto a missing person," she began.

Richard did recall mentioning the matter a few days previously. His mother had been harassing Juliette about the amount of time she spent visiting the fairyland site, and Richard had reduced everyone to tears of laughter by relating the story of his Calgary colleagues and their bombardment by a global network of pixies and peris.

"Well," continued Juliette, "I tracked down that Tasmanian fairy."

"How on earth did you do that?"

"It was easy. You said her fairyland name was Titania and you told me her garden name too. I found her in no time. Anyway, we linked up as friends and she told me all about your case. You know, Marta Greeley never went back to water that bonsai, because it was still wilting at five o'clock in the afternoon. So you can definitely pin the arrival of the murderer at the very moment she stopped the on-line conversation with her cousin—if, of course, it was her cousin at the other end. Well, it was her cousin," she added, contradicting herself, "but not the one that Marta thought she was talking to. Nor the one she was looking at on the screen."

"Hold on," said Richard. "Let me get this straight. Are you talking about the image on Greeley's Facebook site?"

"Of course," said Juliette. "Titania copied several photos from Bluebell's page and sent them to me. She's convinced that the cousins are the villains, and having seen those pale, ice-blue eyes, I must say she could be right. She refers to them as Goneril and Regan."

"Okay, never mind that. What's the problem with the picture on the computer screen?"

"Well it's all wrong," said Juliette calmly. "It can't be the photograph you took."

Richard blinked. His sister sounded so matter of fact. What had she seen that everyone else had missed?

"Why not?" he demanded. "Isn't everything set up the same?"

"Oh yes. The people are posed exactly as I saw them. And the dog is sitting the same way too. Everything is right, except—"

"Except what?"

"It's the dog's face," said Juliette. "Or rather his eyes. He's looking straight at the camera."

"Well, he was looking straight at the camera," said Richard.

"In the Facebook picture he is," Juliette said firmly, "but when you took the photograph that day on the Skookumchuck, Frisk's eyes were rolled sideways the entire time he was sitting there."

"How can you possibly be sure of that?"

"Easily. He was watching me with Purdy, Quasar and MacPuff. He never took his eyes off us for a second. I'd be ready to swear on the Bible," Juliette stated decisively.

"Well," chuckled Richard, "you just might have to."

"Not a problem," said Juliette. "But in future, could we have fewer witticisms being hurled my way? After all," she added sweetly, "where would your case be without dogs and fairies?"

Richard could hear the laughter in her voice as she ended the call.

THE CURIOUS INCIDENT OF
THE BOAT DOG IN THE NIGHT

Edwina Beary sighed. The shoreline, drifting by at a yawn-inducing five knots, had offered little variation for the past hour.

"Isn't there anything but granite and fir trees?" she said pointedly.

Bertram Beary kept his hands on the wheel and his eyes on the water. He was used to complaints from his wife.

He replied, "'Rocks rising perpendicularly from an unfathomable sea.' You're supposed to find them awe-inspiring."

"Well, I don't." Edwina turned away from the land and stared shrewdly at her husband. "That was a dramatic description of the scenery," she said suspiciously. "Are those your words?"

"No. Captain George Vancouver's, and he wasn't impressed either when he charted the coastline of British Columbia in the 1700s."

"You said we were going to a spot where we could picnic in splendid, sun-soaked solitude, and glory in the breathtaking view. I expected something picturesque."

"The view isn't looking towards the land," Beary explained patiently. "It's what you see once you're in the cove. Believe me, you'll love it. I've gone there to dig clams on many occasions. You sit on the beach, gazing out at sky and ocean, all framed in stately pillars of grey granite, and you feel as if you're the only person in the world. The beauty of the cove is that it's surrounded by steep cliffs which make it completely inaccessible by land."

"Well, that's something anyway." Edwina sounded slightly mollified. "It better have a couple of bushes for me to retreat behind, though. I have no intention of using that revolting porta-potty you keep on this boat."

The *Optimist* was a twenty-foot fibreglass clinker-built vessel and very primitively equipped. Beary used it for fishing, but occasionally he put up a large umbrella for shade, set up a deckchair in the stern, and took Edwina on a day trip, which was the only type of excursion they could manage since there was no sleeping accommodation on board.

"There are a few scrubby pines, as I recall," said Beary.

"Good," said Edwina. "Are we nearly there?" she added. "I'm dying for a cup of coffee."

"Just around the next point."

Edwina thawed a little more.

"I'm quite looking forward to our picnic," she said. "It's been hectic, staying with Juliette and the children. A peaceful afternoon with nothing to assault our ears but the murmur of the waves and the odd cry of a gull—that's just what I need."

The *Optimist* forged on steadily, the gray rocks to starboard gliding sedately in the other direction. Beary smiled seraphically as the point came closer. Edwina might be looking forward to her thermos of coffee, but he had secreted a bottle of rum in the cooler. He was looking forward to the picnic too.

A startling noise ahead made them both look up.

"What was that?" said Edwina. "It was almost like a bark."

"Seagull," replied Beary. "They often sound like dogs."

Then, as the *Optimist* chugged around the point and the cove came into view, the noise was repeated in a ferocious volley that exploded on the air with the rapidity of machine-gun fire. Edwina's eyes bulged. She rose from her deck chair and stared at the scene before them.

"Hell's teeth! It's a bloody Armada," said Beary.

Three large boats were anchored in the bay. Furthest from shore was a luxury cabin cruiser that Beary estimated was at least sixty feet long. It was a gleaming white Maxum, the name *Sea Belle* blazoned on its bow. A hundred feet to the right, a Bayliner half the size of the larger boat bobbed up and down on the waves. The third boat was a fifty-foot Carver called the *Highland Heather.* It was the source of the percussive noise that was rebounding off the high granite walls of the cove. A small white dog was standing in the stern, watching the boisterous group of people who were swimming back and forth between the vessels. Every time someone dove off the Carver or climbed back onto the swim grid, the dog erupted into another staccato outburst.

Three people sat at the stern of the boat, apparently indifferent to the antics of the frustrated animal. Two burly men, bare-chested and tanned to the colour of arbutus bark, were drinking and absorbed in conversation. Both had grey hair, dark glasses and airs of entitlement that made Beary think of pictures he had seen of Aristotle Onassis in his prime. The third person was a red-headed woman. As the *Optimist* drew nearer, Beary could see that she was exquisitely pretty, with a glorious figure to match her face, but the set of her body was tense and her eyes were unhappy. Her attention, like the dog's, was on the people in the water.

As the *Optimist* churned by, the dog leapt on top of what appeared to be a kennel in the stern-well of the Carver and eyed the water eagerly. The name, Haggis, was painted in large letters above the entrance to the doghouse. Appropriate, thought Beary.

The animal was a West Highland terrier. The dog burst into another round of barks as a second woman pulled herself onto the swim grid. Her long, black hair trailed in a wet stream down her back as she climbed aboard. She patted the dog, then grabbed a towel and wrapped it around herself. As she turned back, Beary saw her face. She was a ravishingly beautiful brunette who could qualify for a Miss America pageant, except that her face was sullen and her eyes were angry. Beary was intrigued. Two magnificent specimens of womanhood and both so clearly out of sorts. Curiously, he wondered the cause of their displeasure.

He glanced towards the water. Three swimmers remained, two men and a woman. As he watched, the woman darted ahead of the others. She was a powerful swimmer and she streaked through the water, keeping just ahead of a swarthy man who laughed as he chased her. The woman raced toward the *Highland Heather* and, in one swift movement, pulled herself aboard. The second man caught up to the first and both men grabbed onto the stern of the boat. With a peal of laughter that reverberated around the bay, the woman reached down and pushed her pursuers back into the sea.

She straightened up to reveal a tall, lithe body, with a tiny waist and generously curved bust. Her figure was less voluptuous than the brunette's and less lyrically curved than the redhead's, but somehow, mused Beary, perhaps because of the graceful perfection of her movements, far more enticing. He noticed that the men on board the *Highland Heather* had broken off their conversation and now, like the brunette and the redhead, watched the newcomer as she flipped her short brown hair out of her eyes and knelt down to call to the men in the water. Beary reached for his binoculars and focused them on the woman. Her face was not beautiful, or even pretty, but it was riveting. As if sensing she had acquired another admirer, the woman glanced up, and as she did so, the sun glinted and turned her catlike eyes into sparkling gold. Beary was captivated. She resembled a statue of an ancient Egyptian goddess.

But unlike a goddess, he sensed that she was not an object of worship, for as she picked up a beach towel and languidly began to rub herself dry, he had the impression that behind the dark lenses of the sunglasses, all eight eyes aboard the *Highland Heather* were glittering with animosity.

"That's better," said Edwina, coming back down the rocky path that connected the beach to the grove of scrubby pines. Beary had already lugged the cooler off the dinghy and had poured her a coffee from the thermos, which he'd balanced on a nearby rock. He was now arranging a blanket on the loose gravel of the beach so that it nestled in the shade of a smoothly sloped boulder. He placed two float cushions against the rock and settled back comfortably with his own coffee, which, unbeknown to his wife, was adulterated from the bottle he'd hidden behind the rock.

Edwina gratefully took a sip of her coffee, then knelt by the cooler and began to produce an array of plates, sandwiches, fruit, biscuits and hand-sanitizers. Once she had served the food, she sat down on the blanket, with her lunch plate in her lap and her coffee at her side.

"This is nice," she said. "Sunny, but not too hot."

"The cove faces west," said Beary. "It's cool all morning, and even when the sun is directly overhead, there are still patches of shade. By four o'clock, it'll heat up like an oven, though. But by then, we'll be ready to head back."

"You're right about the view," Edwina admitted, eyeing the brilliant stripes of emerald ocean and clear blue sky framed in the towering columns of granite. "If those boats weren't out there, it would be almost surreal. Thank heavens that wretched dog has finally shut up," she added. "I was ready to throttle it."

"You should have let me bring MacPuff along," said Beary. MacPuff had been left with Juliette for the day. "I would have said, 'Lay on, MacPuff,' and Haggis would have been haggis."

"It's too hot for MacPuff, as you know perfectly well. He would have been miserable. I expect that's why that little white rat on the *Highland Heather* is being such a pain. He probably wants to cool off in the water too."

"I don't think we have to worry. The swimmers are back on board, and it only seems to bark when someone goes in or out of the water."

"Let's hope they stay on board. I want to take a swim after lunch."

"Why should the presence of the Armadans stop you?"

Edwina looked indignant.

"I'm not parading in my swimsuit in front of a bunch of strangers."

"Why not? You have a very good figure for a woman in her sixties."

"Exactly—for a woman in her sixties. If they come ashore, my middle-aged figure stays covered."

"Women are so vain," said Beary, patting his ample midriff. "I don't have any qualms about disporting myself in my swim trunks."

"So are you going in?"

"God, no. Too bloody cold. Here, pass me another of those egg and cucumber jobs. I'm still hungry."

Edwina handed him another sandwich and took a bite of her own. For a few minutes, they chewed in contented silence. Then, having finished her sandwich, Edwina picked up her cup and raised it to her lips.

As she began to drink, a loud yelp from offshore caused her to sputter and choke.

"We spoke too soon," said Beary glumly. "What's worse, they all seem to be approaching land."

Edwina looked up to see a series of heads bobbing in the water and progressing towards the shore. On board the *Highland Heather*, the redheaded woman and one of the tanned shipping tycoons were lowering a bucket into a zodiac, which was manned by the other Onassis-lookalike and the lush brunette. Two white pointed ears protruded from the bucket as it bounced its way downward.

By the time the humans had joined the dog in the dinghy, the swimming party was wading ashore. The Egyptian goddess was in the lead, glowing with vitality as she made her sinuous progress towards land. Behind her were two men, the same individuals who had been chasing her earlier. Both were dark and very good-looking. The taller man was rugged and hairy-chested, with black, devilish eyes. He looked like the young Sean Connery, Edwina decided. The shorter man still had to be at least six feet tall, and he had the smooth good looks of a fifties matinee idol.

The taller man hailed Beary and Edwina. "Hello there! You're the people off the *African Queen*."

Beary smiled thinly. His striped umbrella often induced that particular joke. However, he responded with more enthusiasm as the Egyptian goddess sauntered over to greet them. As she reached them, he saw that, although the flat planes of her beautiful bones still bore a remarkable resemblance to Nefertiti, the effect was eradicated by a distinctly turned-up nose and a mischievous twinkle in her green eyes. To his surprise, she spoke with a marked French accent.

"I love your sweet leetle boat, *mon cher*," she said to Beary. "So charming. When we saw you having a picnic, we thought what a lovely idea, so here we are too. My name is Danielle McGarvie," she added, "and these are *mes amis*, Kenneth and Gary." She waved in the direction of the two men who had followed her ashore.

Beary introduced Edwina and himself.

"Who are the others?" he asked, pointing towards the zodiac.

"Gordon, Jill, Jackson and Mattie." Danielle tossed the names off casually as if Beary should automatically know who they were. "They are bringing the food ashore—and Haggis, too, of course."

"So we see," said Edwina dryly.

"Our little dog, he is noisy, yes?" Danielle smiled winningly.

"Yes, he is," said Edwina, not at all won.

"I'm sorry he disturbs you. He gets so upset when I go in the water."

"And out too. We noticed." Edwina's voice was distinctly chilly.

"That's because he is happy to see me back," Danielle explained sweetly.

"We don't mind him at all," Beary purred treacherously. "So you're on the *Highland Heather*?" he continued smoothly, ignoring Edwina's ferocious glare.

Danielle nodded.

"Yes, with Gordon and Jill. We are inviting the others onto our boat for a barbecue tonight. We have lots of wine and food. You are most welcome to join us."

Edwina cut in before Beary had a chance to accept.

"Thank you, but we're only here for the afternoon. We're staying with our daughter's family and we're expected back for dinner."

"Oh, too bad," sighed Danielle. "But please feel free to come if you change your mind."

Beary gestured towards the two darkly handsome men on the beach.

"Your friends are from the other boats?"

"That's right. Gary is on the *Sea Belle*, with his father, Jackson Hughes, who is a beeg, powerful businessman"—a seductive shrug of Danielle's golden shoulders spoke volumes— "and Kenneth Donnelly and his wife, Mattie, own the *Marouska*," she added, naming the Bayliner.

"Are you all cruising flotilla style?"

"Oh, yes. Gordon and Jackson are old friends as well as partners in their shipping firm, and Kenneth is their senior manager. They like to work and play together," Danielle added with a significant arch to her eyebrows. "We, their families, have no choice but to come along. Besides, Gordon and Jackson are determined that Gary and Jill shall marry so they are hoping the holiday will encourage a little romance. They are like two ancient monarchs plotting to enlarge their kingdom," she laughed. "But then, they are businessmen so they discount *l'amour.*"

"How come your sister is marked for the alliance?" Beary couldn't resist being nosy, and Danielle didn't strike him as the sort of person who would mind personal questions. "Judging by the way Gary Hughes was chasing you, I'd have thought your father would have more success pushing you at him."

Danielle burst into another peal of laughter. When her fit of mirth subsided, she replied, "No, no, darleeng. Jill is not my sister. She is my stepdaughter. Gordon is my husband."

With another tinkling trill of laughter, she walked back to meet the zodiac, which was pulling up on the shore. Haggis was the first to leap onto land, and he waddled over to a rock pool and vigorously proceeded to lap the salt water until Jill McGarvie jumped ashore and retrieved him.

"Well, really!" said Edwina, directing a stony stare at Danielle's retreating back. "And you can put your eyes back in your head," she added to Beary. "I fail to see why every male is drooling over that woman. The other two are far better looking. Kenneth Donnelly should be ashamed of himself. What on earth does that creature have that makes her so special?"

"It's the ooh-la-la factor," said Beary. "Some have it, some don't. And she has it in spades—the figure *magnifique*, the eyes *de la chatte*, the nose *retroussée*." Beary gestured extravagantly and rolled his eyes. "You're quite sure you wouldn't like to join their barbecue?" he added hopefully.

"Absolutely not," snapped Edwina. "I have no intention of riding back down the coast in the dark while you try to navigate after drinking your way through several bottles of that Frenchwoman's wine."

With that, she pulled a paperback from her bag, opened it and proceeded to read.

While Edwina enjoyed her murder mystery, Beary lazed on the blanket and watched the fascinating interplay as Danielle exerted her ooh-la-la factor on the male inhabitants of the boats anchored in the bay. While Jill McGarvie and Mattie Donnelly sulkily attended to the mundane business of organizing the picnic, or coping with Haggis when he threw up the hot dogs that his master fed him over lunch, Danielle joined in a lively game of Frisbee with Kenneth Donnelly and Gary Hughes. Gordon McGarvie and Jackson Hughes, whom Beary had mentally christened Ari-Number-One and Ari-Number-Two, appeared to be engaged in business discussions. Any snatches of dialogue that drifted the Bearys' way were comments on stocks or shares or companies or mergers, but in spite of their preoccupation with the vagaries of the market, both men gave the impression that they were covertly watchful of the antics of their shipmates. Haggis, to Edwina's extreme irritation, proved as yappy playing pig-in-the-middle in a Frisbee game as he was when watching his people swim.

She put down her book and poured out the remaining dregs from the thermos.

"Bother," she said. "I should have brought two flasks along. That's hardly enough for a mosquito to wade in."

Beary retrieved his rum bottle from behind the rock.

"Here," he said. "Supplement it with this."

Edwina pursed her lips but she didn't refuse.

"I knew you had a bottle somewhere," she said. "The coffee lasted much longer than I expected. Go ahead. Top it up. I need it after listening to that silly dog all day. I suppose we'd better think about starting back soon," she added, noticing that the sun had dropped in the sky and was beaming into the cove with the scorching intensity of a theatre Fresnel. "I'll have to make another visit to the pine grove, but I'll enjoy this first."

"No hurry," said Beary, who was quite enjoying watching the provocative Danielle stirring up the Armadans. "We'll set off at five-thirty. That's soon enough."

A whoop from the other side of the beach made Beary and Edwina look round. The Frisbee players were staring at a point halfway up the rocky escarpment. Haggis was barking hysterically at the foot of the cliff.

"Someone's aim was high," said Beary. "It's stuck in a crevice. That's the end of that game."

But he had spoken too soon. Danielle broke away and ran towards the cliff. Then, as agile as the cat she had resembled when Beary first laid eyes on her, she began to scale the rocks. In a flash, she reached the ledge where the disc had landed. Then she scooped it up, waved it triumphantly to the watchers on the beach, and slithered back down to the ground.

"Good heavens!" gasped Edwina. "She's a cat-woman! How could she do that?"

"With ease," said Beary. "She used to be with the Cirque du Soleil."

"How do you know that?"

"I met Mattie Donnelly on the path when I went to pay a visit to your pine grove. She told me that McGarvie met Danielle three years ago when she was performing in Vegas. Sounds like I was right to label McGarvie Ari-Number-One. He's a real cutthroat mogul. Mattie Donnelly says he picks up and tosses people the same way he acquires and dumps companies. He's rich, aggressive and arrogant, and he likes to be envied for his possessions. No doubt, with Danielle, he's succeeded in that goal. Of course, the envy is all from the male sex. The women despise him for marrying Danielle. Mattie Donnelly refers to her as the refugee from the circus. She doesn't like her one bit."

"Understandably," said Edwina. "After all, Catwoman has pretty much taken over her husband. I never knew anyone could turn a game of Frisbee into an exercise in seduction."

"Catwoman appears to have packed it in for now," noted Beary, glancing over to the other side of the beach.

The Frisbee game was at an end and the participants had flopped onto their beach towels, as if their brief hiatus had made them suddenly register how the descending sun was baking the beach and transforming the cove into the oven that Beary had predicted earlier. As the heat became suffocating, the boaters became languid and idle. Haggis fell mercifully silent and lay panting in the shade of a log. The air was quiet and still. Yet, despite their motionless state, Beary sensed watchfulness and tension among the people on the shore. He leaned back against his float cushion and turned his eyes toward the ocean. He had been so busy watching the Armadans that he had not noticed the movement out in the bay. A sailboat was gliding gracefully between the *Highland Heather* and the *Sea Belle*.

"Now, that's a beauty," he muttered. "A Catalina 27. Looks like he's intending to anchor."

Sure enough, the sailboat's progress ceased, and fifteen minutes later, another swimmer approached the shore. At first, no one but Beary and Edwina observed the head bobbing through the water, but as the swimmer drew close, Jill McGarvie lazily stretched and prepared to roll over. She started when she saw the sailboat, and then she craned her neck and stared out into the bay. After a moment, she tapped Gary Hughes on the shoulder and pointed towards the water. Then, gradually, every person on the beach sat up to watch the approach of the newcomer.

And a ripple of admiration and unease threaded its way through the assembled boaters as a Greek god rose out of the water and waded ashore.

⟞⊦⊣⟝

With the arrival of a second deity, there was a perceptible change in the atmosphere, though Beary was hard pressed to identify what it was. There were too many intermingled emotions to be able to pinpoint the feeling in the air. Yet it was unfair to blame the Greek god for the strange mix of excitement, anger, gloating and malice that hovered over the strand, for he was godlike only in appearance and proved to be an affable and friendly bachelor, cruising up the coast to visit a sister who lived in Powell River. He walked the length of the beach, civilly greeting its occupants and not ignoring Beary and Edwina who sat a little apart from the rest. He introduced himself as Peter Weldon.

After Weldon had passed five minutes chatting politely with the Bearys, Gary Hughes came over to offer him a beer, and the two men strolled back together.

"Now, that was odd," said Beary, once the men were out of hearing. "Did you pick up the discrepancy in what Weldon was telling us about his voyage?"

"No," said Edwina. "All he said was that he was enjoying seeing the coast. It's his first trip up this way."

"Exactly. And he said he noticed the cove and decided it would be a good spot to stop for the night."

"So?"

"You can't see this cove if you're coming from the south. It's completely hidden. You have to know it's here or you'd sail right past. I bet our little French flirt told him she'd be here and arranged a rendezvous. They're probably just pretending they don't know each other."

"Doesn't she have enough slaves dancing attendance?" said Edwina sourly.

"She's abandoned her other two slaves," observed Beary, nodding towards the group on the sands. "Weldon has all her attention now."

Edwina followed Beary's glance.

Weldon was sprawled on the beach, chatting easily with the Armadans. Danielle, with leopard-like grace, had coiled herself onto a beach towel at his side and fastened her hypnotic green eyes onto his own wide blue orbs.

"He's not exactly reciprocating," Edwina commented. "He's actually rather restrained."

"That could be a smokescreen to fool her husband."

"Well, whatever it is, that woman is trouble." Edwina's bosom heaved indignantly. "Look at the way the rest of them are behaving. Something's brewing."

Beary swept his eyes along the cluster of boaters. Even from a distance, he could see how Gary Hughes and Kenneth Donnelly bristled as Danielle continued to exert her magnetic personality on the handsome newcomer. Beautiful Jill McGarvie was no longer sullen, but was smiling enigmatically, and the anger in Mattie Donnelly's eyes had morphed into something like spite. Even the two Aris had emerged from their corporate cocoon and had their eyes riveted on the interplay between the members of their family and the newcomer on the beach.

Edwina shook her head disapprovingly and went back to her book.

For the next hour, Edwina remained immersed in her Ruth Rendell, while Beary alternately dozed or watched the Armadans. At last, Edwina closed her paperback and decreed that it was time to start back. As she and Beary packed away their picnic utensils, they saw the others were making way too. Haggis had been deposited in the zodiac and Gordon and Jill McGarvie were preparing to take him back to the *Highland Heather.* Edwina declared her intention of visiting the pine grove, so she left Beary to load their gear and set off up the rocky path.

As Beary lugged the cooler into the dinghy, he saw that the pretty redhead had climbed aboard the zodiac. Her eyes held a glint of satisfaction that had not been there before. The zodiac set off, with Gordon McGarvie at the tiller and Haggis firmly ensconced between the two beautiful women. Ari-Number-Two was not on board, so Beary presumed he had decided to swim back to his boat. Three black heads were bobbing in the water, no more than silhouettes against the blinding sun. Beary wondered who had remained behind, but then two more heads came into view. They were closer to shore, but still impossible to recognize. As Beary watched, like voyaging seals, gradually all the bobbing heads converged, and in a little cluster, headed out toward the boats in the bay.

Edwina returned with an inscrutable expression on her face and silently helped Beary carry the float cushions and blanket onto the dinghy. Beary became immediately wary. His wife rarely kept her feelings to herself, and even though he often regretted this trait, he found it disconcerting when she clammed up. He wondered just what it was that he had done. However, once they had pushed off and Beary was manning the oars, Edwina enlightened him. To his relief, for once he was not the object of her ire.

"That woman!" she hissed, worried that her voice would carry across the water. "She's quite despicable. You wouldn't believe what I heard when I was behind my bush."

"I'm sure I will," said Beary. "What did you hear?"

Edwina pursed her lips.

"She must have been swimming just below the rocky ledge. She was with one of the men, and her voice carried up to me quite distinctly. She was making an assignation to meet him back at the beach at midnight. I know it was that Danielle woman. I could tell by her accent. It's unmistakable. I also heard her say that her sleeping pills were like knockout drops so Gordon wouldn't hear a thing. She's actually planning to drug her husband so she can meet her lover!"

"Is she indeed? So I was right to suspect that she had told Peter Weldon about this cove. Did you see him?"

"No, and you can't assume she was with the pretty boy in the sailboat," Edwina pointed out. "I didn't see her companion."

"You must have some idea of who the man was. Didn't he say anything?"

"Not that I could hear, but I think he must have asked about the dog, because there was a pause; then she said something about Haggis sleeping in Jill's cabin, so she could slip away without being heard and she didn't have to go past the cabin because she could climb up through the forward hatch and go across the deck to the stern."

"You might have peeked out from your bush and had a look," grumbled Beary. "Weren't you curious?"

"Yes, but I was busy," said Edwina with dignity. "And by the time I did look out, I couldn't see them at all. It could have been any of the men on that beach."

Edwina furrowed her brow.

"Shouldn't we say something?" she said. "I feel very uncomfortable knowing what's planned and not doing anything. She's going to drug her husband, for heaven's sake."

"A sleeping pill isn't going to hurt him. Anyway, we can't say anything to McGarvie, so the only thing I could do would be to warn her off, and I suspect she'd just get a twinkle in her eye and make some comment about it being our secret."

"Yes, you're probably right," grunted Edwina. "That woman is headstrong and self-absorbed. She wouldn't listen to anyone."

"I guess we'll never know which gallant swain is going to get lucky on the beach tonight, though I'm still willing to bet it's Weldon. By the time they meet, we'll be back at Juliette's and tucked up in the guest room."

"And a good job too, considering the lack of sleeping accommodation on the *Optimist*."

"We could always have our own assignation on the beach," Beary suggested wickedly. "Feel like camping out tonight?"

"Not," said Edwina frostily, "when you've drunk nine-tenths of a bottle of rum. I just hope you're capable of getting the boat home. Don't they have rules about drinking and boating these days?"

"Yes, but you're quite capable of steering," Beary pointed out cheerfully. "Anyway, it was only a mickey, and you drank more than a tenth. I'm still in fine form to run the boat."

But as it happened, neither Beary nor Edwina had to operate a boat that night for when they returned to the *Optimist* and started the motor, an alarming flapping noise under the engine hatch made it apparent that a repair job was called for before the return trip could be undertaken. The cove was to become their harbor for the night.

Once she understood that the *Optimist* could not be fixed until morning, Edwina agreed to join the barbecue on board the *Highland Heather*. It was that, or starvation, so the Bearys got back into their dinghy and rowed across to the Carver. Danielle effusively welcomed them aboard and handed each of them a glass of wine. Noticing Edwina's awed expression as she glanced through the door into the lounge, Jill McGarvie politely offered to show her around the boat. Beary declined the tour and settled himself in the stern-well. A few minutes later, Gordon McGarvie came out from the cabin.

"Engine trouble?" McGarvie took the empty wine glass from Beary's hand and replaced it with a tumbler.

"The V-belt broke," Beary explained. He adjusted his rear end, which was perched on Haggis's kennel. "I have a spare," he continued, "but I couldn't get one of the nuts off. It was rusted so badly it was almost fused into the metal. I've sprayed it with penetrating oil, so I should be able to tackle it in the morning, but we'll have to stay on our boat overnight. Very good of you to come to the rescue and invite us to dinner."

"You're most welcome." Gordon McGarvie poured Beary a large Scotch and filled a second glass for himself. "This'll brace you up," he added. "Better than that French slop my wife drinks."

Beary eyed the bottle. It was Johnny Walker Blue Label.

"Yes, indeed. Very much appreciated."

"Don't mention it. Ye need cheering. It's a bugger when these contraptions break down. We all know what BOAT stands for," McGarvie added dourly.

"Bring On Another Thousand," said Kenneth Donnelly, emerging from the cabin with a large platter of steaks. "Hope you can fix it yourself," he said sympathetically to Beary. "Cost you the earth to get a marine mechanic out here. BOAT really ought to be spelt with two tees."

"Bring On Another Ten Thousand? I hope not," muttered Beary.

McGarvie took the platter and proceeded to lay the steaks on the barbecue that was hanging over the stern. Donnelly continued to address himself to Beary.

"Danielle is making her special gravy to go on top," he announced. His eyeballs did a slow rotation, which Beary interpreted to be an enthusiastic endorsement for the sauce to come. "She is the most fabulous cook. If you had to break down, this was the evening to do it."

McGarvie tossed a piece of gristle to Haggis, whose head had bobbed out from between Beary's legs the moment the meat platter appeared. As if by telepathy, Jill McGarvie stuck her head out from the cabin and chastised her father.

"Don't feed him raw meat," she said testily. "It's not good for him. He's already been sick three times today."

"That's because the wee mutt doesn't have enough brains not to drink salt water," her father retorted.

Jill's response was to sweep Haggis up into her arms and whisk him away into the cabin. Kenneth Donnelly followed her inside, but Beary remained in the stern with his host. He could hear the chatter of the others inside, and there were voices coming from the foredeck too, but the effects of sea air, sunshine, rum, French wine and Scotch were having their effect on him and he was feeling wondrously soporific.

The remainder of the evening went by in a haze. He was vaguely aware of Edwina bobbing back and forth—dutifully helping her hostess in the way Edwinas do, he thought benevolently—and he had a dreamy sense of other people drifting in and out, offering pleasantries along with food and refills. Haggis's kennel proved a prime location, conveniently close to the sources of steak and Scotch, so he drank and ate, and ate and drank, while he watched the granite cliffs of the cove transmute from brilliant gold to soft rose and gradually fade into the all-enveloping night.

After a second serving of thick sirloin, supplemented with Danielle's special sauce and accompanied by another large side-serving of potatoes and salad, the effects of the alcohol were marginally diminished so he decided he would probably be able to row his wife back to the *Optimist*. He was contemplating his level of competency for this task, when he noticed that Haggis had crawled back into the kennel and had wriggled round to face the other way. The dog's head was now protruding between Beary's legs. Beary faintly recognized the hacking noise that began to emanate from the vicinity of his knees, but did not register the significance quickly enough. Without any further warning, Haggis spewed his dinner, and, judging by the lumps of meat in the pile of vomit, other people's dinner, all over Beary's shoes.

"That is the most revolting dog," pronounced Edwina, fifteen minutes later, as Beary carefully navigated the dinghy back to the *Optimist*. "It did nothing but bark and vomit all afternoon. Would you like me to row?" she added, as Beary caught another crab.

"I'm perfectly fine," lied Beary. Edwina continued to chatter.

"It's hardly surprising the dog is so badly behaved when you consider how overindulged it is." Edwina sniffed disapprovingly. "Just like his master who's disgustingly overindulged too. Gordon McGarvie drinks even more than you do and is a glutton to boot. He was complaining about having indigestion from the hot dogs at lunch, but you should have seen the amount of sauce his wife piled on top of his steak—all of which disappeared, because his plate was spotless when he brought it back to the galley. No wonder he was raiding the bottle of Tums on the counter. The only person who seems to take proper care of the dog is the daughter. She's actually quite sweet when you talk with her. Such a beautiful girl too. I can see why Jackson Hughes would be keen to have a merger between the two families. He must be terribly irritated at the way his son keeps bouncing around after Jill's stepmother."

"It's the ooh-la-la factor," carolled Beary, ending the phrase with a hiccup.

"Nonsense," said Edwina. "I don't think the Hughes boy wants to get married, and Danielle is safe to flirt with because she already has a husband. Gary Hughes likes Jill, though. He was sitting with her up in the bow during the party. They were both chatting with the young man from the yacht. They all seemed pretty harmonious, but I got the impression that Jill McGarvie is no more interested in Gary Hughes than he is in her. They're simply friends. The so-called romance between them is all in their fathers' heads."

"Then why does she have a scowl on her face most of the time?"

"Because she doesn't want to be on the cruise. I saw a photograph in her cabin of a very handsome man in full-dress Mountie uniform." Edwina nodded her head firmly, pleased with her own deductions. "I suspect Jill McGarvie has her own plans for her future and Daddy doesn't like them."

"Poor Jill McGarvie," crooned Beary, carefully making his words keep time with the oars. His brain did not seem able to cope with more than one rhythm at once. He ventured a longer sentence. "It must be galling to be rich, good-looking and treated like a company asset."

"True," said Edwina, "but she isn't short on material comforts. You should see her cabin. It's quite luxurious. She has her own washroom and shower. Talk about travelling in style."

"I take it you enjoyed your tour."

"I did. It was fascinating—though I was rather taken aback at the sleeping quarters for McGarvie and his wife. Much less fancy than Jill's. They're up in the bow, and the cabin's nothing more than a wide bunk. But Jill said her father likes it there as he can open the forward hatch and look up at the stars."

"I'm surprised he hasn't put in a periscope so they could enjoy the ocean view too," said Beary.

"You don't have to be sarcastic," said Edwina. "A bit of luxury wouldn't hurt us once in a while. I'm not looking forward to a night cramped on a piece of foam in that tatty little box that passes for a cabin on the *Optimist*. I just hope the McGarvies will take pity on us in the morning and invite us for breakfast."

"They won't have to," said Beary smugly, pulling alongside the *Optimist* with a bump. He grabbed hold and helped Edwina across to the other boat.

"Why not?" asked Edwina.

"Because I had the foresight to ask them for supplies," Beary said, passing over a brown bag that he hauled from the bottom of the dinghy.

"That better not be a bottle of Scotch."

Beary looked indignant.

"Of course not. It's food. I keep a portable butane stove on board, and I always have a supply of bottled water. Tomorrow you will feast on a full English breakfast: coffee, eggs, bacon, sausages and hash browns. Are you sure you wouldn't like to camp out on the beach?" he added, a glint in his eye. "We have lots of time. The others aren't due to get there until midnight."

"The foam in the cabin will do perfectly well," said Edwina.

"If we were on the beach, we could claim the end near your scrubby pine grove," Beary offered temptingly.

He punctuated the sentence with another hiccup. Edwina gave him a withering look.

"I will make do with the porta-potty," she said firmly. "And you," she added, "can sleep on the deck."

Beary was awake by five o'clock. He had slept a sound, alcohol in-duced sleep, but he must have stirred in the night—either that or he was dreaming—for he had a vague recollection of whispering voices, and he was sure he had heard something moving through the water. But in the early morning light, the cove looked shadowy and quiet, and nothing moved on the surface of the sea.

Edwina was still gently snoring, so he crept about silently, set-ting up the butane stove and preparing to brew the coffee. Having set the percolator on the stove, he opened a deck chair and sat back to enjoy the serenity of sea and solitude. He saw that the Catalina was already gone. Weldon must have got underway early. The charms of Danielle McGarvie were apparently not enough to deter the Greek god from his charted course.

There was no sign of life on the other boats, although Beary noticed that the swim-grid gate was open on the *Highland Heather*. Danielle out for an early dip, he wondered, or had she forgotten to close it when she returned from her tryst and left a telltale sign that could alert her husband to her infidelity? Beary hoped he would be able to complete his repair job quickly so that he and Edwina would be long gone before any repercussions started to echo about the bay.

From the corner of his eye, he detected a slight movement on the deck of the *Sea Belle*. Something dark was sliding along the top of the cabin. He squinted and tried to make out what it was. Then Gary Hughes appeared on the bow of the boat. The dark object had been the top of his head, just visible as he climbed along the far side of the vessel. He wore swimming trunks, and a moment later he disappeared down through the forward hatch. Another early morning swimmer? Or was he returning from a night at the beach with the beautiful Danielle? Perhaps Weldon was not the lover after all.

A light breeze sprang up, rippling the water in the bay and causing the *Optimist* to swing on its anchor. Then, as the water in the coffee pot came to the boil, Beary became vaguely aware of another beat amid the rhythmic bubbling of the percolator. Something was bumping softly against the side of the boat. It was too light for a log. Beary could not imagine what it was. He heaved himself out of his chair and looked down into the water. Then he saw the object that had drifted alongside the *Optimist*.

It was the naked body of Danielle McGarvie.

Beary quickly attached a line to the body and went into the cabin to rouse Edwina. It was unlikely that the woman was still alive, but he knew he could not make that assumption, and he needed help getting her out of the water. Fortunately, Edwina, for all her irritating traits, was no shrinking violet and had obtained multiple first-aid certificates during her years as a high-school administrator. She aided him with military precision, and once the body had been hauled into the stern-well, Beary left her to attempt resuscitation while he went into the cabin to send out a Mayday call.

Fifteen minutes later, Edwina came inside to join him.

"It's no use," she said. "She's long gone. What's happening?"

"I'm waiting for instructions. The coastguard has assigned me a channel and told other ships to stay off it."

"Are the police coming?"

"Yes." Beary looked quizzically at his wife. "Your face," he said solemnly, "prompts memories of the way you used to look when our children blotted their copybooks and were attempting to cover up their misdeeds."

"Well, don't you think it's suspicious? You must have seen that nasty bruise on her forehead. She's stark naked, and we know she met her lover during the night."

"We know she planned to meet a lover," said Beary thoughtfully. "We don't know for sure that she did."

Edwina flushed.

"Actually, we do," she said. "I woke up in the night, and while I was using that primitive loo, I heard a laugh—it seemed really close by, but, of course, you know how sound carries across the water. Anyway, I came on deck and looked around. Funnily enough, the first thing I noticed was that a light was on in the cabin of Peter Weldon's sailboat. But I couldn't hear any sound from the yacht, so I glanced across the bay. The moon had come up, and there was a stream of light running across the water and onto the beach."

"And?"

"I saw them there—well, I couldn't see them clearly—but there were two figures, and as I watched, they moved into an embrace."

Beary grinned.

"Tut-tut, voyeurism. You have the most adventurous calls of nature of anyone I know. How much did you see?"

"Nothing else," Edwina said huffily. "I had no intention of watching them. I went back to bed."

"Well, well," murmured Beary. "So she did make it to her tryst on the beach. Still, there's no reason why her lover would pop her off, and presumably her husband was out like a light, so her drowning was probably an accident."

"But she was such a strong swimmer."

"Yes, but she was coming back in the dark. She could have slipped and hit her head on the gunwale as she was climbing back on board. If she'd lost consciousness, she'd have slid back into the water. The bruise is consistent with her hitting a hard, rounded edge, though there's a small vertical mark on her forehead too. Still, that might be from the join where the gate attaches."

Edwina glanced through the glass towards the *Highland Heather*. There was still no sign of activity on board.

"It's rather odd that none of them have noticed Danielle is missing."

"Not really. It's only just six o'clock. The daughter probably never gets up early and McGarvie will be sleeping off the pills."

"Should we go over in the dinghy and let him know what's happened?"

"No. I've been instructed to stay on the radio and not communicate with anyone in the bay. The coastguard and RCMP boat will be coming in from Powell River and they'll be here soon. With any luck, no one from the other boats will stir before they get here."

Beary's prediction proved correct. The coastguard arrived first and removed Danielle McGarvie's body. The police boat purred into the bay soon afterwards, and it was only then that there were signs of life from the Armadans. Jackson Hughes was the first to appear, and he stood at the rail of the *Sea Belle*, impassive and motionless, his eyes following the action in the bay. Kenneth Donnelly emerged from the cabin of the *Marouska*, but his wife was nowhere to be seen. None of the people on board the *Highland Heather* were visible, but the swim grid was now closed, so someone must have come out while Beary and Edwina had been inside the cabin of the *Optimist*. Haggis could now be seen in the stern. He stood on his hind legs and peered over the gunwale, but although he watched alertly, he did not bark or seem agitated.

The police boat drew alongside the *Optimist* and a giant of a man in plain clothes hailed Beary and barked an introduction, rapidly followed by a question.

"DC Small, RCMP. You're the one who discovered the body?"

Beary nodded.

"Coastguard said you seem to think it's a woman from the *Highland Heather*."

"I don't think," said Beary. "I know. Her name is Danielle McGarvie. She's cruising with her husband, whose name is Gordon, and her stepdaughter, Jill."

"You know these people well?"

"No. We only met them yesterday."

"Right. I'm going to break the news to the family. Don't leave. I'll be back to question you later."

The police boat veered away and set off toward the *Highland Heather*. A moment later, Beary heard DC Small's stentorian baritone, amplified through a megaphone, declaring his intention to board the ship.

Edwina's lips compressed into a thin line.

"I really didn't like the way that detective was looking at you," she commented. "Anyone would think you'd murdered the woman. Though, of course," she added, "if you hadn't woken me up to help you, I'd have done a double-take if I'd come on deck and found you with a naked woman, no matter how dead she was. You were certainly giving a good imitation of MacPuff eyeing a plateful of sausages when you were talking with her on the beach yesterday."

"Thanks very much," said Beary. "Well, I don't know about you, but I'm starving. Let's hope the coffee doesn't taste like charcoal. You pour us a cup and I'll get the breakfast back on the go."

Half an hour later, restored with bacon, eggs, sausages and coffee, Edwina busied herself with clearing the dishes and making another pot of coffee. Beary rolled up his sleeves and opened the engine hatch.

"I may as well get this repair job done while we wait," he announced.

By the time he had successfully removed the obdurate nut, Edwina had finished cleaning up. Beary fitted the new V-belt into place and straightened up to see his wife coming out of the cabin with two mugs of steaming coffee. He put the hatch back down and she deposited the coffee mugs on top. Then she set up her deck chair, retrieved her mug and sat down. Beary picked up his coffee mug and lowered himself onto the engine hatch. He glanced across the water. All the boats were still bobbing on their anchors. The police boat had moved from the *Highland Heather* and was now moored alongside the *Marouska*.

"They're taking their time," commented Edwina. "I wonder if they've guessed what she was up to. Surely the fact that she was naked will rouse their suspicions."

"They're police. They're automatically going to be suspicious."

"Do you think they'll find out who she was planning to meet?"

"Probably," said Beary. "I have a pretty good idea. And I don't think it was Peter Weldon after all, even though he was the one most able to slip off his boat without anyone knowing. I believe Danielle was meeting Gary Hughes. I saw him going back on board the *Sea Belle* first thing this morning."

Edwina sipped her coffee thoughtfully.

"Was he really? Now that is interesting."

"Yes. He could have been out for an early morning swim, but it's much more likely that he stayed on the beach after Danielle left and then swam back later. He could go on and off the *Sea Belle* easily enough without his father knowing. The cabins are fore and aft, rather like those on the *Highland Heather*. I had a bit of a chat with Ari-Number-Two during that party and he described his boat. Gary Hughes is in the forward berth, so he could have slipped out the hatch and gone across the deck to get to the swim grid."

To Beary's surprise, Edwina contradicted him.

"I think you're wrong," she said. "I don't believe Danielle McGarvie took Gary Hughes seriously. Kenneth Donnelly is the most likely candidate. He was loaded with sex-appeal."

Beary shook his head.

"Kenneth Donnelly had his wife on board. How could he get away for a midnight swim to the beach? No, it must be Peter Weldon or Gary Hughes."

"I don't think so," said Edwina firmly. "It must have been Donnelly. He could easily have borrowed Catwoman's sleeping pills to knock out his own mate."

Beary was surprised at his wife's adamant tone.

"What makes you so sure it's not the other two?" he asked.

"Well, first of all, Kenneth Donnelly is the only one that would tempt me to transgress—if, of course, I were that sort of person."

"Women!" Beary rolled his eyes upwards. "Instinct versus logic."

"No, it's not just instinct. I was observing them all at the barbe-cue while you were semi-comatose, and the vibes I picked up were between Weldon and Hughes. Danielle McGarvie wasn't even in the picture."

"Good lord," said Beary. "The Greek god and the Hollywood matinee idol. Well, I suppose you could be right."

"I'm sure I'm right. I think they're the two who pre-arranged to meet, and what you've just told me about Gary Hughes climbing back onto the *Sea Belle* this morning reinforces my opinion. He spent the night on Weldon's yacht. And what's more," Edwina add-ed, "I suspect Jill McGarvie knows all about their relationship and sympathizes with them. She and Gary Hughes are both victims of aggressive, bullying fathers who don't care about their personal feelings."

Before Edwina could say any more, the ringing tones of DC Small came booming at them from starboard. Beary looked up to see the police boat drawing alongside. A uniformed constable threw him a line, signalling him to pull the boat in, so, assuming that their interview was about to take place, Beary reefed the boats together and held his arm out to DC Small.

"Coming aboard?" he asked.

Small eyed the tiny space on the *Optimist* and the one deck chair, inhabited by Edwina. He shook his head.

"This is fine," he said. He fixed Beary with a hard stare. "You're Councillor Bertram Beary, right? You're also the father of DI Richard Beary who's with E Division?"

"I am," acknowledged Beary.

Small's bear-like face furrowed into a series of pleats.

"I know your son. Met him on a case a year ago. I just called him up to ask him about you."

"Oh. What did he say?"

"He said you were cagey, wily and very observant."

"Hardly observant last night," Edwina chimed in acidly. "Not after the amount he drank throughout the day."

"Well, we'll pick whatever brains are left," Small said smoothly. "Yours too, ma'am. Your son tells me you have an eagle eye for misdemeanors, both large and small."

"That she does," said Beary. "So what can we tell you?"

"Whatever you know. McGarvie seems to think his wife's death is accidental. He says she often went for an early morning swim. The daughter sleeps in the aft cabin, and she has a vague recollection of hearing the swim-grid gate being opened, though she has no idea when. Mrs. McGarvie had left her nightgown and a towel in the stern-well, so she was obviously intending to go for a swim and come back to dry off there."

Beary opened his mouth to speak, but Edwina beat him to it.

"No, there's more to this than an early morning swim," she said firmly. "You'd better be aware of the other things that were going on." She told DC Small about the assignation on the beach and described all that she had heard and seen. Then, for good measure, she added her own conjectures.

Small listened attentively.

"No, she wasn't meeting Kenneth Donnelly," he said, when Edwina had finished. "He was violently sick soon after he got back to his boat. His wife was up with him for the rest of the night. Too much sun, booze and rich food, by the sound of it. But you're right about the other two. Once we promised not to say anything to his father, Gary Hughes admitted to spending the night on Weldon's yacht, and I imagine Weldon will confirm that when we track him down. Evidently, they've known each other for years."

"Well, what do you know?" said Beary. "That leaves only one possibility."

Edwina was one jump ahead of him.

"Jackson Hughes!" she cried. "Why didn't we think of him? He's a very dynamic, attractive man. I suppose Danielle likes the older type. After all, she married one. But what a slap in the face for Gordon McGarvie! No wonder she needed to put him under with sleeping pills. He'd have gone ballistic if he'd found out."

"My wife's right," said Beary. "You'd better question Jackson Hughes."

Small smiled benignly.

"We already did," he said. "Hughes has owned up to the tryst, though he swears that Mrs. McGarvie was alive when they parted. They were going to swim back to their boats separately."

Beary and Edwina were visibly stunned.

"What on earth made him admit that?" Beary asked.

"When I mentioned that the autopsy would provide DNA matches, Hughes wisely owned up before things got worse for him. He also told us how Mrs. McGarvie ground up her sleeping pills and popped them into the steak sauce."

"What!" exclaimed Edwina. "Everyone's?"

"No, just her husband's. It was highly effective. He was still out cold when we boarded the *Highland Heather*. Well, thank you both. You've pretty well confirmed what we learned from the others. You can be on your way. We'll be in touch if we need anything else."

"But nothing has been concluded about the drowning of Danielle McGarvie," protested Edwina.

Small remained impassive.

"Her death was most likely an accident," he said. "She swam back to the boat, slipped as she clambered onto the swim grid, banged her head and slid back unconscious into the water. It's just too bad Jill McGarvie didn't get up to check on the dog when she heard the gate open. Then she might have seen Mrs. McGarvie trying to come aboard."

He signalled to the constable to untie the line and started to move to the rear of the police boat. Beary was still absorbing what the officer had said; then, all at once, it registered, and he called out hastily.

"What do you mean, check on the dog?"

The constable paused and stopped unwinding the line from the cleat.

"The dog was in the kennel on the aft deck," said DC Small.

"I thought it slept in Jill McGarvie's cabin."

"Usually, but Miss McGarvie said it had been drinking seawater and had thrown up a couple of times so she left it in the stern-well that night."

"Then," Beary said slowly, "you have a conundrum to unravel. There's something here that doesn't make any sense."

Small came back to face Beary.

"And what would that be?" he demanded.

Beary's gaze drifted across the water to the *Highland Heather*, where the small white face of Haggis was still visible peeking above the gunwale.

"Why didn't the boat dog bark in the night?" he said.

Once Beary explained how Haggis behaved whenever anyone dove in or climbed out of the water, DC Small was perplexed.

"How did the woman hope to get back on the boat?" he growled. "She could have dived into the water from the bow, but she couldn't have got back on board that way. Even a monkey couldn't get on a cruiser that size unless it used the swim grid. Perhaps she drugged the dog as well," he mused.

"That would have made no difference," said Beary. "Haggis threw up everything he ate . . . all over my shoes, as a matter of fact. He might have been feeling sickly, but he would have been wide-awake."

"It was revolting," Edwina said irritably. "He'd eaten a lot more than dog food. There were big chunks of steak in the pool of vomit."

"Oh, well, there you are then. The wee mutt probably felt so rotten he didn't have the strength to bark."

Small's tone indicated that the interview was over, and thanking Beary and Edwina for their help, he turned away. The constable untied the line and Beary helped slide the police boat along the *Optimist*. However, his thoughts were still with Danielle McGarvie. He remembered her beautiful catlike eyes, focussed on him with vitality and intensity, and not with the blank stare that had peered sadly at him from the bottom of his boat once he had dragged her cold body from the water. But the image of her face was marred by the ugly bruise on her forehead and the strange ridge that cut across the purple mark.

Beary bent to push the bow of the vessel away. As he did so, his eyes fell on the pulpit of the police boat. At the top of each stanchion holding the round guardrail in place were connections that created a small ridge, and the crosspiece matched the picture in his mind. He stood up slowly, and the image changed to a vision of the lithe and beautiful Danielle climbing the cliff and retrieving the Frisbee with all the showmanship she must have demonstrated during her years with the Cirque du Soleil.

Then, with another illuminating flash, he recalled how Edwina had told him that Gordon McGarvie's dinner plate had been wiped spotlessly clean.

The police boat was gliding forward again when Beary bellowed to the pilot to wait.

Small reiterated the command, and after a moment, the police boat drifted back level with the *Optimist*. Small pinned Beary with a penetrating glare.

"What is it?" he demanded. "Have you remembered something else?"

"Yes!" cried Beary. "Take a close look at the guard rail in the pulpit of the *Highland Heather*. I think you'll find it's a match for the bruise on Danielle McGarvie's forehead. Then go back and question McGarvie again."

"Why McGarvie?"

"Because it will be *his* dinner that Haggis ate."

Edwina caught on immediately.

"Of course!" she gasped. "McGarvie was complaining about indigestion from his lunch—so he didn't eat his dinner! He fed it to the dog."

"Exactly," said Beary, "and if that's the case, he wasn't drugged. He was lying when he said he was out like a light. He must have woken up at some point and realized his wife wasn't there. If he'd gone onto the deck, he'd have seen her nightgown and the towel. They wouldn't have been in the stern where the dog was. They'd have been on the foredeck by the hatch. He'd also have seen the sight on the beach that my wife witnessed. Two lovers locked together in the moonlight. All he had to do was watch and wait for Danielle to return."

Small's eyes narrowed.

"You think he murdered her?"

Beary nodded.

"I'm willing to bet he banged her head against the forward railing. He knocked her out and tossed her away, just as his daughter told us how he tosses away anything that proves to be a bad investment. Then he moved her nightgown and towel to the stern and opened the swim-grid gate, knowing everyone would assume she'd gone for an early-morning swim. What he didn't anticipate were the questions that would be raised by the unusual behavior of the dog in the night."

Small looked puzzled.

"You could be right," he said. "But you still haven't explained why the dog didn't bark. The mutt threw up its dinner, so it wasn't drugged either. How the blazes did Danielle McGarvie get back on board without waking up the Westie?"

"With ease," said Beary. "She was an acrobat."

"What difference does that make? She still couldn't levitate."

Beary pointed to the winch on the bow of the police boat and shook his head sadly. It would take a long time before the exquisite Egyptian goddess faded from his mind.

"Simple," he sighed. "She climbed up the anchor chain."

DIE LIKE A DOG

A Novella set in Fort Benton, Montana

Cast of Local Characters

Josh Henkel (The Colonel)
Shirley Henkel – Josh's first wife (deceased)
Hanna Henkel (Mason) – Josh's daughter by Shirley, now married to Gordon Mason
Frida Henkel – Josh's daughter by Shirley (deceased)
Lindy Henkel – Josh's second wife
Brianne Henkel – Josh's daughter by Lindy

Ruth Mason – elderly widow of Ralph Mason, a Montana rancher
Jackson Mason – Ruth's older son (deceased)
Timothy Mason Sr. – Ruth's younger son, now a violinist with the Seattle symphony
Gordon Mason – Timothy's son, Ruth's grandson, who now operates the ranch
Timothy Mason Jr. – Gordon's younger brother, a musician now living in New York
Robin Tremayne – Timothy's fiancée, a singer from New York
Clint Harrington – Timothy's best man, a lawyer from Seattle
Jack & Ralph Mason, Jr. - Gordon and Hanna's sons, Ruth's great-grandsons

George McEwen – the owner of the local bookstore and coffee shop
Sarah Scott (nee McEwen) – George's daughter, widow of a local rancher
Sally Scott – Sarah's daughter
Liam O'Mara – a rancher whose land abuts The Colonel's property

Jill O'Mara – Liam's older daughter who works in the coffee shop
Rory O'Mara – Liam's son
Erin and Kate O'Mara – Liam's younger daughters

Doc Brady – the town doctor
Joe Kramer – the Chouteau County sheriff
Gareth Jensen – the Henkel family lawyer

THE DOGS

Shep, the sheepdog, commemorated in Fort Benton (deceased)
Blackie, Liam O'Mara's sheepdog (deceased)
Cappuccino, George McEwen's spaniel
Shep, Vietnam War service dog (deceased)
Shep, Sally Scott's German shepherd
Barkley, the Mason family sheepdog (deceased)

DIE LIKE A DOG

The footbridge that crosses the Missouri River at Fort Benton is the most historically significant bridge in Montana. Certainly, it is one of the oldest, built in 1888, a year before the Territory became a State and the first bridge to ford the Missouri in Montana. For seventy-five years, the steel-truss bridge carried traffic—horses, carts and wagons in the early days, and later motor vehicles—but in 1963, a new bridge was built a quarter-mile upstream, and the old steel bridge was closed. The striking quartet of trapezoidal trusses connecting to the east bank remains intact; however, the original swing span that was constructed to allow the passage of steamboats was replaced when the centre pier was washed out in a flood in 1908. Today, the west bank connects to the original structure by a long camelback span, supported, like the original trusses, by concrete piers sheathed in metal plates. The old bridge now serves as a pedestrian feature of the river park, although it can only be accessed from the west side, as the cottonwood-laden east bank is privately owned. So while the traffic in and out of Fort

Benton motors across the Chouteau County Memorial Bridge by the Grand Union Hotel, tourists strolling the river path can walk out over the old bridge and look back towards the unique little town that constitutes the birthplace of Montana.

However, on a Saturday morning in September, tourists are a rare commodity, and the locals, long used to the black metal span yawning over their river, rarely deem it worth the crossing, knowing that they simply have to return again. Walkers and joggers stick to the river path and feel no temptation to turn onto the concrete walkway that leads to the bridge. But children are another matter, and the young Mason boys and their friend, Rory O'Mara, considered it an adventure to walk out along the wooden planking and stare down at the swirling waters below.

As they reached the point where the camelback truss ended and the trio of Baltimore trusses began, the boys turned back to see one of their schoolmates walking her dog along the river path. The German shepherd was bounding ahead, and as it came to the bridge, Jack Mason whistled and yelled out, "Hey, Shep! Here boy!" As an afterthought, he waved to the girl and added, "Sally, come join us."

Shep darted onto the planked walkway. Sally waved back and followed the dog onto the bridge. She was only part way along the camelback span by the time the dog reached the boys. Ralph Mason gave the dog a perfunctory pat and then leaned out over the railing. He liked to see the powerful water surging up and curling around the metal plates.

Jack and Rory started to play with Shep, but Ralph remained mesmerized by the water below the bridge. Something that looked like a sack seemed to be bobbing against the concrete pier.

As Sally reached the end of the first span, Shep abandoned Jack and raced back to meet her. Rory turned to see what had transfixed his friend's brother.

"There's a sack down there," said Ralph. "It's caught on the pier. It's full of some stuff, and there's bits of cloth attached to the back of it."

"No way," said Rory. "A sack wouldn't float." He moved to the railing and stared down into the water.

"Jeez, you moron," he said. "That's not a sack. It's got legs. That's a body down there."

Jack abandoned Shep and came to the railing.

As the boys stared downwards, the body lifted, and an expanse of tan cowhide rose and subsided, its tattooed insignia of interlocking antlers hovering momentarily in view before it glided back under the slate grey water.

"Holy moly, that's The Colonel!" said Ralph.

Jack's eyes bulged and his face went white. Then he gasped as the force of the current rolled the torso against the pier. He felt suddenly sick. He reeled away from the railing and threw up.

"What are you guys staring at?"

Sally's voice behind him made Ralph look round. She and Shep had reached the centre span.

"We gotta get the sheriff," said Rory. "There's a body down there."

"No," breathed Sally. "Are you serious?"

She moved towards the railing.

Ralph stopped her. Even at the age of ten, cowboy-country gallantry was ingrained in his psyche, and he had already seen the effect of the corpse on his older brother.

"Don't look," he said firmly. "He doesn't have a head."

Philippa Beary loved going across the line. The people were friendly, the prices were low and the history was fascinating. However, other than a flight back East for a holiday in New York, her only travels in the United States had been north-south road trips to and from the major cities of the West Coast. Leaving Interstate 5 and venturing into the unknown territory of I-90 was exciting. She was so diverted by the novelty of her surroundings that she had driven several miles before she noticed that the ethereal tones of Natalie Dessay were no longer emanating from the dashboard. She flipped the disc back into the slot. Being on the road imbued her with a glorious sense of freedom and the crystal clarity of Mozart arias suited her light-hearted mood.

Philippa was glad she owned a Jeep. She could already see the mountains far in the distance, pale blue against an even paler sky. She had checked the map and seen that the elevation through the Snoqualmie Pass was over three-thousand feet. The weather forecasts had been good, but it was October, and there could be snow in the higher elevations. As she continued to speed along the highway, the blue gradually transmuted to forest green, and in no time, it seemed the mountains were upon her. To her relief, as she ascended, the road continued to be clear, though there were hard patches of snow on the verge as she reached the vast blue reservoir at the summit. Patches of ice clung to the earth-filled dam at the end of the basin. The water was low here, and big stumps stuck up from the mud bottom.

Once through the pass, the terrain started to change. As she approached Ellensburg, miles of harvested fields bordered the highway. The weather was glorious, the day so bright that the tin roofs on farmhouses glittered as they reflected the sunlight. Where the land had not been irrigated, it was a sea of sagebrush. Cattle grazed; horses stood at fences swishing their tails. A barn painted with the words, *God Bless America*, flashed by. Philippa decided a change of mood was warranted. She flipped out the Mozart arias and substituted a collection of Broadway melodies. With all the grazing cattle and cornfields, she could be in Oklahoma, and it certainly was a beautiful morning. Singing along with the CD, she booted up the speed a little. Other than a brief stop in Bellevue, she'd been driving for four hours and she was ready for lunch and a caffeine fix.

After a half-hour break for a Subway sandwich, she was ready to move on. It was early in the day, but she had many more miles to cover. She tracked down a coffee shop, ordered a latte-to-go and headed back onto the road.

Once past Ellensburg, the land changed again. Now the terrain reminded her of drives through the Cache Creek and Ashcroft Area. It was arid sagebrush country, but instead of the vista of mountains that dominated the British Columbia landscape, she could see miles into the distance. The weather had been mild and in places, yellow daisies and white flowers tinged with mauve created tiny splashes of colour amid the pale green. She flashed by a group of white cows standing amid the sagebrush, as statue-like as the cattle of the Rogers and Hammerstein song. After driving for half an hour, the purple outlines of eroded cliffs appeared on the horizon and glided towards her with the steady progress of a ferry looming down on a speedboat. Before she knew it, she had risen into the hills, and then, with a suddenness that made her gasp with delight, she was crossing the Vantage Bridge and surrounded by a glittering expanse of blue water. She barely had time to take in the spectacle of the Columbia River before her phone rang.

As she exited the bridge, a sign on her right announced a scenic viewpoint. It seemed providential. She pulled off into the parking area and picked up the phone.

It was Detective Constable Bob Miller.

On the bluff high above the parking lot, a man stared out across the river. He was as motionless as the row of steel sculptures that lined the edge of the cliff. He appeared to be looking towards the

Ginkgo Petrified Forest, but his thoughts were directed inwards; the spectacular view made no imprint on his conscious mind for he was remembering the summer of 1992 and wondering how he had been coerced into returning to a town where all the good memories had drowned in a sea of troubles.

A twisted smile crossed his face as the significance of the phrase struck him. He must really be feeling maudlin if he was mentally quoting *Hamlet*. Still, it wasn't inappropriate. Over the years, he'd made as many bad decisions as the Danish prince, failing through inaction as well as misguided action, but it was his selfishness that particular year that had poisoned everything precious from his summers in Montana. He wasn't entirely to blame for the catastrophe that had followed, but he had been the catalyst, and for that, he couldn't forgive himself.

The year of 1992 had been full of promise. He had been seventeen at the time. It was his last summer of freedom before college, and the last summer he could work on his friend's family ranch, for ambition would keep him bound to the city from then on. They had driven from Seattle in Gordon's Ford Crown Victoria. It was an old beater of a car, a startling contrast to The Colonel's gleaming new Chevrolet that the girls had borrowed to drive from Montana and meet them halfway. Was it just the convenient distance that had made them arrange to meet at the Wild Horse Monument? Or was it because the prancing row of steel mustangs symbolized the wildness of youth and because the boys hoped that the romance of the meeting place would make the girls susceptible to the one purpose that dominated their minds.

Hanna, Frida and Sarah. Sarah had been the gentle one, and ironically, given that there was nothing of wildness in her own nature, she had been the only one to walk the length of the monument, eyeing the horses with reverence and absorbing the joyously untamed spirit of the dancing silhouettes. Hanna, the stunning, statuesque blonde whose sensible, down-to-earth personality belied her Miss America good looks, did not even glance at the statues. She had only one focus: she was reunited with Gordon and this was the summer that would decide their future. Her younger sister was blind to the magnificent setting too. Frida's eyes were not for taking in the world around her; they were windows to the wildness of her own soul. He understood that now, but at seventeen, he had not had the wisdom to appreciate that the temperate warmth from Sarah's soft brown eyes promised far greater happiness than the burning heat that blazed from Frida's glittering green orbs. Neither had he been wise enough to realize that Frida's fire was from a burning desire borne of discontent and lack of experience, and that her youth, combined with her nature, made her intensely vulnerable.

He drew his eyes back from the view across the river and looked down the line of horses. He stopped when his eyes lit on the branded pony. As he stared at the metal sculpture, he could visualize the girls as they had stood there years before: Hanna, fair and wholesomely lovely, clinging to Gordon, laughing up at him, oblivious to the view, oblivious to the others, oblivious to everything that did not relate to her determination to acquire an engagement ring by the end of the summer; Frida, a pertly pretty gamin with a halo of short red curls crowning her sharp features, leaning against the piebald branded pony, the strap of her tank top sliding off her shoulder, her cat-like eyes commanding him to see no one but her. Before he gave himself totally up to the promise in that provocative gaze, he recalled how he'd noticed Sarah, quietly watching in the background, warning him that it would not end well. Sickened, he turned away from the horses, cursing the circumstances that had brought him back. Why had he tortured himself by coming up to the monument? Was it some kind of masochistic need to do penance? He tried to blot out the memories and regain his equilibrium. But it was hopeless. Some things could never be eradicated. Consumed with feelings of guilt, he turned from the horses and made his way back to the winding trail that would take him back to the parking lot.

He was about to descend when he saw that there was another car parked by the gate below. He could hear a voice too, a woman's voice, clear and bell-like, although at this distance he could not make out what she was saying. He moved further along but the woman was still screened from view. Resigned to remaining on the hill, he walked back to the horses and pulled out a cigarette. He would wait until the woman had finished her call before he went down. In his current frame of mind, inanimate metal horses were the only companionship he could tolerate. He wondered how he was going to cope with the week ahead.

Philippa was delighted to hear the disappointment in Miller's voice.

"What do you mean?" he demanded. "You can't come out to dinner with me because I'd have to drive three-hundred miles to pick you up? Where are you, for crying out loud?"

Philippa glanced at the sign by the parking lot.

"I'm at the Wild Horse Monument in Washington, whatever that is, and I'm looking out over a breathtaking view of the Columbia River."

"What are you doing there?"

"I'm on my way to Montana."

"Montana!"

"Yes. You remember me talking about my friend, Robin Tremayne, the one who made it to the Met?"

Commendably, Miller managed to recall that the conversation had been about the opera house and not a baseball team.

"The singer you visited in New York," he said. "Yes. Don't tell me she's doing an opera in cowboy country?"

"No, she's getting married there."

"I thought her fiancé was a piano player who worked with her in New York."

"Timothy Mason is a Metropolitan Opera accompanist and répétiteur," Philippa corrected gently, "and he isn't a native New Yorker any more than Robin is. He grew up in Seattle."

"That's Washington. Where does Montana come into it?"

"The Mason family ranch is there. They've owned it since the early part of the last century. Tim's grandfather inherited it from his parents, and now Tim's brother runs it."

"So how come the groom's relatives are hogging the show? Shouldn't the wedding be the prerogative of the bride's parents?"

"Normally, yes, but Robin was an only child and her parents are both dead, so Tim's family has become her family."

"So why can't they all trek into the big city for the wedding?"

"Tim's grandmother's health is frail and the trip would be too much for her. She's ninety-five, and Tim and Robin adore her, so rather than have Granny miss the wedding, everyone is travelling to Montana."

Miller's tone changed from indignant to curious.

"How did Tim Mason progress from a Montana farm boy to a musician growing up in Seattle?"

"According to Robin, Tim's grandmother is a fine pianist. She used to give music lessons when she was younger. Tim's father caught the music bug from her. He won a scholarship and ended up studying at Juilliard. He plays with the Seattle symphony—has done for years—"

"—which is why Tim grew up in Seattle," Miller concluded. "Okay, I get it. But how come his brother is back running the ranch."

"The boys used to spend their summer holidays there. Tim's brother, Gordon, inherited the country-life gene. The moment he was old enough to choose for himself, he moved there . . . which, of course, made Tim's grandfather happy because that way the ranch stays in the family."

"I take it Tim's father was an only child."

"No, he had a brother, but he was killed in Vietnam."

"Well, this is all crappy timing," grumbled Miller. "I finally get back into town and you're in the States whooping it up with the cowboys."

"I won't be whooping it up that much. I'm not just a guest. Robin's asked me to sing at the ceremony."

"That's high pressure. Doing the solo at a diva's wedding. Aren't you nervous?"

"A bit," Philippa admitted, "especially as the wedding rehearsal had to be put forward and I won't be there in time. All I'm getting is a half-hour run-through of my songs with the organist in the church hall the day before the wedding. Still, Robin's a good friend and she asked me, so I could hardly refuse, especially as I was on the scene when they got engaged. I think they look on me as a lucky mascot."

"I thought you were helping solve a murder. Funny sort of mascot. I hope you don't dredge up any corpses to spoil their nuptials. How come your friend had to wait so long to get hitched? Seems to me your trip to New York was over two years ago."

Philippa noted Miller's distinctly grumpy tone, but she ignored it and replied serenely, "Have you any idea how hard it was for them to find a mutually convenient date for a big family wedding? Robin's career has taken off and Tim has a lot of private engagements too. They're very busy."

"Doesn't the Met give them time off for good behaviour?"

"It's not just the Met. They have summer concert tours and guest appearances at other opera houses. Tim's parents have a demanding schedule too. Then there's fitting in with the operations of his brother's ranch and not disrupting the work there—"

"Okay, okay, I get the picture."

Philippa was not to be deterred.

"Part of the delay was due to Tim's grandmother," she continued. "She was undergoing treatment for cancer, so they wanted to wait until she was through the radiation."

"Granny must be tough," said Miller. "Ninety-five and a cancer survivor. They must be a different breed in Montana. Whereabouts is their ranch anyway?"

"Fort Benton."

"Never heard of it."

"Neither had I, but Richard tells me it's a neat little town that is considered to be the birthplace of Montana. It's supposed to have strong links to the Mounties, too. Sir John A. MacDonald formed the North West Mounted Police to deal with the whiskey traders coming up the Whoop Up Trail from Fort Benton. I've read up on it a bit and I'm looking forward to seeing it."

"Well, let's hope it's not still a Wild West outpost. Who's going down with you?"

"No one," said Philippa. "I'm driving my Jeep."

"That's one hell of a trip all by yourself," growled Miller. "God," he added. "I'm looking at Google Maps right now. You're looking at fourteen hours driving. You're not going to try to drive straight through?"

"Of course not," Philippa said sharply. Miller always had difficulty treading the fine line between solicitous and just plain bossy. "I'm stopping in Spokane for the night. Mum and Dad have friends there who offered to put me up, and then I'm driving down to Lewistown the following day as I have a friend who works at the Arts Centre there. I won't be in Fort Benton until Thursday."

"So when's the wedding?"

"Sunday. There's a pre-wedding cocktail party at the hotel on Saturday. Then the ceremony is at the church on Sunday afternoon, followed by a big bash at the ranch that'll probably last well into the night—not that I'll stay late. I'm planning on heading back early Monday morning, stopping overnight at Spokane again, and then driving straight through."

"Well, be careful when you're on the road," Miller admonished. "With the economy the way it is, crime is on an upswing, and there are always nutters running loose looking for pretty young girls who are on their own. I bet you haven't even got an iPhone yet, or a GPS."

"My old cell is perfectly adequate," snapped Philippa, "and I'm quite capable of reading a road map. My parents lent me their copy of *Next Exit*, so I can instantly locate every Starbucks, Subway, rest stop and tourist trap along the way."

"Yes, well if you had an iPhone, you'd have Internet and you'd be able to get information about the tourist traps as you go. Where did you say you were right now?"

"The Wild Horse Monument." Philippa had been preoccupied with her phone call and had not studied the area, but now she looked up to the top of the hillside. "Oh, my goodness! I can see it from here," she said. "It's some sort of horse statues on the mountainside."

"Hold on. I'll Google it."

"I'm sure there will be an info-sign if I walk into the parking lot."

"No, wait. Don't be so impatient. Here, I've got it." Miller paused. Then he continued. "Hey, this is pretty neat. It's outdoor art—a whole series of sculptures of wild horses, all constructed from welded steel plates. There are fifteen of them in total. They were created by a Spokane artist called David Govedare in 1989 for the Washington State Centennial celebration."

"It's too bad they're so distant. They look great from here but I'd love to see them close up."

"There's a trail up the cliff. You can hike up, but it says it's not an easy climb. We should drive down there together some time and go up and have a look."

"Good idea," said Philippa, "but I don't have to wait. I can head up now and have a preview."

"Don't be an idiot," snapped Miller. "You can't go hiking in the middle of nowhere by yourself. Get back in your car and keep moving."

"No way," said Philippa. "I've been driving for four hours and this sounds like the perfect opportunity to stretch my legs. I'll call you later and tell you what it was like. And stop fussing. There's another car in the parking lot, so there must be other people up there."

Miller grunted.

"Yes, well let's hope it's not the Green River Killer."

"Not his kind of vehicle," Philippa said serenely. "It's a steel-grey Cadillac. Besides, they caught him years ago."

She grinned as she ended the call. It would do Miller good to stew for a while. All the same, she thought, she'd make sure her pepper spray was in her pocket and the right way up for easy access. One never knew what one would find up at the top.

The Mason family ranch sprawled over two hundred and fifty acres. Most of the land encompassed wide fields of cow corn, but a smaller portion was used for a ranch where quarter horses were raised. Viewed on a map, the boundaries appeared to form an L-shape, with the longer arm stretching down to the Missouri River. This part of the property, abundant with cottonwoods and pines, was ideal for trail-riding, but one section had been cleared. Here, a small white house stood, its porch overlooking the wide band of moving water, which was sometimes darkly opaque, rippled with wind and current, and other times, a gleaming mirror reflecting the blue and white dappled sky and the tall trees hugging the shoreline. In this house lived Ruth Mason. She had moved there in 1998 after her husband died. She had been seventy-nine when she lost her beloved Ralph, and she did not have the spirit to manage the ranch without him. Luckily, she did not have to. Her grandson, Gordon, had married the beauteous Hanna Henkel, who, in spite of her movie-star appearance, had been raised on a ranch and had a work ethic that rivalled Ruth's own. When it came to discipline, Hanna was very much The Colonel's daughter, even if she had cut all ties to her father after her parents' divorce. Gordon and his new bride were more than capable of running the ranch, so Ruth had retired quietly with her books and her music and left them in charge. The joy of seeing her great-grandchildren born and watching them grow was an immeasurable treasure. She was grateful that the vast estate allowed her that precious mix of independence and familiarity, and although she missed her husband deeply, she was content to wait out the rest of her life in her riverside haven.

Ruth Mason loved both her grandsons. Gordon reminded her of Ralph, for he had inherited many of the characteristics of his grandfather. However, she had a special spot in her heart for his younger brother, Timothy, who had inherited her own love of music. She did not see him often, but he wrote to her regularly— given her age, she had declared herself exempt from the chore of learning to use a computer—and he sent her clippings so that she could follow every step of his career. She had been disappointed when his relationship with a violinist in Seattle had failed to result in marriage, and horrified when he had become ensnared and then discarded by a voracious man-eating diva in New York. The news that he had finally become engaged had been received with mixed feelings when it turned out that his fiancée was another singer at the Met, but once Ruth had met Robin Tremayne, she knew that her grandson had found the perfect mate. It was a musical and emotional partnership made in heaven, and everything she would have wished for him. It was Ruth's desire to see Tim married that had pulled her through her last illness. She was old and weary, and the recent shocks to her system had withered her few remaining resources. Colonel Josh Henkel's death had shaken her badly, and the subsequent worry about Gordon and his family was wearing her down. She would be content to go quietly and join her husband and the son she lost in Vietnam, but she was resolved to enjoy one last family celebration before she gave up the fight. One more milestone and then she could let go. She was very tired and it was time.

It took only a moment for Philippa to pinpoint the trail that led up to the Wild Horse Monument. She set off, glad that she was wearing runners, as the rocky path was steep and, in places, unstable. Although she had deliberately baited Miller, she was not unconscious of the risks of walking alone in isolated areas, and she kept alert for signs of trouble. The air was silent, other than the occasional cry of a hawk or the roll of dislodged pebbles as she walked. If there were other sightseers at the top, they were not making any noise. However, as she climbed higher, she forgot about the possible dangers and gloried in the exhilarating view, which opened up more panoramically as the path rose up the hillside. She was short of breath when she reached the top, but the row of prancing horses stretched out along the clifftop made the effort worthwhile. She was so intrigued by the illusion of a herd of wild mustangs running at the edge of the cliff that she failed to notice the man standing at the head of the herd. She made her way slowly along the line, admiring the craft that had moulded the jagged manes and strutting legs. Each horse had some individual characteristic that set it apart from the rest. One reared on its hind legs; another was a branded pony, dragging his leg as if drawing attention to the marks on his flank.

As she neared the prancing mustang at the front of the herd, she paused to look out at the sweeping stretch of the Columbia River winding between the pink-hued rocks, the bi-colour effect only broken by the silver line of the Vantage Bridge. As her eyes followed the ribbon of highway that traced the route she had taken, she became aware of the smell of smoke. Suddenly she sensed she was being watched. She looked round and gasped. Beyond the sharp-toothed mane of the lead horse, a disembodied face hovered in the shadows, a distorted mask twisted into a grimace of horror.

Philippa froze. Her feet were rooted to the spot, but she forced her arm into motion, sliding her hand downwards and curling it around the canister in her pocket.

The mask glided along the back of the horse and connected with the body of the person who had been standing on the far side of the statue. As the figure emerged from shadow into sunlight, it became human, but the burning eyes riveted on Philippa were not friendly. Her grip on the pepper spray tightened.

The man moved forward, and, in spite of her fear, Philippa registered the fact that he was well-dressed. Expensive casual. He would have been attractive if it had not been for his wild-eyed glare. A modern-day Heathcliff, she thought suddenly. She almost expected him to rear up and toss his mane like the horse that had been shielding him from view, but as the thought flashed through her mind, the man's stunned expression faded and his eyes glinted with bitter amusement.

"I apologize," he said with a mocking bow. "I didn't mean to frighten you. But if it makes you feel any better," he added, "you startled me too. I thought you were a ghost."

Before Philippa could reply, he turned and strode across to the cliff path. Then, as Philippa gaped at his retreating back, he started down and disappeared from view.

George McEwan's attempt to restore some order to the chaos of his bookstore was making little progress. He put down the pile of novels he was shelving and scowled at his friend.

"What the Sam Hill do you want to go stirring things up for?" he demanded. "Nobody is mourning Josh Henkel. His death is long overdue. If I'd had my way, the Viet Cong would have snared him in one of their pits back in the seventies. Unfortunately, the bastard seemed to lead a charmed life."

"That's why we refer to him as The Colonel," said Doc. "He wasn't afraid of anything. That spit-in-the-eye-of-fate attitude can be as effective as an armoured tank."

"And as lethal for others as a dose of Agent Orange."

"Oh, come on," Doc said severely. "Be fair. Henkel came back with a lot of medals and there are survivors today who credit him with bringing them through."

George snorted rudely.

"Yes, and there are a few who said he was the most sadistic khaki-wrapped pile of shit that ever served in Nam. It still rots my gut that he came back and Jackson Mason never made it."

"That wasn't The Colonel's fault. He saved Jackson's life during the Tet offensive. Come to that, he brought him through the entire war. Ruth Mason still talks about the way he looked after her boy. It wasn't Henkel's fault that Jackson was killed right at the end."

George made a noise that sounded like harrumph.

"Henkel wanted to buy a tract of land from the Masons back then," he said. "I remember all the jockeying and negotiating. He wanted to stay in with the Masons in the worst way, so bringing Jackson back safely was high priority. It had nothing to do with kindness—it was all self-interest. He was pissed off as hell that Jackson didn't make it. Henkel never did anything unless it suited him personally."

"Well, you can think whatever you like about his character, but I still don't believe he killed himself."

"Don't you have better things to do than brood over his suicide?" George growled. "Go look after your living patients. And are you going to buy that book you've been fingering," he added, "or are you turning into a parsimonious old bugger like Henkel and figuring you can just borrow it?"

The doctor received the tirade from his friend stoically. He hadn't liked The Colonel either, but he was governed by professional ethics, and the inconsistencies between what he knew and what came out at the inquest had troubled him deeply. When his request for a copy of the autopsy findings had been met, he had become even more concerned at what he had noticed within the report. Still, it was clear that his friend was not interested in the discrepancies he had uncovered.

He paid for the book and listened as George rumbled on.

"The only good thing Josh Henkel ever did was sire Hanna," said George, "but the reason she's so skookum is because of her mother—and look at the crappy way *she* was treated. Shirley never deserved the garbage that Henkel doled out."

Doc nodded soberly. "It broke my heart when Shirley died. She could have had a happy life after the divorce if the Good Lord had only allowed her the time. I can think of at least three good men who were waiting to pick up the pieces." He looked shrewdly at his friend. "You being one of them," he added quietly.

George's face darkened.

"Yes, I was," he muttered. Doc was surprised to hear the intensity in his friend's voice. The pain was still simmering under the surface after all these years.

George went back to reorganizing his shelves, which, thought Doc Brady, was the literary equivalent of shovelling out the Augean Stables. The store was so stuffed with volumes that piles of books formed stools in the corners, barricades in the aisles, and pillars at the end of every shelf unit. He suspected that George was far more interested in collecting than actually selling. At least the musty smell of the dusty old volumes was mitigated by the tantalizing aroma from the adjoining coffee shop, which George also owned. The coffee house was what paid the rent, and that was because George's daughter, Sarah, had taken charge of the management and would not allow her father any involvement other than coming through for a cup of coffee. George was unaware of his friend's thoughts. He continued on the same theme.

"One thing's for sure," he muttered, "no one is going to miss the asshole, especially not his high-maintenance wife and her little-miss-mouth daughter. Now, they have his money without having to put up with him. I bet as we speak they'll be figuring out how to trade in the Montana land for New York apartments and Florida condos."

"Actually," said Doc, "they won't. It turns out Josh wrote a new will before he died. Lindy and Brianne get significant cash settlements, but everything else goes to Hanna."

The book George was holding clattered to the floor, startling the heavily pregnant brown and white spaniel that was sleeping in the corner.

"No!" George looked stunned.

"Yes. Hanna inherits the ranch, and the property west of the river too. That's going to make the Mason family the biggest landholder in the Fort Benton area."

"Well, I'm damned. So in the end, the old bugger tried to put things right. What made him do that?"

"Guilt, I guess. Trying to make up for the way he treated Hanna's mother and sister. Josh must have realized that he had a lot to answer for. He must have finally appreciated Hanna's worth too. I heard that he'd been trying to mend the rift between them."

George picked up the fallen book and scowled.

"No way. A snake shedding its skin is still a snake underneath. If Henkel was trying to do right by Hanna, it'll be because he wanted to piss off Lindy. He probably figured out that the hour she spends in town after her hair appointment isn't just for going shopping."

"You could be right. Still, his new will is going to benefit the entire town." Doc Brady picked up a dilapidated bookmark that had dropped from the fallen book and handed it to George. "Hanna has a sense of commitment to the people who live in Fort Benton."

"She won't perpetuate the boundary dispute her father had with Liam O'Mara, that's for sure," George acknowledged. "Things will be a lot better for him."

"Now, there's a man with a motive," said Doc. "He was out hunting the morning The Colonel died. Alone, too," he added pointedly. "There's no witness to say he didn't stray over the boundary onto Henkel's property."

George's face darkened.

"If Liam was going to commit murder, he'd have done it the day he found poor old Blackie. Liam knew damn well that Henkel had shot his dog, and if that didn't provoke him, nothing would have. Anyway, Joe Kramer is adamant that the shot that killed The Colonel was self-inflicted, and as far as the rest of the town is concerned, that's the way it stays."

"Our sheriff isn't exactly impartial, himself," said Doc. "The Colonel has been trying to bust Joe out of office ever since the Jorgensen case."

George blew his lips out scornfully.

"Are you suggesting the sheriff killed Henkel?"

"No, but I think he deliberately steered the inquest towards a suicide verdict."

"Bullshit."

"It isn't bullshit. There are a lot of unanswered questions."

"Like what?"

"Like the fact that nobody explained the vandalism that happened that day. There was graffiti all over the barn. Somebody who didn't like The Colonel was at his ranch on the day he died, but that's being hushed up. Joe isn't pursuing it."

"Let it be, will you? First you're querying the autopsy results, then talking murder versus suicide, and now you're crying conspiracy theory. Go home, read your book, and quit planting doubts in people's minds. You're going to cause a lot of grief if you keep this up."

He glared a challenge at his friend. Doc was tired of arguing. He shrugged, took the book that he had purchased and left the store. However, he resolved that he would visit Joe Kramer in the morning and have it out with him. The sheriff would damned well have to listen. The Colonel had been murdered. Of that, Doc was certain.

A few blocks away, Lindy Henkel sat fuming in the offices of Jensen, Jensen and Lowther. She could not remember a time when Gareth Jensen had not been her husband's lawyer. He had been there in the days when she had detached Josh from his first wife, and he had handled every family matter of significance since. She considered him responsible for the disaster that had struck with her husband's death. She glowered across the desk and demanded that he sort out the mess he'd created.

"What do you mean, I can't contest the will? I'm his wife, for Christ's sake. Isn't there some law that I get half? And how can he disinherit Brianne in favour of the daughter by his first marriage who hasn't spoken to him in years? Hanna has treated Josh like shit for two bloody decades. What the hell was the divorce settlement for if not to get rid of his obligations to Shirley and her brood?"

Gareth steepled his fingers and let his eyes drift downwards. The surface of his desktop was an infinitely preferable view to the blazing eyes of the exquisitely turned-out harpy who had stormed into his office as he was preparing to take his coffee break, and who was refusing to leave until he assured her that he could help her regain what she felt she had earned through years of marriage to a dictatorial asshole with the sex drive of a goat and the finesse of a threshing machine. Gareth had to admit Lindy had a vivid turn of phrase. He also considered that she and The Colonel had been an exceptionally well-matched pair. Equally callous, equally foul-mouthed, equally self-centered, and equally vain about their appearance.

Gareth tuned out the stream of vituperation and let his mind drift onto the differences between Josh Henkel's two wives. Lindy was far better equipped to deal with Henkel than poor Shirley had been. Shirley's tragedy had been that she was a decent woman married to a psychopathic egotist who was incapable of the feelings that she, being in love with him, tried so hard to project onto his character. Lindy's tragedy was that Henkel, at seventy-four, was aging sufficiently that the physical charms that had lured him into marriage were no longer keeping him in bondage. Lust no longer blinded him to her vapid, grasping nature, and the attraction of Hanna's robust young sons far outstripped any joy he had from Brianne, who was as selfish and shallow as her mother.

Lindy pounded the desk and brought Gareth out of his daydream. He sighed. He was just the unfortunate pig in the middle, and all he really wanted at that point was his cup of coffee. However, not wanting it ruined by the angry virago occupying his office, he attempted to come up with a reply. Procrastination was Gareth's middle name. People like the Henkels wore him out.

"Let me do some research," he said. "I'll look into it and see if there are any options open to us. Be patient. I'll call you as soon as I know where we stand."

Privately, he thought Lindy Henkel was hooped, and he had no intention of doing anything to help her. Hanna Mason was a client too, and a much nicer one.

Lindy stood up, her eyes narrowed to slits that make Gareth think of the gun-ports he had seen when touring the Alamo.

"Do," she said. "I'll be waiting."

Gareth sighed. If only, he thought, Josh Henkel had had the foresight to take his trophy wife with him. Lindy was a legacy that no one deserved.

Philippa had been rendered speechless by the odd behaviour of the man at the Wild Horse Monument. The most aggravating thing, she thought glumly as she plodded back down the trail, was that she would never know who the mysterious ghost was that she resembled so strongly. Judging by the man's reaction, her look-alike was not someone he was overjoyed to see resurrected from the grave. He had certainly made tracks going back down the hillside, for Philippa was only halfway down when she saw his car roaring back onto the highway. She noticed that he was also heading east. Maybe they would run into each other again along the way, but probably not, she reflected. It was a mystery destined to remain a mystery.

Once back on the road, she kept a lookout for the steel grey Cadillac, but she saw no sign of the car or its strange driver. When she reached Spokane, her thoughts turned to the more practical matter of finding her way to her billet for the night. Half an hour later, she pulled up at her destination and the bizarre encounter on the mountainside was soon swept from her mind. Her parents' friends lived in a heritage home in an older part of Spokane and were charming hosts with an endless store of anecdotes about the history of the area. They gave Philippa an abbreviated city tour and wined and dined her at Milford's Fish House. By the end of the evening, her head was reeling from an intoxicating combination of information overload and Pinot Grigio, so she crashed into her borrowed bed and blanked out until morning.

The next day, she thanked her hosts and set off, having ascertained the location of the nearest coffee shop and the entrance to I90 East. While she waited for the barista at Starbucks to produce her caramel macchiato, she texted Bob Miller: *On the road again – heading for Lewiston. Ps. It wasn't the Green River Killer. Horses were great.* Then she took her coffee and headed out to the Jeep.

Once on the highway, the stimulation of caffeine and the promise of another bright day of exploration sent Philippa's spirits soaring. Soon she had crossed the Spokane River into Idaho and was driving along the northern panhandle. She passed Lake Coeur d'Alene and found herself travelling through long stretches of forest, broken by glimpses of snow–capped mountains and sparkling stretches of river that raced exuberantly alongside the highway. Mining towns with letters carved into hillsides flashed by; there were smelters and ski slopes; swampy lakes with masses of bulrushes; here and there a solitary church. Soon, she found herself back in high elevations where snow lay at the side of road. A sign marked the Murray Gold Fields, and before she knew it, she was driving through Lookout Pass. At the summit, she entered Montana.

She pulled over at the first rest stop and, with a sigh, put her watch ahead. Driving back would be easier when she would gain the hour. Then she checked her phone. It had signalled a text message half an hour back on the road. Sure enough, Bob Miller had replied. *Getting that message yesterday would have been nice. Let me know when you arrive so I don't worry all night.*

Philippa smiled. She was glad he thought he had the right to worry about her, but she was also glad that she was not in town. Bob had been away for months, so it was gratifying to be unavailable on his return. It would do him good to wait and fret for a while.

She continued on her way, stopping for lunch in Missoula, having used *Next Exit* to pinpoint another of the ubiquitous Subways that dotted the main arteries of North America; then she set off again. Another three hours to Great Falls, by which time she'd definitely be ready for a latte and a snack. En route, she'd keep her eyes open for a spot halfway where she could stop for a walk.

It was a long day of driving, but she revelled in the solitude and the scenery. She stopped periodically to stroll through rest stops and inhale the unfamiliar scents of clover and sagebrush, but she made good time, especially once the land flattened out and she was back in cattle country. On the long, straight stretches, gleaming blue mirages sprouted on the road ahead, tantalizingly vanishing as she neared them. At one point, a herd of antelope raced across the road, their white tails bobbing up and down as they loped through the adjacent field. The Montana sky was a Cinerama sweep of blue and she suddenly recalled watching a late movie on television when her mother was out and her father, who had a fondness for westerns, had let her stay up. It had been called *The Big Sky*. She was sure it had been set in Montana, and now she understood why. She was beginning to realize that prairie skyscapes could be every bit as spectacular as the landscapes and seascapes of the coast.

The land became hilly again as she approached Lewiston. She arrived in town a few minutes before six o'clock. She had arranged to meet Annie Brandt at the Arts Centre, after which they would drive in convoy to Annie's family home on the outskirts of town. She was looking forward to another evening of visiting, but this time she remembered to text Bob Miller before she joined up with her friend. The answer came back right away: *Already? That's an eight-hour trip. Quit speeding!*

Philippa sighed. It was nice that he cared, but she did wish he could occasionally manage to stop sounding like a cop.

Whenever Robin and Tim came to Montana, they made a point of walking to Ruth Mason's riverside house so they could visit her without the distraction of the multitude of visitors who filtered in and out of the ranch house. The day after they arrived, they arranged to go down for afternoon tea. Robin was particularly happy to go out for a walk, not only because the ranch house was bustling with caterers and decorators, but also because she had found her prospective brother and sister-in-law to be unusually distant and preoccupied. Robin was an exceptionally fine artiste, but with her talent came a high degree of sensitivity to people's moods. The edgy atmosphere in the house had communicated itself to her so strongly that the tension had become infused into her own jaw and shoulders. She could tell a headache was coming on. Fresh air and a walk to the river was a welcome prospect.

While Robin and Tim were walking down to the river, Ruth Mason was busy in her kitchen. She always looked forward to her grandson's visits, and by quarter to three, she had put the kettle on and set out a plate laden with the cookies and cakes that she knew were his favourites.

Ruth beamed when Tim and his fiancée arrived on her doorstep. She greeted them both with hugs and ushered them inside. She waved away their offers of help and insisted they sit in her living room while she bustled off to the kitchen to make the coffee. When she returned with the tray of coffee and treats, Tim and Robin were standing by the fireplace, studying the family photographs that lined the mantel. Robin scrutinized the centre picture carefully and said, "Young Jack is starting to resemble his namesake, isn't he?"

Jack had been named after Jackson Mason, Tim's uncle who had died in Vietnam. Jackson had been a dog handler at the air base in Bien Hoa, and the photograph showed him with the big black German shepherd who had died with him there.

"Not just in looks," said Tim. "Jack's inherited his great-uncle's love for dogs, too."

"He certainly has." Ruth set the tray on the table with a sigh. "The poor lad was heartbroken when Barkley died." Barkley was the ancient family sheepdog who had finally creaked away from old age. It had been Jack's constant companion from the moment he was born and he missed it dearly. Ruth poured a mug of coffee and handed it to Robin. "You know, he hasn't got over that dog's death yet. He's still fretting, even though George McEwan has promised him one of the pups from Cappuccino's litter when they arrive. Jack was more bonded to that dog than he is to his own kinfolk, and my Jackson was just the same with Shep."

Robin looked back at the photo and smiled. The pleasant atmosphere in the river cottage, with its redolent aroma of baking and its surfaces crammed with mementos, was helping her relax.

"Another Shep," she said. "There's a lot of them in Fort Benton. It must get awfully confusing when they're all out walking at the same time and their owners are trying to call them." She noticed an unframed snapshot that had been propped up against the music stand on the piano. She picked it up and peered at it. "I haven't seen this before."

Ruth glanced up. "Sarah Scott gave me that." Robin looked confused. Ruth elaborated. "Bud Scott's widow—George McEwan's daughter—you met her last time you were here." Robin smiled and nodded. Ruth and Hanna had taken her to visit George's bookstore and its charming adjoining coffee shop. Sarah had been there, and Hanna had introduced the attractive brunette as her best friend. Sarah had been as charming as her surroundings and Robin had taken an instant liking to her.

Ruth continued, "Sarah came across the photo in an album the other day and thought I'd like it as it's such a lovely photo of Tim."

Robin turned to Tim. "That's you and Clint with a couple of girls," she said. "My, you look young!"

"We were only seventeen when that was taken," he said. "It was the summer of '92, the last summer I spent working on the ranch. Gordon took the photo. I remember it well. We'd all been down to the river for a picnic."

"Where's Hanna?"

"Packing up the picnic, probably."

Robin stared more closely at the picture.

"Is that Sarah tucked under your arm?"

"Yes. She was pretty, wasn't she . . . in an unobtrusive sort of way. I liked her a lot."

"I can see that," said Robin. "She's not exactly reciprocating, though, is she? Her eyes are locked on Clint, but he's completely besotted with that other girl. It's written all over him. You know," she added, glancing again at the picture, "the girl with Clint looks a bit like Philippa."

"Only superficially," said Tim. "The hair and the tiny physique are the same, but Philippa doesn't have wild eyes. You'd never mistake them for each other if you saw them up close." He turned to his grandmother. "Do you mind if I tuck this picture out of sight?" he asked. "Just in case Clint pops in to visit you. I had enough trouble persuading him to be my best man when he realized the wedding was going to be here. I'd just as soon he didn't see this. He's going to have enough trouble meeting Hanna again. He doesn't need reminders of Frida."

"Why should that photo upset Clint?" asked Robin. "He's been married and divorced twice since then. He can't be still hankering over a summer romance from twenty years ago. And what on earth does it have to do with Hanna?"

"The girl in the photograph was Hanna's sister."

Robin looked surprised.

"What!" she exclaimed. "I never knew Hanna had a sister. What happened to her?"

"She died," said Tim.

Philippa had enjoyed her evening in Lewiston. The Brandt family had proved most hospitable, providing a guest room fit for a princess and a meal fit for at least three kings. Ruefully, Philippa reflected that the only operatic role she'd look right for would be Falstaff if the trend continued throughout the holiday. However, she did not want to dally the next morning, and since Annie Brandt had to be at the Arts Centre by nine, the two young women got up early and breakfasted at a local café, which, Annie swore, served the best flapjacks Philippa would ever taste. Once they'd eaten, they said their farewells and Annie hurried off to her job, having first told Philippa where to locate a coffee shop that would provide a latte for the road.

As Philippa headed down the street, she noticed a sporting-goods store. Thinking it a likely spot to find a gift for her father, she went inside. A friendly-looking clerk around her own age stood behind the counter. He was ringing through a sale for an elderly gentleman who wore a blue wool Pendleton shirt. There was only one other customer in the store, a grizzled, hawk-eyed individual sporting well-worn jeans, a denim jacket and a cowboy hat, which was whipped off his head the moment he noticed a lady had stepped inside. All three stopped what they were doing when Philippa entered and politely offered to help her find what she needed. Having grilled her about her father's fishing habits, they debated the merits of various pieces of equipment until they reached a consensus as to what would constitute the perfect gift. Ten minutes later Philippa was paying for a set of fishing lures that she knew her father would treasure.

The shop's inhabitants proved to be a mine of information. They gave her clear instructions on how to reach her destination: I-91 would take her to a T-junction at Highway 80, where she would come to a sign with an arrow pointing the way to Fort Benton. They also explained what she should see while there, and offered titbits of local colour, such as the fact that the antelopes she had admired on her journey across Montana were not liked by the farmers as they ate weeds, and then deposited their droppings, along with the weed seeds, back in the farmers' fields. Every word was delivered with old-world courtesy. Philippa was charmed. She thanked the trio for their help and left with her purchases. Montana was promising to be a great place to visit. The men in cowboy country were much more gallant than their urban counterparts in Vancouver.

The coffee shop was further along the block. It was large and stocked with pretty items for sale, but having examined the display for possible gifts for her mother, Philippa saw that the souvenirs were imported from China, so she abandoned the shelves, bought her coffee and headed back to her Jeep. She soon found I91, and by ten o'clock, she was racing through miles of fields and open range, here and there inhabited with grazing cattle or capering horses, and sporadically dotted with ranch houses, barns and silos. In places, stark rocks rose out of the ground, eroded and striated so that the different layers were exposed. Much of the time, the highway was straight, cutting between a golden sea of shorn wheat fields that stretched for miles below the pale sky. Periodically, the road snaked down through gulches in sagebrush-covered hills that huddled together like a cluster of crouching dinosaurs.

Philippa negotiated another knot of hills, and then the road flattened out again. She could see a shadowy line in the distance, which after a few miles, revealed itself to be a long gully stretching across the landscape. As she drew nearer, she realized that she had circled back to the Missouri. The gully raced towards her and suddenly the river came into view, with buildings and trees dotted along the far shore. In a flash, she had reached the river and was speeding across a bridge. Glancing up the wide stretch of water, she saw that there was another bridge further along the river, its trapezoidal spans framed in the cottonwood trees on either bank. In the distance, a row of rocky hills glowed pink in the sunlight. Directly ahead, Philippa could see a red brick building lined with long, narrow windows. It overlooked the river and dominated the entrance to town. As she exited the bridge and turned to the right, she realized that she had reached her destination. This was the Grand Union, the refurbished Wild West hotel that was to be her home during her stay in Fort Benton.

As she pulled round to the parking lot, she noticed curiously that there was a statue of a dog outside the hotel. She was surprised. She had anticipated statues of Lewis and Clark, having looked up the town on the Internet and read some of the history, but the dog was unexpected. She pulled into a parking space and resolved to inspect the statue before she went inside. But the moment she got out of her car, the idea went right out of her mind.

For a steel-grey Cadillac was parked at the far end of the lot.

Robin was feeling increasingly anxious to escape from the Mason ranch house. After she and Tim returned from their visit to his grandmother, the tension in the big house had been palpable. By the end of the day, Robin's headache had bloomed to migraine proportions and she had been forced to retire early, well dosed with aspirin. Breakfast the next morning was a muted and uncomfortable affair, so when Tim declared his intention of going into town for a haircut, she snatched the chance to go with him. She wanted an opportunity to tell him what was on her mind.

As they drove into town, she said, "Hanna seems pretty subdued. I guess she's still shocked over her father's death."

"Everyone's shocked," said Tim. "The Colonel is the last person on earth anyone would expect to kill himself. But then, nobody knew about the cancer."

"But what a way to go."

"Not really. If Josh decided to commit suicide, blasting his head off with his shotgun was the predictable method of choice. He was a hard-nosed SOB. Even his own daughter didn't want anything to do with him. If Hanna is subdued, it's probably because she's upset that the boys were the ones who discovered the body."

Robin bit her lip.

"How did his body end up in the river?"

"There's a deck on the riverbank where he always drank his afternoon coffee. It had an open section that served as a dock. I guess he set his chair at the edge, which guaranteed that his body would fall into the water. He was probably thinking up one last way to torment his family," Tim added uncharitably. "If he'd floated down river, his wife would have had a hard time explaining his disappearance. She'd have been hamstrung dealing with estate matters, too. But as it was, his body got caught on the bridge and was spotted by the kids."

"Did they know who it was?"

"Young Jack did. He recognized the insignia on the jacket. I gather he threw up all over the planking."

"That's terrible. Poor kid."

"It wasn't that terrible," said Tim. "I suspect he was more embarrassed than upset, especially as his kid brother didn't upchuck *his* breakfast."

"It must have been upsetting. For heaven's sake, it was their grandfather!"

"Yes, but they didn't really know him and they didn't think of him as their grandfather. To them, he was just The Colonel, a local character that his family wanted nothing to do with."

"They must have been aware of the connection, though."

"Yes, but it meant very little to them. Hanna may have got engaged to Gordon right out of high school, but they didn't marry until 1996, and by then Henkel had already left her mother to marry Lindy. He was much more interested in his trophy wife and his new baby than being Grandpa to Hanna and Gordon's offspring."

"He was still family. Young Jack may be more upset than anyone realizes."

"Young Jack, I've been told, said it was good riddance to bad rubbish. That may have been bravado after the mortifying barf incident, but I suspect he meant it. You see, a week before he died, Josh Henkel shot a neighbour's dog over a property dispute. In Jack's eyes, the dog's death would have been the tragedy, and The Colonel's would have been simple justice. You know, there's a certain irony to it," Tim added. "The Colonel was well-known in Nam for using the expression 'Die Like a Dog' when he dispatched any poor sod from the villages that he suspected of helping the Viet Cong. All those shots in the head. I wonder if those words flashed through his mind before he blasted his own brains out."

"Don't!" protested Robin. "How can you talk like that? You're not usually so callous."

"Sorry. It's just that I've heard so much about Josh Henkel and all the misery he caused. I can't feel sorry for him."

"I still think it's sad that Hanna and her father never resolved their differences," said Robin soberly. "She probably feels guilty that she wouldn't let him back into her life."

"I doubt that. Gordon says Josh was only trying to worm his way back because he was annoyed with Lindy and Brianne. Getting pally with Hanna again would have been the perfect way to upset his second family."

"His illness might have softened him up," Robin said gently, "and he probably did regret that he'd missed out on knowing his grandsons."

"That's possible," Tim allowed. "His daughter by Lindy is a spoiled little madam and the boys are turning into feisty hunting, shooting, fishing tintypes of himself. That must have stung. But can we please stop talking about it? Everything's fine. Hanna and Gordon will perk up once the festivities get underway."

Robin was not reassured, but she fell silent for the rest of the drive.

Tim parked on the street, and once he had gone into the barbershop, Robin set off for a walk along the river. The day was bright, but the wind was cold, so she was glad she had wrapped up warmly. As she crossed the road to the park, she noticed a familiar figure crossing further up the block. It was Sarah Scott. Robin waved and cut over to join her at the edge of the park. Sarah enveloped Robin in a big hug.

"So lovely to see you again," she said. "You must be excited. It's going to be quite the occasion. It must be wonderful to have the whole family together again."

"Well, it is," said Robin, "but it's stressful too. Everyone seems very uptight at the moment. Actually," she continued, "I'm glad I ran into you. You're Hanna's best friend, so if anyone knows what's bothering her, you will. She's so quiet and tense, nothing like her usual self. Is it just the aftermath of her father's suicide, or is there something else going on that I don't know about?"

Sarah frowned. Then she took Robin's arm. "Walk with me," she said. "I'm just heading down to check on Sally. She's playing with Tim's nephews and the O'Mara children."

Robin followed Sarah across the grass. Further along, she could see a group of children throwing a Frisbee while a large black dog raced back and forth barking excitedly. As they strolled, Sarah said, "Hanna's probably upset about the gossip. There's been a lot of talk, and even though the inquest ruled Josh's death a suicide, the rumours just won't die down."

Robin's eyes widened.

"What sort of rumours? Who started them?"

Sarah sighed.

"It's Doc Brady," she said. "He says he gave The Colonel a full physical only three months ago and pronounced him fit as the proverbial fiddle. He says you could have knocked him down with a feather when he attended the inquest and heard that the autopsy report revealed liver cancer."

"Well, I suppose his professional reputation is at stake," said Robin. "It doesn't reflect very well on him that he missed something like that."

Sarah shook her head.

"Doc Brady is a good doctor. People don't believe he's trying to cover up a mis-diagnosis because they can tell he's genuinely puzzled—and that, along with all the talk over The Colonel changing his will and leaving the bulk of his estate to Hanna—well, you know what people are like."

Robin paled.

"Are you saying that people think Hanna and Gordon—" Robin broke off, appalled.

"No one's come right out and accused them of anything." Sarah bit her lip and cast her eyes down towards the grass. "But some people are expressing disbelief that The Colonel would have killed himself, and if he didn't . . ." Sarah shrugged.

"Is there any room for doubt?" Robin asked forthrightly.

"Probably not. Our police chief is convinced it was suicide and I honestly can't imagine him botching an investigation. Joe Kramer is a good man. But you can see, given the rumours, Hanna is feeling extremely sensitive."

Robin nodded but she still was not satisfied.

"I can see that she would be," she acknowledged, "but the way she's acting is so uncharacteristic. Hanna is such an upright, honest person, and she's always tackled problems in a calm, logical way. I can't see malicious gossip getting her down. The Hanna I know would ride it out with her head high. She'd rise above it and she'd talk things through. She wouldn't clam up and shut out the rest of the family. There's got to be more to it than that."

Sarah hesitated for a moment. Then she took a deep breath and continued.

"There is something else . . . and I know it will be worrying her. There was some graffiti sprayed on The Colonel's barns the day he died . . . and Hanna's boys and Rory O'Mara were the ones who did it."

"Jack and Ralph? That's not like them. They're good kids. Is she sure they were responsible?"

"Oh, yes. I was the person who found out what they'd been up to."

They were close to the children now and Robin could make them out clearly. Jack and Ralph Mason she recognized right away. A third boy had a mop of tawny hair that so obviously duplicated the blonde heads of two of the girls that Robin realized the trio must be the O'Mara children. The sweet-faced girl with long, dark hair had to be Sally for she was a miniature version of Sarah. Sarah looked at her daughter and sighed. Then she continued her story.

"I can always tell when Sally has done something she shouldn't," she said, "and I knew she was harbouring a guilty secret the day before Josh Henkel's body was discovered. I didn't say anything, because I knew she'd come to me for advice if it was something serious. But the next day, after the body appeared, she looked so sick and white that I knew I had to say something. Eventually I got it out of her. You see, there was a nasty incident a few weeks ago. Josh Henkel and Liam O'Mara have an unresolved boundary dispute. It escalated, and then went right out of control. Liam was out hunting, and his dog was with him as usual. The Colonel claimed that the dog had gone over onto his property—"

"He shot it. I heard," Robin said bleakly. "That's so horrible."

"It was. Liam was devastated. In fact, everyone in town was horrified . . . and the children were dreadfully upset. I didn't know it at the time, but I guess young Rory O' Mara—" Sarah nodded towards the tow headed youth—"and the Mason lads decided to do something to show The Colonel what they thought of him. They bought tins of spray paint, climbed the fence on the far side of the footbridge and hiked up to Henkel's barns. Then they wrote graffiti all over the walls."

"Was Sally with them?"

"No, but she knew what they were going to do and she was scared for them. She was hanging out with Shep at the town end of the bridge, waiting for them to come back. Gordon saw her there and I suppose he could tell something was wrong. In the end, she admitted why she was anxious, so he hot-footed it back to his car, drove round to the ranch and went in to stop the boys."

"Did he catch them in time?"

"No. I guess they'd all split up to paint different buildings. By the time Gordon got there, they'd made a dreadful mess . . . and they wrote some pretty ugly stuff. Gordon rounded up Ralph and Rory, but I suppose Jack heard him coming and took off, because Sally says he came roaring back across the bridge. He was so white she thought he was ill, so I guess he knew he was for it. Gordon put the other two boys in his car and told them to stay put while he set things right with The Colonel."

"Oh, my goodness," said Robin. "No wonder he and Hanna are so tense. Can you imagine how the rumours would escalate if people knew Gordon was there that day?"

"That's part of it, but I suspect what's upsetting Hanna is that she feels what the boys wrote was the last straw that drove The Colonel past the breaking point. And then to discover that she's named the principal heir. The guilt will be tearing her up inside."

Sarah fell silent. Robin did not know what to say. She turned to watch the children. Ralph Mason and the O'Mara boy had given up on the Frisbee game and were chasing the O'Mara girls across the field. However, Sally and Jack were still tossing the disc for the dog. Shep leapt into the air and snatched the Frisbee in mid-flight. Then he bounded back to the children. Jack knelt down with open arms as the big shepherd approached. Sally watched, beaming with delight as the dog hurtled into the waiting arms and proceeded to wash the laughing boy's face. It was the most natural scene in the world. Sarah's explanation of Hanna's mood was a logical one, Robin thought, as she observed Jack's affection for the animal. The boys' escapade could be the reason for the strained atmosphere at the ranch.

A voice broke into her thoughts. She looked round to see Tim approaching. Although he greeted Sarah warmly, he looked annoyed. Robin didn't have to struggle to figure out why. A small-town barbershop was a natural conduit for gossip. Tim would have been furious to discover that his family was the current target. However, he responded politely when Sarah inquired after his parents and their mutual friends. As the conversation wound down and farewells seemed imminent, Tim's eyes narrowed shrewdly.

"You haven't asked after Clint," he said bluntly. "You are aware he'll be here for the wedding?"

Sarah sighed.

"Yes, of course I am. Hanna filled me in. I gather he's doing all right."

"He's doing well with work. He's a partner in the firm now. Not so great with his personal life. He's divorced again."

"Yes, Hanna told me."

Tim eyed Sarah speculatively.

"It's not going to be too awkward, you two meeting up again after all this time? You are going to come to all the events? Hanna would be really upset if you ducked out on the cocktail party or the barbecue. She's irked enough that Clint is going to be my best man, but she'd never forgive me if his presence kept you away."

Sarah's face became guarded.

"I'll be at the wedding," she said, "but I'm not guaranteeing anything else. I'll see how I feel."

"If it makes you feel any better, Clint's on tenterhooks too. He knows he's not Mr. Popularity in this town. I had quite a job convincing him to come. He'll probably hide out in the Grand Union until the wedding, and it'll take a lot of persuasion to lure him out of his room for the cocktail party." Tim gave Sarah a winsomely hopeful smile. "I suppose you wouldn't—"

"No, I wouldn't," Sarah said crisply. "Like I said, I'll come to the wedding, but don't expect me to form the official welcome committee. If there are any overtures to be made, I shouldn't have to be the person who initiates them. To be perfectly honest, I intend to steer clear of the hotel because Clint's presence will stir up a lot of gossip that will bring back painful memories. I don't need the stress. Between now and the ceremony, I'll be hiding out in the coffee shop."

Accepting defeat, Tim shrugged, put his arm round Robin's shoulder and led her away. Sarah turned back to see a row of round-eyed children watching her curiously. She sighed. Children might have selective hearing when their parents were telling them what to do, but they always heard every word of the adults' private conversations. Rory O'Mara had a wide grin on his face. Sarah ruffled his mop of hair and nodded towards Shep, who was panting eagerly and edging the Frisbee forward with his nose.

"Go on, Big Ears," she said. "Get that game going again."

Once she had ascertained that the owner of the Cadillac was nowhere in sight, Philippa walked over to examine the statue. The dog was a stately figure, sculpted in bronze, his front paws standing on a rail. The base of the statue was rough granite stone, but it was set in an octagon of bricks that commemorated people's pets. The plaque beneath the statue indicated that the dog was called Shep, and the words, *Forever Faithful,* were written under his name. Philippa whipped out her camera and took a photograph, knowing that her father and sister would love the monument. Beary and Juliette were the family dog lovers.

Once she had taken her picture, Philippa retrieved her bags from the back of the Jeep and headed for the hotel. The entrance of the Grand Union was comprised of three wide arches, the outer two framing elegant four-paned windows, and the centre arch containing double doors topped by two transom windows curved to follow the line of the arch. Slinging her overnight bag over her shoulder, Philippa tucked her laptop under her arm and opened the door. Then, using her back to hold it in place, she grabbed her suitcase, and went inside.

Immediately, she was conscious of an eerie quietness. Then she realized it was only the absence of the ever-present Montana wind rippling the cottonwood trees that had created the illusion of total silence. Gradually, other sounds became distinguishable: the muted clatter of knives and forks, someone talking in a distant room, the soft whirr of an elevator. At first glance, the lobby looked as if nothing in it had changed since the mid-eighteen hundreds. Philippa felt as if she had stepped back in time, but as she studied the area more closely, she saw that the furnishings were not all antiques; it was the mixture of leather upholstery and darkly glowing wood that created the illusion of a past age. To the left of the doors was a grand piano, to the right, an armchair and a round table. Beyond these, an open doorway led to a gift shop. The lobby was spacious, with a hardwood floor stretching from the entrance to a staircase, carpeted in red and gold, that swept up to the higher floors. Gleaming mahogany banister rails curved gracefully at the foot of the stairs and the newel posts were topped with tall spindles crafted from the same dark wood. High on the wall by the upper landing was a painting of the hotel in earlier days.

The central section of the lobby featured an area rug with armchairs, side tables and lamps arranged around a magazine-laden coffee table. To the left, an open set of double doors revealed a dining room where tables had been laid for lunch. The right side of the lobby was dominated by a long, curved check-in desk. The most elaborate cashier's cage Philippa had ever seen rose above the counter. It had an arched window, with glass inlays and a small opening where money could change hands. Its intricate moldings and wide cornices conveyed an air of weighty Victoriana, and the ornate pilasters surrounding the window were reminiscent of Greek columns. However, the smiling face inside the aperture was as cheerfully modern as a waitress at the IHOP. The friendly clerk introduced herself as Margaret, efficiently found Philippa's reservation and signed her in.

"You're here for the wedding," she said cheerily, running her finger down a sheet of paper with a list of names.

"Is that the guest list?" Philippa asked.

"Yes. We're catering the pre-nuptial party here tomorrow night, so I need to know who's who, and especially which guests will be staying at the hotel. Hanna Mason has it all outlined for me. She's so well-organized. It's going to be quite the affair."

As Philippa checked in, she noticed a pile of thin, paperback books to the side of the cashier's cage. On the cover was the picture of a dog, identical to the statue outside the hotel.

"Why is there a statue of a dog outside?" she asked. "What's his significance to the town?"

"Ah, poor old Shep," came the reply. "He has another monument on the hillside at the other end of town. That's where he's buried, overlooking the station. His story is in that book, if you'd like a copy."

Philippa nodded and took one from the pile.

"It's a sad tale—" Margaret went on processing Philippa's credit card as she talked— "but we have lots of other fascinating stories too. You'll have to visit the fort while you're here, and our heritage homes—and don't miss the veterans' park. That tells a few tales as well."

"Is it far to the fort?"

"Heavens, no. All the interesting sights are packed into a small area. You could see them in an afternoon. Start with the river walk—you'll find plaques there telling you the history of the town—and then, if you come back along the street, you'll see the fort and the memorial park and some of our historic houses. Oh, and you should check out the footbridge on your way. It was built before Montana became a State."

"I'll do the full tour tomorrow," said Philippa. "Today, I might take a stroll along the river. I need a walk after being stuck in a car for three hours."

"You're probably hungry, then. Our restaurant is open for lunch if you want to eat."

"Actually, I'm not. I had a huge breakfast. But I'd love to have a latte if there's a coffee shop in town."

Margaret looked up and smiled.

"There certainly is," she said. "It's called the Old Fort Coffee House. A real gem. You'll love it. It's owned by George McEwan and it adjoins his bookstore. He'll be at the wedding, and his daughter Sarah, too. . . Sarah Scott, as she is now. She's the widow of one of the town's wealthiest ranchers, but she's also Hanna Mason's best friend. Sweetest lady you could hope to meet. Has a nine-year-old daughter, Sally, who's a little darling too. If you go for a coffee, you might meet her before the wedding. She's often there making sure things are run properly. Her dad's a real character but hopeless as a businessman."

Margaret bent to finish the paperwork. Philippa ventured another question.

"I saw a grey Cadillac in the parking lot," she said. "Is the owner staying here?"

Margaret's eyes widened and if she'd had antennae, Philippa was sure they would have been twitching.

"Now that would be Clint Harrington," she said. "You know him, do you?"

"No. We just met briefly. I recognized the car."

"Well, you're bound to run into him again since you're here for the Mason wedding. He's here for the wedding too."

"He is?" Philippa blinked, startled.

"Oh, yes." Margaret pursed her mouth disapprovingly. "He's Tim Mason's best man. They've been friends since childhood."

Philippa felt a stab of unease. She wanted Robin's wedding to be a joyous occasion, and instinctively, she sensed that the man she had met at the monument in Washington was capable of casting a shadow over the event. There had been an edge to Margaret's voice when speaking of Clint Harrington that added to Philippa's sense of disquiet. Philippa attempted to draw the proprietress out.

"He's rather a strange character," she ventured.

Margaret's cheery face became impassive.

"He hasn't been here for a good many years," she said primly. "I really couldn't say. Now, I'm going to get you some help with those bags," she added, and before Philippa could respond, the proprietress slipped out through the gate and disappeared through the door that led to the gift shop.

Idly, while she waited, Philippa glanced over the list on the desk. As she read the names, she became aware of an imbalance in the list. There was certainly a preponderance of Masons on the list, but no matching groups to indicate any other family branches. Robin, as Philippa knew, had no living relatives, but she had talked often about Hanna Mason and described her future sister-in-law as a family-oriented woman with solid Montana roots. As Philippa puzzled over the anomaly, from the corner of her eye, she noticed Margaret emerging from the gift shop, a lanky youth in tow. She pushed the list back to the other side of the grill and turned to Margaret.

"Isn't Hanna Mason a local girl?" she asked.

"Yes, absolutely. Hanna was born in Fort Benton. Why do you ask?"

"I didn't see any parents or siblings listed for her."

Margaret pursed her lips again.

"Hanna's mother died many years ago," she said, "and she has no siblings. As to The Colonel—"

"The Colonel?"

"Hanna's father, Josh Henkel. Everyone refers to him as The Colonel."

"So what about him? Why isn't he on the list?"

The lanky youth's eyes acquired an avid gleam. They flickered warily between the two women standing by the desk. Then, before Margaret could continue, another voice broke into the conversation. Philippa turned to see a stocky jean-clad woman marching down the staircase. Her weather-beaten face was framed in a profusion of grey curls that sprung out from a shocking pink ball cap with a Key West logo.

"Margaret's being close-lipped because she doesn't want to upset the Masons by gossiping to their guests," the newcomer said cheerily, "but the fact is, Hanna Mason has had nothing to do with her father since her mother died. But even if she had, Josh Henkel wouldn't be attending the wedding."

"Why not?" Philippa asked curiously.

The young porter erupted in a snigger, which was quickly quelled by a minatory glower from the proprietress.

"Because," said the newcomer cheerfully, "his headless corpse was found floating in the river four weeks ago."

With that, she turned away from the reception desk and swept through into the dining room.

Sarah Scott could see that the children were happy playing at the riverside park, so she gave Sally a hug and left her to continue her game with Shep and her friends. Anyone watching Sarah as she walked back to the street would have been struck by the serenity of her countenance. However, under her placid exterior, her thoughts were far from tranquil. The prospect of meeting Clint again after almost twenty years was creating flutters of anxiety and resurrecting feelings that she had thought long dead and buried. Watching the children at play, Sarah had seen the laughing interaction between her daughter, the O'Mara girls and the Mason boys, and she had been uneasily reminded of the relationship between herself and the friends of her youth. The emotions started young, she thought, sadly. Sally might be only nine years old, but she trekked around after young Jack Mason as faithfully as Shep shadowed her own footsteps. Sarah hoped that Jack would prove a loyal friend as they grew to adulthood, and that Sally's sweet face and kindly nature would not be eclipsed by the vivacity of Erin and Colleen O'Mara. Sarah was all too aware that she, herself, had always been overshadowed by the lively Henkel girls.

She took a deep breath and tried to pull herself together. She was shocked at the tide of feeling that had overwhelmed her at the news of Clint's return. Her marriage to Bud had been a good one, and she had found contentment with him. No, not just contentment, she reminded herself firmly. She had been truly happy, and deeply grieved after his death. Perhaps their marriage had not produced the exciting rollercoaster of emotions she had felt around Clint, but it had infused her with a deep, quiet happiness that had made her believe that she was over the infatuation of her youth.

Yet when Tim told her that Clint's second marriage had resulted in divorce, the old feelings had surged to the fore. It was Hanna's fault, she thought bitterly, for pointing out that Clint had twice chosen slender brunettes whose superficial resemblance to Sarah suggested that he had regretted his actions during his final summer in Montana. Hanna's words had planted seeds of false hope and Sarah was determined not to travel that path again. She had to steel herself to endure the next few days. There was no reason for her to see Clint, except at the hotel party and the wedding, and there would be lots of people present on both occasions. She would greet him and move on. She would cope. She was used to keeping her feelings in check and she could do so once again. Once Clint returned to Seattle, she could go back to the peaceful life that she loved, helping her father make a success of his business, raising her daughter, and surrounded by good friends and the loving relatives that she had inherited with her marriage to Bud.

Sarah braced her shoulders and strode along the street towards the Old Fort Coffee House. Bud had left her extremely well off and she had no need to work, but she took pleasure in overseeing the coffee shop where she had worked in her youth. She organized special events to coordinate with the bookstore, and she supervised the small staff, which consisted of three local girls: two high-school students who were part-timers, and one full time employee, Jill O'Mara, who was the older sister of Sally's playmates. Jill was a likeable nineteen-year-old, in spite of her unfortunate habit of constantly changing her appearance to go with whichever book or movie was influencing her at any given time. Her present idol was the Girl with the Dragon Tattoo, a role model that Sarah hoped would soon be changed for something less off-putting to the customers. Still, Jill was reliable and good-natured, so Sarah tolerated her idiosyncrasies.

When Sarah reached the coffee house, she sighed. Liam O'Mara's dilapidated white Tracker was parked outside, which meant Jill would be slipping her father free coffee again. The lower half of the vehicle was caked in mud and a tow bar was tied up against the hood, giving the car the appearance of a battering ram. It suited Liam's personality: scruffy, unpredictable and hard as steel. He was not the most popular stalk in the cornfield, she thought whimsically. No one could empty a room faster than Liam. Sarah was ready to bet he was the only customer in the shop.

When she walked through the door, she saw that her prediction was correct. Liam was lounging against the barista's counter. He was gesturing with the largest size in what appeared to be their most expensive drink and complaining about the shop's collaboration with the bookstore to her father who had come through for his own coffee break. Jill O'Mara, having provided the drinks, sat behind the counter, tuning out the argument by immersing herself in a copy of *People*. Cappuccino, equally indifferent, lay quietly on her blanket in the corner.

"You're not goddam Starbucks." Liam turned up the volume to overcome the jingle as the door opened. "People in town want to chat over their coffee, not feel like they're in a goddam library."

"That's hardly the case, Liam," Sarah interjected quietly as she took off her coat and hat. "The customers have to go through the connecting door to reach the bookshop. It's their choice."

Liam stabbed a calloused finger at the pile of books on the stand near the door.

"Not when you hold book events and then leave all the unsold copies out along with a goddam great sign saying how wonderful they are. And that book is a crock anyway. The woman who wrote that never got near Viet Nam. What the hell gives her the right to write a novel about the guys that served there?"

"She's married to a veteran. The novel is based on her husband's experiences, and it's very good if you could be bothered to read it." Sarah was shocked at Liam's tone. He always tended to be noisy and opinionated, and his temper was legendary, but it was unusual for him to erupt over things that did not affect him personally. Determined to rein in the beast, she turned to her father. "Dad, why don't you take Liam through to the bookshop if you guys want to gossip. I'm going to take over here for a bit. Jill, you can go and have a break."

Sarah's tone was quiet, but there was a determined edge to her voice, and like the children in the riverside park, George McEwan and Jill O'Mara meekly nodded and prepared to leave. Liam looked mutinous, realizing that his hopes of a free refill were disappearing along with his daughter. However, knowing when he was beaten, he followed George through the connecting door. But before he disappeared into the bookstore, he glanced back. Sarah shivered as she saw his lowering expression. Jill was slipping on her coat, but she noticed her employer's reaction.

"Don't mind Dad," she murmured. "It's not directed at you. He's just come back from the hillside by the train station."

Sarah looked surprised.

"The old Shep monument? What was he doing there?"

"Spreading Blackie's ashes."

With a sad, apologetic smile, Jill went out the door. Guiltily, Sarah glanced toward the bookstore. Liam's mood was explained. With a sigh, she went to the latte machine. Jill's father would get his second drink after all.

To Philippa's disappointment, the lanky youth who carried her bags to her room had little to add to what she had learned about the Masons and the Henkels, nor could he tell her about the man she had met at the Wild Horse Monument. He did, however, insist that The Colonel was a "total asshole", though that appeared to be the result of Josh Henkel giving him and his friends a bad time when they were "just hanging out" in town. Since the grin that accompanied this statement implied that the youngsters were doing a lot more than hanging out, Philippa suspected that, in this case, The Colonel was probably well within his rights. She refrained from comment, tipped her young helper and sent him on his way.

Once in her room, she lifted her bags onto the bed, taking care not to bang them against the solid mahogany headboard; then she looked around with pleasure, noting the dark wooden wainscoting, the soft beige walls, the curtains draped back into swags and the richly patterned carpet. Atmospheric period prints adorned the walls. From the windows, she could see the river and the trapezoidal spans of the old footbridge framed in the towering cottonwood trees.

She set her laptop on the desk and tucked the book about Shep on the bedside table. Then she put her makeup case in the bathroom, admiring the black and white mosaic tile as she did so. Once she'd arranged her toiletries, she came back into the bedroom and opened the doors of the wardrobe. One side was taken up with a television set atop a chest of drawers, so she hung up the two dressy outfits she'd brought on the other side and piled the contents from her case into the drawers. Having stashed away her case and bags, she opened her laptop and emailed her parents to let them know she'd arrived safely. Then, eyes gleaming, she texted Bob Miller: *In Fort Benton. Everything fine, other than headless body in river.* That would give him something to stew about.

Since she had her phone handy, she contemplated calling Robin to let her know she'd arrived in town. On the other hand, she was tired, and the prospect of a solitary visit to the coffee shop, followed by a lazy afternoon with her feet up, was singularly appealing. She had no desire to have her plans torpedoed by demands that she come out to the ranch and meet the family. Guiltily, she decided to wait until later to announce her arrival.

A sudden wave of fatigue hit her. A rest was warranted before the walk to the coffee shop. She switched on the bedside lamp and settled on the bed to read about Shep. She was curious to know his story and the book was thin. She could read it in half an hour.

Philippa's eyes were heavy, but she managed to stay awake until the end. Margaret had been right. The story was sad. The tale dated back to the 1930s. Shep had appeared one day at the railway station, the same day a casket was being loaded onto a train to return a man's body to his family in the East. After that day, Shep kept returning to the station. He watched every incoming train, and eventually, the staff realized that the body they had shipped back East must have been his master. Many people tried to adopt Shep, but he refused to leave the station, so for six years, he lived there, watching the trains and being cared for by the railway attendants. Philippa felt her heart lurch as she read the end of the story. When Shep was old and deaf, he had been run over by a train. His paws had been on the rail and he did not hear it coming. Sadly, Philippa closed the book, now understanding the subtitle, *Forever Faithful*. As she was about to put the book back on the table, her phone signalled a text message. It was from Miller: *You're kidding, right?*

Drowsily, she considered answering, but as the thought came into her head, it floated out again and was replaced by a curious sensation that a large dog was curled up at the foot of the bed. And with the image of Shep in her mind, she drifted off to sleep.

If Philippa had been ten minutes later entering the hotel, she would have run into the man who had so intrigued her at the Wild Horse Monument, for moments after she left the lobby, Clint Harrington came out from the dining room. Without so much as a nod towards the woman at the counter, he strode out of the Grand Union and headed down the riverside path. He had decided to bite the bullet and track down Sarah. To meet, one on one, before having to greet each other publicly at the wedding, seemed the proper course of action, and he needed to apologize to her for the mess he had made of things. He should have come back to face her years ago, and Hanna too, but he had hidden in Seattle, buried himself in his studies, and consoled himself with a fellow student whose eerie physical resemblance to Sarah had helped him delude himself that he had recovered what he had lost through his own stupidity. His student marriage had proved a disaster, and it was hardly surprising that his wife had walked out after two years. Her acerbic exit line that he had never understood her was justified. He knew he had merely superimposed another personality onto her face.

Even then, he could have returned, but he kept procrastinating, working hard at his career, deluding himself that success as a lawyer would somehow compensate for his past actions and that he would only go back when he had salvaged his pride and had something to offer. But he had waited too long. Sarah had married Bud Scott and Clint had abandoned all thoughts of return. He knew it was too late now for him and Sarah, but the apology he owed her was long overdue and he could at least try to make peace with her before the wedding.

The shout of children playing brought him out of his reverie. A black German shepherd was darting about the field, chasing a Frisbee, while a group of youngsters hurled it back and forth between them. Clint smiled. Three boys and three girls. They could have been himself, Tim and Gordon at that age, tolerating the company of the girls who, a few years later, would suddenly become the focus of their interest rather than mere hangers-on. Sarah had been a real trouper as a kid. A cheery little tomboy, but even then, she was clever, artistic and venturesome—yet steady, with all the qualities that later made her into the charming young woman that everyone in town loved and admired. He'd loved her too, but Frida had got in the way. If he'd been hit by a tornado, he couldn't have been diverted more violently. It was as if Sarah was obliterated, and yet, deep down, he still cared about her, and arrogantly, had thought she'd be there when he came to his senses. And she would have been, if things hadn't gone wrong—or if he'd had the guts to come back sooner.

He was near to the children now. They were clustered in a circle, facing in towards the dog, but suddenly the dark-haired girl turned and he saw her face. Astounded, he stopped in his tracks. She was Sarah all over again. Sarah at age ten.

The girl stared solemnly at him. Then politely, she said, "Can we help you, mister? Are you lost?"

Dumbly, Clint stared back at her. At last he found his voice. "You must be Sally Scott," he said.

"Yes. Do I know you?"

"No, but I used to know your mother. You look just like her."

"Yes, I know. Everyone tells me that."

"Is your mother around?" Clint's eyes scanned the park, and then swept back to the row of children who had gathered at Sally's side. He noticed that they were eyeing him with a noticeable degree of suspicion. "Is she here?" he repeated.

"Well, yes . . ." Sally paused uncomfortably.

"So where can I find her?"

Sally remained silent. Rory O'Mara interjected bluntly.

"Sally's mom is hiding out at the coffee shop," he said.

"Hiding out?"

"Yeah. There's some guy in town that she's trying to avoid. So as long as that's not you, you're welcome to go over there." He turned back to his friends. "Come on guys," he said. "Let's play."

Clint watched the group of children racing away across the grass. Then, with a sense of weariness born of déjà vu, he turned on his heel and headed back to the hotel.

After Tim and Robin returned from town, Gordon offered to take them riding with the boys. Hanna chose to remain at the ranch house, but as the afternoon wore on, she regretted her decision. Normally she enjoyed some solitude, but in her present frame of mind, it was stressful being alone. She had busied herself baking bread throughout the afternoon, pounding at the dough as if the vigorous movement of her hands could drive the worrying thoughts from her brain, but she was glad when a call from Gareth Jensen came. The lawyer wanted to drop by with some papers. Hanna assented gratefully. The company of the kindly solicitor would be welcome. When she heard a car pulling up outside, she pressed the switch to start the coffee maker and hurried out of the kitchen. Giving her hair a quick pat into place as she passed the hall mirror, she opened the front door.

Then she gasped. The car in the driveway was not the lawyer's conservative grey Buick. It was a bright red Jaguar, and its petulantly pretty blonde driver was the last person she expected to see. Hanna's shocked expression had no effect on the newcomer. Brianne Henkel's cloying smile stayed neatly in place as she slithered out of the car, straightened her short leather jacket and stepped up to the porch.

"What are you doing here?" Hanna demanded.

"We have things to discuss."

"Such as?"

Brianne ignored Hanna's hostile tone. Coolly, she replied, "Such as the fact that we both lost our father last month."

"I lost my father years ago," snapped Hanna, "thanks to your mother. I have nothing to say to you." She remained blocking the open doorway so that her half-sister was compelled to remain on the front steps.

Brianne's smile hardened and Hanna shivered. She recognized the smile. She had seen it many years before when her father walked out on her mother. He had abandoned his family, without empathy and without conscience—and he had smiled as he left. Brianne was indeed The Colonel's daughter.

Brianne was unaware of her half-sister's churning thoughts, and would have been indifferent if she could have known what Hanna was thinking. She continued silkily.

"You don't have to say anything, but you'd better think twice about accepting the inheritance that our father so misguidedly decided to pass your way. You may think it was smart to use your sons to wheedle your way back into Father's will, but you're not going to get away with it."

Hanna's gaze grew as steely as her stepsister's.

"I did nothing to influence our father's will," she said. "I had no contact with him for years, as you well know. If he made changes before he killed himself, it was because of you and your mother. It had nothing to do with me and I knew nothing about it."

Brianne's cornflower blue eyes opened into perfect ovals and she stared, unblinking, at Hanna.

"Oh, really? Your husband knew what was going on. I heard Father ask him if he could take the boys on a hunting trip. He made it quite clear that he was thinking about changing his will."

Hanna felt her jaw clench and her heart started to pound.

"Gordon would have told me. You're talking nonsense. I want you to leave now."

"Oh, I'll leave. I don't like you any more than you like me, but just remember this. You know as well as I do that the suicide verdict was a joke. Our father would never have killed himself, no matter how ill he was. Doc Brady is already asking questions, and if I tell him what I saw when I was out riding that morning, he'll pressure Sheriff Kramer to re-open the case."

Hanna paled but she kept her voice steady.

"I don't know what you're talking about," she said quietly.

"Of course you don't. Your husband was hardly likely to tell you. But you really ought to know about his little secret. You see, as I rode back towards the house, I heard the gunshot . . . and a few moments later, I saw your husband running across the lawn. He was coming up from the river. He not only knew about the changed will; he was down at the dock when our father died. You keep that in mind when it comes time to settle the estate."

Brianne spun on her heel and stalked back to the gleaming red Jaguar. Without turning back, she slid into the driving seat, threw the car into gear and drove away.

Rooted to the spot, Hanna watched her go. As the car disappeared into the trees, she went to close the door, but her hand was shaking so violently she couldn't grip the doorknob. Blindly she turned and tried to focus. She was oblivious to the figure that had quietly moved out from the grove of cottonwoods at the front of the house. But after a moment, she became conscious of a gentle hand guiding her inside.

"Tim and Gordon are still at the stables," said Robin. "I walked back. I heard everything that woman said. Hanna, what on earth is going on?"

By the time Philippa woke up, it was past four o'clock. Too late for a coffee, she decided. Time to shower, change, and then check out the Wild West saloon before going in to dinner. Half an hour later, conservatively dressed in black dress pants and an elegant off-the-shoulder turquoise sweater threaded with silver, she descended the grand staircase and pushed her way through the louvered swing doors of the saloon.

The first person she saw was the stocky, grey-haired woman who'd spoken to her in the lobby when she was registering. The woman had discarded the shocking pink Key West cap, although the fuchsia and green floral blouse she now wore was equally vivid. She was seated on a barstool, next to a bespectacled and balding gentleman whose eyes were glued to the continuous sports coverage on the television over the bar. The woman smiled when she saw Philippa and patted the adjacent barstool. Glad to have someone to talk to, Philippa slid onto the stool and introduced herself.

"Betty McGill," said the woman, shaking Philippa's hand, "and this is my husband, Hal," she added, waving towards the man at her side. Hal acknowledged Philippa with a friendly smile and returned to his sports program. "You're the girl who's going to sing at the Mason wedding, aren't you?" said Betty. "My, but your presence is going to get people talking. You'd better let us buy you a drink."

Philippa blinked.

"How did you know who I was? Are you attending the wedding too?"

"Yes, we're old friends of the Masons, though we live in Washington now. We know all the gossip. Just ask. We'll fill you in. Now, what'll you have? The ale on tap is the best, if you happen to be a beer drinker."

Philippa was about to demur and order wine, but then she noticed the labels on the beer taps and decided to try the local fare. She chose one of the more audaciously named offerings and was presented with a darkly creamy drink that tasted delicious. Montana just kept getting better and better. She supplemented her drink with a handful of nuts from the bowl on the bar counter, then turned to her companion and said, "So why do you say my presence will make people talk? That sounds a bit disconcerting."

"It's your looks," said Betty. "At first glance, you look just like Frida Henkel. A tamer version, of course. You don't have the wild eyes, but the physical resemblance is quite striking."

Philippa's eyes flew wide. At last she had an answer to the question that had hovered in her mind since the strange encounter at the Wild Horse Monument.

"Who is Frida Henkel," she asked, "and where is she now?"

"Long gone," said Betty. "Frida died years ago."

Philippa nodded.

"So that's why Clint Harrington thought he'd seen a ghost."

It was Betty's turn to stare.

"You met Clint Harrington?"

"Yes. Briefly."

"I bet he did a double-take."

"He certainly did. Tell me about this girl. Who was Frida Henkel? And what happened to her?"

Betty McGill extracted a handful of nuts from the bowl and planted them on her napkin. Then she leaned forward and lowered her voice. Her husband was still absorbed in the TV sports commentary and the other people at the bar were chattering noisily among themselves, so her hushed tone seemed overly cautious, but perhaps, thought Philippa, the acoustics in the grand old building magnified any sound that was louder than a whisper. She tilted her ear towards the stream of information and listened curiously.

"Frida Henkel was Hanna Mason's younger sister," Betty explained. "The girls were the daughters of Josh Henkel and his first wife, Shirley, who was a lovely lady—calm, stable, the salt of the earth. The Colonel—that's how everyone here refers to Josh Henkel because he was an army man until he retired to run the ranch—he was a real mean one, tough and belligerent, and restless too. Hanna took after her mother, but Frida inherited her dad's nature. She was bold and aggressive, with the same mean spirit and sense of entitlement . . . and the same—" Betty paused and pursed her lips. "Well, let's just say she'd grown up on a ranch and knew all about the bulls and the cows. She was pretty anxious to start wrangling, but none of the local boys dared lay a hand on her because they were all too scared of her father. Too bad Clint Harrington didn't run scared too."

"Clint Harrington wasn't a local boy then?"

"No. He lived in Seattle, but he was Tim Mason's best friend, so he and Tim, and Tim's brother, Gordon, all used to come out from Seattle to work on the Mason ranch during the summer holidays. Frida was sixteen in the summer of 1992, and since her sister was like that—" Betty held up two tightly crossed fingers— "with Gordon Mason, Frida tagged along and got to know the other boys. Frida set her cap and everything under it at Clint Harrington. He should have known better than to take up with her, given her age, especially since Sarah McEwan was so in love with him that everyone in town ached for her."

"Sarah McEwan? I've heard that name."

"George McEwan's daughter. Her name's Scott now."

"Right. They own the bookstore and the coffee shop. The concierge told me about them. They'll be at the wedding."

"That's right. Sarah's a love. You'll really like her."

Philippa politely steered Betty back to the subject at hand.

"What happened with Clint and these girls who were in love with him?"

"Sarah was quiet and shy, and Frida was vivacious and willing, so it was pretty predictable. Clint was a randy teenage boy—well, let's face it, blind with lust like they are at that age—and he took advantage of what was on offer . . . and, well, it all escalated from there."

"What happened? Did Frida get pregnant?"

"No, nothing like that. But after a few weeks, Clint wised up to the fact that he was entangled with a sixteen-year-old viper with enough poison in her system to fell a herd of bison. Like I said,

Frida was a real spiteful one under the pretty exterior. I guess once Clint had got rid of enough wild oats to get his vision working again, he could see that he'd bypassed a diamond in favour of a rhinestone. Even though Frida was determined to hang on to him, he detached himself firmly at the end of the summer and headed back to Seattle."

"So what happened? You're not telling me she killed herself over a failed teen romance."

"No. Frida wasn't the suicidal type . . . not in that sense. But her home life was going into a tailspin, and the combination of rage over being dumped by Clint and havoc at home . . . well, she went haywire. Total rebellion."

"What was going on in her home life?"

"Her parents' marriage was breaking down. Josh had been having an affair with the woman who's now his second wife. She was a shipper/supplier in Great Falls—only twenty-seven years old—a real piece of work." Betty rolled her eyes upward. "Josh was fifty-five at the time. Shirley finally wised up to what was going on, so there was nothing but friction in the house. Josh's solution to her distress was to arrange the least generous settlement he could get away with and to file for divorce. He jettisoned his family without so much as a blink. Hanna was away at college so it didn't affect her the same way, but Frida was in the centre of things. Shirley had rented a house in town as she intended to remain in Fort Benton while Frida finished her last year of high school. But just after the divorce went through, Shirley had to go to Idaho to stay with her ailing mother, so Frida ended up back at the ranch with her father and his new wife who was expecting a baby. Frida was already in a paddy over her break-up with Clint Harrington, and her father's indifference to her and her mother was the final straw that pushed her over the edge. She was angry and defiant and wanted to hurt her father back, but of course, she only ended up hurting herself.

She started hanging out with the wrong crowd, including a young lout who introduced her to drugs. Josh was livid because she was defying him at every turn. After all, he was The Colonel. He wasn't used to people disobeying his orders. Two months later, without consulting Shirley, he kicked Frida out of the house and told her not to come back."

"So where did she go?"

"She went to Seattle with her boyfriend, but he soon abandoned her. It was downhill from there—drugs, prostitution, and ultimately AIDS, though no one knew what was happening at the time. That all came out much later. When Shirley returned home, she was frantic. She contacted Tim and Clint in Seattle, but they had no idea where Frida was. Shirley pleaded with Josh to help track Frida down but he refused, so she set off herself. She never made it. She had an accident on the panhandle. Killed outright, poor lady. She was probably so blinded by tears she wasn't fit to drive. And do you think Josh Henkel displayed an ounce of grief? Folks round here figured he was just pissed off that he'd already split his assets in the divorce when, if he'd waited a bit longer, he could have kept the lot."

"What a sad story," said Philippa sincerely. "How did they discover what happened to Frida at the end?"

Betty stabbed a neatly manicured figure in the air.

"Well, that was Clint Harrington," she explained. "He was so driven by guilt once he heard what had happened that he made it his personal mission to track Frida down and put things right. But by the time he found her, it was too late. After that, he never returned to Fort Benton. Figured he wasn't welcome and that folks blamed him for what happened, which a lot of them did. And still do. Amazing he has the guts to show his face here again. Still, I guess he felt he couldn't turn down his best friend, and at least he doesn't have to worry about meeting up with The Colonel. That's another bit of drama that's stirring up the town, though we can't blame Clint for that one."

"I heard about that," said Philippa. "A headless corpse in the river? What happened?"

Betty elaborated with gusto. Philippa listened intently.

"Are you serious?" she said when Betty had finished. "Are people really suggesting that his death wasn't suicide?"

"There's talk. Mind you, I wouldn't put it past Josh Henkel to kill himself and deliberately set it up so that his family would have nothing but trouble in the aftermath. He was a mean old bugger, that's for sure. I wouldn't worry about your friend," she added. "The gossip will die down soon enough. Nothing'll happen to the Mason family. Everyone round here loves them too much. It'll pass."

Betty popped a handful of nuts into her mouth and leaned back. Her husband turned from the television set and slid off his barstool.

"Well, if you've finished gossiping," he said to his wife, "we'd better hustle in there and have some dinner. You're welcome to join us, young lady," he added to Philippa.

"Thank you," said Philippa. "And thanks for forewarning me about the family skeletons," she added to Betty. "I'll certainly watch what I say."

Betty's face broke into a mischievous smile and she stared over Philippa's shoulder towards the louvered doors.

"You'd better start watching right now," she murmured. "One of the main players just came into the saloon."

Philippa swung round and looked towards the doors. Clint Harrington met her gaze and stopped in his tracks.

"Good God!" he exclaimed. "You again! What the hell are you doing in Fort Benton?"

Betty took her husband's arm and steered him towards the door.

"Come along, darlin'" she said. "I think our young friend just found herself a date for the evening."

She winked at Philippa and followed her husband out of the saloon.

Sarah Scott stayed to close up the coffee shop, so by the time she and Sally were home, it was five-thirty. Good job Sally's favourite dinner was Annie's Mac, Sarah thought, whipping up a salad to go on the side. As she served up the macaroni, closely watched by Shep whose large black head kept inching closer to the table top, Sally looked up and frowned at her mother.

"Are you going to the party tomorrow night?" she asked.

"I don't know. Probably not. Why?"

"Just wondered."

"Eat up," urged Sarah. "You must be starving after running around all day with your friends. All that fresh air must have given you an appetite."

"Maybe you should go," said Sally as her mother sat down with her at the table. "I can stay over at the O'Maras if you do."

Sarah gave her daughter a hard look.

"What brought this up?" she asked.

"There was a man who wanted to come see you today. Only Rory told him you were hiding out from someone, and I think the man figured it was him. So he went back the way he'd come."

Sarah set down her fork. She felt a hollow feeling in her chest.

"What did he look like?"

Sally delivered a remarkably accurate description. "He looked sad," she concluded. "I felt kind of sorry for him. I thought, maybe, if he was here for the wedding, you could talk to him at the party. Then he wouldn't feel so bad."

Sarah did not reply. Sally looked up and raised her eyebrows.

"So are you going to go?" she asked.

Sarah pulled herself together and picked up her fork again.

"We'll see," she said. "Now hurry up and finish your dinner."

Philippa's expression was glacial as she returned Clint Harrington's stare.

"You are the rudest man I've ever met," she said acerbically. "If you want to know why I'm here, you can change your tone and ask politely."

"Sorry." Clint grinned. "I keep putting your back up, don't I? It isn't intentional. It's just that you remind me of someone—"

"Frida Henkel. Yes, I know. And the memories aren't good ones."

Clint's grin morphed back into a glare.

"You know, you're really getting to me. You come out of no-where, looking the spitting image of Frida. You scare the hell out of me at the Wild Horse Monument, and now you pop up here and seem to know all about me. Who are you anyway?"

"I'm a friend of Robin and Tim's. I'm here for the wedding."

"I can't believe Tim told you about Frida Henkel."

"No, Tim didn't say anything, but I've heard all the gossip. You're a hot subject in this town."

"You'd think after a couple of decades people would find some-thing else to talk about." Clint climbed onto the barstool vacated by Betty McGill and scowled at the row of beer taps. "Can I buy you a refill?"

Philippa decided to sample a different local brew. Clint or-dered two of the same.

"I guess there's bound to be talk when you've come back af-ter such a long time," said Philippa, as the bartender served their drinks, "but it seems to me that the death of this man they call

The Colonel is another reason why everyone is digging up the past. You're being over-sensitive thinking it's all about you," she added. "You should stop looking for slights and try to use your time here to mend a few fences, particularly with Hanna Mason and Sarah Scott."

Clint took a long draught of his drink and thoughtfully set the glass down on the counter.

"I was going to," he said, "but Sarah wants nothing to do with me." He told Philippa about his encounter with the children on the green.

"I wouldn't go by what kids say. They can get the wrong perspective on things pretty easily. She might give you the cold shoulder, or she might not. You won't know until you try. You know the saying about faint hearts never winning fair ladies."

"What's the use? Sarah and I are fated never to get together." Clint drained his glass and glowered towards the flickering images on the television screen. "Let's face it, it was all my fault, so I don't know why I keep thinking I can put things right. Give me another," he added, turning towards the bartender.

"Well, if you're determined to dramatize yourself and do the doomed Heathcliff act, you'll never get anywhere," Philippa said tartly.

"You know, you may look like Frida, but you're sure as hell nothing like her." Clint grinned suddenly, belying his irritable tone. "Which is probably a good thing. She was all sugar on the surface and mamba venom underneath. You have a real sharp tongue, but I bet there's a kind heart below that prissy surface. Want to have dinner with me tonight?"

Philippa blinked at the abrupt shift, but before she could answer, her phone signalled a text message. It was from Bob Miller: *You were kidding, weren't you? R u OK?*

Philippa excused herself, drained the last dregs of her on-tap ale and texted a reply: *Not kidding. Am OK. Having a great time.*

She had barely put her phone away before it rang again. This time the message said: *So what are you doing now?*

Philippa shrugged apologetically to Clint and tapped in a speedy reply: *Sampling Moose Drool and Pig's Ass Porter.*

Then she turned off her phone and smiled at Clint Harrington.

"Why not?" she said. "Lead the way."

She slid off the barstool and followed her escort to the dining room. Bob Miller could wonder about that one all night.

The following day, Philippa slept in past eight o'clock. She stretched lazily; then, eyeing her cellphone on the bedside table, she leaned over and turned it on. Immediately, it buzzed a text message. Philippa grinned and looked to see what Bob had messaged this time: *On-tap beer. Right?*

"Know-it-all," said Philippa. She was about to put down the phone when it rang. Expecting it to be Bob Miller, she answered the call and was surprised to hear Robin's voice. Before Philippa could formulate an excuse for not letting her friend know she had arrived the previous day, Robin cut her off.

"Philippa, thank goodness I caught you. I really need to talk with you. Somewhere away from the ranch."

Philippa felt a rush of apprehension. Other than her sister, Juliette, Robin was the most calmly balanced person she had ever met. To hear the distress in her friend's voice was alarming, especially as the wedding was only two days away.

"Robin, what's wrong? What on earth has happened?"

"I'll tell you when I see you. Let's meet for coffee before your rehearsal? Afterwards I'll take you over to the church hall and introduce you to the organist."

"All right. What time and where?"

"There's only one coffee house across from the riverside park. Just go up the main street and you'll see it. You can't miss it. It's called the—"

"Old Fort Coffee House. The concierge told me. I'll be there."

Robin rang off. By now wide-awake, Philippa put her phone down and threw back the bed covers. It was time to get up. As she showered and dressed, she pondered the reason for the call. What could have happened to upset Robin so badly? With a growing sense of unease, she headed down to the dining room. The breakfast buffet was a generous spread, but she was still full from yesterday's dinner, so she made do with fruit and a croissant. Then she put on her coat and headed out the front entrance. She had the best part of an hour before she was to meet Robin, and she would occupy herself with a walk through the riverside park and a tour of the local sights.

Once outside the hotel, she pulled her coat collar high around her neck and tied her scarf firmly in place. Then she retrieved her toque from her bag and pulled it over her hair. The day was bright and sunny, but there was a distinct chill in the patches of shade and the wind was gusting ferociously. Overhead, the branches of the cottonwoods were rustling and shaking in the breeze, and the fallen leaves were hurtling across the road. Philippa had no desire to end up with sinusitis right before the wedding. Voices had to be protected. Once snugly wrapped in wool, she strolled down to the river and turned towards the footbridge.

The sporadic gusts seemed even stronger by the water. The sign at the info centre was swaying back and forth and the river was rippled by the wind. A statue of Lewis and Clark held pride of place on the riverbank, although further along, Philippa found a cowboy statue and a keelboat that had been used in the movie, *The Big Sky*.

Her progress was slow because she paused to read the interpretive signs along the way. As Fort Benton was located at the point on the Missouri where the steamboats stopped and the stage-coaches began, it had been the trade centre for the American and Canadian West from the 1850s until 1887. There was a lot of history in the little riverside town. By the time Philippa had learned about Fort Campbell and the fur trade, the Lewis and Clark Expedition, the Nez Perce War, the Great Northern Railway and the Coulson Steamboat Line, her brain was so overloaded with information that she gave up reading the signs, and simply let her eyes drift onto the sparkling water.

As she continued along the path, she noticed three flagpoles, their flags flapping so hard that they were beating against the poles. As she drew nearer, she could hear the poles squeaking as if in protest. A sudden gust lifted the flags, and they uncoiled and waved gracefully on the breeze. Amazed and delighted, Philippa saw that the Canadian flag was flying between the United States and Montana flags.

By the time she reached the end of the river path, it was ten-fifteen. Philippa realized that a visit to the fort would have to wait, but she just had time for a walk through the war-veterans' park. It was easy to locate, its entrance flagged by a white monument topped by a statue of a soldier. She entered the park and explored the field, reading the inscriptions on the various stones. Every branch of the military appeared to be honoured. There was a circle of mock periscopes, each one bearing a plaque dedicated to a ship in the US Navy. Both World Wars were commemorated, along with the Korean War. Philippa also found the dog memorial mentioned by the hotel proprietress. More than 4000 military working dogs had served in the Viet Nam War and had saved over 10,000 American lives, yet they were ultimately left to their fate overseas. Philippa felt saddened as she read the inscription: *They were our heroes, our best friends and companions and we will never forget them.*

Deeply moved, Philippa saw that there were stones honouring individual dogs. One stood out by virtue of its name, though it was hardly unexpected, given that the dog's hometown was Fort Benton. Shep, a German shepherd, had served in Vietnam. His dates were 1966-1975. Nine years old. Presumably killed in service, and perhaps, thought Philippa, that was preferable to being parted from his handler and abandoned in Southeast Asia.

Philippa sighed and glanced at her watch. Robin would be at the café soon. It was time to move on. She left the park and turned onto the street. The wind was still gusting ferociously and she found herself following a bouncing knot of tumbleweed as it rolled erratically along the road. About the only things that weren't in motion that day, she reflected, were Lewis and Clark, the lone cowboy and Shep.

Philippa strolled down the sidewalk, delighting in the Old West atmosphere. The town's buildings alternated between late-nineteenth century wooden houses and clusters of three-storey buildings in red, white or salmon coloured brick, some of which bore wooden balconies that seemed designed for western-movie shootouts. However, when she reached the coffee shop, she saw that it was located in a freshly painted white bungalow, very much a contrast to the ancient-looking red brick structure that nestled against it on the southern side.

As she walked up the steps, the door opened and a young woman emerged, ruining the Wild West illusion. She was needle-thin, encased in black leather and pierced with glittering studs. Her black-ringed eyes and spiked hair complemented the Goth fashion statement; however, the girl's friendly smile contradicted her otherwise startling appearance and she politely held the door for Philippa to go through. Philippa thanked her and stepped into the coffee house.

It was a cheery space, with tastefully colourful décor. Behind the counter, a woman was grinding fresh coffee, which gave off a headily welcoming aroma. The soft strains of a tune that Philippa recognized as a theme from the movie *Anonymous* drifted from a speaker at the corner of the room and competed with the steady groan of the grinder. The shop was warm, so Philippa pulled off her toque and stuffed it into her bag. When she looked up, she saw that the woman behind the counter had turned and was gaping at her with the same stunned expression that Clint Harrington had displayed at the Wild Horse Monument. Philippa wondered how many other people were going to react this way during her stay in Montana.

Deciding to take the initiative, she gave a friendly smile and said, "Yes, I know. I bear a resemblance to someone who used to live in this town, but it's purely coincidental. I'm a visitor from Canada who's here for Tim and Robin's wedding."

The woman at the counter relaxed and managed a half-hearted smile, but her face remained guarded. Before any words could be exchanged, a jingling sound heralded another customer and Philippa turned to see Robin entering the shop. Uneasily, she noticed the shadows under her friend's eyes. However, Robin covered her fatigue well. Maintaining her usual gracious manner, she inquired whether or not Philippa had met the café owner, and when the answer was negative, introduced them.

Philippa eyed Sarah Scott curiously, wondering if she still carried a torch for Clint Harrington. Probably not, she decided, since Sarah had married and had a child. A good husband and a young daughter would have obliterated the memory of a teenage crush by now.

Unaware that Philippa's mind was drifting, Robin chattered on about Sarah's influence on the bookstore. "Sarah is a genius when it comes to selecting stock and organizing promotions." Robin waved towards the pile of paperbacks on the table by the door. "Those are from the book launch last month. Hanna and Gordon said the event was fabulous and the book is excellent. It was written by the wife of a man who served in the same unit as Gordon and Tim's uncle."

Philippa picked up a copy and turned it over to read the back cover.

"Oh!" she cried. "It's a novel about the war dogs. I was just looking at the memorial, but I didn't realize Tim's uncle was a dog-handler in Viet Nam."

"That's why Gordon and Hanna were so interested in the book," said Robin.

Sarah smiled.

"Yes, they were. They came to the launch and brought the boys with them. They bought a copy for themselves, and young Jack bought a copy as a birthday present for his great-grandma—with his own money yet."

"Have you read it?" Philippa asked Robin.

"No. Too sad for me." Robin was very softhearted. Philippa often wondered how she survived in the world of professional opera.

"There was an initiative to bring the dogs back," Sarah interjected. "A few handlers did manage to have their dogs returned to the States, but the majority were either euthanized or abandoned. Not a glorious episode in our history."

"Did Tim's uncle bring his dog back?" Philippa asked.

"No," said Robin. "Shep and Jackson were both killed in action. In a way, it was just as well," she said sadly. "From what I've been told, Jackson loved that dog so much he'd never have abandoned him. Perhaps it was better that they went together."

Sarah smiled ruefully. "Ruth Mason told me once that Jackson shared everything with Shep. If she served up sausages, Jackson would do One-for-you-and-one-for-me all the way through the meal."

"You can see why Ruth is so close to her great-grandson," said Robin. "It's as if Jackson is living all over again in young Jack. He's a real farm boy . . . a hunting, shooting and fishing tintype of his great uncle, with the same passion for dogs."

"He certainly has that," said Sarah. "My Sally adores Jack, but she's always worried that he's only her friend because he loves our dog—another Shep," she added for Philippa's benefit.

Philippa nodded. "There are a lot of—"

"—Sheps in Fort Benton," Sarah and Robin chorused.

All three broke into laughter. The noise disturbed the sleeping spaniel in the corner and it heaved itself upright and looked indignantly at the trio by the counter.

"Sorry, Cappuccino," said Sarah. "Go back to sleep. Now, what can I get you ladies?" She turned to Philippa and Robin and assumed her official role.

Robin and Philippa ordered lattes. Philippa pointed at the array of pastries under the glass counter top. "Could I have one of those too," she added. "I haven't eaten since breakfast." She turned to pick up a book from the table by the door. "And I'll take this too. I'd like to read it."

Sarah rang the items through and made the coffees. As she placed their order on the counter, the door opened and a young couple came through. Sarah attended to her new customers and Robin led Philippa to the small lounge at the end of the shop, which was divided from the brightly covered café tables by a set of black iron railings. The shop was split level, and they had to go down two steps to the lounge, so the area was relatively private. The room held two comfortable leather sofas with patchwork quilts for throws. Between them was a small bookcase overflowing with paperbacks. The end tables were covered with magazines and the walls were lined with local artwork. One of the larger paintings depicted the Shep of the statue standing on the station platform watching an incoming train.

Once they took off their coats and settled with their drinks, Robin explained why she had wanted to meet privately. With a growing sense of horror, Philippa listened as her friend described the rumours that were being spread and the tension in the Mason household. Robin concluded by repeating the conversation she had overheard between Hanna Mason and Brianne Henkel.

"Hanna is beside herself. She's ready to pass up her inheritance, just because she's terrified that Gordon is implicated in The Colonel's death."

"That's foolish. The stepsister could be making it all up."

Robin shook her head.

"No, that's the trouble. Hanna knows that Gordon was at the Henkel ranch that day. He found out what the boys were planning and went around to stop them. He was too late, because the paint was already all over the barn walls when he arrived, but he did retrieve the boys and bring them home."

"Did he talk to The Colonel while he was there?"

"He refuses to talk about the day. All he will say is that he caught the boys in the act and brought them home."

"So given his silence, and the fact that Brianne Henkel claims to have seen him coming up from the river right after the gunshot, Hanna has made up her mind that her husband killed her father."

Robin nodded. "Yes, but I'm sure she's wrong. I think fear, and her love for her family, is causing her thinking to be skewed. Gordon's a good man. He'd never do anything dishonourable. I know there has to be some other solution."

"What does Tim think about it all?"

Robin's face shadowed.

"I tried talking to Tim, and he clammed up as well and refused to discuss it. He's never shut me out like this before. The whole thing has become a nightmare for me as well as for Hanna. How can I go forward with the wedding when I feel like this? I don't know what to do."

Philippa looked at her friend, amazed.

"Robin, Tim is as solid as they come. You've just said that he and Gordon are good men who wouldn't do anything wrong. Why would you be having second thoughts about your wedding?"

Robin looked utterly miserable.

"I can't help it. It's like a wall between us. I can't get beyond it. That's why I've come to you."

"But how can I help?"

"You're clever at unravelling mysteries."

Philippa opened her mouth to protest but Robin quieted her with a gesture and continued: "You'll be at all the events. You could talk to people, dig for information without being too obvious. You're an outsider, and people might tell you things they wouldn't pass on to Hanna."

Philippa set her mug on the table and shook her head.

"Robin, just because I helped sort out that mess in New York doesn't mean I'm qualified to figure out what's going on here. Surely you're not expecting me to play amateur sleuth and start ferreting out stuff about your future in-laws."

Robin sat forward and looked Philippa in the eye.

"That's just what I want you to do. I want you to find out the truth."

Philippa returned Robin's level stare.

"From what you've told me, there are so many reasons to query the suicide verdict that I'm amazed the police chief hasn't called in the entire Mason family for questioning. What if the truth is something you don't want to hear?"

"There's no other choice," said Robin. "I won't rest until I know what's going on. Obviously, I can't go to the police, so I've come to you. Now—" Robin set down her cup and stood up— "we should get moving if we're going to be at your practice on time."

Robin put on her coat, her air now brisk and professional. Philippa sighed. Robin might feel better for having unloaded her burden onto her friend, but Philippa's mood was far from calm. She remembered Bob Miller's reply to her headless-corpse text message. He was not going to be impressed to hear that The Colonel's death might not have been suicide—and he'd go ballistic if he knew that the family Philippa was visiting might be harbouring a killer. Not that Philippa had any intention of telling him. But she wished she had texted back: *Yes, just kidding.*

Philippa felt she had been handed an impossible task. However, she could not ignore her friend's plea and she had to admit that her curiosity was piqued. Gathering information would not be easy, but she could capitalize on her resemblance to Frida Henkel and use it as an icebreaker to get people talking about The Colonel.

From what Philippa had heard of her look-a-like, Frida had exuded glamour and sex-appeal well beyond her years, so, when dressing for the party that evening, Philippa donned the flashier of the two cocktail dresses she had brought with her, put on what her father would have described as full war-paint, and emerged from her hotel room ready for action. By the time she reached the top of the grand staircase, the clamour of voices from below indicated that the party was in full swing. As she descended, Philippa felt glad she'd worn the sequined dress for she could see enough glitter in the lobby to light a fairground. When she reached the bottom of the staircase, she peered through the crowd, trying to pick out someone she knew. After a moment, amid the sea of faces, she saw Betty McGill, whose rosy countenance matched the scarlet velvet of her evening jacket. Betty caught her eye and waved her over.

"Well, don't you look stunning!" she exclaimed, as Philippa reached her side. "Midnight blue is gorgeous with your hair. You're doing the Grand Union proud."

"So I should. It's such an elegant hotel. I feel as if I've stepped back in time. Don't you love staying here?"

"Oh, we're not booked in here. We just come to eat or visit the saloon. We're staying at the RV Park at the other end of town. Once the wedding is over, we're heading South."

"You're in a motorhome?"

"Yes. We take a trip every year. Only way to travel. No packing or unpacking, no worrying about bed bugs, no having to stop for a bathroom break and finding turds left by their namesakes in public toilets. Can't beat it. So," she added, abruptly changing the subject, "how was your dinner with Clint Harrington? He's quite a hunk, isn't he?"

"Yes," said Philippa, "but a rather distracted hunk. I suspect he spent the entire evening trying to decide whether to come on to me or to use me as a sounding board over his regrets for not coming on to Sarah Scott when he had the chance. For someone who's supposed to be a hotshot lawyer, he's pretty indecisive."

"Ah well, he wasn't the only young man who got knocked out at the knees by Frida Henkel. She had a way of looking at them that had all the boys puffing like The Little Train that Could, our present police chief being one of them," she added, nodding towards a tall, well-built man who was staring unashamedly at Philippa.

Philippa glanced round to see where Betty was looking. The man met her gaze for a moment, and then turned away. Philippa felt uneasy. The man's fair good looks spoke of country-boy hospitality, but his eyes had not been friendly.

"That's the sheriff?"

"Yup. He was at school with Frida. He had the hots for her just as bad as Clint Harrington, but luckily for him, she wasn't interested. That girl was nothing but trouble. Just like her old man."

Before Philippa could comment, she felt a hand on her arm. She turned to see Robin at her side. Robin looked stunning, in a cream cocktail dress slashed dramatically with one diagonal green stripe across the bodice. Her tawny hair was swept up, revealing jade earrings in the shape of eagles in flight. Philippa was not surprised at her friend's elegance, but she was astonished to see how excited, vibrant, and happy she looked. The tension of the previous day seemed to have melted away. Curiously, Philippa wondered what had triggered her friend's change of mood.

Robin flashed an apologetic smile at the older woman.

"Excuse me, Betty, I need to borrow Philippa for a moment." She whisked Philippa away and guided her into the dining room. Then she pointed towards a dignified-looking gentleman at the far end of the room.

"That's Doc Brady," hissed Robin, "and you won't believe this. He just pulled me and Hanna aside and apologized for the fact that he upset us by questioning the results of the autopsy. He says he's now perfectly satisfied that everything is in order. You can't imagine how relieved we are."

Philippa was bewildered.

"But what about the conversation you overheard between Hanna and her stepsister? How can that be explained away?"

"That's okay, too. Doc Brady had a talk with the sheriff. Joe Kramer knows that Gordon was at the Henkel ranch that day— and that he went down to the deck by the river—but The Colonel was already dead by then. He must have shot himself just before Gordon reached him."

"So were there witnesses?"

"I've no idea, but it doesn't matter. The case is closed. What's more, The Colonel had been on the deck for over an hour, so he couldn't have seen the graffiti. That means Hanna can stop worrying that the boys drove him to suicide. I told you, it's all resolved. Forget everything I said yesterday. Just come and enjoy yourself— in fact, come and meet Doc. He's a grand old character."

Robin led Philippa over to the grey-haired man. She made the introductions, then excused herself and slipped away. Philippa saw the startled look in the doctor's eyes and braced herself for the predictable comments.

"My," said Doc Brady, "the resemblance is remarkable."

"So I've been told."

"But only skin deep, so your friend tells me. I gather you're an opera singer like Robin."

"I wish," said Philippa. "I mean I am an opera singer, but certainly not in Robin's class."

"Well, Robin speaks very highly of you. I'm looking forward to hearing you sing tomorrow. I must say your appearance will turn a few heads, though. What a good job we're meeting you at the party tonight. That way, when you sing at the wedding, we'll be seeing you as yourself and not viewing you as an echo from the past."

Philippa felt smug. Doc Brady had given her the perfect opening to talk about The Colonel. Robin might be satisfied with the doctor's about-face, but Philippa was inclined to be sceptical. She asked, "Was Frida Henkel as difficult a character as I've been told?"

Doc sighed and shook his head sadly.

"Frida was her own worst enemy," he said. "She was so different from her sister. Hanna inherited their mother's kind nature and their father's disciplined character, but in the gene-pool shuffle, poor Frida landed the weaknesses from both sides: her father's callousness and overdriven libido, and her mother's emotional vulnerability."

From the corner of her eye, Philippa noticed that the sheriff had entered the dining room. Uneasily, she was conscious that he was looking her way again. Deliberately, she turned her back and focussed on Doc Brady.

"Josh Henkel must have been vulnerable too," she said, "if he ended up committing suicide."

Doc Brady frowned.

"Cancer has made tougher men than Josh opt for a quick exit."

"I heard that you gave him a checkup a month ago and found him entirely fit. I was told that the autopsy report knocked you for a loop."

"Nobody likes realizing they've missed something so important. It's never fun to admit you've made a mistake."

"That's true," Philippa said brightly. "So you no longer think that the pathologist made an error? You don't believe there was a deliberate cover-up?"

Doc Brady looked sternly down at Philippa. "No, I don't, young lady," he said, "and please don't put words in my mouth."

Stiffly polite, Doc Brady excused himself and moved away.

Philippa watched him go, noticing that he paused to talk with the sheriff. No doubt, the doctor would be filling him in on who she was. She shrugged and glanced around the room, looking for familiar faces. As her eyes swept the area, she saw Clint Harrington making his way towards her. He was eyeing her appreciatively.

"You look stunning," he said, when he reached her. "Can I get you a drink?"

"White wine would be great."

Clint nodded and disappeared into the crowd. Philippa became aware of a potent smell of aftershave overpowering the various perfumes and food odors that were mingling throughout the room. She turned to see a huge mountain of a man in a pinstriped suit peering down at her through horn-rimmed spectacles.

"So are you the little lady that Clint had to square things up with?" he boomed cheerfully.

"No. That's not me. I only met Clint a few days ago. How do you know him?"

"Through Gordon Mason. Gordon and I own a sporting-goods store in Great Falls. Clint was down for a couple of days doing legal work for us."

"Great Falls? That's not far from here, is it?"

"Less than an hour's drive. Clint figured he could combine the business trip with a detour up here. Said he had unfinished business to settle. Know it was something to do with a lady. Wanted to deal with it before he came for the wedding."

Philippa blinked.

"I'm confused. I met Clint when he was driving out here, and that was only two days ago. And he got here before me. How could he have spent two days in Great Falls?"

The man laughed.

"No, not this trip. This was last month. He was mighty angry because he'd discovered that a letter he'd written years ago had been hijacked by Gordon's jerk of a father-in-law. Don't know the details, but it was all to do with a woman. Still, if it wasn't you, my lips are sealed. Hey, here he comes. Guess I'd better not ask him if he put things right with his lady friend, seeing as he's getting you a drink." The man winked. "I'll leave that to you to sort out."

He maneuvered his bulk through the crowd by the dining-room doors and disappeared into the other room. Clint worked his way over and handed Philippa a glass of wine. Philippa's eyes narrowed.

"You talked a lot about Sarah Scott last night," she said, "but you didn't tell me that you made a special trip here last month so you could break the ice before the wedding."

Clint looked at her coolly.

"I suppose Bradley Peterson told you that."

"Yes. He said you made a side trip from Great Falls last month just so you could talk with Sarah."

"Do I detect a note of jealousy in those pretty soprano tones?"

"Not at all. I'm just curious. Did you come here to see Sarah?"

"I planned to. I lost my nerve. So are you going to drink that wine or gape at me like a goldfish?"

Before Philippa could gather her wits and reply, she was startled to see the sheriff materialize at Clint's side. Joe Brady was another hunk, thought Philippa. About the same age as Clint Harrington, equally tall and handsome, but the expression on his face was far from congenial. She seemed to be afflicted with good-looking men with touchy tempers.

"You're Philippa Beary?" The man's voice was brusque.

Philippa nodded.

"I'm Joe Kramer, the Chouteau County police chief. Can we have a word?"

Philippa's eyes widened, but she did not resist as the sheriff took her elbow and steered her towards the front entrance. It was obvious that he needed privacy for whatever he wanted to say. Curious to know why he had singled her out, she followed him outside, barely noticing the chill in the night air.

The statue of Shep loomed out of the darkness, gleaming a soft gold in the light spilling from the lobby windows, but the cottonwood trees and the slow-moving river had disappeared into a wall of blackness. The hum of voices from the party was muted, although the gravelly tones of a country singer bewailing his lost love were just audible over the rustling leaves and the sporadic noise of traffic from the bridge. The sheriff moved Philippa away from the entrance doors and the music faded. Now, only the sound of the wind in the cottonwood trees filled the night air. Philippa glanced back towards the hotel. Elongated triangles of yellow light marked the swag-draped windows, but the brick walls had melted into the night. The effect was surreal: Victoriana on black velvet.

Suddenly conscious that the sheriff was speaking to her, Philippa pulled herself back to the present and turned to face him. His voice was smoothly mellow, but his message was terse and crystal clear.

"Have a good time at the wedding, Miss Beary, and enjoy your sight-seeing before you head back to Canada. But a word of warning. While you're here, stick to socializing and don't nose around asking questions. And tell your cop friend to butt out too. You stay out of our business, and we'll make sure you have a nice visit and a safe return home. Get it."

Without waiting for a reply, Joe Kramer strode back into the hotel. Stunned, Philippa watched him go. As she stared after him, Clint Harrington came out through the lobby doors.

"My God," he said. "You still look like a goldfish. You obviously need another drink. Come on. Back inside before you freeze."

Clint put his arm around Philippa's shoulders and led her back into the hotel. Neither of them noticed the car that was pulling into the parking lot. Neither did they see the woman who was watching them as they passed by Shep's statue, still bathed in the golden light from the windows. They disappeared inside and were swallowed up by the bustling crowd.

Sarah Scott watched them go. Then she pulled into a parking space, reversed back out and drove out of the lot. Unnoticed by the crowd in the hotel, the car turned onto the main street and disappeared into the night.

The next hour passed in a blur. Philippa smiled outwardly but inwardly she was seething. There was only one explanation for the sheriff's outburst, and she was determined to phone Bob Miller and find out what he'd done to cause her to be rapped over the knuckles. She had planned to leave the party early, since the last thing she wanted was to talk for hours and strain her voice, but now she was even more anxious to get away. As soon as she could politely excuse herself, she returned to her room so she could call Miller in private, but to her frustration, after several tries, she only got through to his voicemail. Finally, leaving voicemail and text messages for him to call her, she gave up, got ready for bed and soothed her irritation by reading the book she had bought at the coffee shop.

At first, she could not relax and drowsiness eluded her, but by eleven o'clock, she was tired enough to set the book aside and settle down. She turned off the bedside lamp, yet the story of the service dogs still hovered in her head, and as soon as she lay back on the pillow, she drifted into a troubled sleep. In her dream, she strolled through fields of sagebrush that were overrun with black German shepherds whose shapes twisted and turned until their silhouettes became jagged and they were no longer dogs, but metal horses, closing in on her and threatening to crush her between their ser-rated flanks. As she recoiled, drawing her arms in tightly around her body so as not to be struck by the flying metallic figures, the horses receded and dissolved into a solid black sheet. She stepped towards the dark wall and saw her image in the gleaming surface, but as she stared at the reflection, the eyes in the palely gleaming face grew wild. Terrified, she turned to run, but the image had stepped out of the mirror and was now standing in front of her, blocking her way.

Sweating and rigid, Philippa woke with a start. Glancing at the clock on the bedside table, she saw that it was only six o'clock. Restlessly, she remained in bed for another half-hour, but finally, unable to sleep, she got up. So much for being in great shape to perform, she thought fretfully. Then her professional instincts kicked in and she pulled herself together. A leisurely soak in the bath would soothe her stiff muscles and do a lot to restore her spirits. She padded into the bathroom and turned on the taps in the vast white tub.

By the time she was out of the bath, it was still only seven-thirty. However, she felt human again, so she dressed in comfortable walking clothes and started down for breakfast. Halfway down the stairs, she could smell the tempting aroma of bacon waft-ing through the lobby, so she knew that food was already being served. The dining room was empty except for the staff members, who were setting out the buffet on a long table that stretched the length of the end wall, and two elderly couples who were filling their plates from the platters as each one was put in place. The smaller tables had been set with white tablecloths and each one held a vase with a single rose at its centre. Without the crowds of the previous evening, Philippa was able to admire the room's elegant wainscoting and the long windows, gracefully framed in cream velour swags. A huge painting of Fort Benton in the early days graced the longest wall, but the other walls were decorated with shimmering wall sconces and smaller prints or lithographs on local historical subjects.

Philippa helped herself to a generous serving of eggs, bacon and sausages. The wedding ceremony was not until one o'clock and she never liked to sing on a full stomach, so a big breakfast this early would fuel her up nicely and be well digested before she had to perform. She bypassed the white-clothed tables and slid into one of the booths that lined the right-hand side of the dining room. Predictably, she had no sooner started on her breakfast than Bob Miller called. Between mouthfuls, Philippa indignantly relayed the warning she had received from Sheriff Kramer.

"What have you been up to?" she demanded.

Miller seemed cheerfully indifferent to her fractious mood.

"It's your own fault," he said. "You text me about a headless corpse and tell me you're not kidding. You drop hints but don't fill me in. What am I supposed to do? Knowing what a buttinsky you can be, I was worried that you might be getting involved in something dangerous, so I called the local station, told them who I was and said I had a friend down here who'd mentioned the case, and I asked if there was anything I should be worried about. I had a nice chat with the cop at the other end, but I guess the police chief got wind of it, and you were warned off."

"How could you interfere like that? You made me feel like a perfect fool."

Miller's tone became serious.

"Actually, I'm sorry I did," he said. "I had no intention of stirring things up. Given the reaction I caused, I'm getting bad vibes about the situation. The whole thing has a bad smell to it and I'll be glad when you're back home. Don't go sticking your neck out."

"I had no intention of sticking my neck out." Philippa was about to continue when she became aware that the couple at the nearby table was staring at her. She lowered her voice. "Look. Can I call you back in ten minutes? Let me finish my breakfast and go up to my room. It's pretty public here."

Miller agreed and they ended the call. Philippa went back to her breakfast, assiduously avoiding the curious stares of the other diners. She demolished the rest of her meal with downcast eyes, resolutely studying the intricate pink curlicues on the carpet that vaguely reminded her of wrought-iron gates. Then she drained her coffee cup and stood up.

Five minutes later, she was back in her room. She pulled out her cellphone and tapped in Miller's number. He picked up right away. Philippa came right to the point and relayed everything that Robin had told her. Her annoyance had faded, and she had to admit it was a relief to be able to talk to Miller about the situation.

"Honestly, Bob," she concluded, "if Robin hadn't told me about the rumours, I wouldn't have known there was any question about the suicide verdict—and even though she says everything's fine now, I think there's something very odd going on. I didn't want to stumble on a mystery, but I'm involved now whether I like it or not. I'm ready to bet that Doc Brady was warned off, just the way I was, and for some reason, he's knuckled under."

"Look. Stay out of it. If you hear anything inadvertently, pass it on to me and let me check it out."

"I can tell you're taking this seriously," said Philippa. "Your associate down here obviously doesn't think Josh Henkel committed suicide."

"He's sceptical," Miller admitted. "I can understand why Robin is worried about her future in-laws, but if it makes you feel any better, I gather there's an awful lot of suspects besides the Masons. For starters, there's the non-grieving widow who was supposed to be at the hairdresser at the time of her husband's death but has a ninety-minute window of opportunity when she could have returned home."

"Really? I didn't know that."

"There's also a money-grubbing daughter who was riding on the estate at the time of her father's death."

"That I knew, because she claims she heard the shot and saw Gordon Mason running up from the river."

"Yes, well, she could be lying. There's also a neighbour on the adjacent property who hated Henkel's guts because he shot his dog, and there are several town citizens who have reason to be relieved that Henkel has gone to his maker. I can tell you this much, if I'd been investigating the case, there's no damn way I'd have let the inquest get away with that suicide verdict. There are far too many unanswered questions."

"So your Montana colleague does think there's something sinister going on?"

"Pretty well. That's why I'd like you to stay out of it. If you want to talk about the case, phone me."

"Why would the police chief risk his job allowing a cover-up?" said Philippa. "It's a pretty dicey thing to do, just because he's glad the man's dead. How much power does the sheriff have anyway?"

"Lots. The Chouteau County Sheriff's office covers five towns and all the rural areas in the county. It also covers coroner duties, search and rescue, and a bunch of other departments."

"Now, that's the other thing that's troubling. Doc Brady originally challenged the autopsy report, but now he says it's okay. If there is a cover-up, he and the sheriff are in it together, but how on earth would they be able to get the coroner to bend the rules?"

Miller's voice hardened.

"I don't know, but my buddy did pass on one significant bit of information. There was a train crash in Great Falls just before Henkel died and the pathologist who would normally have performed the autopsy was called away to help. A young med student who had just qualified handled the post mortem, and he left town the next day."

"He disappeared?"

"No. He was due to go to Vermont to take up a position there."

"What are you suggesting? That he missed something due to his lack of experience?"

"Not necessarily. He might have been spot on, but reports come in on computers these days, and you know as well as I do that files can be altered very easily. I'm going to track the guy down and make sure his verbal report is consistent with what was presented at the inquest. And in the meantime, you keep your mouth shut and stay out of trouble. I'll tell you what I find out after you come home, but you let me do the investigating. Deal?"

"Deal," said Philippa. She was very happy to hand over the sleuthing to someone with official connections. There was something about the whole situation that was making her extremely uneasy, and for once, she felt out of her depth. With a sense of relief, she ended the call. She felt less alone now that she had talked with Bob. But with a sudden wave of longing, she wished desperately that he were there with her.

⥤╪⥢

Philippa felt restless after her conversation with Bob Miller. She had several hours before she had to change for the wedding, so she decided to stretch her legs and walk along the river. The fresh air was invigorating and she felt better for the outing, but once she returned to the hotel, she still had time on her hands, so she went up to her room and tucked up on the bed to read more of her book.

Sarah Scott had been right about the novel. It was a moving and engaging read. Although the book was fiction, Philippa suspected that the stories of the soldiers and their service dogs were based on real-life incidents. There were two main protagonists, both passionately committed to the dogs they worked with, which was hardly surprising since the dogs had saved their lives on more than one occasion. Their commanding officer was a remarkable character too—far from likeable, yet his toughness had got his men out of several tight situations. War could make heroes out of people that were often detestable in civilian life, Philippa thought ruefully. She had reached the part of the book when the Americans were starting to evacuate Vietnam. The hero was worrying about his dog, but he had heard that an initiative was underway to quarantine some of the dogs with a view to sending them back to the States. Having read the information on the monument in the memorial park, Philippa read on uneasily. She hoped that the dog in the novel would prove to be one of the lucky ones, but she had a horrible feeling the book was not going to have a happy ending.

Sighing, she saw the time. Eleven-thirty. Time to freshen up, change and set off for the church. She put the book aside and slid off the bed. Half an hour later, as she checked her appearance in the full-length mirror, there was a tap on her door. She opened it to see Clint Harrington standing in the corridor. He looked particularly dashing in a dark grey suit and a deep pink shirt that, Philippa acknowledged, could only be worn by a man with a strong macho image. Clint was eyeing her with an equally approving look.

"Nice outfit," he said. "Can I give you a ride over?"

Philippa mentally viewed the gleaming silver Cadillac and responded with a smile.

"Why not?" she said.

⊱⊰

The wedding went off beautifully. To Philippa's relief, her voice struck an immediate love affair with the acoustics of the country church and her songs, floating ethereally over the congregation, drew blissful smiles from the sea of faces in front of her. The ceremony invoked the prerequisite number of handkerchiefs and Philippa needed every ounce of self-control to prevent herself from tearing up until her final song was over.

Afterwards, as the guests drifted outside, Philippa found Clint waiting for her. She demurred when he offered to drive her out to the ranch.

"I don't want to stay late," she said. "I'm leaving tomorrow at the crack of dawn. Besides," she added, noticing Sarah Scott chatting with Hanna and Ruth Mason by the church door, "you have unfinished business to attend to. Turning up with me is hardly going to help, is it?"

"Maybe I need you for moral support. A lot of people wouldn't even look my way at the party last night."

"I'll come with you if you promise to ask Sarah Scott for a dance once the party gets underway."

"What if she tells me to get lost?"

"That's a chance you'll have to take. Of course, it'd be a whole lot easier if you just went over now and said hello. Come on, I'll even go with you."

Hanna had moved on to talk with the reverend, but Sarah still stood by Ruth Mason. Philippa was struck by how pale and frail the elderly woman looked, yet her air of serene contentment was so radiant that she glowed with an ethereal beauty that made her as lovely as the young woman standing beside her.

Clint hesitated. Then he nodded. Philippa nudged him forward, but as they approached, Sarah Scott slipped away and joined her daughter who was standing in a circle of immaculately dressed children solemnly sporting suits and party frocks. Sarah took Sally's hand and whisked her towards the row of cars parked by the curb.

Clint shrugged.

"She saw us coming."

"Oh well, you can try again at the party. Come on. Let's get over there. I haven't eaten since breakfast and I'm always ravenous after I sing."

As Clint drove over the bridge, Philippa glanced downriver towards the camelback spans of the old crossing. She thought of the well-behaved children she'd seen at the church. They had all seemed cheerful and happy, but she wondered how much they were inwardly troubled by the memory of the grim discovery they had made while playing there. Thinking of the children reminded her of the long history of friendship between their parents.

"Did you and your friends have much to do with Josh Henkel when you were young?" she asked Clint. "Did you visit the girls at the Henkel Ranch?"

"Not really. The Colonel had a reputation for being a real mean bastard and we avoided him if we could. Besides, the Masons were the hospitable ones. Tim's grandparents loved to have the kids around, so Sarah and the Henkel girls hung out at their place."

"Were the girls scared of their father?"

"Hanna was. Frida wasn't, but then she was a little spitfire, all piss and vinegar just like her Dad—which was why what happened to her was so tragic. She was so sure of her father's love for her that she figured she could defy him and get away with it, and when he cast her off like a bag of garbage, she fell apart."

"Did Josh Henkel show any remorse after she died? I presume you got in touch with him to let him know."

"I wrote to him, but he never replied."

"Did you contact Hanna?"

"Of course I did. I wrote to her at her college address, and I enclosed a letter for Sarah, because she was off on a gap year and I had no idea how to track her down. I never received a reply from either of them so I assumed that they wanted nothing to do with me." Clint's jaw stiffened and his eyes grew hard. "I found out much later that the letters had never reached them."

"Why not?"

"Henkel had gone to the college to tell Hanna what had happened to her sister. I suppose he had a modicum of conscience about parental duty and figured he should give her the details himself. The bastard saw my letter in her box in the hall and pocketed it. I went all those years thinking Hanna and Sarah hated me for what happened to Frida, and they went all those years thinking I didn't care."

"Have you made your peace with Hanna?"

"Yes. We talked after the cocktail party. She promised to talk to Sarah and let her know what had happened, but judging by the way she acted at the church, it's too late. Look, can we talk about something else? This is getting depressing."

"Sorry. Henkel really does have a lot to answer for, doesn't he? You must have been furious when you found out what he'd done. Was that why you decided to take a side trip here from Great Falls?"

Clint turned and glared at Philippa.

"What the hell sort of question is that?"

"A logical one. If I'd learned that someone had intercepted an important letter and caused me a lot of grief, I'd have wanted to face them and tell them what I thought of them."

"I told you. I contemplated coming. Then I changed my mind. I lost my nerve."

Clint swung the Cadillac onto a road that branched off to the right. They proceeded more slowly, for the side road was narrow and wound its way through stands of cottonwood trees. He fell silent as he negotiated the curves. Soon the road straightened out and the entrance to the ranch came into view. As they passed under the wooden archway, Philippa saw a series of targets lined up in the field to their left. Clint followed her glance.

"We used to practice shooting there as kids," he reminisced.

"Hunting's big in Montana, isn't it?"

"It's big in North America," said Clint. "The hunters in the United States form the largest armed force in the world—and there was a time when it counted. Ever read about the Battle of New Orleans?"

"Yes, actually. My parents told me all about it after their trip to Louisiana."

Clint rounded another corner and Philippa saw a series of buildings ahead. She could also see cars parked in an adjacent field. As the Cadillac drew nearer, a crowd of brightly dressed wedding guests came into view. They were congregating by a pavilion, which had been decorated with balloons, banners and silver bells. Philippa could hear the strains of a band playing, though the tune was muted by the shrill chatter of voices.

As soon as Clint parked the Cadillac, Philippa found herself whisked away, and the rest of the day passed with introductions to a bewildering parade of people who complimented her on her singing and praised the beauty of her hometown—which, Philippa thought wryly, would not have happened before Vancouver had been advertised to the world by the 2010 Olympics. She also noticed that people tactfully avoided mention of her resemblance to Hanna's deceased sister.

Philippa enjoyed the party. The food was delicious, the band was excellent, the children's efforts on the dance floor were adorable, and the local men gallantly ensured that she herself made regular turns around the floor. Best of all, she was thrilled to see Robin's radiantly happy face and to realize how much her friend was loved, not only by her husband, but by every member of his family. However, Philippa was disappointed at the coolly polite reception Clint Harrington received when he spoke to Sarah Scott, and she could not help noting Ruth Mason's increasing pallor as the afternoon wore on. She was also uncomfortably aware of the guarded looks flashed her way every time she caught a glimpse of Doc Brady or the sheriff.

By the time Robin and Tim were ready to depart, the party was winding down. As the couple made their farewells, Philippa noticed that Ruth Mason was missing and that her son, Gordon, had also disappeared. Hanna remained, but she looked anxious. Robin's eyes were moist as she enveloped Philippa in a hug and she confided that the elderly matriarch was feeling unwell and had retired to lie down upstairs. Philippa was not surprised. It was amazing that Tim's grandmother had lasted the course as long as she had.

Once Tim and Robin had left, the guests began to filter away. With a cursory wave in Clint's direction, Sarah Scott gathered up her daughter and slipped out. Philippa was ready to leave too, and she asked Clint to fetch her coat. Once he moved away, she went over to Hanna Mason.

"Is Sarah really indifferent to him?" she asked.

"No," said Hanna, "but she's afraid of being hurt again. He left it too long. The letter business wasn't his fault, but he should have tried again. And it hasn't helped that he's been here with you. The resemblance is unfortunate, because it reminds Sarah of the way things were before."

"He isn't at all interested in me, you know," said Philippa. "If anything, my resemblance to your sister has been a source of fascination and anathema to him, but we've struck up a friendly alliance while I'm here, if only because we're both outsiders. I know he's made a lot of mistakes, but I believe he really has been carrying a torch for Sarah all these years."

Hanna shrugged as Clint returned with the coats. Forced to let the conversation end, Philippa thanked her hosts and followed Clint outside. The sky was an inky black canopy, with no stars to break the oppressively opaque surface, and the path to the parking lot was lit only by the glow from the pavilion. The solitary howl of a coyote drifted up from the river, breaking the stillness of the night. The air was frigid, and Philippa was glad to reach the warmth and security of the Cadillac. They drove back to the hotel in silence, and this time, Clint did not linger by her door as he said goodnight. Once more glowering like the hero from a Brontë novel, he turned away and disappeared into the shadows of the dimly lit hall.

Philippa got ready for bed and set the alarm on her cell-phone for six o'clock. She had packed her bags before the party, so there was little for her to do in the morning. She planned to breakfast early and leave immediately afterwards. She fell into bed, feeling suddenly exhausted and dreading the long drive awaiting her in the morning. Sleep came right away, but her rest was fitful, and once again, she was besieged by dreams of dogs, wild horses, and an eerie redheaded doppelgänger who threatened her with a shotgun. In her dream, she escaped into the river, but the current swept her away and she struggled to stay above water. The black girders of the old bridge raced towards her, and as she scrabbled against the concrete buttresses, her fingers began to bleed—and then the river claimed her and she sank down below the green water. She looked up toward the surface and saw the black girders overhead, starkly outlined against the pale Montana sky. It was peaceful letting go; strange that she must be drowning, yet she could still breathe as she drifted downwards. Then her alarm startled her out of her nightmare. It was morning.

Shaking off her fatigue and the feeling of malaise, she dragged herself out of bed and headed for the shower. By seven o'clock, she was downstairs and ready for breakfast. She would eat and get on the road right away.

However, her plans were derailed the moment she entered the dining room. Betty McGill and her husband were sitting at a corner table. Their faces were solemn, and as Philippa entered, they looked up. Gravely, Betty told Philippa the reason for their subdued manner. Ruth Mason had died in the night.

⋙⊹⋘

As soon as she'd finished breakfast, Philippa retrieved her bags from her room and checked out of the hotel. Abandoning her hopes of an early start on the road, she set off for the Mason ranch. She would not stay long, but she felt it imperative to stop by in person to express her condolences.

The sky was already light when Philippa drove across the river. It promised to be a glorious day, with delicate wispy strands of cirrus clouds forming lace-like patterns on a sky that was rapidly becoming a child's-picture-book blue. No storms and thunder from the heavens to mourn Ruth Mason's passing. The day was as serene as the gentle woman had been in life.

As Philippa passed under the log-framed arch that marked the entrance to the ranch, she heard the sound of gunshots. A solitary individual was firing at the targets on the range. She recognized the slight figure right away. It was young Jack Mason. Even at a distance, she could read the anger in his body language, but she was willing to bet that there were tears in his eyes. There had been too much loss lately in his young life. Impulsively, she pulled over and got out of the Jeep. The boy did not notice her walking across the grass. He was too intent on his task. When she called out, he turned, startled, and lowered his rifle. He stared at her, waiting for her to speak.

"I just stopped to say how sorry I am about your grandmother," said Philippa. "I heard the news this morning."

Jack looked at her suspiciously.

"You're the singer—Robin's friend—right?"

"Yes."

"Gran-gran wasn't my grandmother. She was my great-grandmother," Jack muttered.

"Yes, of course. I only met her this weekend, but I liked her very much. She was a gracious, lovely woman."

Jack stared miserably at the ground.

"She shouldn't have died. It's all my fault," he said bitterly.

Philippa was shocked at his tone. She wondered if his parents were aware of his feelings, or knew that he was out here trying to cope with his sorrow alone.

"Your gran-gran was old and ill," she said. "It's a miracle she lived as long as she did. Why on earth would you think it was your fault?"

Jack raised his eyes and stared tearfully at Philippa.

"Because it was. She was doing really well again. It was only after she found out that she had the relapse. It was my fault." Suddenly his expression hardened and the fury in his eyes made Philippa quail. "My fault and The Colonel's," he spat.

Turning back toward the target, he raised his rifle and began firing again, shouting with every hit. Horrified, Philippa heard the angry cries and watched him chambering the round with expertise after every shot. Having emptied the clip, he removed it from the rifle and began to reload it. As he slipped the bullets into the slot, he noticed that Philippa was still standing there. He turned to her, eyes blazing.

"Go away! Just leave me alone!"

There was no point in staying. Philippa returned to the Jeep. As she drove away, she could still hear the shots on the field and the sound of the boy's voice. She could no longer make out the words, but she did not need to. They were etched on her brain. "Die like a dog!" Chilled and shaken to the core, she made her way to the ranch house. Condolences were no longer the order of the day. She now realized why Gordon Mason had refused to talk about the day of Josh Henkel's death. But if young Jack were ever to recover, it was time the truth was faced.

When she reached the farmhouse, Gordon opened the door. He did not seem surprised when she asked to speak to him alone. He led her into a small front parlour and closed the door behind them. Philippa guessed that the room was reserved for visitors who came on business, for it contained nothing more than a desk, a bookshelf and two wing chairs. She noticed a small stack of books piled on the desk and recognized the volume at the top of the pile. It was the novel about the service dogs in Viet Nam.

Gordon waved her towards an armchair, but Philippa remained standing. She came straight to the point.

"The Colonel didn't commit suicide, did he? He was murdered, and Hanna has been terrified that you were the one who killed him. But you didn't, did you? You're just covering up for the family member who killed him. Brianne was way off target when she said her father had been murdered because of money. It was much simpler than that. Josh Henkel died because he killed a dog."

Gordon's face was ashen.

"How did you know?"

"It's the only scenario that makes sense. You went to Henkel's ranch to bring the boys back, but you only managed to corral two of them. Young Jack eluded you and found his own way back. But before he returned, he went to see The Colonel, and when you went down to square things and apologize for the graffiti, you saw what Jack had done. Your son was already depressed over the death of his own dog, and when he heard about The Colonel shooting Liam O'Mara's dog, it drove him right over the edge."

Gordon's expression changed and his eyes became guarded.

"You think The Colonel died because he shot Blackie?"

Philippa blinked.

"Yes. What else could it be?"

Gordon was silent for a moment. Then he went to the desk and picked up the book at the top of the pile.

"Robin said you bought a copy of this. Have you read it yet?"

Philippa blinked. The question was unexpected.

"Not all the way through," she replied. "I got as far as the section where the hero was trying to arrange for his dog to be brought back to the States."

"So you know there was a movement to bring some of the service dogs back from Asia."

"Yes, but from what I read, not many of them made it. I didn't find out whether the dog in the book survived. Did he?"

"No. The commanding officer gave the soldier two options. He could either turn his dog loose or have him put down."

Philippa flinched, but she kept her voice level. "That was a heartbreaking choice, but I don't understand how any of this relates to The Colonel's death."

"You said it yourself. Josh Henkel died because he killed a dog. The hero of this book is based on my Uncle Jackson."

Philippa's eyes widened.

"I was told your uncle died in action, along with his dog."

"That was the sanitized version. We'd never have found out the truth if it hadn't been for the book. You see, the woman who wrote it was married to a man who'd served in the same unit as my uncle. The author's husband knew what had really happened over there. He'd remained quiet, convinced by his platoon leader that it would be kinder to let my grandparents believe their son had died in action. However, he told his wife Jackson's story, and many years later, she used it in her book. Perhaps she never realized how thinly she'd disguised a true story, but to us, it was crystal clear who the characters were, particularly as she'd dedicated the book to her husband and acknowledged that much was based on his recollections of his time in Viet Nam. We recognized his name right away, because my uncle had mentioned him in his letters. Even some of the incidents that Jackson had described were outlined in the book."

"So what was the truth? How did your uncle die?"

"He refused to leave without Shep. The Colonel was determined to get Jackson on that boat, and I guess he had no comprehension of how deep the love was between man and dog. He saw Shep as an obstacle to his command being obeyed."

Philippa paled.

"Oh, my God! He shot Jackson's dog?"

"Yes."

"What did your uncle do?"

"He repeated the phrase he always said to his dog: 'One for you, and one for me.'" Gordon fixed Philippa with a look that made her quail. "And then he shot himself."

Philippa was stunned. Speechlessly, she stared back at the steel-eyed man.

"Josh Henkel had a lot to answer for," Gordon said grimly. "Frida, Jackson, Shirley. Every one of them died because of him. He deserved what he got."

Philippa looked grave, but she found her voice.

"Maybe he did," she said quietly, "but don't you think Jack should have some counselling? He needs to come to terms with what he did."

Gordon laughed bitterly.

"You still haven't figured it out, have you? Jack didn't do anything other than spray paint Henkel's barns. He didn't fire that shot."

Gordon's eyes glittered. Warily, she met his gaze.

"Then who did?"

"I did."

Philippa gasped. From the corner of her eye, she sensed movement. She turned to see Sheriff Joe Kramer coming into the room.

"You just don't give up, do you, Miss Beary?" Kramer turned to Gordon. "You'd better let her read the letter," he said. "She'll just keep stirring up trouble until she knows the truth."

Silently, Gordon went to the desk and took an envelope from the drawer. He opened it and pulled out a folded sheet of lilac notepaper. He handed it to Philippa. It was a handwritten note, the letters elegantly sloped, reflecting a hand that had been well-trained in the art of penmanship. It was signed by Ruth Mason. Curiously, Philippa began to read.

The book was a present from my grandson, and I know he would never have bought it for me if he'd understood the anguish it would cause. I recognized Jackson as soon as I started to read. The hero was so obviously my son and the commanding officer was unmistakeably Josh Henkel . . . Josh, who had promised faithfully to look after my boy and bring him back after the war. The story in the book was clear enough—many of the incidents could have come straight from Jackson's letters—and when I saw that the author's husband was Jackson's friend who served alongside him throughout the war, there was no doubt in my mind. I think I went a little mad with the grief of knowing what my boy must have suffered, and at that moment I resolved that Josh Henkel would face retribution before I left this earth. I went out to the shed where I keep poison for the rats and filled a vial with some of the strychnine. Then I walked over to the Henkel Ranch. I knew Josh had coffee on the river around that time, and I went down to join him on the lower deck. He was surprised to see me, but perfectly civil and he offered me coffee. Before I accepted, I told him what I had learned and asked him if it was true. I had to be sure that I was right. I had to learn the truth from his own lips. He was startled, but not in the least upset. He gravely told me that he had acted in the boy's best interests, that he thought once the dog was no longer an issue, that Jackson would obey the command to leave. He apologized, and said that he had kept the truth from me in order to save me more grief, and then he patted me on the hand as if that was all that was needed to put things right, and reiterated the offer of coffee. I accepted, and as soon as he had left to refill the pot, I slipped the strychnine into his cup.

He died very quickly, but I was more shaken up than I realized, and I was still sitting there, in shock, when Gordon appeared. He had come to apologize for the boys' behaviour, but when he saw what I had done, he was terribly distressed. I told him to call the sheriff, but he insisted that I let him deal with matters. He made me leave the way I'd come and walk back to my cottage. I didn't realize what he intended to do, but of course, now I know that he took Josh Henkel's shotgun and staged the suicide, trying to cover up for my actions. He assures me that everything is all right, and that this is the best solution for the family, but I am writing this in case things go wrong. I want no one to suffer for what I did. I have no regrets, and I know I have very little time left on this earth, but at least I can pass on, knowing that my loved-ones are no longer blighted with the presence of the man who has brought nothing but grief to my family.

"The pathologist wasn't fooled," said Joe Kramer. "He called me in and told me the results, and I investigated and uncovered the truth. But it was a pretty hard call. I could have pulled Gordon in for conspiracy, but I'd have also had to arrest a ninety-year-old woman who was dying of cancer. Sometimes, the law doesn't provide all the answers—and every cover-up isn't always the result of incompetence or corruption." He fixed Philippa with a steady gaze. "You still want to stir up the shit around this town?"

Philippa stared mutely at the two men. Then the silence was broken by the ringing of her cell-phone. It was Bob Miller.

"I don't know where you are or who you're with right now," he said tersely, "but I'm reiterating what I said before: steer clear of trouble. I just had a talk with the Vermont pathologist. Someone went into the computer and altered that autopsy report. Josh Henkel didn't have a brain tumour, or any kind of cancer. He was as healthy as a horse until he was murdered. And it wasn't the gunshot that did it. His system was loaded with strychnine. The Colonel was poisoned."

"I know that now," said Philippa quietly. "Don't worry about me, Bob. I'm at the ranch, but I've just come to say goodbye. I have to make one quick stop in town after I leave here. Then I'm coming home."

Philippa drove back to town and parked in front of the Old Fort Coffee House. Even though she told herself that she didn't bear any responsibility for her Wild Horse Monument acquaintance, she hated the thought that her resemblance to Frida Henkel had hampered Clint's attempts at reconciliation with Sarah Scott. Before she left, Philippa wanted to put things right.

However, when she entered the coffee house, the only person behind the counter was Jill O'Mara. Sarah, Jill informed her, had left a moment ago. She had taken the children to place a wreath for Blackie at the Shep monument on the hillside.

Philippa looked at her watch and sighed. So much for her early start. She ordered a latte and asked Jill to have it ready in twenty minutes. Then she pulled out her cell-phone and called Clint Harrington. He was still at the hotel, though he had checked out and was almost ready to leave. He sounded surprised when she said she needed to see him. However, he agreed to meet her, and did not demur when she asked him to come to the monument on the hillside. Then she asked Jill for directions, hopped in her car and drove towards the north end of town.

The hills ahead were so closely tumbled together that it seemed as if a long grey ridge enclosed the town, and far to the left, Philippa could see a freight train snaking its leisurely way along the base of the rocky escarpment. The day was quiet, but a bouncing knot of tumbleweed hurtled across the road in front of the Jeep, belying the tranquillity of the scene. The Montana wind was still blowing vigorously.

As Philippa drew closer, the breaks in the hills became more distinct, and soon one solitary rise stood out, towering above the station. At the very top, clear against the marbled sky, the silhouette of Shep rose majestically from the promontory. Below his image, Shep's name was spelled out in letters as big as the dog himself, and in front, a needle like projection marked his grave.

Philippa drove around to the small parking lot behind the rise and pulled over to the verge. Only one car was in the lot. Through the windscreen of the Jeep, she could see Sarah and the children walking up the path that led to the monument. Sarah's long dark hair was tossing in the wind. The gusts, which had been strong in town, were ferocious on the hillside, and the wind buffeted the Jeep so that it creaked and rocked with every blast of air. Philippa was content to sit inside the vehicle and wait.

The walking figures disappeared over the rise and Philippa mentally willed them to remain where they were until Clint arrived. She checked her watch impatiently. It would be frustrating if her detour proved to be an exercise in futility. However, five minutes later, Clint's Cadillac pulled into the parking lot and Sarah had not yet reappeared. Clint parked on the far side of the lot and got out of his car. Philippa opened the door of the Jeep, but another gust hit and the door flew back at her, so she had to struggle to get out. By the time she had managed to extricate herself, Clint was standing in front of her. His eyebrows were raised quizzically, alleviating his usual sardonic stare, but with his dark hair tossing in the wind, he still resembled a brooding Heathcliff.

"You wanted to see me?" Clint thrust his hands in the pockets of his coat and eyed Philippa suspiciously. "What's up?"

"There's something you need to see at the monument," said Philippa.

"And what would that be?"

"Do me a favour. Just walk up and look. I'll wait here."

Clint gave her a long, hard stare. Then, without another word, he left her and set off on the path. Was it her imagination, or had she picked up a flash of comprehension in his eyes? Philippa hoped so. She watched as he disappeared over the top of the hillside. She waited a few moments, and to her relief, he did not reappear. Then she returned to her Jeep and drove out of the parking lot. She coasted slowly down the sloping road that curved around Shep's hillside. When she reached the bottom, she stopped and looked up towards the monument.

The distant scene that met her eyes could have graced a Hallmark card. Shep's silhouette was surrounded by a cluster of children, and a little way off, a man and a woman stood side-by-side watching the youngsters play. Philippa sighed contentedly. Whatever Bob Miller might think, sometimes it was good to be a buttinsky.

She was about to pull onto the main road and head back to the coffee shop, when her cell-phone buzzed and signalled a text message. Telepathy must be at work, she thought. It was from Bob Miller.

Have tomorrow off. Will meet u at the Wild Horse Monument at noon. Convoy home and stop in Seattle 4 dinner. OK?

Smiling at her phone, Philippa texted back: *OK.* Then with a last look at Shep and his entourage on the hillside, she set off for the Old Fort Coffee House. A latte for the road never sounded so good. It was time to go home.

AUTHOR'S NOTE

The stories in this book were inspired by places I have visited and events I have attended, but with one notable exception, the characters are entirely a product of my imagination. Anne Kent in "The House of Once Before" is the one exception and her character is based on the person named in the dedication at the front of this book. *National Post* columnist, Barbara Kay, has encouraged my writing ever since I sent out review copies of my first book. After reading *To Catch an Actress*, she contacted me to say how much she had enjoyed it and gave me permission to quote her endorsements. She continued to be supportive after my second book was published, and subsequently when I was visiting Montreal, we arranged to meet. We discussed mystery writing—Barbara also had a manuscript in the works, later to be published as the intriguing mystery novel, *A Three-Day Event*—and when I told her my intention to use Montreal as a setting for a future story, she laughed and asked if my outspoken protagonist, Bertram Beary, was going to meet an equally outspoken newspaper columnist on his travels.

A couple of years later, Barbara and her husband were downsizing, and she wrote a column about their new home, which happened to be a house that she had visited and loved in her youth.

The next time we were in touch, I commented that her move would make a great set up for a mystery story. She reminded me that we had joked about Beary meeting an outspoken lady columnist and suggested that this was my chance to make it happen. And so "The House of Once Before" was born, with an imaginary set of characters as the first occupants of Barbara's new home. It was great fun to create a literary mystery for a female protagonist who, like Bertram Beary, never fears to say what she thinks and refuses to hide behind the veil of political correctness. Thank you, Barbara, for stepping into my story and making it special.

I should also include a few words about Fort Benton, Montana, where "Die like a Dog" is set. Philippa's stay at the Grand Union Hotel and her walk along the Riverside Park mirrors our own exploration of the town. We were deeply moved by the two Shep monuments—one of which now includes a brick in memory of our late husky, Max—and the story of Shep, along with the memorial park with its tributes to human and canine sacrifice, suggested the theme for the story. The Grand Union Hotel is every bit as charming as described in my book and it is well worth a visit if you are travelling to Montana. Also worth visiting is the warmly welcoming Wake Cup Coffee House which inspired my fictitious Old Fort Coffee House.

Some final acknowledgements are in order for several people who have supported my artistic ventures. These include Holly Fynn and Maureen Worthen, who will be particularly amused by one of the stories in this book. My gratitude also to Luman Coad, master puppeteer, who helped me navigate some of the problems of publication, and competitive cyclist, Craig Premack, who provided me with essential details about racing bikes. Thanks, as always, to my husband, Hugh Elwood, for his help and support, and to Lorraine Meltzer for her thoughtful editing and ongoing encouragement.

Elizabeth Elwood is the author of the Beary Mystery Series. She is also a playwright whose plays have entertained audiences all across Canada. Her first play, *Casting for Murder*, is shortly due to premiere in the United States. Born in England, Elizabeth resides in Vancouver, British Columbia. Visit her website at www.elihuentertainment.com

Books

To Catch an Actress and Other Mystery Stories
A Black Tie Affair and Other Mystery Stories
The Beacon and Other Mystery Stories
The Agatha Principle and Other Mystery Stories

Plays

Casting for Murder
Renovations
Shadow of Murder
Body and Soul

Watch for the next book in the Beary mystery series.

After Rebecca and Other Mystery Stories

Made in the USA
San Bernardino, CA
25 February 2017